Conecuh

Conecuh

Herb Hughes

Books From The Pond
2019

This is a work of fiction. Names, characters, businesses, places, organizations, events and incidents are either the products of the author's imagination or are used in a fictitious manner.

First Printing: 2019

ISBN: 9781096009511

Books From The Pond
1207 E. Forrest St., Ste. D-105
Athens AL 35613

www.herbhughesnovels.com

Cover art: Mutt Suttles

Dedicated to the memory of Pat Ryan, Portroe, Ireland, a gentleman and a friend.

Conecuh

Cah-NECK-ah.

Conecuh

August, 1861 ~ A Forest Near Sepulga, Alabama

The southern summer stilled the air around and between the trees, raising dust from the ground not by breeze but by the sheer will of the heat. The air was soaking humid, oppressive. The pines loved it. Caleb had never seen them so green.

Raising a hand in the air, Caleb motioned that they should hold their fire. He pointed toward Arlis then jerked his musket to the left. He pointed at himself and jerked his musket to the right. Arlis nodded his understanding. Caleb held up three fingers, the count of three. Arlis nodded again.

Moving in slow motion, the two men brought the barrels of their muskets up and over the bushes, brushing the top tips of the leaves to keep the barrels low and unseen. They took aim.

"One," Caleb whispered under his breath.

His face nestled into the bushes, Arlis could not see Caleb. He could only smell the bitter sweetness of the leaves as he listened for his friend's whisper.

"Two."

Caleb flexed his fingers under the long, heavy barrel, steadying it for the shot. The wood of the stock was polished smooth from years of use, with slight indentations where his fingers came to rest.

"Three!" he said, almost out loud.

Two shots rang out at virtually the same instant, the sounds so close together that, if they had been heartbeats, the heart would have ruptured.

The bird to the right took to the sky, its wings taking it quickly away. A circular plume of black feathers meant the bird on the left would not escape. As the small, dark body at the center of the circle fell from the pine limb, the airborne feathers began their lazy, zig-zag fall to the earth, twirling around and around as they drifted downward.

"Well, I'll be," Caleb said. "Your ball sent feathers a'flying, but I plumb missed. You always were a better shot."

"I was trying to take his head off."

Caleb raised an eyebrow. "Take his head off? I was just aiming for the middle and hoping."

As they walked to where the blackbird lay on the ground, sweat beaded down their faces and ran along their chins in the afternoon heat.

"You sure done it!" Caleb said. "I wish I could shoot like that."

The iridescent black feathers and soft, almost weightless down on the bird's chest lay still in the stagnant heat. Blood oozed from the red stump where the head should have been, hiding the blue and green tints of the feathers around its neck.

"How do you do that?" Caleb asked. "I didn't ruffle a feather, but you hit him right where you was aiming."

"My eyes are pretty good, I reckon. I could always see far away stuff other folks couldn't. But it might be more luck than anything." Arlis shrugged.

"Twarn't luck," Caleb said as he leaned his musket against the trunk of the pine tree. "I've known you too long." He unsheathed his hunting knife and bent over the bird.

"What are you doing?" Arlis asked.

Caleb glanced up with a quizzical look on his face. "Gutting him," he said, shrugging his shoulders.

"It's a blackbird. It ain't fit to eat."

"It shouldn't die for no reason. Maw taught me never to take one of God's creatures without making good use of him. That's the right of it."

"You just go ahead then. I ain't eating that awful thing. Blackbirds taste like liver. I hate liver."

Caleb looked down at the small body in his hands. "We can't walk off and leave him on the ground to rot."

"Why not? If you shot a polecat, would you eat him, too?"

"That's different," Caleb protested. "I'd be protecting myself."

"What? That polecat's gonna raise a musket and shoot back?"

"No. Worse. If he squirts you with that stinky stuff, you'll wish you'd been shot instead."

With a smile and a shake of his head, Arlis turned away. He looked at the few puffs of white cloud drifting slowly across the sky and asked, "Are you going to fight?"

"The Yankees?"

"Yeah. The Conecuh Guards are in the thick of it up there in Virginia. Whipped them good at a place called Manassas. We lost several of our own, though."

"I heard. They marched away in a parade last April like they was going on a picnic. The next thing you know, they're getting shot full of holes."

"And putting holes in the Yankees, too." Arlis kicked the dirt a moment, sending up a small puff of dry dust. "So, are you going?"

"I don't reckon I know. Maw and Paw need me here to work the farm, but lots of men from Conecuh have done joined already. The old folks are whispering, like those still here are cowards or something. I ain't afraid. Maybe I'll go ahead and enlist and show 'em."

"You'll be marching away from Emily," Arlis needled. His grin broadened.

Caleb's hands stopped moving. He looked up at Arlis and said, "Emily Rose?"

"Only Emily under fifty years old around here, other than your sister."

Caleb stared at the ground and thought a moment. "She wanted to sit beside me in church last Sunday."

"I've seen her smiling at you. That girl's smitten."

"But she's…" Caleb stuttered. "She's, well… I'm just a farmer's son. We don't have nothing and ain't likely ever gonna have nothing."

"Your daddy's a traveling preacher. Preacher's son counts for something."

"I don't know. She makes me feel all messed up inside like my innards turned into jelly or something."

"Uh, oh. You got it bad, Caleb. That's exactly how it starts. My granddaddy told me. I 'spect that's the way Emily's feeling, too. Maybe it's time you started sparking that girl."

"Won't matter none if I go off to war. She'll have lots of time to find somebody else. Somebody with money. She's pretty enough to have her pick. Any man in the county would jump at the chance to be sparking her."

"Who's she going to pick from? The way everybody's going off to the war, there won't be nothing left but old men and little boys." Arlis looked back at the sky and the distant horizon. "I don't know about the war. I'm no coward, but I ain't too keen on getting myself killed so's some rich cotton farmer can own slaves."

"Me, neither." Caleb opened the blackbird's small body. "But what choice do we have? The Yankees are fighting against Alabama. We can't stand against our home. We've got to stand up and protect it. Besides, the way you shoot, it's the Yankees who need to worry about getting killed, not us."

With a practiced hand, Caleb had the bird gutted in seconds, dropping the entrails to the warm dirt beside the pine tree. The bird's body was lowered into his hunting bag.

"Let's go," Arlis said. "There's got to be something else we can shoot for supper." He took a couple of steps but realized Caleb was not following. Instead, Caleb was digging in the earth. "What?" Arlis asked as he shrugged his shoulders. "What are you doing now?"

"Gonna bury his innards by this root. They'll go into the soil, feed this old pine."

Arlis rolled his eyes back into his head. "What has gotten into you, Caleb?"

"Maw said the least we can do is make full use of any critter we kill. I don't aim to eat the guts, so's I'll leave them for this here tree. It don't care how it gets nourished. Besides, it don't taste things. Leastways, I don't think it does."

"Your momma must have been raised by injuns. They say the Great Spirit tells them they have to use every part of anything they kill."

"Injuns? I don't know about no injuns. We've got to respect God's critters. Think about it, Arlis. That's the right of it. You know that's what God would want."

"I know no such a thing. What I do know is you're having blackbird for supper because I ain't eating that awful thing. If God wanted me to eat blackbirds, he would have made them taste like chicken breast, not chicken liver. That's enough of this. Let's go find something worth eating so I won't starve tonight."

"Just a second. This old orange Conecuh dirt is hard to turn up. Rocks all in it. I hate farming in this stuff."

"Preacher Sam says the rocks help separate the soil and make it better."

Caleb stopped digging and glanced at Arlis. "Absalom?" Caleb glanced back at the rocky soil, shrugged his shoulders, and said, "My daddy's a better preacher than a farmer." He stabbed at the dirt again.

"You go ahead and dull your knife. I'm going to find some real supper." Arlis turned and walked off. He didn't look back this time. If Caleb was not coming, he could darn well eat blackbird for supper.

March 9, 1862 ~ Rose Residence, Forks of Sepulga Community, Alabama

"Hurry, Momma," Emily said as she sat in her chair and waited for her mother to finish braiding her hair. "Caleb's going to be walking by any moment. It's almost time for church."

"There's a little time, yet, Girl. My, but it's shameful the way you run after that boy."

"He's not a boy, Momma. He's a man. Full grown. And I'm a grown woman. Almost."

"You're as obvious as a cat in heat, Girl. You've got to be ladylike, coy."

"He's going off to war, Momma. I ain't got time to be coy."

Mary Rose looked at her daughter. Emily was no longer the little girl she had been a few short years ago. She was a young woman, slim and pretty. Mary glanced at the small mirror on the dresser. Her own face was thin and pinched. Her dark hair, pulled back in a simple bun, showed more than a few stripes of gray. She returned her gaze to her daughter. Emily Rose was every bit as pretty as Mary Rose was plain. But Mary remembered a time, many years ago, when she was considered one of the prettiest girls around. It seemed like only yesterday. Better to let her daughter enjoy life at this age, enjoy being one of the prettiest girls in the county. It would change soon enough.

Mary lifted the braid and inspected her handiwork. With a clip still hanging from the side of her mouth, she said, halfheartedly, "It's still shameful for a young lady to chase after a man. You know that. I taught you that all your life."

"Things are different from when you were young, Momma. What's really shameful is this stupid war. Caleb has to go far away and get shot at. He could get hurt, even killed. That's shameful. I ain't got time for social quibbles right now."

"The other ladies around here will sure have time. They'll whisper their gossip long after Caleb's gone."

"Only rich folks gossip, Momma. We ain't rich folks."

"Girl, where have you been all your life? Rich folks only gossip about other rich folks. Poor folks are worse. They gossip about the rich folks *and* the poor folks. They even gossip about the poor folks' animals."

"Let them talk. I don't care what they say. I'll still walk around with my head held high."

Thomas Rose, a smile on his face, appeared in the doorway. He took his floppy brown hat off, and said, "While you've got your head in the air, Girl, be careful you don't trip on something. You might fall face first in a fresh cow patty. You best be listening to your momma."

Emily looked up at her father. He was dressed in his usual homespun brown britches and shirt. He had a friendly smile, a plump face, rounded shoulders, and muscular arms that spoke of years of hard labor on a farm.

The family's lone slave, Nathaniel Whiteeagle, walked in behind Thomas. The brown-skinned man wore his usual clothes as well, black pants and jacket. The jacket would give way to a dark shirt in warmer weather, but in mid-March, it was still cool enough to cover the shirt with his jacket. He also wore a black bowler with an eagle's feather sticking out of the band, but as he stepped through the door, he reached up and lifted the hat from his head as Thomas had done. Men did not wear hats inside the Rose home.

Where Thomas was smiling, a little bulky, and stood with a slouch, Nathaniel stood tall and straight, his body slim but muscular. He held his countenance rigid, his lips giving away nothing. Emily knew when Nathaniel was smiling only by looking into his eyes. If it hadn't been for the difference in the color of the two men's skin, everyone would have assumed that Thomas was the slave and Nathaniel the slave owner.

Emily jumped up, one of her braids flying out of her mother's hands, and wrapped her arms around her father. A great big smile was plastered onto her facc. "Daddy! How long have you been listening to us?"

The men hung their hats on wooden pegs in the wall by the front door. Thomas turned around and said, "Long enough to know that you've been embarrassing us by chasing after that farmer boy again."

"Farmer boy? Now, just exactly what is it you do, Daddy?"

Thomas' wrinkled his face.

"Ahhhh, words spoken with the thrust of a dagger," Nathaniel said. There was no smile on his lips, but his eyes danced with humor. Thomas laughed out loud.

"Why, your daddy's the best farmer in Conecuh County," Mary said. "Leastways, to my way of thinking."

"Caleb will get it all figured out," Emily said. "He's smart. I promise. He'll be the best farmer in the county someday. Just like you, Daddy."

"I don't know for sure if I would say I was the best. There's some who raise more crop, and some who've got larger herds. But I make us a decent living."

"Those others have lots of slaves to do their work for them," Emily said. "We don't have no slaves."

Nathaniel frowned. He cocked one brow and turned his head slightly sideways as he stared at Emily, his best menacing look pasted onto his brown face.

"You don't count, Nathaniel. You're more like family. Why, you even eat at the dinner table with us, like a brother would." Emily threw her arms around Nathaniel and hugged him as well, but Nathaniel did not try to hug her back as Thomas had done. He stood rigid and endured the girl's hug. Still, Emily could see a twinkle in his eye. *Am I the only one who notices?* she wondered.

"Yes, well, don't be spreading that tale around none, Girl," Mary said. "Nathaniel *is* like family, but some's around here might get pretty upset if they knew."

"Your momma's right," Thomas said. "Serious right."

"I know, I know. I don't tell nobody. I've never even told Caleb."

"Speaking of Caleb," Thomas said, "I saw him passing by, headed to church."

"OH!" Emily screamed. "I've got to go. I've got to catch up."

She turned toward the side table by the rocking chair. A small, worn black book rested on the lace cover that draped the table. Her mother had made the cover by hand, stitching the lace border all the way around. Emily had always marveled at her mother's handiwork. The small cover was so pretty, but there was no time to admire it as she hurriedly reached for her Bible. In her haste, she missed and knocked it to the floor.

"You might want to be a little gentler with the Lord's Word," Thomas said. The admonishment was accompanied with a smile.

Emily smiled back at her father. "Maybe He'll forgive me," she said. She picked the Bible up then burst through the front door as her mother shouted, "I need to pin those braids up."

"They'll have to hang down today," Emily shouted over her shoulder as she rushed into the road, quickly out of earshot.

March 9, 1862 ~ Union Church, Forks of Sepulga Community, Alabama

"Caleb," Emily called as she ran after him. "Caleb!"

Thomas and Nathaniel put on their hats and stepped outside, along with Mary. Thomas added his Sunday jacket then took his wife's offered arm as they walked toward the road to join their daughter. They were quickly left behind by the running Emily.

Nathaniel walked behind them. Slaves were welcome at Union Church, but they stayed on their side, in pews designated for them. It was a good arrangement. Everyone got to hear the word of the Lord, and the slaves caught up with each other after a long week of serving their white owners.

"Caleb," Emily shouted again as she continued to run, closing the distance between them.

Not too far ahead, Caleb stopped and turned around. As Emily came to a stop beside him, he said, "Good morning, Emily."

"Walk me to church?"

Caleb glanced ahead at his family and motioned for them to go on. He turned back to Emily and said, "Sure. That would be nice. I looked for you when I walked by." They started walking side-by-side, a respectable distance between them since there was family before and after. Besides, Caleb would never disrespect Emily by getting too close.

"Momma was still doing my braids."

"She did a right nice job, too."

Emily smiled and said, "Thank you. I heard something, Caleb. Arlis' momma told my momma y'all are going to join the army."

"That's right. We're going down to enlist next Saturday. We'll train for a time then we'll leave next month."

Emily stopped and turned around to face Caleb. Her hand rushed to her mouth, so she spoke around it. "But, Caleb. I thought you and I… I mean. Why do you have to go? I want you here so I can see you."

They faced each other and stared into each other's eyes, silent for several seconds. "I reckon I've got to," Caleb finally said. "Everybody else is gone or going. We've got to stand up for Alabama. Besides, Maw and Paw need the money." He could see tears forming at the edges of her eyes. "It won't be forever. I promise. Seeing you these last few months have been the best part of my life. By a long shot. But it's something I've got to do. I won't be gone too awful long. Only three years. That's if we don't win the war sooner. But…" He stammered to a stop, took a deep breath, and then continued, "If you can't wait for me, I'll understand."

"Of course I'll wait for you." Emily swiped at the corners of her eyes with the back of her hand, trying not to be too conspicuous about wiping away her tears. "Three years? That's forever. Please be careful. I don't want you to get hurt."

"I'll be fine," Caleb said. He wished he felt as strongly about it as he sounded. "Arlis will be with me. He's the best shot around these parts. Why, he'd kill any Yankee who got close to us."

Emily turned silent. Just the mention of the word 'kill' did something inside her. Caleb was walking straight into a war, a place where people killed other people. It seemed so bad, so useless, so wasteful.

She turned her head behind her enough to see her parents and Nathaniel closing the distance between them, so she started walking again. "Come on, Caleb. We don't want to be late to church."

The rough-sawn pew of the Union Church was worn slick-smooth with time. It was their favorite place to meet. Everybody from some distance around could see them, but no one could see the backs of Caleb's and Emily's hands touching at their sides. Emily's full and flowing Sunday dress hid where their hands rested.

Her soft skin stirred Caleb in ways he had never felt before. He began to wonder if going off to war was such a good idea after all. *Too late now,* he thought. He wasn't a blowhard, but he and Arlis had already told people they were going to join. They would look like deadbeats if they backed out now.

It was Baptist week, the Methodist service having been the week before, and Caleb's father, Sam Garner, Absalom Garner to those more formal, was preaching this Sunday. Before he started the sermon, however, he said he wanted to make an announcement. That was unusual. Sam almost always went straight into talking about God and the Bible. He rarely discussed local news.

"You all know my oldest son, Willis, is in the Confederate cavalry," Sam said from the pulpit. He was not a large man, but his voice was deep and strong, perfect for a preacher. "I am not alone. Many of you have seen your sons going off to war. Now more of Conecuh's young men will be marching away. Two more of my sons will be a'going with them. Caleb and John are going to join next week. I want to pray for all three of my boys. And for your boys, too. But not just for them. My friends, let us pray hard for all of Conecuh County's sons, for all of Alabama's sons, and for all of the Confederacy's sons…" He hesitated as his eye roved over the crowd. "So that God will grant us a quick victory and bring our boys back home safe and sound." There was a chorus of 'amens.' "Please join me as we bow our heads in reverence to the Lord."

As they nodded their heads forward and closed their eyes, Emily's hand moved from barely touching the back of Caleb's hand to holding his hand, palm-to-palm. This was something new, something wonderful. She squeezed gently. A warm tremble worked its way through Caleb's body. He squinted his eyes open and looked around to make sure no one could see them then he squeezed back, being careful not to squeeze too hard.

As Sam was nearing the end of his prayer, requesting God's intervention on behalf of the great Confederate cause, Caleb saw Emily squinting her eyes open as well. They looked at each other and smiled. It was all he could do to keep from laughing out loud. In the middle of his father's prayer? That would have been a disaster. He almost choked himself in his effort to stay quiet.

Finally, Sam sealed the request to God with a firm 'Amen!' The congregation, both black and white, echoed the 'amen' as Emily slipped her hand out of Caleb's. Everyone lifted their heads. Reverend Garner dove straight into his sermon, a lesson on how each person had to do their part to help God help them.

Eyes were no longer closed, and heads were no longer bowed so they could not hold hands, but they kept their hands back-to-back, touching ever so slightly. For once, Caleb wanted his father's sermon to last all day. It didn't.

March 15, 1862 ~ Hawthorn Place, Sparta, Alabama

It was a fine day, a Saturday. The late winter sun filtered through the budding leaves of the grand old oaks that stood sentinel over the landscape. Abstract patches of sunlight swayed gently across the front lawn in the light breeze. There was a briskness in the air, but the walk to Sparta had lasted much of the morning. Jackets had long since been taken off.

"This is the place, sure enough," Arlis said. "We might as well go on in. We're later than I expected after you took so long to say goodbye to Emily."

Caleb glanced at Arlis and said, "Saying goodbye was hard. I mite near changed my mind about joining."

Arlis smiled but did not respond. The three young men climbed the few steps to the front lawn of Hawthorn Place. As they walked across the grass, they stared at the whitewashed clapboard rising high above them. None of them had ever been this close to a mansion, to a home so huge you could raise three or four families in it.

Caleb looked at his younger brother, John, then at Arlis before turning around and staring at the four large rectangular columns that reached up as high as the trees, holding the gabled roof so far above the ground that it provided no protection from any rain that rode the wind at an angle. They stared at the railed porch jutting out of the second floor. There was a door that opened onto the porch, a door with no other purpose on this Earth than to let the residents of the house stand on their perch high above the ground and look out over their lands.

"You gentlemen here to enlist, or inspect the building?"

The three of them lowered their gaze to see a Confederate officer standing on the front porch, smiling. He was not much older than they were.

"We heard tell you was paying a fifty dollar bounty to everyone who joins," Arlis said.

"You heard right, young man," the officer answered. He stepped down off the porch, walked over to where they were standing, and extended his hand. "I'm Second Lieutenant John Guice."

"My name's John, too, John Garner," Caleb's brother said as he extended his hand. "This here's Caleb, my older brother."

"And I'm Arlis Johnston," Arlis said after Caleb and the Lieutenant finished their handshake.

"Welcome to Hawthorne Place," Lieutenant Guice said. "I hope the building passed your inspection."

The three of them gave an awkward smile then Caleb said, "We were thinking about joining the Conecuh Guards."

"All three of you from Conecuh County, are you?" They nodded. "That's real fine, men. I've got the papers inside. Come on in, and we'll sign you up." John Guice turned, but when he put his foot on the first step of the front porch, he realized the three young men had not moved. He turned and looked at them. "Sign up's inside," he said as he nodded toward the wide front door.

"We're still thinking," Arlis said. "What about the fifty dollars?"

"Yes, Sir," Caleb said. "Could you tell us some more about that?"

"Why, of course," Lieutenant Guice said as he took his foot off the step and turned around to face them. "You join today for three years of service, and we'll train you right here before you leave. Bivouac's out back. We'll provide you with a tent so you can stay dry. You'll stand beside your friends from right here in Conecuh County while all of you learn how to fight the Yankees. In a few weeks, when you're ready, we'll put you on a train to Virginia. You'll ride along with the other new recruits from Conecuh County. When you get up there, you'll be joined with the 4th Alabama infantry. That's the Guards' unit. Once you've settled in, you'll be paid fifty dollars Confederate. Cash money."

"Maw and Paw need the money here," Caleb said. "Not in Virginia." He had little feel for where Virginia was but understood that it was a long way from Conecuh County, Alabama.

The Lieutenant nodded then said, “We can take care of that for you. Caleb, wasn’t it? The Confederacy will make sure that money gets to wherever you need it to go.”

“How can we be sure?”

A broad, friendly smile stretched across Lieutenant Guice’s face. “We need brave young men like you three. That’s why we’re offering the bounty. If we didn’t make sure you got the money fair and square, the word would get out and nobody else would join. That’s the last thing the Confederacy needs. You have my word as an officer, Caleb. I will personally make sure your bounty is delivered as you wish.”

Caleb thought about his father and mother, Sam and Sarah. Neither he nor John would keep any of the money. If they both joined, as they planned to do, their parents would receive a hundred dollars. It would be more money than they’d held at one time since Sam had a falling out with his father and left South Carolina, many years before Caleb was born. Maybe it would be enough to turn the farm around, make it productive. He glanced at John and nodded. When John nodded back, Caleb realized his brother was likely thinking the same thing.

“Tell you what,” Lieutenant Guice said. “Before we go inside, I’ll show you boys something that might help you make up your minds. Step this way. It’s on the chimney at the side of the house.”

Lieutenant Guice started walking along the front of Hawthorn Place, the three young men following. Caleb looked at the whitewashed clapboard siding. A mansion! It was right there, so close he could reach out and touch it. He wanted to but dared not.

Turning his head away from the house, Caleb looked out across the gently rolling fields. It was early spring, not yet fully turned to green. Shadows from the trees danced around in the light breeze. It was a beautiful setting.

Growing up he had heard stories about wealthy plantation owners sitting and sipping drinks in the late afternoon sun while black servants waited on them hand and foot. Any thought that the stories might be false flew away as he looked at the cultured grounds around him. Everything was too perfect. The stories had to be true. This was how rich folks lived.

Lieutenant Guice turned the corner and walked along the side of the country mansion. They could see tents set up in the backyard. There were other young men, rifles on their shoulders, walking along, their steps in perfect unison with each other.

Guice stopped beside a tall chimney covered with whitewashed plaster. He turned to face the three young men and said, "Here they are." He pointed at the chimney.

Caleb looked closely. There was writing on the whitewash, pencil writing. It was all over the lower part of the chimney. The writing meant nothing to him, strange symbols that had hidden meaning for other folks to share. Caleb could not share with them. He lowered his head and stared at the ground.

"These brave men..." Guice started. He stopped as he looked at Caleb. "Raise your head, Caleb. No need staring at the ground. Why, these brave men deserve your attention."

Caleb looked up but did not look at the chimney. He stared at the Confederate officer and said nothing.

"He don't mean no disrespect, Sir," Arlis said. "It's just, well... He don't read." Caleb frowned at his friend, but Arlis ignored the look and continued. "I read pretty good. Had four years of schooling. Them's names. I know the Thomas boys. And the Robinsons. It looks like they might have writ their names themselves."

"That's right," Lieutenant Guice said. "All of us volunteers signed this chimney last April when we first came together as a unit. I'll rejoin them as soon as this recruiting trip is over. These are your friends and neighbors here, a brave and fearless group. They're up in Virginia fighting for you right now."

Caleb wanted to say that the soldiers were not fighting for him. They were fighting for the slave owners. But he held his tongue. He knew that many of them were fighting for home, for Alabama. Like he would be when he joined.

"They've proven brave and strong in battle," the Lieutenant continued. "Why, if we had a few more like them this war would be over by now. You wouldn't have had your chance for glory." Lieutenant Guice placed his hand on the chimney and smiled. "You boys look like you're every bit as brave as these young men. We need more men like you. That's why we're offering a fifty dollar bounty. As soon as you report for duty in Virginia, you'll get paid fifty dollars Confederate. That's a lot of money. Are you ready to sign the papers? Are you ready to help us drive the Yankees out of our homeland?"

"Fifty dollars is fifty dollars," Arlis said. "Granddaddy and Granny sure need the money. I reckon I'm ready if you are, Caleb."

"But…" Caleb stammered as he hung his head again. "I can't sign no papers if I can't write."

"Hold your head up high, Caleb," Lieutenant Guice said. "I can tell by your hands you've worked hard all your life. You were working and taking care of your family while others were going to school. Well, that's nothing to be ashamed of. As a matter of fact, helping your family is something to be proud of. And you can help your larger family, your friends and relatives right here in Conecuh County, by joining the Confederacy."

Caleb glanced at the chimney, at the dozens of graphite signatures dashed across the whitewash.

"Not everybody has time for schooling," Guice continued. "Not being able to read or write is as common as dirt around here. But you were born an Alabamian, by God. And your state needs you to stand up and protect it." Guice rapped his knuckles against the signed chimney. "Like these men here are doing."

"Maw and Paw need the money," Caleb mumbled.

"All you have to do is join us," Lieutenant Guice said. "I can read the signup papers to you. You make your mark and your friend, here, can witness it. When you do, you'll be standing tall as a sworn Confederate soldier. Why, you might be the very one who makes the difference, Caleb."

May 5, 1862 ~ Countryside Near Williamsburg, Virginia

Gray-brown mud splashed up from his pounding boots, splattering the legs of his uniform as he charged forward, toward the earthen wall of Fort Magruder. Corporal John Murray leaned this way and that to make sure he stayed behind those in the lead, avoiding an open firing lane that might allow a ball to find his chest. The strategy had always worked before. Corporal Murray was not only alive, he had never been wounded.

The strategy broke down, however, when his fellow Union soldiers suddenly turned to retreat. The blue-clad soldiers in front of him were in full run to the rear, trying to get away from too many Confederate muskets. He turned and ran himself. From his rear position in the charge, he was now leading the retreat.

"They are too well entrenched," he heard the Captain shout from somewhere behind him. "Fall back! Form a line along the road. We'll hold there till the reserves arrive."

The road? Murray thought. *Out in the open? To hell with that.*

The road the Captain referred to, the one the Union troops had crossed when the attack began, was a few steps in front of Murray. Beyond that, there was a field with a small patch of trees in the middle, an island of cover. That was his target. He could hide behind the trees as long as the Rebels didn't get too close.

"The Rebs are leaving the fort," a man immediately behind him shouted. "They're coming!"

Things were confused, as retreats invariably were. Soldiers stumbled and fell. Others stopped to turn and fire then rejoin the helter-skelter running after their muskets were spent. This caused several collisions and more confusion.

Corporal Murray did not stop to fire as he continued to lead the retreat. He had but one objective. When he reached the edge of the road, he kept running the short distance across the field to the relative safety of the small clump of trees.

"Form a line and fire on my command," the Captain shouted.

A ragged, haphazard line began to form. Soldiers stood in the face of greater Confederate fire and loaded their muskets. Some fell, moaning and rolling about on the ground. Others fell and stayed still. Corporal Murray continued to run.

Murray stumbled into the trees and slumped behind a thick trunk. He took several deep breaths then turned and peered around the edge of the bark, trying to see what was happening back at the road. There was too much smoke, too much confusion. Everyone was focused on the Rebs. He was sure that no one had seen him continuing into the trees.

The Union soldiers tried to follow orders, but the Confederate force greatly outnumbered them. Several men broke ranks and began to run for the trees. Corporal Murray saw them coming and decided he could not afford to be seen hiding behind his own lines. He could make excuses later, say he got lost in the smoke of battle and separated. He would even tell them he had somehow gotten behind the Confederates and had to weave his way back through the danger of enemy positions.

But right now he did not want to be found. He ran through the clump of trees, dodging trunks large and small. On the other side of the island of cover, the trees gave way to the field that surrounded them. It was a short distance across the open grassland to the larger forest. He never slowed down, crossing the open stretch in mere seconds.

As he once again caught his breath behind the trunk of a large tree, he looked back. He was sure he had gone unseen this time as well. The others who broke from the line had stopped as soon as they reached the small island of trees, where he had left only moments ago. No one was coming toward the forest. Time to find a safe spot until the reserves came in. Once the battlefield had been secured by the might of the Union, he would return, circling so that it would appear he was coming from the danger of enemy positions. He would claim that he charged ahead and became trapped when everyone behind him retreated.

To make sure he could not be found, he wandered deeper into the woods. Besides, he wanted to see what he could find in the relatively flat countryside of the James Peninsula.

On the other side of the forest, he looked out from the cover of the trees to a whitewashed house in the middle of a weedy field. The land was uncultivated, the spring weeds almost as high as his knees, but he could tell by the weathered furrows in the earth that the field had been cultivated at some time in the past. As he looked more closely, there were other tell-tale signs. He had no doubt this field had raised crops as recently as the previous year. Early May and it was abandoned to weeds? Why?

He looked back at the house. The whitewash appeared to be wearing thin in several places. It was not a grand plantation, but it was not a home for poor folks, either. The whitewash should have been newer, fresher. Was the house abandoned, left to suffer the ravages of war should a battle turn this way?

No. As he was watching, a colored girl carrying a pot came through the front door and ran to a small stone wall not far from the house. A well. She laid her pot on top of the wall and quickly jerked her head this way and that, looking all around. Too well hidden in the trees to be seen, he held himself rigidly still. Hidden or not, movement might catch her attention.

The dark-skinned girl pumped the crank hard, trying to lift the bucket as quickly as possible. Although the battle was some distance behind them, the sounds of cannon and musket were unmistakable. It was easy to see that this young colored girl was frightened.

She hurriedly filled the pot then let the wooden bucket drop back into the well, banging against the stone walls as it fell. His eyes followed the smooth, almost silky movements of her body as she ran back to the house and rushed through the door.

She wasn't the prettiest of girls, but she wasn't bad. He had always been intrigued by colored women's dark skin. He tried to imagine what she would look like naked. Would her nipples be reddish-pink like a white woman's? Or were they a different color? Would her body be shaped like a white woman's? Or were the darkies shaped differently somehow? There was only one way to find out.

He was well away from the battle, and there was no one in the open field, right or left. He hunched over to make himself less visible and ran through the tall weeds, stopping at a corner of the home, hiding behind the whitewashed wood as he took another look around. There was no one, not even livestock. In all likelihood, the stinking gray backs had long since appropriated the farm's animals to feed their pathetic soldiers.

Corporal Murray crept along the side of the home, tracing his fingers along the clapboard siding as he took small, quiet steps. The wood was cracked and rough, the whitewash old and in desperate need of a new coat. The home was as neglected as the uncultivated field that surrounded it. *No man at home*, he thought. *Probably gone off to war. Or already dead.*

He reached the first window and slowly raised his eye to the corner. When he peeked inside, he saw an older white woman, late thirties or early forties, brushing a young white girl's hair. The girl couldn't have been more than eight or nine. Possibly the older woman's daughter. They favored.

The colored girl, the slave, tended a pot in the fireplace. She was in her late teens, ripe, well built, not older than twenty at the most. He didn't expect to see a man. Judging from the small farm's condition, it was doubtful a man had lived here in months. But he looked around just in case. He saw no one else downstairs.

Staring at the slave's dark skin, John Murray wondered if it felt like a white woman's skin when you touched it. Would she sweat under a real man? Would she respond to him? He was determined to find out.

His army's commander, General Hooker, had a reputation as a drinker and a womanizer. Murray could identify with this man, even if he had never met him. But the whores who followed the camps, known as "Hooker's Division" or, simply, "The Division," were unattractive and too well used. They were useful only for scratching an itch that soldiers built up after days of marching and fighting. And they were all white girls. This colored girl was different. Her face was not painted in any way. She was naturally attractive. And her body was perfect!

Corporal Murray could see through the window that the front door was latched with a piece of wood that slid through a metal bracket. The wood bar was not wide enough or thick enough to stop him.

He ducked under the window and crept along the side of the building, around the corner then to the front door. After taking a couple of steps backward, John Murray lowered his shoulder and leaped toward the door. The simple wood latch gave way, the door flying open and slamming against the inside of the front wall. Splinters skittered across the floor as the women looked up in shock.

Murray moved quickly. He shut the front door. Since the latch was now broken, he pulled a table over to block it on the inside.

"Please," the white woman begged, her eyes wide with fear. "We don't want no trouble. Please." She reached her arms around her daughter as though that might protect her.

Murray looked at the stairs, momentarily worrying about someone being on the second floor. He quickly realized there was no need to worry. When he burst through the door, neither woman had glanced at the stairs in hopes of help. They were alone.

Up close the slave girl looked even better as she stood there with her eyes wide, as filled with fear as the white woman's. He drew his pistol and took a step toward her. She dropped the long wooden spoon she was holding. It clattered to the floor as she started to step backward. When she bumped into the wall, she stopped. Tears were forming around the edges of her eyes.

"Please don't," the white woman said. The little girl was too shocked to react as her mother continued to beg. "We don't help the Confederates. I promise. We don't do nothing for them…"

John Murray turned his pistol toward the white woman and little girl and said, "Shut up! You stay right there, the two of you. Keep your face turned toward me so I can watch you, make sure you don't do something stupid. The little girl can turn away, but she stays. If you try to run, I'll shoot both of you. The little girl first so you can watch her die." It was a hollow threat. He would never hurt a child, but as long as the mother believed him, that was all that mattered.

The mother turned the young girl's head around and held it so all the girl could see was the opposite wall. But she never took her eyes off the Union soldier as she did. The little girl heaved a couple of heavy sobs then started to cry loudly.

With her back to the wall, the slave began to slide down to the floor. Corporal Murray grabbed her and snatched her arm around violently, sending her sprawling across the floor.

"Stand up!" The pistol was spun around and pointed directly at her. She rolled over and slowly drew herself up to her feet, crying as she stood. Unlike the little girl, her crying was muted, more like muffled sobs from a heaving chest. Still, tears streamed down her face. "Pull your dress off," Murray commanded as he waved his pistol back and forth to make sure the colored girl wouldn't forget who was in command. Her tears only strengthened his resolve. "Let's see what a colored girl looks like when she's naked."

Murray whipped his arm back around and pointed the pistol toward the mother and daughter. "NOW! Or I shoot the little girl first."

Her face wrinkled in fear and shiny with tears, the slave pulled her dress up and over her head then let it fall to the floor at her feet. She stood there in her hand-sewn underwear, her head bent and her eyes cast down as teardrops fell onto the haphazard heap of cloth that was her dress.

"Get it all off! I want to see every inch of you." When the slave was completely naked, John Murray said, "Turn around. Let me see your ass." She complied. "Oh, yeah. You look real good, girl. Now, show me what you do for your white masters. Lay your back over that table."

The girl leaned against the table but had trouble getting on top. John Murray's drive had been watered. He wasn't in the mood to wait. He reached out and grabbed her arm then lifted her up and slammed her back onto the table. The slave screamed from the pain and reached around to rub the mistreated arm, but Murray slapped her arm away. It had blocked his view of her dark-skinned body. He smiled. This was going to be good.

Once again, he turned his pistol toward the white woman and her crying daughter. “Shut that girl up! Either of you move, you’re both dead. You understand?”

The white woman nodded in quick, short jerks of her head but said nothing as she tried to console her daughter. The little girl quieted but continued to sob as she stared at the opposite wall, eyes blank with incomprehension.

Murray slipped his belt off and unbuttoned his pants as quickly as he could. As he rammed himself into the slave, again and again, he continued to hold the pistol toward the mother and daughter. *This is so much better than the whores*, he thought.

The excitement of what he was doing swirled in his head. He didn’t last long. As soon as he finished, he pulled out and stood in plain view of the mother while he smiled. “If I didn’t have to leave,” he said, “I’d hang around and do the both of you just for the hell of it. But I can always come back. And if any of you ever breathe a word of this to anybody, that’s what I’ll do. I’ll come back at night and slit your throats, all of you. The little girl will go first, Momma, while you watch. Right after I rape her. I’ll rip her open then I’ll slice her up right in front of your eyes. Do you understand me?” There was only silence. “DO YOU?” he shouted.

The white woman was holding onto her little girl’s shoulders as the girl started crying out loud again. She squeezed them gently as she nodded. “We understand.”

John Murray turned to the slave and said, “You, too. You understand?” She nodded through her tears, which were coming hard and heavy. “Good. As far as all of you are concerned, this never happened. You’ll never talk about it again as long as you live.” He reached down and squeezed the slave’s nipple, hard. When she winced and jerked away, Murray said, “You’re a damned fine piece of tail, girl. You could make a good living with that thing.”

Then he was gone.

July 1, 1862 ~ Alabama Hospital #2, Richmond, Virginia

When Lieutenant Guice walked into the ward, the first thing he noticed was the stains on the floor, splotches of dark, muted colors. The stains were different shades of dark, caused by different things splashing onto the rough-sawn wood boards. He had been in too many hospitals, had seen the stains every time. He didn't want to think about what caused them, but couldn't help it. Thank goodness the soles of his boots were thick.

But his boots could not help with the smells. The odor of blood and urine and vomit and feces and other foul things wafted through the air. Flies, perhaps drunk on the odors, buzzed around in thick groups. Guice swatted at the ones directly in front of him as he walked between the cots.

The stains and smells and flies, however, were not the immediate problem. John Guice was here for another task, the part of his job he dreaded with every emotion he owned.

"Good morning," he said as he stopped beside Caleb's bed. "I'm sorry this happened to you. Unfortunately, dysentery is all too common in the camps."

"It's okay," Caleb responded. "I'm a mite better, now. It's been something awful, but I'm holding down a little food. And I ain't turning the sheets brown anymore. Not making much of a difference from here, am I?"

"I'm sorry…" Guice gave Caleb a confused look.

"Back to home, you said I might be the one to make the difference. Hard to make a difference when your insides is a'coming out at both ends."

The lieutenant smiled then said, "You'll get your chance."

"Yeah, I reckon I will. I'll be back with the Guards right soon. What happened to you?"

John Guice absently touched the bandage around his head. “Got hit beside my left eye at Gaines Farm. It was a hell of a thump. I was out cold for several minutes. I’m still having headaches, but I’ll be fine. It didn’t break the skin. Not as bad as the ball I took last summer at Manassas. Square in my left hip.”

Caleb winced. Guice smiled then lowered his head and stared at the floor again, momentarily not speaking.

“You was the one getting on me for staring down at the ground,” Caleb said. “Now you’re doing it, too.”

Lieutenant Guice looked back up at Caleb, eye-to-eye. “I’m... Caleb, I’m glad you’re better. But that’s not why I’m here. There’s... something else.”

Caleb could see the reluctance in Lieutenant Guice’s eyes. “What’s wrong?” He said, his voice rising. “Tell me!”

“The fighting at Gaines Farm was the fiercest of the war. So far, that is. The way the armies keep waltzing around each other, though, there may come a bigger battle one of these days.” Guice hesitated, reluctant to deliver his message.

“I heard tell we won the battle,” Caleb said. “And I heard the Yankees are leaving Virginia.”

“That’s correct. McClellan gave up on trying to take Richmond.”

“That’s good news, then,” Caleb said. “So what’s wrong?”

“It’s your brother, John,” the Lieutenant said. “He got hit. It’s, well, he’s in a bad way. The doctors don’t expect him to survive. I’m... I’m sorry.”

“No. How can that be? John’s my little brother.” Caleb stared at Lieutenant Guice. As the seconds ticked away, both men remained silent. When Caleb found his voice again, he said, “It’s my fault. If I’d been there, I might could have kept him safe.”

“As sick as you were? If you’d been there, you’d have died before the day was over. You can’t blame yourself. There was nothing you could do to change things. What’s meant to be is meant to be.”

Caleb looked down through the ward at the sick and wounded Confederate soldiers. There were a few empty beds, but not many. “Maybe he’ll pull through. Maybe he’ll make it.”

"For your sake, I hope so. It's not looking good, though. You need to prepare yourself."

"Prepare myself?" Caleb mumbled as he stared at Lieutenant Guice. They once again fell into silence. John dying? How could this be? Going home after the war had been a given for both of them. There was never any consideration of anything else. They talked about what they were going to do when the fighting was over, how they were going to make a success of the farm no matter which side won. Now John might not be going home at all?

"I, ah, should be getting back," Lieutenant Guice said, "I need a lot of rest so these headaches will go away for good. I look forward to welcoming you back to camp in a few days." The Lieutenant smiled a thin, strained smile then quickly turned and walked out. He did not look down at the floor as he left.

What about me? Caleb thought. With almost three years of enlistment left, there would be many battles in his future. Would he survive? Or would he be buried somewhere in Virginia, maybe next to John? *What about Emily? What would happen to Emily if I don't make it home?* Caleb had never questioned that he would see Emily again. Now, things were different. His brother was dying, and the question was there. This was real. This was war.

August 29, 1862 ~ Thoroughfare Gap, Virginia

"You hear that?" Caleb asked. He was standing beside Arlis as the 4th Alabama infantry assembled in the early morning mist on the dirt road at Thoroughfare Gap, preparing for the march forward. The rows were still forming behind them.

"You mean all them cannon firing in the distance?" Arlis said.

"Yeah. Muskets, too. Awful early in the morning for that much shooting."

"I heard there was some awful fighting yesterday afternoon at a farm owned by a man named Brawner. Glad we weren't part of it. Both armies practically toe-to-toe, out in the open, loading and firing, loading and firing. South Alabama boys could have told them how stupid that was. You'd go hungry if you hunted that way. Animals are too smart to stand there and get shot at. Lots of people hurt and killed, they say."

"And we're a'headed right into it this morning," Caleb said. "I 'spect we'll see plenty of action before today's over."

"True enough. Word is it's going to be big today. Won't be like when we whipped them here yesterday. That was only a skirmish. Lieutenant Guice said it would be bigger than the first battle they fought here at Manassas, over a year ago. A lot bigger."

"This land has had enough blood spilled on it. Including some of the Lieutenant's blood."

"That's right. He said he got shot in the butt the last time we fought here. There's worse places to get shot. I hope he stays safe this time."

"I hope we all do." Caleb looked away from the soldiers around him and into the distance, at the trees climbing the gentle slopes to the side, the leaves still carrying the dark green of late summer. "May not, though. I may see John again before sundown. He hadn't been buried two weeks, yet."

"You're going to be fine. I'll be there to watch out for you."

Caleb turned around and stared Arlis in the eyes. "I should have been there for my little brother. Now he's dead. Lieutenant Guice said things are meant to be, but meant to be or not, he was too young to die." Caleb was silent for a moment as he turned back around and gazed into the distance once again. "Wouldn't that be something? If I died today? Three months out and Maw and Paw already lost both of us."

Arlis' brows cocked, and his eyes narrowed as he said, "Don't talk like that. God will watch over us."

"I was supposed to be watching over John. My momma said to make sure he made it. Instead, I was in the hospital squirting my guts out at both ends. He stayed alive for seven weeks, a lot longer than the doctors thought he would. But he kept getting worse and worse. Worse and worse."

"Like the Lieutenant said, Caleb, it was God's will. There warn't nothing you could have done about it even if you hadn't been sick. You can't change God's will. We've got to think about today, about getting through one more day."

Caleb could see between the soldiers in front of him that the column had started moving. "Here we go," he said. "If I'm not here come dinnertime, it's been good being your friend. We had a lot of good hunting trips together."

"You hush up. There's lots of trees around here, so we'll have some cover to help us. We'll be fine." The two men smiled at each other. "All we've got to do is whip the Yankee's real quick and we'll be back in Alabama hunting again a'fore too awful long."

"If you shoot today like you shoot on our hunting trips," Caleb said, "You and me may both be here come tomorrow morning."

August 29, 1862 ~ Forest Around Stuart's Hill, Virginia

"I didn't know it got this hot all the way up here in Virginia," Caleb said. He was standing behind a tall oak in a patch of trees on Stuart's hill, immediately south of Brawner's farm.

"This uniform don't help none," Arlis said as a drop of sweat dripped from his nose.

"Yeah. I'd like to take it off and jump into the Sepulga River, back home."

"That would be a dream, sure enough."

"They're charging!" someone to their left shouted.

"Look at those fools!" Arlis said from behind a tree. "Charging uphill across an open field. I hope our officers never do that to us." He fired his musket then jerked it down to reload.

"I don't have to worry about hitting my target," Caleb said as he leaned around his tree and raised his musket. "I just shoot into that big mass of blue, and I'm bound to hit something."

Union soldiers fell like straws in the wind as they charged across the field, climbing the hill toward the trees. The Confederates could not load their muskets fast enough.

The lead edge of the blue wave reached the trees. A Union soldier hid behind a pine tree that was not quite as wide as he was, reloading his rifle. Caleb leaned out from the cover of his tree trunk, took careful aim at the part of the blue uniform that was beyond the edge of the pine, and sent bark and wood flying as his ball splintered the side of the tree, a mere inch away from hitting its target.

The Yankee soldier ducked, at the same time putting his arm over his head to protect himself from the spray of bark and splinters. He finished loading and lifted his musket. Thinking this was his chance to get a shot in before the Rebel could reload, the Union soldier leaned out from behind the pine. He never pulled the trigger. Arlis' ball hit him in the chest, lodging inside the man's heart. He was dead before his body heaped on the ground, his eyes open wide in shock.

"They're running," somebody shouted.

Caleb could see Union soldiers turning and running down the grassy slope of the open farmland, running back toward Chinn Ridge as fast as scared legs would carry them. The soles of their new boots flashed in the air as their legs pumped up and down, scattering side-to-side to miss the bodies of their comrades.

"That wasn't a real attack," someone else said. "They were trying to find out where we are."

"I 'spect they know now," Caleb said as he looked out at the bodies of Union soldiers scattered across the field.

Caleb and Arlis walked over to the Yankee Arlis had shot and looked at his grizzly body. Blood was everywhere.

While Caleb was struggling to stay alive in the hospital, Arlis had been in the thick of it at Gaines Farm, hitting his target with almost every shot he took. Arlis had no idea how many Yankees he had killed. He didn't try to keep track like some soldiers did. But in the rush and confusion of battle, he had never been this close to the results of his handiwork. This was a new experience for him. The dead Union soldier stared into the tops of the trees with unwavering stillness.

"That Yankee's sure enough mustered out now," a soldier to their side said.

"Thou shalt not kill," Arlis said, reciting the sixth commandment as he looked down at the man's open eyes and all the splattered blood.

"What?" Caleb asked.

Arlis turned and looked at Caleb.

"I killed one of God's creatures. Does the Great Spirit expect me to use his dead body? I ain't gonna eat him. We ain't got time to bury him and feed him to the trees. What am I supposed to do with him?"

"You don't do nothing," Caleb said. "You didn't willfully take his life. Just had to be. It's kill or be killed out here. All we can do is try to stay alive ourselves. We'll have to let God sort this mess out. I'm sure that's what my daddy would preach. Come on. We got to get back into position. They'll come get their dead soon enough. Be thankful it wasn't you or me."

Arlis stretched his neck to look at the sky above, glancing at the patches of blue and white between the clusters of dark leaves. He said nothing more as they walked back to their line and knelt behind the trees.

"We're on the move," an officer shouted sometime later. "Forward, men."

August 30, 1862 ~ Henry House Hill, Virginia

"I thought we was both dead last night," Arlis said as he leaned on his rifle and took several deep, hard breaths. "Staring at 'em eyeball-to-eyeball across that open field. Fighting till the sun went down." He took some more deep breaths before continuing, "But it's been worse today. I'm plumb tuckered out. I don't think I can go another step."

Caleb slowed his heavy breathing enough to get a few words out. "At least we weren't toe-to-toe today. They've been using their toes mostly to run away from us. Look yonder, in the distance. They're retreating, headed back toward Washington. These guys here are trying to cover their retreat. We've got them beat!"

"We've been giving them a pretty good licking, but you and I could still get shot. I can't run no more. I'm plumb wore out."

"Come on Arlis, We've got to make it up that last hill yonder, where that rock chimney is. We can sit there and pick them off while they're running away." Caleb pointed to a battered but still standing rock chimney, the house no longer surrounding it. The chimney was all that was left of the old Henry house. "We've sure enough got 'em whipped. Come on."

They lifted their rifles and started toward the hill, but Arlis stopped when he saw a mass of blue coming in from his left. "Look," he pointed. "More damn Yankees. That's a bunch of Ohio boys. I've seen that flag before."

"Don't matter where they're from. It only means there's more bullets to dodge."

The man on the other side of Arlis grunted loudly then fell to the ground. Arlis looked down at him then back up at Caleb. "We're out in the open, again. A dumb animal's got sense enough to hide so's we won't see him, but here we are in this open field, ripe for the shooting. We can't hide behind blades of grass."

"Just bend over and lower your profile," Caleb said. "Let's get up that hill to the chimney. Maybe we can hide behind it. If one of us gets hit, the other one will have to drag him up the hill."

"We'd be too easy a target if we was toting someone," Arlis said, "If one of us gets hit, the other one better run faster."

September 2, 1862 ~ Conecuh County Courthouse, Sparta, Alabama

This was not a shopping trip. News of a major battle had filtered through the community. Families from all over Conecuh County, including the Rose family, had made their way into the county seat to find out how the Confederate soldiers, their loved ones, had fared.

Thomas and Mary Rose walked down the dirt street arm-in-arm. Nathaniel was nearby, looking out from beneath the brim of his black bowler, keeping an eye out for the family as he always did when they were away from home. Emily looked at the goods in the store windows and trailed some distance behind, trying to look as though she were in town on her own. Everyone knew better, of course. The townspeople knew Emily and her parents well. They also knew Nathaniel and his black bowler with the eagle's feather. Emily had seen how white people kept a respectable distance from Nathaniel. Most black people, too. *He does have a menacing look,* she thought. *Tall and strong. High cheek bones and rigid facial features. But that's silly. They don't know him like I do. Why, he's as nice as can be.*

The Conecuh County courthouse was surrounded by scattered groups of people, mostly white, milling about talking to each other. Slaves were there, too, but tended to gather in groups behind the white people, far enough away so that normal conversation could not be overheard.

Thomas turned to Nathaniel and said, "You don't have to stay with us. You can go talk with your friends if you want to."

Nathaniel looked around at the people in the dirt streets, the groups of slaves standing around talking with each other. He turned back to Thomas and said, "I will see them at church on Sunday."

Thomas nodded and smiled. There was something comforting about Nathaniel's devotion to his owners.

The Mayor of Sparta, a childhood friend of Thomas', turned from the group he had been chatting with and stepped over to meet the Rose's as they walked up.

"Morning, Bob," Thomas said as they stood in front of the courthouse.

The Mayor looked both ways then glanced behind him before saying, "If you don't mind too terrible much, Tom, when you're in town, in front of other folks, call me Mayor. Out of respect, you understand. It's, well, I have to keep up a certain image. In front of other folks. You know how it is."

Thomas looked at his friend and cocked his eyebrow then said, "Why, we've known each other since we were little boys, Bob… ah, Mayor. I don't know how it would make any difference, but if that's what you want, that's what you'll get."

"Thank you, Tom." The Mayor glanced around again, making sure no one had heard the exchange. He looked at Mary and tipped his hat then said, "Afternoon, Mary."

"Good afternoon, Mayor," Mary replied, accentuating the word 'Mayor.' She suppressed a smile, but Thomas could see the mischief in her eyes and hear the slight tint of sarcasm in her voice.

"Nathaniel," the Mayor said as he nodded toward Thomas and Mary's slave.

"Mayor, Sir," Nathaniel nodded back.

As Emily walked up, the Mayor said, "Well, I declare! This must be little Emily. You sure have grown up, young lady. And you keep getting prettier every day."

Emily smiled and curtsied.

"Word is," Thomas said, "That this new battle at Manassas is the biggest of the war."

"Is it over, Daddy?" Emily asked.

"Yes," Thomas said. "People riding the trains say it ended a couple of days ago. Rumor is we won, but we don't know for sure."

"The final word should come from Montgomery any time," the Mayor said. He glanced at the north end of town as he spoke. "I wish we had telegraph in Sparta. Why, they ought to make telegraph a priority in every county seat."

"That would cost a lot of money," Thomas said. "I 'spect the government is spending most of their money to put soldiers on the field."

"Hmm," the Mayor muttered as he continued to look into the distance to the north.

Thomas tipped his hat. "We're going to look around town for a spell. It was good to see you again, Mayor."

"Good to see you, Tom." The Mayor reached out and shook Thomas' hand, using both his hands to do so, and smiled warmly.

When they turned to walk away, Emily saw Caleb's parents and sisters walking toward the courthouse. "Good morning," Thomas said.

There was something about Caleb's father. Emily thought he looked older, much older than he had only a few months ago. And he looked tired, as though he had been carrying everyone's sins for far too long. The hollows of his eyes were dark, and his mouth curled down at the sides, fixed in a partial frown. Perhaps age had moved faster for this man than it had for others.

"Morning," Sam replied.

Mary Rose and Sarah Garner smiled knowingly at each other. It seemed to come from the heart, needing no words to accompany it. Thomas mumbled something as though he was having trouble talking. "John was a fine young man," he finally said. "He will be missed."

Emily was uncomfortable watching her father. It was awkward for Thomas. He had never been good at this sort of thing. He had extended his sympathy to Sam and Sarah after church services more than once, but he could not seem to let it go.

"It was God's will," Sam said. "We can't argue with God's will. We must accept it. Sarah and I will be reunited with John someday."

The way you're aging, it won't be long, Emily thought, but she held her tongue. It was like that all through the county. If somebody died, no matter how accidental, it was God's will. That attitude allowed Southern soldiers to perform great feats of bravery on the battlefield. They knew that if their day had come, it didn't matter what they did. And if their day had not come, they would be safe regardless of what happened. Might as well charge straight into the fire-spitting muzzles of enemy rifles. If God didn't want them to die, he would save them no matter the odds.

Emily had never said anything out loud, but she questioned whether God wanted all these men, on both sides of the war, to come home to heaven all at once. It seemed to her that charging the enemy would create more souls for God to deal with than staying back in their camps. Looking at it that way, things weren't necessarily meant to be. Maybe these people were right, but she didn't think so. All that truly mattered, though, was that God watched after Caleb, kept him safe from enemy fire.

"It was good seeing you," Thomas said. Emily had been lost in thought and had missed the conversation. The two families smiled at each other and parted.

"We've been in town for hours," Emily said. "When is the rider coming? I've got to know if Caleb's okay."

"Won't be long," Thomas said.

"When is this war going to be over?" Emily asked as she looked to the sky. "We keep winning battles, but the war won't end. Don't the Yankees know they're whipped? I want Caleb to come home. Now!"

"He hasn't been gone all that long, Girl," Mary told her daughter. "Why, he just left last May."

"That was forever ago," Emily said. "Way back in the spring."

"I'm afraid this war might take a long time, Girl," her father said. "We've got to be patient. We've won most of the battles so far, but none of them have been that big. That is, before this one. It's like they've been pawing at each other, trying to find strengths and weaknesses. But I 'spect this battle was…" Thomas stopped in mid-sentence as Nathaniel nodded sharply at him. "What?"

"Hooves," Nathaniel said. "Coming fast." He pointed toward the north edge of town, toward the dirt road that led to Evergreen and eventually to Montgomery.

"I don't hear anything," Thomas said. He stood there a moment and looked in the direction that Nathaniel had pointed. "There it is! I see dust a'flying. Beyond the trees there. It's got to be a rider. This may be it."

"I hear it now," Emily said. "Oh, please, God, let Caleb be safe."

"And let us win the battle," Thomas added.

The rider, a young boy, pulled to a stop in front of the courthouse, dismounted, and ran to where the Mayor was waiting. Everyone in town fell silent as the young boy handed the Mayor a piece of paper. The Rose family turned and walked back, joining the people gathered around the front of the courthouse. The slaves backed away to let the white folks get in closer. Except for Nathaniel. He stayed close to the Rose family.

"The word from Virginia," the Mayor called out in a voice that seemed stronger than his years would indicate. Emily crossed her fingers as she held her hands to her neck, directly under her chin. "Everyone is aware that there has been a second battle at Manassas. This engagement was much larger than any battle we've seen before." He read the handwriting on the paper for several seconds then looked up at the crowd and raised his voice, "It was a clear victory for our Confederate boys!"

Cheers and whoops rang out from the crowd. Several hats flew into the air. Small boys chased after the hats, hoping to get a halfpenny for their return. Horses, the few that were there as some of the whites and most of the slaves had walked into town, skittered back and forth at the sudden burst of sound. People began talking to each other, a bee buzz of congratulation swelling throughout the gathering.

The Mayor's smile disappeared as he looked back down at the paper in his hand. He waved his arm for silence and, one by one, the groups standing around the courthouse stopped their conversations. All eyes focused once again on the Mayor.

"Please, friends, I… I must continue. The 4th Alabama infantry was in the thick of the action. And our own Conecuh Guards distinguished themselves. They fought bravely," he added, though there was nothing written on the paper he held to indicate that was the case. "I must tell you, we have lost two of our own in our great cause."

Emily's eyes widened as she sucked in a huge breath. She held her breath as she reached down and grabbed each of her parent's hands, squeezing them so tight that Mary wiggled her fingers to try to ease the grip.

"I regret to inform you that we lost Sergeant Jasper Newton Stinson," the Mayor continued.

A gasp went up on the other side of the dirt street. Emily turned to see Mrs. Stinson's knees buckle as she dipped to the ground, her face pale and stunned. Her husband held her up, kept her from crashing into the dirt and gravel.

"We also lost Private Joseph Stallworth."

Emily relaxed her grip as a scream rose from someone in the crowd only a few feet away. A woman was crying heavily, another mother's heart breaking.

"Please give your condolences and your charity to the families of these two young men. Let us bow our heads in prayer to help guide their souls." The Mayor looked over the crowd to ensure that heads were bowed before continuing. "Our Father, we beg you to accept these boys into your arms…"

The prayer was short. When it ended, the Mayor called out again, "There were wounded as well. Among the officers, Lieutenant John Guice. I deeply regret to say that he lost his leg."

Gasps were heard throughout the crowd, including Emily's. She had not known John Guice personally, but the Guice family was well respected. Caleb had spoken highly of the Lieutenant. And Caleb's few brief letters were written by John Guice, as dictated by Caleb.

"His service to our noble cause is now over," the Mayor continued. "When he returns home, I want you all to welcome him with open arms. Let us never forget his sacrifice.

We'll remember every time we see his pants leg hanging slack, Emily thought, but she said nothing.

"Also, among the enlisted men, the wounded are Corporal Alfred Christian, Private Charles Floyd, Private Jessie Goff, Private…"

The list went on. Ten wounded in all, counting Lieutenant Guice. The Conecuh Guards had suffered heavily. Emily felt bad for them, for the soldiers and for their families. How could you stand there and listen to the Mayor shouting out for all to hear that your son was suffering from a wound or, much worse, had been killed on some field far away from home, his body to be placed in a grave so far away they would never travel to see it?

At the same time, she was happy that Caleb's name had not been on the list. The happiness, however, was tempered by the fact that there would be other battles to come. How many times would she stand on the streets of Sparta listening to the casualty list? How many times would she have to suffer through this? And, worst of all, what would she do if Caleb's name was called out? She didn't know, but she knew one thing. She would not cry out loud or fall on the ground like the others. She would be strong. She would do something to show that strength. But what?"

April 23, 1863 ~ Trail From the Sepulga Trading Post, Sepulga, Alabama

There was no letter. Hearing from Caleb had become rare. When a letter did come, it was short, a few quick sentences. Arlis could write Caleb's words, but he labored over the individual letters so, taking long seconds to properly construct each one. It was nothing like Guice's easy, flowing script, smooth consonants and vowels that fell out of the pen quickly and beautifully. But Lieutenant Guice was no longer a part of the fighting, no longer there to write Caleb's letters.

"It's been a year since he left," Emily announced to the spring breeze that fluttered the pines to the sides of the trail.

Nathaniel, the supplies they had purchased from the trading post slung over his shoulder, heavy but not slowing him down the least, walked beside her, slightly behind as was the habit of a slave. It was easy enough to realize who Emily was talking about. He could barely hide his own disappointment when the clerk had checked the postal bin and dryly stated there was nothing for the Rose family. He could think of no encouragement to offer.

"I've tried screaming in the woods," she continued.

"Screaming in the woods?" Nathaniel repeated. His brows cocked.

"Yes. It sounds silly, doesn't it? But I did. I went out one night after Momma and Daddy went to sleep. When I was deep into the pines, I screamed at the world to stop this stupid war."

"I'm afraid the world isn't listening."

"No. It isn't. And I felt so stupid afterward. I went back inside and lay on my bed until the sun came up. But I'm not stupid. War is stupid. Why doesn't the world listen?"

"You aren't rich."

"What?"

"The world only listens to fools with money."

"Then we've got fools listening to fools," Emily observed.

Nathaniel snorted a short laugh. "Yes. And the everyday fools will continue to listen as long as the rich fools who are running the war still have money, regardless of what side they're on. When the fighting takes the rich people's money away, the little people will start to listen to other people. Perhaps those others will want the war to end."

Emily turned and looked at Nathaniel and said, "Yes, but how long will that take?" Then she turned back around. She didn't expect an answer. Nathaniel didn't offer one.

They walked along in silence a few minutes. A hawk soared well above the tops of the pines, lazily drifting back and forth. It started to lower its circles, closing in on something below. Suddenly, it swooped down. As soon as it arced inches above the ground, it was on its way back skyward, a field rat in its talons.

Without turning around, Emily said, "And how many more soldiers have to die before we start listening to the politicians who believe in peace?"

Nathaniel glanced to the sides then turned his head enough to take a look behind them, a constant habit as he walked. "I'm afraid the cloth is dyed," he said with finality. "The war is engaged and will not end until one side sees more hope in surrender than in continuing to fight. Even if we elect politicians who want peace, the fighting will not stop as long as both armies have even a faint hope of victory."

July 2, 1863 ~ Big and Little Round Tops, Gettysburg, Pennsylvania

"I'm so almighty tired of marching," Arlis said. "Twenty more miles this morning alone. I feel like I've walked around the world since we joined the army. Twicet."

"In this heat, too. It's got to be ninety degrees out here. I'm thirsty and my canteen's empty."

"Mine, too. There's a creek down there. We could fill up our canteens if they'd let us."

Lieutenant Lee came running down the line, shouting at his men to form up.

"What for?" Arlis asked him. "We need to rest. And we need water."

"No time for that," the Lieutenant said. "This hill right here in front of us is Big Round Top. That hill over there is Little Round Top. That's where the Yankees are. We've got to get after them, fast and hard. This may be the key to winning the battle, men. And the Conecuh Guards are going to be a critical part of it!"

The Lieutenant didn't wait for a comment. He continued down the line, getting the 4th Alabama ready for the charge.

"So we've got to climb the side of this hill," Arlis said, "about halfway between the bottom and the top, then down the backside. Then we cross the field between, and those of us who ain't dead by then will charge up the second hill. We'll have to work our way around all those big rocks. And there ain't enough big trees to give us decent cover. I wish this war was over and I was home."

"I heard talk that whoever wins this battle wins the war," Caleb said. "I don't know if that's true, though. Maybe wishful thinking."

On Lieutenant Lee's command, the 4th Alabama began to move forward. They formed a line along the slope of Big Round Top, not quite reaching the top. There were two more regiments to their right, reaching the top and beyond, and several to their left, stretching all the way down to the creek. It was a formidable line of gray.

Going downhill was easy, but they were peppered with scattered sniper fire from Yankee sharpshooters as they crossed the field between the two hills. Lieutenant Lee gave the command to charge. Exhausted and close to dehydration, they tried to run up the slope of Little Round Top.

A volley of rifle fire burst from the Union troops at the crest. There were more shots than Caleb could remember hearing at one time, coming from well-entrenched Union soldiers who enjoyed the advantage of high ground. Many of the charging Confederates fell. The rest of the gray wave backed up, hiding behind the meager cover on the slopes. They fired when they could and tried to regroup.

Over the course of the next hour and a half, the Confederate troops were ordered to charge the hill twice more. Both attacks were repelled. The combatants were often within arm's reach of each other. Caleb bent down and took a canteen from a fallen Yankee soldier. It was almost full. Between attacks, he and Arlis hid behind a rock and drained the canteen.

"Oh, dear Lord," Arlis said. "Thank you for sending that canteen to us. I don't know if I'd have made it another step without water."

Caleb looked back at the body of the Union soldier. "Just as well. I don't reckon the Yankee who owned it will ever be a'drinking water again."

Suddenly, there was a burst of shouting from up the slope, not far away. Caleb and Arlis looked up at a sea of blue, Union troops with bayonets fixed, charging toward them. The Yankees were running downhill from Little Round Top, like angry blue ants pouring out of a mound, charging the entire Confederate line.

Musket balls began flying in from their right, a direction that was supposed to be clear. Confused, dismayed, and almost sick from being tired and dehydrated, the Confederate troops retreated toward Big Round Top.

Caleb stopped and hastily fired his musket at the charging soldiers then turned and ran downhill, trying to reload as he did. Arlis was beside him but stumbled and fell. Caleb reached down to help Arlis get up like they had helped each other many times before. When he pulled, Arlis did not immediately rise to his feet. Instead, his friend stumbled and fell again.

"I'm hit," Arlis said. "My side."

Caleb grabbed Arlis' arm and pulled it behind his neck then attempted to lift Arlis and carry him. Arlis was thin but tall. He was not light. Arlis tried to help, but shock and pain coursed through him. They could not move fast enough. The Yankees would be on them in mere seconds.

Caleb kept dragging. He couldn't leave Arlis to the Yankees. A Yankee prison would be bad enough, but this was a battlefield. In the heat and passion of war, a bayonet might be used instead. It was far easier and left the charging soldier unencumbered with a prisoner.

Caleb knew he was too slow. The Yankees were closing. He grimaced as he thought about a bayonet slipping into his back, between his ribs, but he couldn't leave Arlis behind. He just couldn't.

A soldier jumped into Caleb's peripheral view, on the other side of Arlis. Caleb reached for his blade, but as he turned, he saw that the soldier was wearing gray. It was Sam Little, the iron man of the Conecuh Guards. Sam grabbed Arlis' other arm and said, "I'll help you. Afore we all get kilt."

"Thanks, Sam."

With Sam's help, they could almost run full speed. Sam Little was called the iron man because he could be depended on. He had never missed a battle. He had never been in the hospital. He had been present for every single roll call. He had never even been on furlough.

There was little energy left in Caleb's legs, but he seemed to run faster than he thought he could, trying to keep up with Sam. He consciously willed one leg at a time to lift and move forward then go down so the other leg could lift.

Thinking about each step kept his mind off Arlis. How badly was he wounded? Would his friend make it? He couldn't imagine going through the horrors of war without Arlis beside him, but he couldn't think about that right now. It was one leg up, out, and down. Then the other leg up, out, and down.

Somehow they stumbled around the rocks and bounced through bushes and young trees and made it downhill, across the field, and over Big Round Top. Caleb was amazed they made it without getting hit in the back by a musket ball. They were such easy targets. He never knew that Arlis had been hit by a sniper to the side, not the Union soldiers who were pursuing them with fixed bayonets. He never found out that the Union soldiers chasing them were out of ammunition, and that it was the only reason he was still breathing at the end of the day.

July 9, 1863 ~ Conecuh County Courthouse, Sparta, Alabama

"How many times do we have to come down here and listen to them call out the dead and wounded?" Emily said. "Isn't this war ever going to end?"

"It may end all too soon, Girl," Thomas Rose said. "The politicians and the newspapers declared a victory at Gettysburg, but General Lee is retreating. They called it a 'strategic' retreat. It doesn't sound much like the kind of strategy a winning army should be using. It's not just Lee's army that's faltering, either. The Yankees captured Vicksburg over on the Mississippi River. They outnumber us. Not enough gets through the blockade, so they're better equipped. And they keep putting fresh fish on the field. We've got no more boys to send to the front."

Mary coughed then hung her head and said nothing. Tears began to leak from Emily's eyes. Nathaniel stood to the side, quiet and observant.

"The Conecuh Guards were in the thick of the battle in Gettysburg, Pennsylvania," the Mayor called out loud and clear. "My friends, our boys acquitted themselves well in defense of our great cause. The Richmond newspapers have announced the tremendous Confederate victory at Gettysburg, but it was not without great sacrifice."

Emily had learned to hate that word, 'sacrifice.' She was crying long before the first names were called out.

"We lost three of our own. Those who are no longer with us are 1st Lieutenant William Lee…" Gasps rose from the crowd as they always did, particularly for the officers. "3rd Sergeant John Robert Richey and Private William T. Coleman. Please bow your heads as we beseech the Lord to guide their souls into his heavenly bosom."

Caleb was still alive! Her heart always fluttered when the list of dead was finished, and Caleb's name was not on it. At the same time, however, Emily wondered how many more times she would have to endure the horrible suspense of the death list before this war was over.

"Taken prisoner by our enemy are Sergeant James Cotton, 2nd Corporal Joseph A. Thomas, Private John J. Daniels, Private..."

The list went on. Seven soldiers from the Conecuh Guards captured. By now, Emily had learned that many of the captured soldiers were those who were wounded and left lying on the battlefield as the Confederate army retreated. She knew that many would die before reaching home, before ever being released from a Union prison.

"And, finally, the wounded," the Mayor continued. "1st Sergeant Andrew J. Mosely, 2nd Sergeant Alfred H. Floyd, Private and Reverend George A. Wood, Private Archibald D. McInnis, Private Arlis Johnston..."

Arlis! Emily's heart fluttered when she heard his name called. Her knees felt weak, but she didn't allow them to bend. She stopped crying and looked around to see if Arlis' grandparents were there. She didn't see them. Arlis had been brought up by his grandparents, but they were getting old. They didn't get around like they used to.

She listened intently as the Mayor finished the list. Caleb's name was not called. Caleb was alive, uncaptured and unhurt! But Arlis... Emily chewed on her lip. Arlis told her he would protect Caleb, make sure Caleb made it home safe and sound. How serious was his wound? The list did not say. It rarely did. Sometimes the next thing you knew, the soldier sent a letter from a camp near some distant battlefield. All too often, however, the soldier never left the hospital alive. A letter with a mourning cover came, the envelope's black edges revealing the sad tale that would be inside.

A few of the ones who survived would be coming home. Mostly amputees. The rest would be returned to the Guards as soon as they could walk and lift a musket. She didn't know about Arlis, but it meant that he might not be in the next battle. That also meant he wouldn't be there to watch after Caleb. She worried and chewed her lip some more.

July 13, 1863 ~ Falling Waters, West Virginia

"They've got their backs to the river," Corporal John Murray said. "They're trapped pigs, ready for slaughter. This should break the backs of the damned Rebels."

"Water's too low," a private said. "They'll cross into Virginia and get away again."

"Not if we get after them," Murray said. "We can't afford to nibble here and there. We've got to go after the Rebs with everything we've got before they cross the river."

"You?" Corporal Stan Gerszewski said. "You're no account, a deadbeat. Just because you can turn the ladies' eyes with your looks, that doesn't make you a good soldier. I've seen you hiding behind others and running away from the fighting."

"What are you talking about?" Murray countered. Gerszewski had been a thorn in Murray's side for the entire war. "I'm not a hospital rat like some of the others. I've been in every battle this unit has ever fought. I've been right in the thick of it." He looked around at the other men in the group. "I know the rest of you have seen me fight. Tell this idiot how brave I was."

No one said anything for several seconds then a private said, "I ain't got time to keep up with others in the middle of a battle. Hell, all I'm trying to do is keep my head on while taking the Rebels' heads off." Several amens murmured through the group as their hats dipped up and down, soldiers nodding their agreement.

"You ain't never been hit in battle," Stan Gerszewski said. "Not the slightest little wound. I don't think I've ever even seen you dirty. Now, that's a trick after all we've been through."

"That doesn't mean I'm not as brave or braver than the rest of the men," Murray shouted back. "I keep myself clean. I'm not a pig like you, Gerszewski."

Corporal Gerszewski laid his musket against a tree and lifted his tightened fists. "Who are you calling a pig, you jackass? I say you're a coward, and I can back it up."

Corporal Stan Gerszewski was a big man, thick boned with huge fists. Murray knew he had little chance in a fair fight, but he had to silence the man. His right hand fell to his side and fingered the bayonet that was strapped there. It would not be a good idea to use it. For one, there was no handle. If he tried to grip the ring, and it slipped in his hand, he could end up slicing himself. But it would also look bad if Gerszewski fought with nothing more than his fists, and Murray slid a blade into his guts. Still, he wasn't about to let the big Polish man beat him to a pulp. If it came down to it, he would have to claim self-defense. Before he was forced to pull the bayonet, however, they heard the Lieutenant shouting for them to form a line.

Stan Gerszewski gave John Murray one last look, a look of total disgust and disdain, lowered his fist then retrieved his musket and fell in with the others.

Moments later, the officers cried, "CHARGE!" The men moved forward. As soon as they were in range, a volley thundered from the Confederate line along the river. Smoke filled the air.

Corporal Murray lagged back and was some distance behind the others. Stan Gerszewski was leading the group. Murray wanted to put a ball in his back but knew he couldn't afford to. It would look too suspicious for a charging Union soldier to be shot in the back. But he also knew that Gerszewski would turn around for the sole purpose of checking on him, to see if Murray was lagging back, avoiding the fight. Gerszewski was determined to get Corporal Murray in trouble. John Murray couldn't afford to let that happen.

Murray was a crack shot, one of the best in the regiment. He had his musket up and ready when Corporal Gerszewski turned around to check behind him. Confusion reigned. Musket fire was constant, and a gunpowder haze was everywhere. No one would be the wiser.

July 23, 1863 ~ Manassas Gap, Virginia

When they loaded Arlis onto the medical wagon, days ago in Pennsylvania, the driver said it did not look as though any organs had been hit. The ball did not pierce the intestine, either, so the driver thought that Arlis had a fair chance to live. Caleb hoped it was true. You could never be sure, though. Lots of small wounds would turn into bad ones, festering until the soldier went crazy. Most of the time they got sane again when the fever broke. All too often, however, the festering got worse until they died.

The driver said Arlis would likely be taken to General Hospital at Howard's Grove in Richmond. Eventually. Three weeks later, Caleb still had no word. They were a retreating army, being pursued by the Yankees. News about wounded comrades in Richmond was a luxury no one had time to provide. If Arlis wasn't too bad, he might have been moved to an Alabama Hospital by now, perhaps the same one where Caleb had spent weeks being sicker than he'd ever been in his life.

With Arlis gone, Caleb mingled with the remainder of the 4th Alabama as they retreated. This was not marching. Marching was the last word Caleb would use to describe the rag-tag way the defeated Confederates meandered through the fields and trees. Stagger was a better word. They staggered through the Virginia countryside. The soles of their worn out shoes barely cleared ground each time they lifted a foot for another step, but somehow they continued to move. It was all Caleb could do to put one foot in front of the other, again and again.

Many of the men were bandaged in one place or another, often multiple places, and virtually all of them hung their heads as they stumbled along. Somehow, though, they moved fast enough to avoid the bulk of the Yankees.

Caleb could hear a skirmish not far to the rear. While the Conecuh Guards were not in the main fighting in Manassas Gap, it was close enough so that a ball occasionally whizzed overhead. Caleb kept glancing to the side as he trudged along. The Yankees pecked at them, sharpshooters and sporadic raids.

He heard the sound of a musket being fired, much closer than the fighting to the rear. Several more musket shots shattered the air around them, all close by. He began to run toward the nearest tree as he glanced in the direction from which the shots had come. A scattering of blue soldiers sprang from the bushes, a Yankee raid. Caleb didn't stop to shoot. When there was a surprise attack, Arlis taught him, always look for the nearest cover first then fire when he was safely behind it. Arlis also taught him to run fast. It was harder to hit a running target.

Caleb was a couple of steps short of the tree when his leg gave out, and he stumbled and fell. He tried to get back up but couldn't put any weight on his leg. Looking down, he could see a hole in his pants, his right thigh. Blood was all around the hole and still dribbling out. He dropped his musket and grabbed his thigh, above the wound, squeezing with both hands to try to stop the bleeding. Balls whizzed all around him as the Guards and other companies in the 4th Alabama returned fire.

"Hang on," Sam Little shouted. "I'll try to stop the bleeding. You fire back when you can."

Sam pulled a strip of cloth from his blanket roll and reached under Caleb's leg at the same time that Caleb lifted his musket. Caleb aimed and fired, but the shot sounded odd like he was at the end of a tunnel. All of the sounds of battle began to drift away as though the war was traveling to another place. There was a white edge to the trees. Even the blue-clad soldiers were white on the side as they ran here and there. Everything was turning white. There was a brief moment when all he saw was white with thin edges of color that suggested soldiers and trees. Sounds turned into silence. That was the last thing he remembered.

August 26, 1863 ~ Rose Residence, Forks of Sepulga Community, Alabama

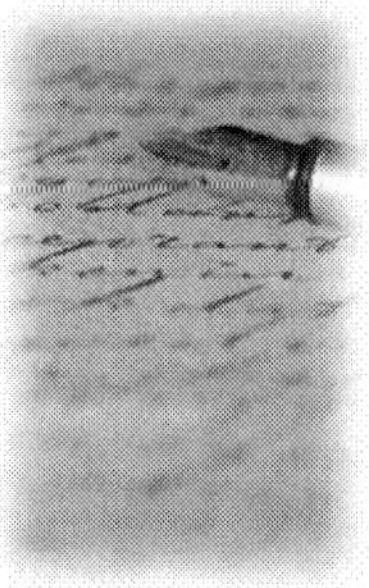

As Thomas and Nathaniel rushed into the house, Thomas called out, "Girl. Where are you? Got a letter for you." The door closed behind them with a thump as Thomas held up a piece of paper, offering it to an empty room.

Moments later, Emily rushed in. "A letter for me?" Excitement rushed out with her words.

"I sent Nathaniel to the general store for some tar. The post office there had a letter for you. It came all the way from Richmond."

"It must be from Caleb, but Arlis is wounded. He wouldn't be writing a letter for Caleb if he's still in the hospital. Maybe he's okay now. Maybe he's back with the Guards." She looked at the letter her father held in his hand. Excitement quickly gave way to concern. Arlis had not been with the Guards while he was wounded, not there to protect Caleb. Something bad could have happened. "Maybe Caleb's hurt." She gasped and put her hand over her mouth as dire possibilities ran through her head. "Oh, Daddy, what could it be? I'm scared."

"Now, don't go getting riled up just yet. There's not been a major battle, so there's no casualty lists, no need to go to Sparta. Maybe this is nothing more than an everyday 'how do' letter. The address looks like Arlis' handwriting. It's poor enough, but it's readable. By the way, if Arlis can get by writing like this, Caleb could, too. You need to teach that boy his letters when he gets home."

"Daddy!"

"Okay, okay. I don't think anything's bad wrong, Girl. It's not a mourning cover. It ain't black around the edges."

Thomas reached out and offered the letter to Emily. Reluctantly, she took it. She looked at the back then the front. There was no paper stamp glued to the envelope. It was ink-stamped with a simple circle and the letters "PAID 10" on the inside of the circle. There was a postmark from Richmond with a date of August 11, 1863. In Arlis' roughly constructed letters, each one a different size from the last, it was addressed to "Emily Rose, Sepulga Post Office, Alabama." There was no return address.

Mary Rose came into the room to see what the fuss was about.

"It's a letter from Richmond," Emily said to her mother. "It's from Caleb. I hope. It might be something bad about him."

"You won't know till you read it, Girl," Mary said. "No need to jump at things."

Emily stared at her mother then her father and Nathaniel. They all stared at the letter in her hands. She looked down and slid her fingers along the envelope, feeling for clues. There was a single piece of paper on the inside, folded once along the middle. She could feel nothing else. She looked back up at her father.

"Go ahead and open it," he said, trying not to look as nervous and anxious as he felt.

With her stomach in a knot, Emily took a small knife from the table and carefully pried the flap open. She pulled out the letter from the inside and ran her fingers across the rough surface of the cream-colored paper. There was a pinkish cast to the color. With one last glance at her parents and Nathaniel, she unfolded the paper and began to read aloud.

"Dear Miss Emily, This here is Arlis. I got wounded at Gettysburg. It was not bad. I'm okay now. Caleb helped save me. Caleb got wounded at Manassas Gap."

Emily sucked in a deep breath, glanced up at her parents, then looked back down at the letter and continued to read aloud as tears rolled down her cheeks.

"I was not there to watch for him. I was in the hospital. He has a small flesh wound in his leg. The doctor said he will be okay. Please let his folks know. I am back with the Guards now. Caleb will be back soon. Don't worry none. He will be fine. This time I will be here to watch out for him. Sincerely, Private Arlis Johnston, CSA"

"Thank goodness he's okay," Thomas said. "He'll have a scar he can show off for the rest of his life."

"Thomas!" Mary said.

Emily stared at her father as the tears flowed from her eyes. Thomas only shrugged. He knew it was a stupid thing to say, but there was no need to compound it by saying something else stupid. He couldn't think of anything that was better, so he finally said, "I need to take care of the roof. Before the next rain gets here. Come on, Nathaniel. I'll need a hand." The men turned, took their hats off the pegs, and walked out the door.

April 19, 1864 ~ Rose Residence, Forks of Sepulga Community, Alabama

The wooden spoon clattered across the floor. There were small streams of buttered grits on the edge of the table, the floor, and Emily's dress.

"I'm... I'm sorry," Thomas said as Mary dabbed at Emily's dress with a damp rag.

"It's okay, Daddy. It's an old dress. I can get it clean again."

"You're as nervous as a sinner at church," Mary said to Thomas. She coughed once before continuing, "You might as well go ahead and tell him."

Him? Nathaniel turned his head and looked at Mary. Her eyes gave away only enough for Nathaniel to know that Thomas had something to say. And, apparently, what he had to say was meant specifically for the family slave. He turned his eyes back to Thomas.

"Yeah," Thomas said. "Might as well." He pushed his breakfast plate to the side and set his elbows on the table with his hands folded together in front of him. "You see, Nathaniel, this war... well, it ain't looking so good. The chances are better than even that we won't win. If we don't... You know Lincoln has already declared the slaves free. As of last January."

"Yes, Sir," Nathaniel said, setting his fork down on his breakfast plate as he listened.

"And even if we was to win somehow, there's talk that the slaves might be set free anyway. Over a period of time, of course. It wouldn't happen right away."

Nathaniel nodded his head though he had heard nothing about the Confederacy voluntarily freeing their slaves.

"Mary and I had a serious talk about it last night. I ain't never bought no slaves. You came to us when Mary's brother died. But you've never really been like a slave to us, you understand."

Nathaniel said nothing, and his face gave nothing away as he sat with his hands on the table, palms down, on either side of his plate.

"We think you ought to be able to leave if you want to. Go up North where you can be a free man. I can give you a horse and a little money to help, enough to buy whatever tickets you might need and get you set up somewhere where it's safe."

"I see," Nathaniel said. "What about the Home Guard? It would be difficult for me to travel all the way to the North without being captured by them."

"The Yankees are all over the South," Thomas answered. "Pensacola. Mobile. Nashville. They'll be easy enough to find. I can give you your papers saying you're free. Show them to the Yankees. They can help arrange your passage. We'll be fine here."

Nathaniel glanced at Mary then Emily and finally back at Thomas. "Have I done something that makes me unwelcome here?"

"Why, no!" Thomas said, waving his hands in front of him. "Nothing at all. It's like Emily said. You're like family to us. But down here in the South..." His words trailed off.

"We felt like we ought to let you be a free man," Mary said. "You've done nothing wrong. Why, you've been wonderful to us. But it's the right thing to do."

"Nathaniel," Thomas said, finding his voice again. "This war won't go on forever. We can't guarantee it'll be safe for former slaves when the war is over, and the Confederate soldiers come home. We don't know what it's going to be like. It might be fine. But it might not."

Emily was stunned. This was the first she had heard of this. Nathaniel leaving? It was a shock to her, but her parents were right. He deserved a chance to be a free man. There was no good reason to hold him back. Especially if his safety was involved. She said nothing as a few tears dripped from her chin.

"So I am not being sent away for any particular reason? You are offering me a chance to be a free man up North, nothing more?"

"Yes," Thomas said. "We would never run you away. We want to do what's best for you."

Nathaniel took his dinner cloth and wiped the tears from Emily's chin then dabbed her cheeks dry. He turned back to his plate and picked up his fork. "I'll stay," was all he said as he started eating again.

May 3, 1864 ~ Evening Campfire, Outside Gordonsville, Virginia

"More cornpone," Arlis said in disgust as he looked at the cornmeal cake on his tin plate. "They ain't even made proper. They got no milk. It's only water and cornmeal. And we got no long sweetening to pour on them. It's awful, downright awful. I'd give a month's pay for some of Momma's fried chicken right now. Along with some mashed taters and gravy. A slice of Grandma's apple pie would, sure enough, be heaven."

"Apple pie?" Caleb said. "You can forget that. Nobody would give you a slice of an apple for the worthless script we get each month, much less a pie with real sugar in it. Confederate money was worth something back when we joined, but it's worth less and less each day it seems like."

"Yeah, you're right about that. And the food we're a'getting is worse and worse each day. I'm so hungry I can't see straight. Heck, Caleb, I'd even eat a blackbird right now." Arlis fingered the trigger of his musket. "You ain't seen none around here, have you?"

"I wish we had time to hunt them. But I ain't seen nothing around here. No squirrels, no rabbits, no birds of any kind, black or otherwise. I guess the animals were smart enough to skedaddle out of Virginia while we was fighting in Tennessee. They must have known we was a'coming back. There ain't nothing but fighting and death around here."

"I've seen a heap of that," Arlis said. "Too much. But I reckon I'll see a lot more."

"It's been two long years. I'm sick of this war. I'm sick of getting shot at. And I'm sick of shooting people I don't even know. If I did know them, we might even be friends."

"We're lucky we made it this far with no worse than we've been hit. Lots of Guards hadn't made it."

"And some of them just left and ran away. Didn't like fighting, I guess. I'm wondering if maybe they was the smart ones."

"If they was the smart ones," Arlis mused, "You and I would be the dumb ones cause neither of us is a deserter."

"Yeah, that's for sure. Besides, it don't make no sense. You can't go home. If you do, you'll get executed. Or spend the rest of your life in prison. If I was to take French leave, I'd have to go out west someplace where they don't know me. I'd never see Emily again. That can't be."

The friends chewed on their tasteless cornmeal cakes while they stared into the darkness around their tent. After several minutes Caleb said, "I heard we're setting off for another big battle at first sunlight, a day or two East of here. A place called Wilderness."

"You heard right, I 'spect. There won't be any animals to hunt there for sure. Except for the animals what shoots back. It seems God's other critters got better sense than we people do. They get out of the way when trouble's brewing."

"Yeah, the only thing left in those trees will be a few of us soldiers. And what's left of us will be mostly walking dead."

"Or just plain dead," Arlis said.

May 6, 1864 ~ Directly North of Orange Plank Road, Wilderness, Virginia

The wilderness was mostly bushes and bramble, thick and hard to get through. Most of the mature trees had been cut down decades earlier in support of the iron industry. The lower level growth was high enough and thick enough so that the landscape was confusing, easy for an army to lose their way. As Major General Charles W. Field's division of Confederate troops moved through the darkness, they lost their way several times. This caused them to arrive behind schedule. They entered the battle late, at six o'clock in the morning, but their arrival tilted the balance. The Union troops, tired and confused themselves, many of them raw new recruits, fell back several hundred yards, the Conecuh Guards in hot pursuit.

Caleb and Arlis were firing and charging, rushing through the thick foliage amid hazy clouds of gunpowder smoke. Musket blasts could be heard from every direction. They burst through a dense cloud of smoke and stopped charging immediately. A large group of Union soldiers was directly in front of them, only a few feet away. The Yankees were looking in a different direction, firing at Confederate soldiers in the distance, behind and to the right of Caleb and Arlis.

Caleb reached out and grabbed Arlis by the arm. "We've come too far. The Guards are behind us. We've got to get back."

As they spun around to run away, Caleb saw one Union soldier turn his head and look at them. The man began to shout and point.

Caleb had become accomplished at firing while half turned around then reloading on the run, his back turned toward the Yankees. He did not like it, but he was good at it. Experience was a great teacher if you lived long enough to learn from it. He fired once then turned to catch up with Arlis.

They ran as fast as they could. Arlis turned around to fire but kept running, not looking where he was going. He was running straight toward a young, firm oak tree. Caleb shouted, “Tree!” just in time for Arlis to dodge to the side and miss the trunk.

“Thanks,” Arlis cried out, but he never broke stride as they ran toward their own lines.

They were side-by-side as they jumped a large rock about two feet above the ground. Their feet stayed on the top long enough to press against the hard surface and propel them over the back of the rock in one long leap. Their feet touched the ground at the same time, but when Caleb kicked forward with another hurried stride, Arlis fell to the ground.

“Arlis,” Caleb called out as he stopped running. “Don’t stumble now. They’re almost on us. Let’s go.” Arlis did not move. “Here, I’ll help you up.” Caleb rushed back, reached down and grabbed Arlis’ arm. It was limp. Caleb tugged at the arm. Instead of rising, Arlis rolled onto his back. His eyes were wide open, staring up at the sky but focused on nothing. A last gurgle of blood bubbled from the front of his uniform, where his heart would have been. The gray was mostly red.

“Arlis! No! You got to get up. Come on!”

Arlis didn’t answer. Caleb stood there, frozen, staring down at his friend’s unseeing eyes. There was a thump against the side of his knee. His leg jumped forward. He could not remember making an effort to move, but his leg had moved as though he was starting to run.

Then there was pain. It was severe, far worse than his memory of the flesh wound he had suffered at Manassas Gap. This pain was deep. The ball had found more than just muscle.

His knee collapsed beneath him, and he fell to the ground, half across Arlis body. He looked up. Three blue-clad soldiers were standing over him. The youngest of the three was little more than a kid. The boy held a musket aimed at Caleb’s chest, his fingers and hands twitching nervously on the weapon.

With sweat pouring off his forehead and streaming from his nose, Caleb’s attention was taken from the young soldier by the severe pain inside his knee. His eyes closed. If he were going to die, he would die beside his friend. *That’s the way it should be,* he thought as he slipped into darkness.

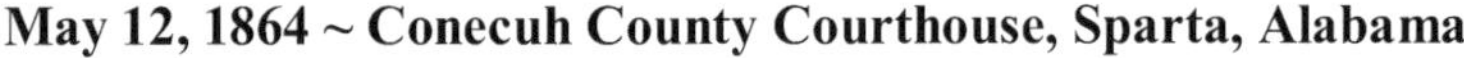

May 12, 1864 ~ Conecuh County Courthouse, Sparta, Alabama

The crowds had thinned. Even though Conecuh County was not occupied by the Union, there were far fewer slaves than there had been in the early days of the war. *Perhaps the owners are reluctant to let slaves leave the plantation,* Emily thought, *for fear of them running away.* After all, Lincoln had declared them free well over a year earlier. And, in fact, many had run away, trying to find the freedom that was promised up North. Many of those never made it, perishing in the effort.

Emily looked back at Nathaniel. She smiled. He acknowledged her with a stoic look and a nod.

There were fewer whites, as well. The casualty and desertion counts had risen. Many families who had suffered the death or maiming of their heirs no longer came into Sparta to listen. Some, knowing their sons or husbands had run away, were ashamed to be seen. Others had become numb to the process, choosing to stay home and find out by word of mouth. Or hoping to hear nothing. After all, no news was good news. Or so they hoped.

In addition to the losses, Sparta was dying. A couple of stores had closed. Others were not doing as well as they had in the past. Evergreen, situated directly on the Montgomery to Mobile road, was more convenient, and the telegraph lines ran through it. It was slowly growing at the same time that Sparta was slowly declining.

Emily was tired of the war, tired of the casualty lists, tired of growing older while Caleb was far away, in danger where she could not help him. Tears did not fall as readily. She turned to her father and said, "We've been through Manassas and Gettysburg and Chickamauga and so many other battles. I sometimes feel like screaming my lungs out, but it wouldn't help. I just want this war to be over."

"I don't think it'll be long, Girl," Thomas said. He didn't elaborate.

"We can't win," Emily said. She had not said it before, but now it was out. "Not anymore. They all need to come home. What's the point of fighting to the last man? There's no sense in it."

Thomas shook his head and stared at the dirt street. He had no answer. He was afraid of what would happen if the war didn't end soon. He was also afraid of what would happen if it did. The South would pay dearly either way.

"There's never been any sense to this whole war," Emily continued when Thomas did not speak. Before she could say anything else, the Mayor began to shout over the crowd noise.

"Please, ladies and gentlemen, let me have your attention." The paper he held shook from the tremble in his hand. "We lost three more of our young men, and a fourth, Private Newton Snowden, is believed to be mortally wounded. The doctors do not believe he will survive."

A woman cried out, and Emily watched as she fell to her knees. Those around her tried to help her up, but she stayed on the ground, refusing to be consoled. "I need to be there," she screamed. "I need to be there to help him. Hear me, dear God! I need to be there."

"Please," the Mayor said. He looked around and waited for the noise to subside. When the woman had sunk into low sobs, he continued, "Also killed are Private John Russell Johnston…"

Once again Emily heard crying and deep gasps. She wasn't sure if it was one woman or two. As the commotion slowly died, the Mayor spoke again, "Private Arlis Johnston…"

Emily froze. There were screams around her. Or perhaps it was loud crying. Or even some other kind of noise. It sounded so tinny, so distant, almost as if coming from another world. *Arlis dead? Who was going to watch after Caleb?*

Her eyes fogged with tears she thought were long dried up as she sought her mother's and father's arms. They hugged briefly as the Mayor said, "Please. I must continue." He looked down at Emily with pity in his eyes. His lips mouthed "I'm sorry," but there was no sound. Then he turned back to the crowd and said, "Private Caleb Garner," almost under his breath.

Her world suddenly stopped. *How could this be? The war was almost over. Caleb made it this far. How could it be? This couldn't be happening now.*

Her knees began to buckle. Nathaniel was suddenly beside her. Thomas put his arms around her, but she didn't want help. She needed to be strong. Gently moving Thomas' arms away, she straightened her legs and stood tall even though her knees felt as though they were molasses. Emily Rose would not cry. She would not slump to the ground. She would not fall apart like all the others. Emily Rose would stand strong.

She had always wondered what she would do to show her strength if this day should ever come. She wondered no more. As though a vision had been sent from heaven, in that instant she realized what she would do. She would go to Virginia and find his grave. She would say her last goodbye to Caleb once she was there. Only then, when she was all alone by his side, would she let her tears flow freely. She looked to the north, into the distance, and willed her tears to stop, to wait behind the dam of her strength for the right time and place.

May 14, 1864 ~ "Punch Bowl" Holding Area, Belle Plains, Virginia

The land had been raped. It hadn't happened overnight, but it had happened. Most of the trees had been cut down over the years to build the docks that lined the Potomac on the other side of the "Punch Bowl." The few original trees that remained after the docks were built were now gone, cut down, the logs and limbs used for supports for the shelter tents that meandered haphazardly down the slopes on all sides. A few scrub bushes dotted the unique landscape, a bowl-shaped area not far inland from the Belle Plains Landing. The bushes were outnumbered by the tents.

Union cannon sat sentry on the lip of the bowl, overlooking the Union supply landing on the Potomac as well as the thousands of Confederate soldiers who lived, although temporarily, inside the "punch bowl." The gray-clad soldiers lay in their tents or milled about outside with nothing to do but eat, sleep, and wait. It was mostly sleeping and waiting. The eating never seemed to be enough.

On the slopes of the punch bowl, blue uniforms were sprinkled in with the gray and brown. Union soldiers sat with and talked to the Rebel prisoners, making friends and helping where they could. There was no war here. Soldiers on both sides were passing their time day-to-day, waiting to be sent somewhere else.

Caleb could no longer lie in the confining tent with the pain of his wounded leg and stare at the underside of the canvas. It made him think about Arlis. All the time. A few days of that was a few days too many. So he found a tree limb that fit and hobbled around on it.

With the limb under one arm, Caleb limped over to where a group of soldiers was sitting on the dirt banks of a trench. Two unarmed Union soldiers sat with the group. Caleb hobbled up and pulled the limb out as he stood on one leg. One of the Union soldiers jumped up and took the limb then helped Caleb ease down to a sitting position on the dirt edge of a dug-out area. Caleb nodded his thanks but, still reluctant to talk to a Yankee, said nothing.

"The biggest fish I ever caught," a Confederate soldier said, "Was longer than my arm. Catfish. Caught him with my bare hands in a creek back home. I reached up under the rock where he was hiding and snatched him out by his gills." He was a big man, tall and thickly muscled. He wore a hat with the 4th Alabama insignia on the side, but Caleb did not know him. No doubt, however, that he was talking about an Alabama catfish. Perhaps it was pulled from a creek not too far from Conecuh County.

"You ought to see the walleye up in Michigan," one of the Union soldiers said. He talked funny, stretching out syllables in strange places. "Their eyes glow green at night. Makes it easy to find them. I've caught walleye as long as my arm, but most of them are smaller."

"Walleye?" Another Confederate said. "I've never heard of them. What do they look like? Does they taste good?"

Caleb sat and listened as the conversation went on and on, covering almost anything other than the war.

The Union soldier that had given him a hand looked at the bandage on Caleb's thigh. "Your wound is bleeding," he said.

When Caleb glanced down, he saw that, indeed, blood was oozing out from under the bandage. A week and a day had passed, and it still bled from time-to-time. Even though the pain had subsided somewhat, it hurt all the time, throbbing deep inside his knee, especially at night when he was trying to sleep. There had been no rest, nothing more than a few short, fitful naps since being captured. That wasn't good.

"You need to see the doctor," the Union soldier said. "Come on. I'll help you."

With the Yankee supporting Caleb's bad side, they limped up the slope.

His curiosity got the best of him. Caleb finally asked, "Why are you helping me? I'm a Confederate soldier. You're Union."

The soldier shrugged his shoulders and said, "You're hurt." He glanced at Caleb then introduced himself. "I'm Sergeant Major James Ross from Battle Creek, Michigan."

Neither soldier had a free hand for shaking, so Caleb nodded his head and said, "Caleb Garner. Conecuh County, Alabama. Every Union soldier I've met in this war was trying to kill me. Never had one help me before."

"If we met on a battlefield, I'd be trying to kill you, too. No sense in that here. We need to set the war aside for a short time and look at each other as fellow Americans."

"The guards that brought us here didn't think that way. One of them kept slapping me with the flat side of his pig sticker. I couldn't move fast enough, and he didn't want to help me. I thought any second he was going to turn that blade around and slide it between my ribs so he wouldn't have to waste time on me anymore."

"Bad egg," Sergeant Major Ross said. "There are plenty of those out here. On both sides. It's amazing what a little power will do to a man. Here's the med tent, ah… I've already forgotten your name. I'm terrible with names. But I can remember Conecuh County. That's a hard one to forget. I'll call you Conecuh."

Caleb smiled and said, "That's fine. In fact, now that I think about it, I like being called Conecuh. Has a nice sound to it."

James Ross smiled back and helped Caleb hobble over to the med tent.

There was a short line in front of the tent, so they took their place at the end and waited, Ross making sure that Caleb did not fall over as he stood in line. Half an hour later they were inside.

The doctor looked at Caleb with what seemed to be a scowl on his face then, scissors in hand, reached down to cut off the old bandage. "Dirty," he said as he cut. "This thing hasn't been changed in a week. Most doctors reuse bandages. I don't believe in doing that, but no choice out here. I've got some clean linen, though. I use boiling water." The old bandage fell away as the doctor finished cutting all the way through. "My patients have less infection, but most of the other doctors don't believe me. A lot of them use that adhesive plaster mess. Not me. It'll rip a man's skin off."

The doctor looked at the wound and became quiet. It was dark red and raw where the ball had entered, but there was no black or green, something Caleb had learned to watch for. The doctor felt around here and there, punching and poking and squeezing, almost bringing Caleb off the table at times.

"Ball's still in there," he finally said. "Looks like it lodged somewhere inside the knee. Don't have the tools or facilities to get it out here. Too delicate an area to go digging around. But it may well be damaged too severely to fix. Hard to say for sure. I suspect they'll amputate when you get to Hammond Hospital. May be all they can do."

Caleb glanced at James Ross. Losing his leg? Emily wouldn't want a man with one leg. But what could he do? Caleb Garner was a prisoner of war, at the mercy of the Union army. Running away was not possible on one leg and a tree limb.

The doctor cleaned the wound in silence, covered it with some sort of salve, and then turned and reached for a bandage on the shelf behind him. After he tied the clean bandage tight, he stood and said, "What's your name?"

"His name is Conecuh," Sergeant Major Ross said, a smile on his face.

"Interesting name. Well, that's about all I can do for you, Conecuh. At least in this place. There are some good doctors at Point Lookout. If they do have to amputate, chances are it will save your life. Good luck." Without waiting for a comment, he turned toward the tent entrance and called out, "Next."

May 30, 1864 ~ Union Camp near Mechanicsville, Virginia

"At ease, Corporal," the Captain said. His look was stern, unhappy.

"Yes, Sir," John Murray replied as he relaxed his stance.

The Captain took his hat off and set it on the table inside his tent. He rubbed his beard as he paced back and forth, staring at nothing in particular. Corporal Murray did not like the look on the officer's face. Something was up.

The Captain stopped and turned and looked Murray directly in the eye. "This unit has seen a lot of action. Few of us have gone completely unscathed." He rubbed his beard again then continued, "You happen to be one of those few."

"Just lucky, Sir," Murray shrugged.

"Perhaps. Others think differently. Some of the men say they've seen you hiding behind others and running away from action."

"No, Sir! I'm a fighter. I don't hide, and I don't run. I have been separated from the squad a couple of times, in the confusion of battle. But I've always found my way back."

"Three times, according to the record. In your reports, you state you had to sneak through Confederate troops to return. Three times without being captured? That's quite an accomplishment."

"I can move through the woods quietly, Sir. And I have a good sense of direction."

"Which makes me wonder how you got separated to start with." Corporal Murray did not like the way the Captain was talking, but he held his tongue a moment as he listened. "We've also had reports of serious war crimes during each of your three absences."

The Captain's look was forceful, piercing. It was difficult for Murray to avoid breaking eye contact. He had to defend himself. "I resent what are you insinuating, Sir. We have reports of war crimes every week. You can't have an army with tens of thousands of men without a few criminals. Why, I'm one of the bravest soldiers you have, Sir. And no one has more integrity than me."

"For your sake, I hope so Corporal, but you seem to be the only one who thinks that way."

"I don't understand." John Murray put a sincere, quizzical look on his face and asked, "What proof do you have that I have been anything other than an example for all Union troops?"

"That's the problem, Corporal Murray. I have no definitive proof. All I have is a fist full of hearsay reports that say you shy away from combat. Plus the fact that serious crimes were committed nearby each time you were 'separated' from your unit."

"Sir, I would never do anything to embarrass our brave Union army and our great country. I beg you to bring my accuser in right now. I want to meet him face-to-face. We'll see if his lies hold up when he looks me in the eyes."

"*Accusers.* There are many of them. In fact, virtually everyone in your platoon. And many from outside your platoon. They would hardly fit into this tent, Corporal. The most vocal of them was Corporal Stan Gerszewski, a top rail soldier whom I respected deeply. Unfortunately, he is no longer with us.

Murray started to talk but stopped and held his tongue as the Captain continued, "The fact is, I cannot find a single person who will vouch for your actions during the heat of battle. I tried, but no one can recall ever seeing you in close quarter fighting." The Captain stroked his beard again, then shrugged and said, "But, as I mentioned, I have no undeniable proof. Because of that, I cannot waste time on a court-martial. We're about to enter another engagement at Cold Harbor. It promises to be a drawn out affair. As far as you are concerned, I can no longer trust you in battle. You are being transferred."

"Transferred? To where, Sir." Murray tried to look hurt and defeated, but this had the potential to be good, perhaps very good.

"To a place where there is no combat to hide from. You will be highly visible to your commanding officer. You will do your job, or you will suffer the consequences."

"As you command, Sir. But, please, let the report show that I fully and vehemently deny the accusations you have stated. I have been a model soldier."

"For what it's worth, I will add your statement to the file. You are to report to the recruiting depot at Elmira, New York, on Monday, June 13th."

"Yes, Sir. I will be honored to assist with the new recruits."

"No, Corporal Murray, you will have nothing to do with new recruits. Elmira is being refitted to accommodate Confederate prisoners. You will be in the guard detail, a position for which, I believe, you are much more suited."

June 2, 1864 ~ Rose Residence, Forks of Sepulga Community, Alabama

Emily rolled over in her bed and faced the wall. Looking at blankness seemed to be fitting. She was fully dressed. Her mother forced her to get up every morning and put fresh clothes on. But she didn't want to. What was the point?

Her heart ached to go to Virginia, to find Caleb's grave and say a final farewell. Thomas said no. He told her the war was still raging in Virginia, said that it was too dangerous for a young lady to be moving around the countryside by herself. She would have defied him and gone regardless, but Thomas had explained that Caleb would have been buried by the Yankees in a mass grave. It was doubtful the site would even be marked. There were hundreds, perhaps thousands of mass grave sites. She would have no way of knowing which site was Caleb's final resting place. That meant she would not be able to do the one thing she believed she should do. Lying on the bed, she felt only total despair.

Footsteps pounded the earth outside the house, heavy boots striding fast and hard against the ground. Someone was running, getting closer and closer, coming toward their front door. Emily heard a quick, hard knock on the door, but told herself she didn't care. Whatever it was, it didn't matter. Caleb was gone. Nothing mattered anymore. Nothing would ever matter again.

The door to her room opened, and Mary rushed in. "Girl," she said through a cough, "Come quick. You've got to hear this." She turned and rushed out of the room as quickly as she had rushed in.

Emily did not want to get out of bed. How could anything be important anymore? She decided not to get up.

A few minutes later Nathaniel Whiteeagle walked into the room and stepped over to the bed, standing by her side. He placed his hand on her shoulder and said, "Emily, your mother sent me to fetch you. This is not helping at all. You need to get up. We have a visitor who has something important to tell you."

"Nothing's ever going to be important again."

"I believe you told me, Miss Rose, that you were going to be strong. As I recall, you said you would not roll around and cry like the other women who lost their loved ones."

"I am strong."

"Tell me, then, Miss Rose, do you think a strong woman lies around in her bed all day doing nothing but feeling sorry for herself? Would a strong woman refuse to acknowledge an important visitor?"

Emily said, "Yes," But it lacked conviction.

Nathaniel put his hands on his hips and said, "Come on, Emily. It is time to get up. It is time to be that strong woman you claim to be."

Emily rolled over and looked at Nathaniel. His face was as impassive as ever, but his eyes were firm. "You're right. As usual. Okay, I'll get up."

Nathaniel backed up to let her roll out of bed. She swung her legs over the side and put her feet on the floor then stood. Pushing her untended and stringy hair to the back, she followed Nathaniel out of her room and into the parlor.

Thomas, a huge grin on his face, was standing beside Mary. How could he smile? How could anybody smile? The world had come to an end. There was no possible reason left for anyone to smile.

Nick Stallworth was standing in the door. He had joined the Conecuh Guards at barely fifteen years old, the youngest man who ever served with the guards. No doubt Nick had lied about his birthday, but sixteen months later the Army discovered his actual age and discharged him as a result of the conscript law. He was something of a local hero, but an important visitor?

"Nick here has something to tell you, Girl," Thomas said. Her father was beaming. How could any news make him act that way? How could it put such a happy smile on his face? Caleb's death had upset him, too.

"Miss Emily," Nick said as he nodded and removed the Confederate hat he still wore even though his days with the Guard were long behind him. "It's Caleb." He grinned from ear-to-ear. "He's alive."

"Alive? Wha… OH!" she screamed as realization sunk in. This time her knees did buckle. She couldn't stop them as she slumped toward the floor. Nathaniel caught her shoulders and eased her down to her knees. That was okay. Better to be on your knees when talking to the Lord. She closed her eyes, put her hands together, and thanked God for bringing Caleb back from the dead.

Nick waited while she said her prayer. When she finished and stood, with Thomas and Nathaniel helping, he continued, "It's not all good news, mind. He's been captured by the Yankees. And he's wounded in the leg. But he was still alive at last sighting. The officers thought he had been killed, but Sam Little saw the Yankees take him. Sam was the last one to get away. He got them to change the records. Caleb's officially listed as a prisoner of war, now."

"Then he can come home!" Emily exclaimed.

"Home?" Nick looked confused. "No, ma'am. He's a prisoner. Of the Yankees."

"But he can take the loyalty oath and come home. I've heard about it. All he's got to do is take the oath, and the Yankees will set him free."

Thomas' smile turned into a grimace. "Well…" he said, but words failed him. He didn't finish the statement.

Mary only stared at her. Pity mixed with tears shown in Mary's eyes.

"No, ma'am," Nick Stallworth said. "Caleb would never take the oath. He would be considered a deserter. If he tried to come back, he'd go to jail. I know Caleb. I don't reckon he would ever pledge allegiance to the Yankees, even if they held a knife to his throat."

"Oh," Emily said, her quickly rising hopes suddenly dashed. Then the seed of an idea sprouted in her head.

"Caleb's strong," Nick said. "He's strong inside. He'll survive. He'll be home as soon as the war is over."

"I can't wait that long," Emily said. "If he can't come to me, then I'll go to him."

June 13, 1864 ~ Hammond Hospital, Point Lookout Prison, Maryland

Curling his upper lip in disgust, the doctor said, "Infection has set in. We'll have to amputate."

"No!" Caleb cried. He had held his tongue up to this point, but he did not want to lose his leg. If he ever made it back to Alabama, he would need both legs, for farming and for being the man Emily would still love. "You can't take my leg. It'll get better."

"I can't? Balderdash! Not only can I take your leg, but I am also obliged to do so. That is my job. You should be thankful that there's a lull in the battles in Virginia right now. Otherwise, Union soldiers would have the priority in Hammond Hospital. Your leg would have to be amputated in one of the tents on Pennsylvania Avenue, where you run a much greater risk of dying."

Pennsylvania Avenue was not a road. It was the center row of tents in the Point Lookout prison camp, where thousands of tents were laid out on the sand in a rectangular grid to house thousands more prisoners than the area was built to accommodate. It was a filthy place, a flat sandbar only five feet above sea level. It often flooded. There was no relief from high water, no safe ground the prisoners could go to. If you wandered even a short distance out of the appointed grounds and stepped over the deadline, a shallow ditch scratched through the sand; you were subject to being shot by one or more of the Union guards, most of whom were black and were hell-bent on punishing white Southerners.

But it didn't matter. Hammond Hospital or a tent on Pennsylvania Avenue made little difference to Caleb. He did not want to live the rest of his life, however long, with only one leg. He didn't even want to try. "Just let me die of infection," he said. "I want to be buried with both my legs."

The doctor tilted his head and gave Caleb a questioning look. "I've got half a mind to grant your request." He leaned back in his chair and looked out a side window, over the waves in the ocean, as he continued, "You know, you and your people ruined this place. My family and I used to come down to Point Lookout for a getaway every summer. We rented one of the cottages. Those were such wonderful times. I taught my children how to swim right here in this ocean. We used to wander through the stores to pass the time. This place had everything. Now? It's a prison for your type and a hospital where we try to patch up our own boys. These Union boys are the North's best and brightest, the sons that you and your type have injured. All because you want to make slaves out of the darkies. Yes, I could easily let you die from infection. But, unlike you, I swore an oath to heal. It doesn't matter how disgusting you Rebels are. I have to do what's best for you."

"I don't own no slaves," Caleb said. "We're poor folks. Farmers. I don't reckon I cotton to the rich folks what own colored men and women. I'm not fighting for them. I'm fighting for Alabama, where I was born. And the money. I sent all my money home to my maw and paw."

The doctor looked away from the window and wrote something on a piece of paper beside the bed. He turned to Caleb and said, "Admirable. Be that as it may, I've got to do what I am sworn to do. As I said, now is the best time. I'll go arrange for the operation. I should be back in fifteen minutes."

"NO!" Caleb screamed, but the doctor ignored him. He only nodded at the two Union guards then walked out of the room.

"You can't let him do this to me," Caleb said to the guards as he looked first at one then at the other. "You can't. Let me go back to the tents. Please. I would stop our sawbones if our shoes were swapped. I swear I would. I'd rather die. Here and now. You can't let him cut off my leg!"

The two soldiers looked at each other then looked away. Neither said anything.

Caleb tried to keep the tears from flowing, but couldn't. He rubbed his eyes with the backs of his hand and his bare arms. It was too hot in mid-June in Maryland to wear his uniform, so he was dressed only in his drawers and undershirt. They were relatively clean. He had washed them in the bay only two days earlier.

The prisoners were allowed to wash themselves and their clothes in the bay, as well as try to catch fish, crabs, or anything else that moved. Since there was never enough food, they had to supplement their diet the best they could.

It wasn't long before the doctor returned. "You are lucky on several accounts," the doctor said. "I understand Confederate surgeons are low on medicines. They sometimes use whiskey as an anesthetic. Sometimes nothing at all."

An assistant walked into the room, carrying a wooden case with intricate carving on the top and sides. The doctor turned to the assistant and indicated a table beside the bed. "Place the amputation kit on this table." He pulled a key from his pocket and unlocked the kit, lifted the lid, and pulled out the amputation saw. He held the saw up in front of Caleb and said, "Can you imagine someone sawing off your leg with this while you were wide awake?"

"NOOOOO!" Caleb screamed again. He tried to climb out of bed.

The doctor nodded to the two guards. "Please," was all he said. One of the guards grabbed Caleb's arms, and the other grabbed his legs. They were well fed and far too strong for Caleb to resist. "Now," the doctor said, holding up a bottle of liquid, "First we will administer…"

A young soldier rushed into the operating room. "Sir," he said. "Rebel cavalry ambushed one of our camps. Dozens of wounded. Serious. They're coming across the bay right now. Be here in a few minutes. They'll need immediate attention."

"Damn!" the doctor said. "Almost everyone is gone. Things were so quiet we thought it would be a good time to get some rest." Then he turned back to Caleb and said, "It appears you will get your wish soldier. If you want to die of infection, then so be it." He turned to the messenger and said, "Send riders out to any doctor within an hour's ride and get them down here right away." As the young soldier was rushing out of the room, the doctor turned to the two guards and said, "Get him out of my sight. And out of my hospital. He can rot in Hell for all I care. We've got to worry about our own boys."

June 15, 1864 ~ Rose Residence, Forks of Sepulga Community, Alabama

"You can buy a prisoner's freedom," Emily said. "In church, I heard Mrs. Anderson talking about how her second cousin in Georgia bought his son's freedom. Please, Daddy, you've got to let me go."

Week after week Emily had thought about traveling to the North and finding Caleb. But what would she do when she got there? She couldn't break him out of prison. That was impossible. Would they even let her visit Caleb? Could she beg for his release? The prisoner exchanges that were so common in the early part of the war were no longer being carried out. The Yankees had stopped them because Confederate soldiers went right back to the front, even though they agreed not to fight anymore. Many had been captured more than once. There were no answers until she happened to overhear Mrs. Anderson at church. It was the answer she had been dreaming about, praying for.

"How are you going to buy his freedom, Girl?" Thomas asked. "You ain't got no money."

"I do, too," Emily said. "I've saved some money." She turned and ran into her room. Moments later she came rushing back, holding some bills and waving them through the air in front of her. "I've got fourteen dollars saved."

Thomas shook his head and let it hang down. Emily glanced at Nathaniel. She could tell by his expression that something was not right. She turned back to her father. His eyes watering at the edges, he lifted his head and looked at her.

"What is it, Daddy? What's wrong?"

"Girl, the Yankees don't take Confederate money."

"Oh." She looked at the bills in her hands then let her arms drop to her sides. "I didn't think of that. I..."

Speaking softly, Nathaniel said, "You'll need Federal currency. And you'll need a lot more than fourteen dollars."

"How much?"

"I ain't for sure," Thomas said. "I've heard rumors that it could be done, but I don't know how much it would cost. A lot, I suspect. It might depend on what his rank is, and which prison he's in."

"There was a rich man in Montgomery," Nathaniel said. "His son was captured back early in the war, and he bought his freedom for seven hundred and fifty dollars. I heard it from one of the slaves at church quite some time ago. This slave had previously belonged to the man in Montgomery and knew of the story first hand. Since Caleb is a private, I would think that amount would be more than enough, but if you've only got fourteen dollars…"

Emily felt her chest flutter. "Seven hundred and fifty dollars? In Yankee money? That's impossible." She sank into a chair and stared at the air in front of her with her mouth open. Tears ran down her cheeks.

"I'm surprised," Thomas said. "Seven hundred fifty dollars? I would have thought it would have been more. That means, ah… It's not impossible."

Emily's head snapped up. She stared at her father. "What?"

Nathaniel's head whirled around as well. Both of them stared in anticipation of Thomas' next words.

"I've been, well, ah, this war was… Oh, come with me." Thomas turned for the door. He called over his shoulder, "Get a couple of shovels out of the barn, Nathaniel." Emily and Nathaniel glanced at each other momentarily then rushed after Thomas.

Stepping off ten paces due south from the back corner of the horse barn, Thomas Rose stopped then turned around to face Emily, who had followed his every move. "It's down here, Girl," he said as he pointed toward the ground. He was smiling.

Nathaniel took the shovels from his shoulder and handed one to Thomas. They thrust the blades into the rock-filled orange dirt. The thrusts of the shovel blades did not go deep. Too many rocks. But they continued to work, and within a few minutes, they had a hole almost two feet into the earth.

Nathaniel struck something that had a different sound to it.

“That’s it,” Thomas said.

They dug more carefully, working around the thing in the ground. After a while, Nathaniel lifted a tin box out of the hole. He dusted dirt from the top then handed the box to Thomas.

“Let’s go inside,” Thomas said as he looked around. “I’m sure nobody’s a’looking, but no sense taking chances.”

Emily followed Thomas toward the house. Nathaniel filled the hole and smoothed the top then tried to make it look natural. Satisfied, he went into the barn and hung the shovels from their hooks. By the time he got inside the house, Thomas was almost finished counting the money as he and Emily sat at the dining table.

“Eight hundred and thirty-two dollars,” Thomas said. “United States banknotes. That’s most of everything I saved for my whole life, back before the war. I changed some to Confederate currency. Had to make it look good. Besides, we needed some Confederate money. But I saved all this in case... Ah…” He hung his head then continued, “I sort of had a feeling from the start, you know.”

“But what if we’d have won?” Emily asked. “It’s not impossible that we still could.”

Thomas shrugged his shoulders and said, “Federal money will always be good up North. But that’s not important now. What’s important is bringing Caleb home.”

“Oh, Daddy!” Emily shouted as she jumped up. She put her arms around her father and hugged him from behind before he could stand.

Thomas brought his hands up and patted his daughter’s arms. “We got word that the prisoners are in Belle Plains, Virginia. It’s on the Potomac River, across from Maryland. We’ll have to buy his freedom there. You’ll need Confederate money, too. For traveling. I’ve got three hundred of that in my mattress. You may not need that much, but you never can tell the way prices have been going up.”

“When can we leave?”

“Well…” Thomas hesitated, once again hanging his head as though he was praying. He looked back up and said, “You know your mother’s been sick. She’s gotten worse this last week or two. I’ve got to stay here with her. Besides, we've got to watch after the farm. There are raids about, and lost souls wandering around right now. Things aren't as safe as they used to be. If we left, we could lose everything."

"I'll go by myself, then," Emily said. "I can do it. They'll let a young lady pass. I've heard they have ladies' cars on the trains."

Thomas glanced at Emily then at Nathaniel. "Maybe, but a young lady by herself in the middle of a war might be in danger. Serious danger. We can't take that chance."

Tears began to well up in Emily's eyes once again. "You've got to let me go get Caleb."

"Yes, I agree. But you can't go alone, Girl. We've got to find somebody to travel with you, someone the Union soldiers won't bother when you cross into the territory they're occupying. It's got to be the right person. This is going to be dangerous."

The tears leaked a little but dried quickly as Emily started to think. "Who can we get?" she thought out loud.

With his face as stoic as ever, Nathaniel Whiteeagle said, "I'll go."

June 27, 1864 ~ Rose Residence, Forks of Sepulga Community, Alabama

Emily held the new dress against her body and twirled around the room as she looked at her smiling reflection in the mirror. "It's beautiful, Momma. I'll never be able to sew like you."

"That's because I stayed at home and learned to sew instead of running off to Virginia."

Her mouth opened, but Emily's retort caught in her throat. This was not a time to say something ugly to her mother. Instead, she walked over and sat on the sofa beside Mary and took her mother's hands in hers and said, "That's because Daddy was here, Momma. He wasn't in Virginia. There was no war when y'all were courting. If Daddy had been in a Union prison and there was a chance you could get him free, you would have gone, too. You know you would have."

Mary turned away from her daughter and looked out the window, to the tree limbs baking in the summer heat, leaves unmoving in the still air. "I would have," she admitted. She coughed loudly then continued, "But that doesn't make it any less dangerous. I am so worried for you, Girl. There's lots of people who would kill you without a second thought for the money you'll be carrying."

"I'll hide it somewhere."

"You'll hide it right here," Mary said as she held up some homemade underwear. I sewed pockets on the inside of all your underpants. You can hide the Federal money in these pockets. If somebody goes as far as searching in your underwear, you'll already be…" Tears started rolling down Mary's cheeks. She coughed loudly again before continuing, "Either dead or as good as dead."

"I'll be fine, Momma." She held up the underwear and inspected the pockets. "This is a wonderful idea. I can put a little in each pocket, and nobody would ever suspect I was carrying that much money. And besides, what would happen? The other passengers aren't going to bother me on the trains. There are too many people around. I'll be in crowds of people the whole trip. When I get to Richmond, there will be plenty of soldiers there to protect me. General Lee is keeping Richmond safe. Besides, Nathaniel will be with me the whole time."

"He's a colored man. There's only so much he can do. He's not allowed to carry a gun. What would happen if some of those Yankee soldiers came after you?"

Emily's face wrinkled in confusion. "Why, Nathaniel is a free man in the Yankee's eyes. They wouldn't do anything to us."

"You are so naïve, Girl. That's one of the things that worries me. This is a war and a bad one. These men, on both sides, have not been home in a long time. Some of them haven't seen their families for years. They're fighting, killing and being killed. They don't respect the same things they respected before. War changes things. It changes people, even good people. Sometimes it turns them into animals."

"Don't you worry none, Momma. We'll be on the train all the way to Richmond. There won't be any bad people on the train. Even if we did run into a bad apple, Nathaniel would take care of it. He's fast and strong. Just look at him. Nobody would bother him. And they won't bother me if I'm with him."

Mary put her arm around Emily's head and pulled her daughter to her breast and hugged her and said, "I hope so, Girl. Lord, God, I hope so. But these aren't normal times. People are doing things now they wouldn't have dreamed of doing ten years ago. And they're not even thinking twice about it. I'll be praying for you every day."

July 6, 1864 ~ "Hellmira" Prison, Elmira, New York

With a light screeching of metal upon metal, the train stopped at the Elmira station at six o'clock in the morning. The sky was bright, but the red tint of early morning still lingered. As early as it was, the streets were crowded with onlookers. It appeared that everybody in Elmira, as well as many from the surrounding countryside, had come into town to see the first contingent of Confederate prisoners. This would be quite a show.

The murmur in the crowd grew as everyone stood on their tip-toes and looked around the heads in front of them, trying to get a glimpse of the captured enemy soldiers disembarking from the train. Nothing happened. Major Henry V. Colt of the 104th New York, the prison camp commander, stood in the street beside the train with several of his men and waited.

The crowd murmur rose to a buzz. People began talking louder and louder so they could be heard over those around them. Even though it was Wednesday, most of the women wore their Sunday best. The men were dressed in suits. This was a special occasion for the town, not something to be missed and not something to dress lightly for, regardless of the heat.

A Union soldier stepped down from the first car, and the drone of conversation began to die. He stepped to the side then turned ninety degrees to face the path he had taken in leaving the train car. He was followed by a second soldier who took the opposite side. The two faced each other, holding their rifles in front of them.

At last, the first Confederate prisoner emerged, the moment the town's people had been waiting for. He took one step out of the train and stopped, looking over the crowd. To everyone's surprise, he smiled broadly then marched down the steps to the street where he passed between the Union guards. Why was the man smiling? He was going to prison. What was there to smile about?

Southern soldiers, dressed irregularly, strangely, emerged one after the other. Some wore dark or medium gray. Others were in brown or a dark brownish red. Most were in some stage of undress; britches with undershirts, britches with no shirts, even nothing but their drawers. There seemed to be few dressed alike, and even fewer in clothes that were not ragged and tattered. Their skin, caked in weeks of dirt and sunburned from years in the open, was almost as black as the Africans they were fighting to keep enslaved.

The raggedness of the Southern soldiers was in stark contrast to the beautiful Victorian mansions and neat commercial shops of downtown Elmira, to the village green and tall elm trees that gave the town such a clean, natural look. These men were ugly and ragged, dirty, invaders to the residents' pristine environment. Still, many of the Confederates smiled and laughed as they were assembled into four columns.

They began the two-mile march to Barracks Number Three, continuing to laugh and joke as they went. Why were they joking? Barracks Number Three was a prison, their home for the duration of the war. Unless they died first.

"Just look at them," John Murray said to a man beside and behind him as Murray stood guard to the side. "They're disgusting."

The man had been writing on a pad. He looked up and said, "What? Oh. I don't know. They're obviously lower intelligence, but they are good physical types. Tall. Lean. Muscular. There seems to be an inordinate number of older and younger soldiers among them. Not many of the middle age group." He scribbled something quickly then looked back at Corporal Murray and extended his hand. "Charles Fairman from the Advertiser. Glad to make your acquaintance."

Murray turned back to take the man's hand and said, "Corporal John Murray, Barracks Number Three guard detail. Pleased to meet you."

"So you'll be looking after our Southern guests, eh?"

"Guests? They're stupid and filthy. Vermin! That's all they are. Look at our Union soldiers." Murray pointed at the guards walking alongside the Confederate columns. "They are neat and clean. Nothing like these sorry Southerners. I'll be watching after them, all right."

Fairman raised his brows and shrugged.

The lead men of the four columns marched past where Murray and Fairman stood. There was a bounce in their steps. “Look at them,” Murray said. “Walking along like they’re going to a picnic. They’ll think picnic when I’m finished with them.”

“They do seem to have an extraordinary amount of liveliness to their marching. Perhaps they believe Elmira will be an improvement over their last incarceration.”

“If that’s the case then I’ll need to provide an education to all four hundred of them.”

“Only three hundred ninety-nine,” Charles Fairman said. “I understand one of the prisoners passed away in transit.”

“It’s a damned shame they didn’t all pass away in transit. Then we wouldn’t have to use our resources to house and feed vermin like this. A waste of good food, I tell you. They don’t deserve it.”

“Ah…” Fairman started to protest but hesitated. He was not sure he wanted to get into a prolonged discussion with this man.

“Look at what they’re doing to our boys down at Andersonville. You’ve heard the stories about that, haven’t you?”

“I have read some disturbing accounts.”

“They’re true. And it’s even worse than what you read. I’ve talked to some of the men who were exchanged. They’re starving our soldiers to death. On purpose! The Rebels deserve nothing better up here. I’m going to make sure they don’t get anything better.”

Charles Fairman raised his eyebrows and shrugged then turned back to look at the ragged men marching down the streets. Several of the Confederates marching directly in front of them had smiles on their faces.

July 17, 1864 ~ Train Station, Sparta, Alabama

"That should do it," the old man in the home guard said as he handed the travel pass to Emily. His name was Carter something or other. Emily couldn't remember the last name. What was it? She glanced at his signature on the travel pass. *Oh, yes. Captain Carter McInnis.* The man had volunteered for the Confederate infantry but was too old for service. He was a natural for the home guard since he had military experience. He had served with the Union in the Mexican war. And, of course, he had had plenty of stories to tell, stories about war, cactus, desert heat, and Mexican women. The stories about Mexican women were always punctuated with a wink to Thomas.

"And this will do for both of us?" Emily asked. They had left home in plenty of time, but the stories had drug on so. She was starting to worry about the train leaving. "Nathaniel doesn't need a separate pass?"

"Why, of course not, young lady. I wrote your domestic's name on your pass, right where it says 'Traveling With…' The colored boy won't need nothing more."

The sunlight glinted in Nathaniel's eyes as he gave the old man a sideways glance, but he held his tongue. He was used to it.

"Thank you," Emily said as she folded the pass and placed it in her purse.

"Much obliged," Thomas said as he tipped his hat and turned to leave.

"You folks are sure welcome. You're lucky you caught me in Sparta today. Everything seems to be moving to Evergreen. I spend a lot more time up there nowadays. Well, I hope you have a pleasant trip, young lady." There was another story wavering on his tongue, but the family and their slave had turned around and were going out the door. "Folks always in such an all-fired hurry nowadays," he mumbled to himself as he turned his attention back to his newspaper and cup of coffee.

Steam escaped from the engine in small wisps. The train was not ready to leave, but it wouldn't be long. Nathaniel lifted Emily's two bags up to the steward in the door of the baggage car as Emily hugged her mother goodbye. Mary coughed then said, "You be mighty careful, Girl. I don't want nothing to happen to my baby."

"I'll be fine, Momma."

"Let's go over the plan one more time," Thomas said.

"Oh, Daddy, we've been over it a hundred times. I know what I'm supposed to do."

"Okay, Miss Smarty, where are you going?"

"Richmond, Virginia, to visit with your Aunt Millie Hanson."

"Well, yesss… But no." Thomas pointed toward the train they were about to board. "Where are you going on this particular train, the Alabama and Florida Railroad?"

"Why, the capital, of course. Montgomery. Then we change trains."

"To what?"

"Oh, Daddy."

"Just humor me. It's the last time. Besides, it'll delay you getting on the train a few more minutes."

Emily smiled at her father then said, "Okay, Daddy. We change to the Montgomery and West Point Railroad in Montgomery, but their station is in a different place because the two railroads are owned by different companies. We've got plenty of time to sort all that out since we'll spend the night at the Exchange Hotel and catch the train in the morning. We can't go through Atlanta because the Yankees are in that area, so we get off at Opelika then travel to Columbus…"

As Emily recited the different legs, including the railroad companies, Nathaniel's lips remained stone still, but his eyes radiated a smile. Once she was finished with all the legs of the trip, she said, "In Richmond, we'll stay with your Aunt Millie."

"Now, you be nice and polite around Millie. I haven't seen her since I was a little boy, but we've passed letters back and forth a few times. Family matters, of course. I don't want her thinking your momma and I raised a heathen."

"Don't be silly, Daddy. You know I'll be nice. Why, I always am."

Thomas smiled. “Yes, I know you are. Okay. Finish now. What do you do in Richmond?”

“First, we get travel passes to cross the border from Brigadier General John Henry Winder’s office. Then Nathaniel and I will borrow some horses if we can. If Aunt Millie can’t help us with horses, we’ll rent some and ride out to Belle Plains, Virginia, where the Yankees are holding Caleb. I’ll meet with the officers and buy his release.” She shrugged her shoulders as though nothing could be simpler and said, “Then we’ll come home.”

“Who will come home?”

“Me and Caleb. Nathaniel will travel somewhere up North where he’ll be safe from slavery. He has the paper you wrote him giving him his freedom sewn into his jacket. He’ll pull it out when we get Caleb released. Since he’ll be a free man, the Yankees will let him in.”

“Mary and I appreciate everything you’ve done for us, Nathaniel Whiteeagle,” Thomas said.

“We’re going to miss you so much,” Mary added.

Nathaniel, unused to displays of emotion, looked uncomfortable. He shrugged his shoulders, an awkward move as it was something he rarely did, and said, “And I will miss you as well.”

The train whistle blew, saving Nathaniel from further discomfort. The steward called out, “All aboard.” It was a Sunday, and they were the only ones standing at the Sparta station.

Thomas hugged his daughter as he whispered to her, “Take care, Girl. We love you, and we want you and that farmer boy to come back home, safe and sound.”

When he let go of Emily, Thomas nodded to Nathaniel, a nod that conveyed much. No further words were needed. Then Emily and Nathaniel boarded the train.

“This is the ladies’ car,” the steward said as they entered the passenger car. He pointed to a seat by a window and added, “Your seat is right here.”

Emily wasn’t sure why it mattered where she sat. Most of the seats were empty. “Thank you,” she said as she started to slide between the rows.

She stopped when she heard the steward say, “You’ll have to ride in the back car, with the luggage. It’s that way.” He pointed toward the rear of the train.

“But he’s my domestic,” Emily said. “I will require his services while we’re on the train.”

“I’ll take care of anything you need, ma’am. Slaves aren’t allowed to use white seats. He’ll have to go to the back.”

Emily was stunned. She sat down and shared supper with this man. And he wasn’t good enough to ride with her on a train?

Before she could protest further, Nathaniel said, “Those accommodations will be fine. I will have your bags ready for you in Montgomery, ma’am.” He tipped his black bowler, turned, and walked out of the passenger car.

“Mighty fancy hat for a nigger,” the steward said as he watched Nathaniel leave.

Emily frowned and turned away from the steward. She ignored him as she took her seat. The few ladies in the car were watching her every move. She ignored them as well. Instead, she looked out the window and waved at her parents.

Sitting by herself, the minutes seemed like hours as she waited for the train to leave, to take her to places she had never seen before. But it was only a few minutes. Before long she was waving her last goodbye to her parents.

As the train slowly pulled out of the Sparta station, Emily thought about her trip. Evergreen was only a few miles away and Gravella just five miles beyond that. Once the train reached the county line on the other side of Gravella, she would be further away from home than she had ever been in her life. And Richmond was forever far away after that. Even though there were many things to fear, to worry about, this was the most exciting adventure she had ever been on. By far. She wished Nathaniel was in the ladies’ car with her so she could share the excitement. Good times were always better when they were shared with someone.

July 17, 1864 ~ Point Lookout Prison, Maryland

"Big tide's coming in," Charles Pearson said. "They'll be scurrying out of their hidey-holes. We'll eat good tonight if we move fast enough."

"I guess I'll go hungry," Caleb said as he leaned on his crutch. "I ain't chasing nothing nowadays." Caleb could hobble around without the crutch, but it hurt so to put pressure on his leg. He used his crutch almost all the time.

The infection had gotten better. Perhaps it was the salt air and the salt water. Or perhaps God was smiling on him. Whatever the reason, Caleb was thankful. The wound no longer bled or oozed. There was no pus and no clear liquid. Scar tissue had almost closed over the hole. But he could still feel the ball down inside his knee, every time he bent his leg too much or straightened it too much.

"Don't you worry, none," Charles said. "I'll catch one for you. A big one."

"You better watch out Charlie," another prisoner, Danny Talley, a big man from Georgia, said. "Those niggers on the wall will shoot you if you cross the deadline while you're a'chasing. And they'll laugh about it. The officer of the day pays them ten dollars for every prisoner they can shoot for breaking the rules."

"Name's Charles, not Charlie. I'll thank you to keep that straight."

"Charles, then. As if it made a big heap of difference in this place."

"It makes a difference to me," Charles said. "And I don't worry none about no guards. I'm too fast. I'll catch the little buggers long before I cross over the deadline."

Another prisoner said, "Sometimes they don't care if you cross the deadline or not. I heard tell that one of the prisoners got shot while he was sleeping."

"He must have done something to make 'em mad," Charles said.

"Don't take much to do that," Danny said.

“Maybe he was snoring too loud,” Caleb said.

Charles pulled a small Bible from the pocket of his ragged shirt and held it up in front of him. “Just pull out a Bible and hold it up,” he said. “Everybody respects the Bible. Even those darkies walking the wall.”

“I wouldn’t bet my life on it,” Danny said. “Besides, you’re about the only one who has a Bible in here.”

Charles looked toward the ocean. “Here it comes,” he said. Seawater was creeping higher, already covering the sand along the sides of the prison. It was rising inside the tents closest to the shore on both sides, the Atlantic Ocean to the east and the mouth of the Potomac River to the west. The occupants from the flooded tents were moving toward the middle of the prison camp, toward higher ground. “They’re going to start coming out any minute. Let’s walk down to where the tide’s coming in. Keep your eye out.”

Everyone surveyed the ground as they walked toward the flooded sand. Suddenly, there was a burst of tiny gray motion, a family of rats scurrying away from their flooded home. The chase was on as dozens of prisoners went after them. Caleb could only stand with his crutch and watch from some distance away.

Charles Pearson was small, wiry, and fast. He had quick hands as well. The black guards were laughing loudly and pointing down at the melee as most of the other prisoners ran around and fell into the sand, coming up empty-handed. Charles didn’t. Within moments he was walking back toward Caleb with a plump rat in his hands. Caleb could see money changing hands between the guards on the wall. There were still a few guards who had the bad sense to bet against Charles Pearson.

“Told you,” Charles said as he walked back to the middle of the prison, where Caleb was still standing. “Let’s get him gutted and cooked while those other fools are still chasing. We might get him eaten before they catch anything.”

Wood was rare enough on the sandy peninsula, so fires were shared by many prisoners. Charles wanted to finish before the others came back.

Caleb may have had trouble walking, but his hands still worked perfectly. He had the rat skinned and gutted in seconds. Charles was the expert on cooking. He pulled a small pouch from his pocket and sprinkled a few precious grains of salt on the meat then placed it on a hot stone in the fire. It didn't take long to cook the small body.

"Never thought I'd ever eat a rat," Caleb said as he was chewing. "Not all that bad, though. Better than blackbird."

"Don't know," Charles said. "I ain't never ate a blackbird. But I'd sure enough do it if one got close enough to catch. I'd eat almost anything. They don't give us enough to keep body and soul together in this place. The Yankees can't beat us on the battlefield, so's I guess they're going to starve us to death instead."

Danny Talley came walking back, dangling a small rat by his tail. "Glad y'all have eaten because this one's too small to share."

"I'm just proud you caught one," Charles said. "We might could catch some more."

"Tide'll be falling soon," Danny said. "I don't guess we'll see any more get washed out of their holes."

"Oh, well," Charles said. "We'll have to wait till the next high tide. Or till the little buggers get hungry themselves and come sneaking out." He pulled his Bible from his shirt pocket, flipped it open to the ribbon-marked page, and began to read.

"You read that thing near about all the time," Danny said. "You're going to be God's right-hand man up there in heaven, ain't you?"

"Don't you be irreverent with the Lord's word," Charles said. "Elsewise, I won't be a'seeing you again when I get to heaven."

"I don't think God is that spiteful," Caleb said. "Leastwise, that's what my daddy preaches. He says the Lord is forgiveness and love."

"That's true enough," Charles said. "But no sense taking no chances. So your daddy's a preacher?"

"He travels around doing some preaching here and there, usually at the Union Church back home, on Baptist weeks, but he's mostly a farmer, I guess."

"Raised by a preaching farmer, eh? You've probably been missing your Bible reading." Charles closed the Bible and offered it to Caleb. "Here. You might as well catch up a little since you don't have one."

Caleb stared at the black leather-bound book in Charles' hand. He reached out momentarily then pulled his hand back and stared at the sand where he sat. "I don't read," he mumbled.

"You're a preacher's son, and you don't read the Bible?" Charles said. "Why, my daddy was a gambler and a drunk, but I still read the Bible every day. I pray for his soul, too. Lord knows he needs it."

"It ain't that I don't want to read it," Caleb said. He hesitated a few seconds then finally said, "I can't read it. I don't know my letters. Never had time to learn. We was always so busy with the farm." He shrugged his shoulders. "I didn't have no chance."

"You and thousands of others," Charles said. "Not uncommon at all. Why don't we change it? We got all the chance in the world in this place."

"What? What do you mean?"

"He means," Danny said, "He's going to spoon feed you the word of the Lord."

Charles waved off Danny's words and said to Caleb, "What are you doing right now? And what else have we got to do around this place other than chase rats, which you can't do on your stick? Maybe bathe in the ocean once every week or two. That leaves you plenty of time for learning to read."

"Learning to read? I can't learn to read. I'm too old. Why, I'm just a dumb farmer."

"You're a scared farmer, not a dumb one. But you're only afraid of learning to read out of ignorance. I've been around you long enough to know you're pretty smart, Caleb. You're more than smart enough to learn to read. I mean, seriously, what else you got to do while this war winds down? Come on. I'll show you the secrets, and your ignorance will disappear. We can start right now. Do you know what the alphabet is?"

"It's all the letters," Caleb said. "I know there's twenty-six of them, but I don't know what they all are."

"I'm going to show you," Charles said as he opened his Bible. "Today is Sunday, the Lord's day. I can't think of a better day for you to start learning how to read the Bible. Now, this here is the letter 'A'…"

July 17, 1864 ~ Montgomery, Alabama

Downtown Montgomery drifted slowly past Emily's window as the train rolled through the city. Great wood and brick buildings, shining with plaster and white paint, stood tall and proud, centers of commerce and government. People were walking along the busy streets or stopped and talking in pairs and groups. Others were sitting, reading or doing what appeared to be nothing. Horses were everywhere; tied to posts, bearing riders in the streets, and hitched to wagons. A busy place even on a Sunday afternoon.

While Montgomery had been the provisional capital of the rebelling states, the permanent capital was moved to Richmond early in the war. Still, Montgomery's importance was underscored as the Confederacy's historic birthplace. Situated on road, rail, and river, it was an important business center for the region. And, with Confederate soldiers dotted in the crowd, it remained firmly controlled by the South. The city was not being ruled by Union soldiers like so many other Southern cities in July of 1864.

Emily had tried to imagine Montgomery from the descriptions her parents and others had given her. The reality was better than the picture her head had jumbled together. And busier. Her heart beat faster and faster as she looked at all the amazing sights that her eyes beheld. She had never seen buildings so tall and streets so wide. She had never seen so many buildings or so many people in one place. It was like a vision she couldn't have imagined, but this wasn't a dream. This was real.

Six hours after they started, the train pulled to a full stop at the Alabama and Florida Railroad station. Emily stepped off the train onto a wooden platform. Wrought iron posts held up a canopy that kept the hot summer sunlight from baking her. She looked around the platform for Nathaniel and saw him outside the baggage car, holding her two bags. He nodded as he walked over. They stepped out of the station and onto the well-trod dirt streets of the city. Thank goodness it had been dry.

"Montgomery in only six hours!" Emily said. "That's amazing. I've always wanted to visit." She twirled in the street, looking over the cityscape all around her. "It's so big. There must be thousands of people here. Half of them are out in the streets right now." She looked around at the Sunday afternoon crowd as people milled about. Most of the stores were closed. Still, there were dozens of people standing and talking, dozens more riding along the streets. "Why would they move the capital of the Confederacy away from such a bustling city?"

"Many reasons," Nathaniel said. "To be close to the war front. To be nearer the bulk of the South's manufacturing capability. To be in a much larger city with more and better accommodations. To get away from South Alabama's oppressive heat. And to get away from the great swarms of Alabama mosquitoes. Take your pick."

"Richmond is larger than this?"

"Yes. Several times larger."

"Oh, my. That is big. Well, shall we get some dinner? I'm starved."

"Of course, but we won't be eating together anymore. Not on this trip. You might do well to remember that Nathaniel Whiteeagle is a slave. Specifically, your slave."

"Oh. I hadn't thought of that."

There was that flicker of a smile in Nathaniel's eyes. "Your father said to stay at the Exchange Hotel. He said they had the best rooms and would have accommodation for domestic slaves, as well. So I will be close by."

"Okay. Shall we get a carriage?"

"It's close enough to walk. We need to save our money."

"But my bags…"

"I can carry them." Nathaniel picked the bags up as easily as lifting a handful of cotton. "Besides, the Lord has blessed us with this beautiful day."

"The Lord must like it warm," Emily said with a smile. She turned her head back toward their destination. "We will enjoy His beautiful day while we walk through this magnificent city."

The Montgomery summer afternoon was hot, but the walk was short. The Exchange Hotel was four stories high, almost as tall as the old pines back home in Sepulga. It was wide and deep, which made it look taller than the pines, and it seemed to take up almost as much space as the entire downtown area of Sparta. *How could any city need so many hotel rooms?* Emily wondered as she stared at the rows and rows of windows. *Were there that many travelers in the world?* She felt small, insignificant, as though her life had been missing key ingredients all these years.

"Are you okay?" Nathaniel asked.

"Yes, of course. I just… It's a large building. I was admiring the architecture. The columns are so massive. I've never seen columns so large, not even at the best of plantations."

"They are quite large."

"Have you ever been to Montgomery?"

"Yes. A long time ago."

"What did you do when you were here?"

"I stood over there." Nathaniel nodded toward the wrought iron fence that surrounded the artesian well in the center of Court Square. "Chained to the fence while I was auctioned off."

"Oh." Emily's hand went to her mouth. "I'm sorry. I…"

"There is nothing for you to be sorry about. It is the world we live in. The world I live in. I cannot remake the world, not by myself, so I make the best of it."

Emily glanced at Nathaniel then at the wrought iron fence. "Yes. You're right, of course. My mother inherited you from her brother, who died of consumption. They were rich. Is he the one who bought you in the auction here?"

"No. It's a long story. And not very interesting. Shall we check in?"

"Yes, of course." Emily turned back to the Exchange Hotel, situated on the corner of Montgomery and Commerce Streets. "Which side is the front? There are columns on both sides." She looked at each entrance then said, "I suppose it doesn't matter as it appears people are entering on either side. I'm sure we'll see the registration desk as soon as we enter. Shall we?"

They stepped out of the radiant heat of the sun and into the lobby, cooler because of the ground floor's tall ceiling. With her footsteps clicking loudly on the stone floor, something she thought quite pleasant, the announcement of her arrival, she walked over to the registration desk.

Behind the desk, a young man in a suit smiled warmly. "Will you be staying alone, ma'am?" he asked.

"Yes, thank you. Ah…" After having endured the steward on the train, Emily was apprehensive asking about accommodations for Nathaniel. "We will also need a place for my domestic."

"Yes, of course, ma'am. We have a room available in the ladies section for you. And we have rooms for Negro slaves when they are accompanied in travel by their owners. The Negro accommodations are nearby, close should you require his services. Let us know, and we can summon him for you." The clerk wrote something down then pointed to the register. "Please sign here. Will you be taking dinner in your room?"

"Yes, thank you. And what about dinner for Nathaniel, here?"

"We will see to it right away," the clerk said then he turned and snapped his fingers, summoning a bellhop. "Please take Miss Rose's bags up to her room." He handed her the room key.

The bellhop reached out to take the bags. When Nathaniel let go of the first one, the bellhop almost went to the floor with it. He glanced down at the bag then up at Nathaniel, who was holding out the second bag in one hand as though it was nothing. The bellhop gulped, took a deep breath, and reached for the second bag. Straining under the weight of both bags, he stumbled his way toward the stairs, glancing back at Nathaniel as he did. Nathaniel kept his expression neutral, but Emily could see the twinkle in his eyes.

"Please have someone knock on my door at six o'clock in the morning," Emily told the clerk. "We don't want to be late for our train." She did not need a wake-up knock. She could not remember the last time she had slept past five in the morning. But she couldn't resist. It felt good to have someone cater to her whims. Emily turned to Nathaniel and said, "I will meet you in the lobby at seven o'clock sharp tomorrow morning. Good evening."

"Good evening, ma'am," Nathaniel said as he bowed. Emily smiled and turned toward the stairs.

Walking to the stairs became one of those moments for Emily that is forever burned into memory. People had called her pretty, cute, lovely, and other such words as long as she could remember. But when she looked in a mirror, she thought she was quite plain. She had always assumed everyone was being kind, pandering to a young girl.

At that moment, however, when she turned toward the stairs to walk after the bellhop, dressed in the beautiful dress her mother had made, she knew she was wrong about the reflection in the mirror. She knew that she was not a good judge of her own looks. Every man in the lobby, strangers she had never seen before and would never see again, was looking at her with that unmistakable look. She knew what it meant. Some of them had their mouths open. A cigar fell out of one man's mouth. He quickly retrieved it from the floor, but never took his eyes off her until he burned his fingers by placing them on the wrong end of the cigar.

There were young men and old men, single men and married men. Those accompanied by a lady turned away quickly enough, so as not to create a problem for themselves. But their brief look had spoken so much without the first word passing through the air.

As good as the admiration made her feel, it mattered not the least. There was only one man in her life. Caleb Garner. Still, she had her confirmation that everything she had always been told was true. She smiled delightedly as she walked straight ahead, following the struggling bellhop. It didn't take long to catch up to him.

July 17, 1864 ~ Barracks Number Three, Elmira, New York

"He ain't moving," one of the prisoners said.

A second prisoner placed a hand on the chest of the emaciated man lying still on his cot. After a few seconds, he said, "He ain't breathing, neither."

Another prisoner, dressed in ragged undershorts and undershirt only, hobbled up and stood beside the cot. He had a bandaged foot and was using a crutch to keep it above the floor. The cloth of the bandage had been white at one time. It was now a dingy tan, streaked with brown. "That's three today," he said. "So far. Day ain't over yet."

"What the hell are you doing?" Corporal John Murray shouted as he came over to where the men were standing.

"Private Newsom, here, he's dead," the first prisoner said.

"Serves him right. Filthy Rebel." Murray turned to the guards by the door and shouted, "Get another stretcher crew in here. Tell them to get this dead animal out of my sight." He turned back to the prisoners standing around the dead man's cot and said, "Only three of you scum today. That's a shame. Maybe we'll have better luck tomorrow." He looked down at the dead man, curled the corner of his lips in disgust, and said, "One less mouth to feed."

The soldier using the crutch looked up and said, "Won't make no difference. Y'all don't feed us nothing much, no ways."

Murray shoved his arms forward, palms out, catching the rail-thin man hard in the chest. The crutch fell to the side and clattered against the next cot before bouncing onto the floor. Too weak to keep himself steady, the prisoner fell backward. His bandaged foot slammed hard against the side of the cot as he fell. He curled in a ball on the wood floor and screamed in pain. The other prisoners who were standing around the dead man's cot backed away, their eyes wide with fear.

Murray held up his hands in front of him and said, "Look what you've done, you fool. You've got my hands dirty from your filth." He kicked the man in the back with his heavy boot. There was another weak scream. The other men backed even further away until they were lined against the wall.

"It's Sunday," one of the men said, "The Lord's day. Please."

"Sunday? God doesn't give a damn about you. You Rebels are nothing but stupid, filthy pigs. You're not worth the sweat from a Union soldier's ass. Let this be a lesson to you."

Two Union soldiers came into the barracks with a stretcher. With cloth strips wrapped around their hands, they lifted the dead Confederate soldier and placed him on the stretcher. It wasn't hard. The man's body was so slight it weighed well under a hundred pounds. They lifted the stretcher and left. One of the men was whistling "Always Stand On The Union Side."

When the body was gone, Murray turned his attention back to the soldier writhing in pain on the floor. The man was sobbing, tears flowing out of his eyes. John Murray spat on the man. "You're disgusting," he growled in a low, menacing tone then turned and walked away.

The rest of the prisoners were silent as they watched him go. When Murray was out of sight, they helped the man with the injured foot get off the floor and onto his cot. One of them said, "I could almost put up with that blasphemous animal if they'd feed us more."

July 18, 1864 ~ Montgomery, Alabama

The clerk insisted they take a carriage even though it was only a few blocks to the Montgomery and West Point Railroad station. "The dust in the street," he said, "If you walk, it will get all over that beautiful dress you're wearing, ma'am."

She thanked the clerk for his thoughtfulness and his wisdom. They rode the few blocks down Lee Street, toward the Alabama River.

The train station was grand, even nicer than the Alabama and Florida Railroad station from the day before, but they could see from a couple of blocks away that things were not quite the way they should be. The scene was chaos. Soldiers were everywhere. Citizens were shouting, waving their arms through the air. Riders pushed their horses here and there, but nobody seemed to be going anywhere.

"Montgomery and West Point Railroad Station, ma'am," the driver said.

"There seems to be some confusion here," Emily said. "Is it always like this?"

"No, ma'am. I don't know what's going on," the driver said as he opened the small side door of the carriage to let Emily step out. "There's an awful lot of soldiers here. Don't know why. Here, I can help you with…" The driver turned to the baggage rack in the rear, but Nathaniel had already retrieved the bags and was waiting to the side.

Emily paid the driver then they worked their way through several groups of soldiers and walked into the station. The people standing in front of the ticket booth were more of a mob than a line. A railroad company clerk was standing off to the side, talking to several of the people in the crowd and shaking his head. A dozen people were talking back at him all at once. A man in a suit, a railroad company spokesman, stepped behind the counter and held his arms up. The crowd lowered to murmurs then became quiet.

"Please," he said, "I have an important announcement to make. The Montgomery and West Point Railroad regrets that the train will not run as usual this morning." He stopped as several people in the crowd shouted questions. "I cannot give you the details," he resumed. "But the Confederate army can."

The train executive stood back, and a Home Guard officer came forward. He was an old man, with gray hair on the sides and a wide brim Confederate hat covering his bald head.

"I regret to tell you," the old officer said, his voice scratchy but steady, "That there's been a Yankee raid near Opelika. Those devils are right here in Alabama. Right now as I'm talking to you." The quiet of the crowd was gone as people erupted into gasps and questions and exclamations. There were several inappropriate words, the kind that parents whipped their children for uttering. This time it was the parents speaking the words.

The old Home Guard officer held his hands up for quiet then continued, "They're tearing up the track. Miles of it. Word is they've also torn up some trestles. Civilian passengers won't be able to take the train. You wouldn't get to your destination anyway. We're putting as many soldiers on the train as we can. They'll travel until they reach the damaged track. That's where they will meet with other troops from other areas and, by God, drive those damned Yankee vandals out of Alabama." Cheers erupted from a few people, disappointed grunts and moans came from others.

For the most part, Montgomery had been spared the destructive touch of war. This was a significant inconvenience, but not something that brought the blood-and-guts reality of war home to their eyes. For the few who understood the full implications, that the South was losing their infrastructure amidst the flowing of blood on both sides, there was little reaction other than contemplative silence.

A man in the crowd asked, "How long will it take to get the rails fixed?"

The railroad executive stepped forward once again. "We don't know the extent of the damage, or how much more damage they'll be able to do before we can run them off. From what we've heard, we're guessing it will be several weeks before we can get things back in order. Perhaps a month."

More groans. Emily turned to look for Nathaniel. He was standing quietly behind everybody, as a slave would be expected to do. She walked over to him and asked, "What are we going to do?"

"We could go home…"

"But Caleb… No. We can't leave him in prison. It's terrible how they mistreat prisoners. I've heard the stories. Many of our boys are dying."

"Or we could take the train toward home but continue past Sparta, all the way to Pensacola. From there we could try to book passage on a Union ship. The North has control of Pensacola. That has both advantages and disadvantages. But the boat trip from Pensacola to the Chesapeake Bay would be a lengthy one. And we're not sure the Union would allow civilian passengers. I'm not even sure we could get into Pensacola. So we may get there and have to turn around and come right back to Montgomery."

Emily stared at Nathaniel but said nothing. A tear rolled down her cheek. Several more rolled down until the liquid on her face became two tiny streams.

Nathaniel tried to ignore the tears and said, "Or, the final option, we could purchase two horses and ride to a different town, somewhere safe from the raids. It would need to be a place from which the track to Richmond has not been destroyed. We would sell the horses there. If we were lucky, we might get our money back, or most of it."

The tear streams stopped. "What about time? Where will we go, and how long will it take?"

Nathaniel nodded toward a framed map hanging on a post to the side. "There is a map of all the railroads in the South. Let's study it. Well, you study it. I'm not allowed to read, of course. It's against the law."

"Yes, I know. It's so stupid. I also know you can read. And you understand maps better than I do, so you'll need to look, too."

"I will try to be inconspicuous," Nathaniel said.

They stepped over to the map. Emily glanced at the train lines connecting Alabama and Georgia and groaned. She traced her finger along the glass that protected the map. "If we ride east, along this track, we may run into the Yankees. We'll have to take a line that's further south. The closest point is Chunenaggee, here, but that spur goes into Columbus. It puts us right back where the Yankees might be."

"We can't take that chance," Nathaniel said, avoiding looking directly at the map. "We'll have to ride further south."

"We could go to Eufaula then take the train to Macon. It's a long ride, but that line should be safe. Surely they will capture the Union raiders before they destroy the track all the way to Macon."

"Perhaps. I'm not sure we want to risk that, though. The safest route appears to be Thomasville, Georgia. The train from there goes straight to Savannah. That looks like our safest option."

"And the longest horseback ride. Do you see this scale of miles, here? If I'm reading it correctly, it's about two hundred miles from Montgomery to Thomasville. How long would it take to ride that far?"

"By horse… I'm not sure. A week or so, perhaps. But I promised Thomas I would keep you safe. There is fighting on the other routes, or could be soon. The Thomasville route appears to be the safest, even if it is a long ride."

Emily stood staring at the map. She didn't immediately respond.

"Don't you agree?" Nathaniel asked.

"Yes, I suppose so. I was thinking about how hard this is going to be on my… Well, you understand. I'm a good rider, but two hundred miles?" Emily turned around and looked at Nathaniel, "There will be sores."

While Nathaniel's lips did not move, his eyes smiled.

July 27, 1864 ~ Rural Southwestern Georgia

Meandering through a gently rolling, almost flat terrain, the dirt trail was pocked with gullies made in wet weather, where wagon wheels had plowed through the mud in a topography that did not drain well. Even though it was dry, and had been for days, the footing was tricky because of the depth of the gullies. In the South Georgia heat, the horses plodded along as best they could to the side of the trail and out of the gullies, as long as the bushes did not block the way.

"It's too hot to dress like a lady," Emily said. "I wish I was a little girl. I could strip down to my unmentionables and be a lot cooler."

Nathaniel said nothing. He only rode along and looked carefully side-to-side as he had done the entire trip, occasionally turning his head to see behind them. He perked up. "Riders ahead," he said. "Sounds like two of them, maybe more."

"How do you do that? I don't hear anything."

Keeping his eyes on the road in front of them, Nathaniel was quiet. After traveling a few more feet, they could hear a conversation. Then they saw them, two men on horseback coming around the trees in a curve not far ahead. There was a flash of light on one of the men's chest, a reflection of sunlight. Emily looked more closely. A badge. Another light flashed. Both of the men were wearing badges.

"Local Sheriff," Nathaniel said. "They'll want to see our travel pass. Smile and be friendly. Another day on the road."

The Sheriff and his deputy stopped a few feet in front of them. The Sheriff was tall, round in the middle but otherwise only slightly stocky. He had a long, shaggy mustache and fluffy sideburns. A shotgun lay across his lap. "How do, stranger," he said to Emily. "Where you from?"

"Sepulga, Alabama," Emily answered, smiling as pleasantly as she could. "I'm Emily Rose."

"Alabama, eh? Welcome to Georgia, Miss Rose. You're a long way from home, young lady. Where you going?"

"Richmond. Going to visit my daddy's aunt, Mrs. Millie Hanson. She lost her husband a while back. We're going up to help her."

"Sorry to hear that. But I'm pleased to meet you. I'm Sheriff Tate, Rufus Tate." The Sheriff glanced back at his deputy, a slender man with a face like a hound dog and long, droopy brown hair. "This here is Deputy Henry Satterfield. Riding to Richmond, eh? That's an awful long way for a lady to ride a horse."

"We were taking the train, but the Yankees tore up the track. There was no way to get through from Montgomery, so we're riding to Thomasville to catch the train there."

"I see. Who's your boy, there?" The Sheriff nodded at Nathaniel, the first time he had acknowledged the black man's presence.

"Oh, this is Nathaniel Whiteeagle, our domestic. He always travels with us." Emily nodded and smiled.

"Whiteeagle, eh? Indian name. You an Indian, boy?"

"My grandfather was a Cherokee," Nathaniel answered, as respectfully as he could.

"Well, sir, you're the brownest Indian I've ever seen. You do have high cheekbones, though." The Sheriff turned back to Emily and continued, "I don't mean to trouble you, none, Miss, but I'm going to have to see your travel pass." Sheriff Tate brought his horse alongside Emily.

"Of course, Sheriff Tate." Emily pulled her small purse from the saddlebag and slid a paper out of the purse. She placed the travel pass in the Sheriff's outstretched hand.

Rufus Tate looked over the single sheet of brown paper, seeming to read every word. Finally, he looked up and said, "Signed by Captain Carter McInnis of the Home Guard. Well, I don't know the gentleman, but it looks official. It's got a stamp on it." He folded the pass then handed it back to Emily. "Everything seems to be in order."

"Thank you, Sheriff. Well, we'll be on our way. We've got a long way to go."

"Hold on, young lady. I'm not quite finished," the Sheriff said. He turned his attention to Nathaniel and looked him over carefully.

"What's the matter, Sheriff Tate?" Emily asked.

"Well, Miss, I find it mighty curious that a pretty young lady like yourself is traveling alone with a big buck nigger like Mr. Whiteeagle here."

Nathaniel's stoic face did not change. Emily's brow wrinkled, and anger flashed in her eyes. "What are you insinuating, Sir?"

"Oh, I don't guess I'm insinuating anything. Unless there's something to insinuate. You know, Mr. Whiteeagle is a well-built man. He looks like he's in fine shape. A darkie like him could work all day long, day after day."

Nathaniel stared ahead, not acknowledging he had heard the comments.

"Yessiree, that darkie would be worth a substantial amount of money at some of the plantations around here. Maybe twenty-five hundred or three thousand. Maybe even more. An enterprising owner could stud this one out for a good fee."

"What are you saying?" Emily shouted. Her face was turning red. "I'm going to report you to the authorities…"

"That would be me, ma'am. I am the authority." The Sheriff raised his shotgun and pointed it at Nathaniel. When he did, Deputy Satterfield pulled his pistol from its holster. "The two of you are under arrest. Your big black boy, here, for running away from one of the local plantations. I'll find out which one will pay the most to have him back then we'll know which plantation he escaped from." The Sheriff smiled broadly.

Emily was in shock. She stared at the Sheriff with her mouth open but said nothing. Nathaniel's face never changed.

"We're going to have to take you two over here to the jailhouse."

"Jail?" Emily said. "You can't do this. Why, the Home Guard..."

"Move along in the direction you were already going, Miss Rose. The jail's coming up here soon. Follow Deputy Satterfield, and I'll be right behind you with my friend, here." He patted the shotgun. "Come on, now. I'll explain as we move along."

The dog-faced deputy began to lead. There was nothing else they could do, so Emily and Nathaniel fell in behind.

"You see," Sheriff Tate said from behind them, "I'm not only the Sheriff; I'm also the head of the Home Guard here. Now, Southwest

Georgia is darn near perfect for growing cotton. There's a lot of plantations around, but there's a shortage of slaves to work them nowadays. With old Abe declaring them free, seems like these boys want to try to run away about all the time. Why, we get several escapes a week, sometimes eight or ten darkies at a time. Not many of them get by me, but enough do so that the plantation owners are willing to pay a good price for a slave that's captured. Old Nat Whiteeagle, here, since he's a runaway slave from somewhere else, would be worth a lot. With the Yankees raiding here and there, we can't take him back to where he came from, so I'm going to find out how much he's worth around here."

"What about me?" Emily asked. "I'm not a slave. Why are you taking me to jail?"

"Well, Miss Rose, I would have thought it would be obvious to someone with your intelligence. Young lady, you are under arrest for aiding and abetting a runaway slave."

"What? I have done nothing of the kind!"

"We'll see about that. Just keep riding."

Emily realized there was no need to talk to this man. Conversation was getting her nowhere, so she decided to follow Nathaniel's lead and keep her mouth shut.

They veered from the main trail onto a less traveled path. Some minutes later Emily saw a building off to the side, immediately behind a group of pine trees. It was made out of stone, though crudely. The building had one wooden door and an open window with no glass or shutter. A wide old oak tree with enormous limbs stood close by. The ground around the building was littered with various wood and rusted metal pieces of this and that. It was in no order and seemed to be useless, junk. There was a small wood house, the lumber gray and warped with age, off to the side with a woodshed next to it. There were no other buildings.

"Here we are," Sheriff Tate said.

"Where's the town?" Emily asked. "This is only a couple of buildings. It's not a town."

"It's all the town we need. We've got our jail and our office right there." He pointed to the stone building. "Deputy Satterfield's house is right here." He pointed toward the small wood house. "He cooks your meals there and brings them over. And our storage building is over there. Plus the outhouse out back, of course. We don't need anything else. Our purpose here is not to have stores and streets and lots of townsfolks. Our purpose here is to keep the plantations running as smoothly as they can at this point in the war. The owners pay well." Sheriff Tate smiled broadly.

"You can't sell me as a slave. I'm a white woman. There's no need for you to arrest me or put me in jail."

Sheriff Tate's head snapped back in mock surprise. "Young lady, did you not hear me? You are guilty of aiding and abetting a runaway slave. That's a mighty serious crime here in Georgia. I think we're going to have to keep you in jail for a long, long time."

July 28, 1864 ~ Point Lookout Prison, Maryland

"That was pretty good," Charles said. "Not as many mistakes this time."

"It was pitiful," Caleb said. "I can never remember what comes after 'j.' Or 's.' And I get 'm' and 'n' backward half the time. Why is this so hard?"

"Because there's twenty-six of them," Danny Talley said. "All different. That's a lot of things to have to put in a particular order."

"It's not as bad as trying to juggle twenty-six apples at once," Charles said with a smile.

Caleb lay back on the canvas covered sand. Unable to straighten his wounded leg, he took up more space to the side than the other prisoners. With six people in a four-person tent, they were beyond crowded. His crooked leg rested on top of Danny's stomach. Having to make accommodation for Caleb's leg made the crowding worse. Still, no one complained. They were all in the same misery. They tried to help each other out as best they could.

"I wonder what's happening back home," Danny said. "I wonder if my wife and kids are okay. If I was there, we'd be out weeding our vegetable garden about now. Milking the cow. Collecting eggs. I sure do miss all that. And I miss my family so."

"Where do they live?" Charles asked.

"Southeast of Atlanta. Near Milledgeville. It's out a ways. Countryside. Nice and peaceful."

"I'm sure they're fine," Charles said. "They'll be looking forward to seeing you when this war is done."

Danny grunted.

"What about you?" Caleb asked Charles.

The smaller man picked up his Bible and said, "This is my family, my peace and my solace."

"You don't have nobody back home?"

"Never married. Never found the right one. My family's all gone."

"All of them?" Danny asked.

"I was the baby. My parents were older. They passed away about two years apart, not long before the war. That was back in South Carolina. My brothers were both killed in the war, one at First Manassas and the other at Second. That ground's a sad place for the Pearson family. I had a sister, too, but she took sick and died before I was born. She was only eight years old. So I'm the only one left. I got a few friends back home, the ones who hadn't been killed in the war yet." He turned to Caleb and said, "You?"

"Got the prettiest girl in Conecuh County waiting for me back home. Her name's Emily Rose."

"Nice name," Danny said. "It even sounds pretty."

Caleb smiled and said, "It is. And she is. I'm glad she's safe back home in Sepulga. It's too deep in the South, and there's nothing much there. The Yankees can't get to it and wouldn't waste their time if they could. I don't know what she sees in me, though. My prospects aren't all that good. I'm just a farmer."

"You're right 'bout not having no prospects," one of the other prisoners said. "None of us do. We ain't likely going to get off this sandbank alive. Might as well drown in a high tide. It'd save a lot of suffering."

Everyone was silent for a couple of minutes. Trying to break the gloom inside the tent, Charles turned to Caleb and said, "You know all the letters. When I show you one, you say what it is right away. And you can read and spell a lot of simple words. Knowing the order of the alphabet is not so important to reading, but you still need to know it. So you can order things by how they come in the alphabet. It's called alphabetizing. Tell you what. There's a song they created years ago. You can learn the alphabet better if you use this tune. Sing it like me."

Charles started singing the alphabet song. A few letters later, Danny and one of the other three in the tent joined in. Within minutes, they could hear prisoners in adjacent tents singing along as well. The gloom disappeared. Caleb couldn't help but smile as he joined in. The tune was not familiar to Caleb, but it appeared as though everybody who had gone to school knew it. And it was easy to pick up.

This went on for some time. Finally, after many times through, Charles pointed his finger at Caleb. "You got it!" he said. "All the way through. No mistakes. See? Even old dirt farmers can learn."

Caleb smiled. "Yeah," he said. "I guess I can learn. And maybe I'll be able to read like other folks someday. But what good is it in here?"

"You think we're going to spend the rest of our lives in prison?" Charles asked.

"Lots of folks dying in here," Caleb said. "They're already spending the rest of their lives in prison. We could take sick easy enough. Or get starved to death."

"Or get shot," Danny added.

July 29, 1864 ~ Rural Jail, Southwestern Georgia

"I've been shopping you around, boy," the Sheriff said from his desk as he looked into the cell where Nathaniel sat impassively. "Got several plantations interested. Three of them are coming out to look you over tomorrow."

Emily was in the adjacent cell. There was a stone wall between them and bars in front. While Emily and Nathaniel could not see each other, they could easily talk to each other. They could also pass things back and forth, but they had nothing to pass.

"You can't do this!" Emily screamed from her cell. She had tried Nathaniel's stoic approach, but it had broken down after less than a day of confinement. "You'll never get away with it. Let us go, or my father will bring the entire Confederate army down on you!"

"Well, young lady, based on the story you told me, I don't believe your daddy has any idea where you are. And right now the Confederate army is busy getting whipped by the Yankees, way too busy to travel down to South Georgia."

Emily fumed. The Sheriff looked at her from the corners of his eyes then continued, "When they're finished getting whipped, things are going to be different around here. The Yankees will come in and tell us all what to do. But they'll need local help. The man who has the most gold will be able to work with them, maybe get himself elected to a pretty high office. Mr. Whiteeagle, here, represents a nice stack of gold to me. I'll put that with what I've got stashed away, and I'll be someone to be reckoned with. Hell, I might even be Governor of Georgia before I'm through."

"You couldn't get elected to pick up garbage," Emily shouted.

"You obviously don't understand the power of gold, young lady. Those Union officers aren't the lily-white do-gooders some people think they are. A few pieces of gold in the right hands speaks awful loud. And you don't seem to understand your situation very well, either. I can't have you running around talking, now, can I? Not now, not later. But that problem can be solved. All I've got to do is tell everybody how you've been laying in a haystack with this here darkie. That's a hanging offense in Georgia."

"You're a liar!" Emily shouted. "I did nothing of the kind!"

"And I could say otherwise. But I won't, as long as you don't make me mad enough to forget the gold. You see, if I hang you for tossing the hay around with this here darkie, then I've got to hang him, too. Not that I wouldn't enjoy seeing his legs twitch around, but if I hang him, I can't sell him." Sheriff Tate pointed his finger at Emily. "But you better be careful. There's other things I can do. Now, you're going to be here for a long time. You best be doing what I tell you to do. Otherwise, you'll disappear down here in South Georgia. Forever."

Emily was stunned into silence, but Nathaniel broke his. "YOU, Sir," he shouted. "Will do nothing to Miss Rose, or I will find you somehow and some way. Whatever it takes. When I do, I. Will. Kill. You."

Sheriff Tate cocked his head sideways and stared at Nathaniel several seconds before saying, "You know, boy, I'd almost be worried except a darkie can't move around freely in this part of the world. And besides, I keep my friend with me all the time." Rufus Tate patted the scattergun leaning against the wall. "Even when I'm sleeping. You'd be dead long before you could make good on your threat. But, now, that brings up another point. I don't let a white man talk to me like that, much less a nigger. I do what I damn well please, boy. And you're going to find that out right now. There's a penalty in this town for threatening the Sheriff."

Rufus Tate opened the front door and called the deputy inside. Then he stepped over to the front of Emily's cell and pulled his pistol, holding it in the air. He turned to Nathaniel and said, "Deputy Satterfield is going to come in there and put the cuffs on you. And you're going to cooperate nice and polite, or I'll take care of my problem with this young lady right here and now." He lowered the pistol and aimed it at Emily's chest.

Nathaniel held his hands in front of him, palms out in a show of surrender. He said nothing as the deputy locked the cuffs around his wrists then led him outside.

Sheriff Tate opened Emily's cell and put cuffs on her then led her outside as he said, "Wouldn't want you to miss the show, Miss Rose. This will be educational for you."

Henry Satterfield cut off Nathaniel's shirt. He was in a hurry. Emily winced as she thought the knife would cut Nathaniel open, but the deputy was adept with a blade. The shirt was off quickly with no blood drawn. Then he lifted Nathaniel's cuffed hands and placed them over a large metal hook that dangled at the end of a thick rusty chain. The chain hung from a huge limb that stood out from the centuries-old oak in front of the jail building. Sheriff Tate turned a crank to the side. As he did, the chain became taut. The Sheriff continued to turn the crank, lifting Nathaniel off the ground. He stopped when Nathaniel's toes were the only thing touching dirt.

"On a charge of threatening a duly appointed sheriff, I declare you guilty. The penalty is a hundred lashes. We'll see how much sass you've got in you after I get through carrying out your sentence, boy."

Sheriff Tate walked to the other side of the tree and picked up a whip hanging from a makeshift wooden fence. He walked back and let the whip out, pulled it behind him, and then brought if forward, popping the end across Nathaniel's back with deathly precision. He had done this before.

Nathaniel grunted loudly but did not cry out.

"Quiet one, eh? You think you're not going to give me the pleasure of hearing you scream? Well, boy, we'll see about that. I suspect you'll be howling like a wolf before I finish all one hundred lashes. You see, before I became Sheriff of these parts, I was an overseer. The plantation owners hereabouts weren't too happy with the way I whipped you boys. I got a little carried away at times. Just having fun, you understand. But they didn't like me killing off their property. Too expensive. After they thought about it, though, they decided the same traits that made me a bad overseer would make me a good Sheriff. So there you have it. I'm good at this. And you're going to do more than grunt before I get through with you."

Sheriff Tate pulled the whip back and popped it again, harder than before. Nathaniel grunted again, but Emily could tell he would be screaming soon. "Please," she said through her tears. "He doesn't deserve this."

"Of course he does. He's got a multitude of sins to atone for. Not the least of which is being born a black man. Why, he's not much better than a monkey. You hear that monkey? Here's another one for you."

The third lash, the hardest one yet, slapped across Nathaniel's back. His body rocked forward with the force of the blow. The grunt turned high pitched as breath fled from his lungs.

"Almost screamed for me on that one, didn't you. A couple more and we'll be there. Then you'll be singing a song for the rest of the afternoon as I drag that hundred lashes out nice and slow."

Sheriff Tate heard the thudding of hooves and looked up at the same time as Deputy Satterfield. A rider came in at full speed. "Sheriff Tate!" the rider, an older man, called out as he drew his horse to a stop. "It's the Buchanan place. An escape. Six of them. You've got to come quick before they get away."

"Damn," Rufus Tate cursed. "Interrupting my fun. I thought we were going to have a whole week without a single attempt." He turned to Nathaniel and said, "You boys never learn, do you? Well, this is why they made me Sheriff. I'm the best tracker around. I'll have to finish with you tomorrow. Let's see, that's three lashes, so I still owe you… Oh, what the hell. We'll do the whole hundred tomorrow morning. Saves trying to subtract." Sheriff Tate smiled as he turned the crank to lower the chain.

Nathaniel was rudely thrown across his cot then Deputy Satterfield tossed salt on the three deep lashes. Nathaniel's back arched in pain as his breath strained out. Somehow, he managed to stifle the scream in his throat.

"Salt's good for keeping the infection down," Sheriff Tate said. "We wouldn't want you to take sick and die. You wouldn't be worth nothing to anybody dead. The training's good for you, too. When I'm finished, whoever buys you will have a docile, hardworking slave. There won't be no more uppity talk coming from your mouth. Now, it's late, and the Buchanan place is a long way from here. I'll be tracking these six darkies through the night, maybe all night long, but I'll be back tomorrow morning. The Deputy, here, will make sure y'all don't cause no trouble while I'm gone."

Emily could not see Nathaniel from her cell, but she could hear his breathing. It was regular but hard. A hundred lashes? By tomorrow afternoon, Nathaniel's breathing would be ragged at best, if he breathed at all.

~ O ~

The reddish-orange light of sunset filtered through the slit beneath the door and poured through the glassless window. Deputy Satterfield said, "I've got to go home a spell, get some vittles. Maybe I'll bring y'all something back. You be good, now." He smiled and left.

"Nathaniel, are you okay?"

"I've been better."

"I'm sorry. Stupid question. I wish I hadn't gotten you into this. I should have insisted I go on this trip by myself. I never dreamed we would run into somebody like Rufus Tate. He's crazy! Both of them are crazy."

"Don't blame yourself. I let him get to me. I opened my mouth when I knew better. Besides, I volunteered to go with you in the first place. It should have been an easy trip. There was no way to foresee the Union raid. If we had been on the train to Richmond as we planned, we wouldn't have had this problem. But the raid happened, and we have a problem."

"What are we going to do? You can't go through that beating. You just can't."

"A beating is a beating. He's taking it easy. He won't swing that hard because he still wants to sell me. There is a more serious problem."

"What could be more serious than you getting beaten like that?"

"I am worried about what the Sheriff plans to do to you."

"Me? Why, he'll have to let me go. And as soon as he does, I'll find the real Home Guard and bring them here."

"Exactly. I'm sure the Sheriff knows that."

"Oh!" Emily said as realization dawned on her. "Yes. He wouldn't want me to tell anyone. Do you think he was serious about…"

"About you disappearing forever? We have to assume it's a possibility. There are several possibilities, and none of them are good."

Emily became silent. Sometime later, Deputy Satterfield returned, a tin plate in each hand. The plates held a piece of dark bread and a splattering of something lumpy and brown. Beans, Emily guessed. He passed them into the cells then went back outside.

Emily stared at her tin. She was hungry and took a couple of bites of the bread. She couldn't bring herself to try the undercooked beans. There were several globs of hog fat mixed in. It was so disgusting she avoided looking at it.

A few minutes later Deputy Satterfield returned with a large tin cup, sat in his chair and started sipping. The pungent, slightly sweet smell of moonshine permeated the jail. He continued to sip and said little as he stared at her. In the two days they had been there, Satterfield had proven he was not a conversationalist.

An hour later the sunset was gone. The open window showed only black. The Deputy lit an oil lamp sitting on the desk and another hanging from the wall. Satterfield had continued to eye Emily as he sipped his homemade whiskey, but eventually, the moonshine was gone. He set the empty tin down on his desk and stood, wobbling as he did. Without a word, he opened the door to Emily's cell.

Emily backed up. She didn't like the look in his eyes. Once inside, he reached through the bars and locked the cell from the outside then stuck the keys in his pants pocket.

"What are you doing?" she said.

Satterfield didn't say anything. He looked at her with a strange expression on his face, inching slowly closer. She tried to move away, but his arm shot out. The man was fast. He grabbed her shoulder and pinned her to the wall. He was also strong. She couldn't get loose no matter how much she wiggled. The rocks dug into her back as he pressed with his hand.

The smell of moonshine was strong. As repulsive as it was, it was the best thing in the deputy's breath. Up close, the air he exhaled and the other smells from the man were rancid, beyond repulsive. Emily gagged. His other hand ripped at her clothes.

"HELP!" she screamed as loud as she could.

The back of his hand came across her cheek, hard. The back of her head pounded against the stone wall. She was dazed and lost her balance, but he held her up.

"Might as well shut up," Henry Satterfield said. "Ain't nobody going to hear you out here. Even if they did, they wouldn't do nothing no ways. Anybody around here would laugh at you. But you can go ahead and struggle. Fight all you want, little lady. That's the way I like it."

The stone wall had staggered her. She heard his words but had to think to understand them. She was still struggling with consciousness. Everything was foggy. She was aware of Nathaniel shouting, but she couldn't see him in his cell. She couldn't understand what he was saying, either. As the Deputy jerked her blouse back and forth, full consciousness slowly came back. She could feel a trickle of blood run down the side of her neck, behind her ear.

The deputy was having trouble. He didn't want to take the time to unbutton the blouse, but her mother had made her clothes well. The blouse was not ripping. Instead, he succeeded only in jerking her head around in circles.

"Damn it!" he said. "Get this stupid shirt off. Unbutton the damn thing, or I'll beat you senseless." His fist came around and slammed into her jaw. "NOW!" he shouted.

He held her from behind, in an awkward position, so the force of the blow was less than it could have been. Still, her head rocked, and her jaw was racked with sharp pain.

"Please," she pleaded. When her head steadied, she could see the front corner of the cell. Nathaniel's arm was reaching through the bars on the front and slapping against the rock wall on her side. His fingers motioned toward him. *Go to him? How?* she wondered. She was being held so tight it hurt her chest as he pawed at her buttons and breasts. Then a flash of inspiration hit her, and she realized what Nathaniel wanted.

Worried that the deputy might see Nathaniel's hand motions, she twisted around some more. "Please don't hit me again. I'll take it off. Please."

"Do it! Quick!" Satterfield let her go as he waited for her to get undressed.

She turned her back to the corner where Nathaniel was motioning, putting the deputy behind her. Gathering all her strength, she crouched then shoved against the floor with both legs, thrusting her body back-first into Satterfield. Slowed by the moonshine, the deputy stumbled backward and fell against the corner. Nathaniel's muscular arm found his neck, closing and squeezing hard. The deputy tried to scream, but nothing more than strained breath came out of his throat.

"The keys," Nathaniel growled. "Find the keys." His voice was tense because of the pressure he was exerting on Satterfield's neck.

Emily stayed back as far as she could as she reached into Henry Satterfield's pants pocket. The deputy tried to stop her, but Nathaniel pulled on his neck so hard Satterfield's arm could not extend. All he could do was slap at her hand with his fingers. She rushed to the cell door and, after several moments fumbling with the key, was finally able to unlock it. Deputy Satterfield's head went limp as Emily unlocked Nathaniel's cell. Nathaniel let go and the deputy's body slumped to the floor.

"Is he dead?" she asked.

"No. He's unconscious. He'll come to soon enough." He grabbed the deputy's cuffs from the desk and cuffed Satterfield around a cell bar. Then he ripped a piece of cloth from the cot and gagged Satterfield's mouth.

"That animal deserves killing," Emily said.

Nathaniel glanced at her momentarily but turned back around and locked Deputy Satterfield in the cell. "If we kill him, they would waste no effort to find us. This way, they're embarrassed, but they're not going to do an extensive search. The South's in disarray right now. Union raids everywhere. Slaves are escaping and rebelling. They can't afford an extensive search for you and me as long as there is no serious crime."

"But Rufus Tate knows we're going to Thomasville."

"It is unlikely they would go that far as long as the deputy is alive. I seriously doubt there's telegraph anywhere around here, but they wouldn't contact the authorities in Thomasville if there were. They don't want the light of day shining on their operations here. There's no telling how many laws these two have broken. And they need to stay here to help track down the runaway slaves. There's going to be more and more of those as this war draws to a close."

"Then we need to go quickly. My purse! It's got what's left of our Confederate money." Emily pulled her purse from a wooden box that was under the desk. She rummaged through it then said, "The money's gone."

"Not surprising, but they didn't get much. We spent most of it on the horses. We'll get some back when we sell them in Thomasville."

"I've still got the Federal money," she said. "Thank God he didn't get far enough to find that. For a lot of reasons."

Nathaniel glanced at Emily and nodded then snatched his hunting knife out of the box.

"Glad he didn't take this." Nathaniel slid the blade into the leather scabbard sewn into the inside of his right boot. He grabbed Emily's two bags from the corner beside the desk. The Sheriff had searched them but found only women's clothes, something he had no use for. They were no longer neatly folded, but she didn't think anything was missing.

Hurriedly jerking the handcuff keys off of a nail on the side of the wood desk, Nathaniel said, "I've got the cell and cuff keys. We'll drop them into the first creek we get to. They'll have to saw through the bars to get the deputy free. It'll slow them down. Sheriff Tate will expect us to go south. If he chases us at all, that's the direction he'll head, so we'll go east first then south. We've got to cover our tracks, make sure he doesn't know we've gone east."

"He said he's the best tracker around."

Nathaniel stared at Emily before speaking. "In that case, we had better hope he doesn't want to take the time to follow us. All the more reason to leave Satterfield alive."

August 12, 1864 ~ Point Lookout Prison, Maryland

Putting as little pressure on his wounded leg as possible, Caleb crawled out of the tent. He used the tent support to pull himself to a standing position. Having done it so many times before, it was automatic. He could go through the process while thinking of other things. Or thinking of nothing at all.

Across the expanse of the peninsula, there were rows and rows of tents, every possible variety, and a few men up and moving around in the morning breeze that came in from the ocean. The smell of dead seaweed and salt were strong in the air. He heard stirring and turned to see Charles Pearson coming out of the tent behind him.

"It's a fine morning," Charles said. "The Lord has given us another beautiful day."

"Beautiful days don't matter none when you're a prisoner in this place," Caleb said.

"Would you rather be standing here in the rain, the thunder and lightning?"

"No. We did that last week when the Lord decided not to give us any beautiful days."

"Don't speak no blasphemy, Caleb. The Lord is watching you every second of every day. He had his reasons for all that rain last week. Wild animals get thirsty. So do the plants and trees and insects. Or there could be some other reason we can't even imagine. Remember, the Lord works in mysterious ways."

Caleb only grunted. He didn't know what to think about the Lord's mysterious ways, but he knew it was true. His daddy had taught him that all his life.

Danny Talley came up behind them. Morning pleasantries, as pleasant as they could be in a place like Point Lookout, were passed around. Danny had never been an early riser until finding himself in prison. He was a large man before being captured. He liked to eat, so he learned to get up early, before reveille, and get in line quickly. He theorized that the first people in line got larger portions than the stragglers.

"You want to do some reading before breakfast?" Charles asked Caleb. "We might have time."

"We can do some reading after we eat. Let's get in line early so we won't have to wait so long. They'll be bringing the rations out soon. Won't be enough, but I'm so hungry, I'll take what I can get." Caleb turned and hobbled away.

Charles and Danny caught up with him quickly. Even though Caleb was no longer using a crutch, he was slow as he limped along. He could still feel the ball in his knee, but if he didn't stretch his leg out all the way, or didn't bend it too much, it hurt little. So Caleb kept from bending or straightening his knee any more than he had to as he struggled along, one slow step after another. It was hard to call it walking, and he knew he looked pathetic, but what did it matter in this place?

"Just as well, I guess," Charles said. "You're reading good. You're a quick learner."

"I sound like a little kid. I read slow, and I mess up every other word."

"That's not so. You're doing fine."

"The Bible's not the easiest book for learning your reading," Danny said. "When you master the Lord's written word, you'll be able to read anything."

"Danny's right," Charles said. "If you can read the Bible, everything else is child's play."

Caleb briefly wondered why the Lord would make his book so hard to read, but let the thought go. He was sure the Lord had his reasons.

Other than reveille and roll call, there was little need to rise as early as the summer sun unless you wanted to stand in the ration line for hours. The guards did not start passing out the pitiful portions of meat until eight o'clock. Even so, many of the prisoners were already in line while the sky and the sand still glimmered with the red of first light. The line was long by the time Caleb hobbled up and took his place, Charles Pearson and Danny Talley directly behind him. As the minutes passed, more and more prisoners came in search of food. Before long, the line behind the three of them was longer than the line in front.

As did virtually all of the other prisoners, Caleb and Charles and Danny started eating as soon as the food was dipped into their offered tins. Only a few steps later they were cleaning out their empty plates with their tongues. A quick rinse in the ocean was all that was needed.

By noon the beautiful day had become a raging hot devil, one of the hottest of the summer. Caleb and Charles worked on Bible reading in the shade of their tent to escape the withering rays. Most of the other prisoners stayed in their tents as well, at least the ones who were still sane enough to realize they needed to avoid the radiant heat of the sun. Even the sport of rat chasing had stopped. No one had the energy, not even the rats. It would be picked up at dusk when the temperature finally started to drop.

"Caleb Garner," a deep voice called from outside the tent. "Charles Pearson. Daniel Talley. The three of you stand at attention before me."

Caleb and Charles glanced out of the open end of their tent. A large black man with mutton chop sideburns and wearing a Union uniform with sergeant's stripes stood a few feet away. There was a zigzag scar on the left side of his forehead. Two other black guards stood behind him, both carrying muskets with bayonets fixed.

They couldn't afford to take the time to wonder why their names were being called. No need to suffer the punishment for a delay. Charles took his Bible back from Caleb and placed it in his pocket as they crawled outside. Danny was right behind them.

"Attention!" the big man shouted.

They stood as rigid as they could, but with Caleb not being able to straighten his injured leg, he leaned to the side. It was the only way to keep from falling over.

The big guard glanced down at Caleb's leg, at the wound that was still red from inflammation, and cocked his eyebrow before returning to the paper he held in front of him. He started to read, "By order of the Secretary of War of the United States of America, the Honorable Edwin

McMasters Stanton, you are hereby notified that you are to be transferred to the Federal prisoner of war facility at Elmira, New York. You will leave Point Lookout on Monday, August 15th, and will travel by boat to Baltimore, Maryland. There you will be placed on a train for transfer to Elmira." He lowered the paper he was holding and stared at Caleb and Charles and Danny then said, "Be prepared to leave immediately after morning rations next Monday. That is all."

The big guard turned on his heels and marched away, the two slender guards falling in immediately behind. They stopped at another tent, and the big man once again called out the names of several prisoners. Apparently, it would be a big group. Made sense. Lookout Point was crowded beyond reason.

"I sure hope they got more food in New York," Caleb said.

"May not," Danny said. "I heard tale they started calling the place 'Hellmira.' That don't sound none too encouraging."

August 12, 1864 ~ Thomasville, Georgia

"That was a long way out of the way," Emily said as they ambled into the edge of Thomasville, Georgia, late in the afternoon. "I am so tired of riding. I almost hope I never see a horse again."

"Better to go out of the way than risk being caught by Sheriff Tate. Even if he came this far, he probably gave up and went home days ago."

"Call him Rufus Tate. He doesn't deserve the title 'Sheriff.' As far as I'm concerned, he's nothing more than a common criminal hiding behind a badge. If the Yankees do take over like he says, I hope they hang him. No amount of gold can erase that man's evil. Satterfield, too."

"We need to find the train station, see when the next train leaves. I suspect we have missed it for today. We'll have to find a place to sleep tonight. That could be a problem for me in such a small town."

There was no one at the train station. The bill on one of the posts that held up the canopy showed that the passenger train left at five o'clock the next morning, arriving in Savannah at six o'clock that evening. The cost was nine dollars per ticket.

"Thirteen hours to travel the two hundred miles to Savanah on the train," Emily said. "It took us over three weeks to travel the two hundred miles from Montgomery to Thomasville. Of course, a fair part of that time was spent behind bars."

Nathaniel grunted but said nothing. There was no need to explain that, concerned about her stamina on such a long ride, he had slowed the trip on purpose.

"If the damned Yankees hadn't destroyed the rails," Emily continued, "We would have reached Belle Plains and bought Caleb's freedom by now. He and I would be on our way back home. You'd be on your way to freedom up North."

"Nothing to be done about that now," Nathaniel said. "I'm thankful we're not still in a small jail in the middle of nowhere, Georgia."

"Amen. The train from Savannah arrives at nine o'clock tonight. Whoever runs the station will be back before then so we can buy our tickets and be ready."

"First, we need to sell the horses. There is a stable over there, across the street and down a couple of blocks." Nathaniel pointed toward a wide wooden building with large double doors. One of the doors was pulled open. "Maybe they will give us a decent price."

Nathaniel followed behind as they rode to the stable, as a slave would be expected to do. Appearances were important in a small town. Once inside, they were met by an older man dressed in simple brown britches and a brown undershirt. Emily could see that the shirt had been a light color at one time, probably white, but it was filthy, as were the britches. The stable had the strong smell of horse manure. So did the older man, but his smell was mixed with human odor as well, days or even weeks of hard work and no bath.

"How do, Missy," the smelly man said. "Name's George Harwell. What can I do for you?"

"I'm Emily Rose. This is my domestic. We need to sell our horses. What would you offer us for them?"

"Sell your horses? Why, whatever for? You going to walk back to the plantation?"

"Oh, we're not from around here. We're catching the train to Savannah."

George eyed Emily warily. "Savannah? You want to sell your horses and get on the train to Savannah? Where you from?"

Emily let out an exhausted breath. Any number of easy lies flitted through her mind, but she decided to stick with their original story since it was mostly true. After all, she had always been taught that honesty was the best policy. "No, we're not spies or Yankees or anything of the kind. I know it sounds strange, but we were on our way to visit my daddy's Aunt Millie in Richmond. She lost her husband, and we're going to help. But we couldn't catch the train in Montgomery because the Yankees tore up a lot of track, so we bought horses and rode to Thomasville. Now we need to sell the horses." There was no need to get into buying Caleb's freedom. The story was long enough as it was.

George, apparently satisfied with her story, shrugged then said, "Let's have a look." He walked around the horses, patted them here and there, looked at their teeth, then turned to Emily and said, "I'll give you a hundred dollars for the pair of them."

Emily's head snapped back. She glanced at Nathaniel, and he shook his head, almost imperceptibly. She turned back to George and said, "Why, we paid twice that much for them. We can't accept that. Are you trying to take advantage of us?"

"No, ma'am. Not at all. Horses might be worth more in Montgomery. And these two have been through a long, rough ride. You can tell by looking at them. Tell you what I'll do; I'll bump it up a quarter. I'll give you a hundred and twenty-five. Best I can do."

Nathaniel's head shook again. "No thank you," Emily said. "We couldn't take anything less than a hundred seventy-five. We'll go elsewhere." She turned to mount her horse.

"Why, you drive a hard bargain, Missy. I reckon I can split the difference with you. One fifty as long as you throw in the saddles."

Emily took her foot out of the stirrup and set it back on the ground. "We have no use for the saddles on the train. One hundred sixty. I won't go a dime lower. Do you want me to ride out of here or walk out?" Nathaniel's eyes flashed a smile.

George scratched the back of his filthy neck, glanced up at the ceiling briefly then said, "I reckon you can walk. Hold a second, and I'll get your money. You come near wiping me out, Missy."

"You learn quick," Nathaniel said as they walked back to the train station. "You'd make a good horse trader."

"It couldn't have gone on much longer. Another round on those negotiations and I'd have thrown up from the smell of that place. And that man. But we lost forty dollars on those horses. He'll turn right around and sell them for two hundred this week. Our forty dollars will be in his pocket."

"He has to make something out of the deal. That's the way commerce works. There's a restaurant a couple of doors down, right across from the train station. Looks like it's still open, but it'll be dark soon. Why don't you get us something to eat before it closes? I'll take our bags over to the station and wait for you."

After ordering and receiving their supper, Emily stepped out of the restaurant with a small bag in her hand. She stopped in her tracks when she looked across the street to the train station. Henry Satterfield, the filthy man who had tried to rape her, held a pistol on Nathaniel. There was a group of white men with him. They were tossing a rope over one of the wooden rafters of the railroad station. The rope had a noose at the end.

August 12, 1864 ~ Point Lookout Prison, Maryland

"I was starting to get used to this place," Danny said. "I sorta wish we weren't leaving."

Caleb looked around at the fourteen-foot wooden parapet wall and the guards walking along, rifles on their shoulders. "I was brought up roaming the forests around Sepulga. Me and Arlis would go hunting any time I wasn't farming. We could wander for miles around and not meet another soul. I don't think I could ever get used to this."

"Maybe a change will do us good," Charles said.

"Elmira?" Danny said. "I don't know. It might be out of the frying pan and into the fire."

"No way to know," Caleb said. "I don't think the place has been open too long."

"Everything ought to be nice and new," Charles said. "But whatever it is, we'll make the best of it. I'm happy the three of us are going together."

"Amen," Danny said. "If we've got to be prisoners for the rest of the war, at least we'll be prisoners together."

"What about being exchanged?" Caleb said. "They used to do prisoner exchanges. I'd sure like to get swapped with some Yankee so's I could go home. I ain't going to do no more fighting with this leg."

"They don't do exchanges no more," Danny said. "That devil Grant put an end to them."

They ambled along the sand in silence for a couple of minutes. While they were near the perimeter, they stayed well inside the deadline. Nobody wanted to take a chance.

Charles broke the silence when he asked Danny, "How do you know it was Grant. And how is it you know so much about what's going on outside?"

"I wander around, talk to all the new prisoners. Best way to get news in a place like this. But I heard the tale about Grant before I was captured. Everybody was talking about how he didn't want Southern prisoners to get back on the battlefield, so he stopped the exchanges. Maybe it's true. Maybe not. Might be. Marsh Lee keeps trying to get us exchanged. I'm sure of that. So the only reason they ain't doing exchanges any more has got to be Grant."

"General Lee is a good man, sure enough," Charles said. "I bet he thinks about his men in prison all the time. I wouldn't be surprised if one day he didn't try to break us out."

Caleb looked around at the expanse of sand that made up the peninsula. "I don't think he could do it here," he said. "We're surrounded by water on three sides. There ain't nothing but Yankee ships floating out there. Marsh Lee's men can't march on water. And that little stretch of land to the north goes on up into Maryland. Too long a way to march an army around. Besides, the Confederate army has got to stay in Virginia and protect Richmond."

"Yeah, I 'spect you're right," Charles said. "I reckon we're stuck here for a few more days. Ain't no way Lee could bring the Confederate army up to New York, either, so we'll be stuck up there till it's over."

"Damn," Danny said. "You got my hopes up for half a second then turned right around and smashed them."

They walked as far north as they dared go on the bay side of the compound, so they turned to walk east, toward the Atlantic Ocean. A few steps later, Danny said, "Look. Over there. A small dog has wandered past the wall. See him? Sniffing around those bushes. He's inside the deadline."

"Oh, no, you don't," Charles said. "I'm hungry enough to eat a dog, sure enough. But that's a killing offense. Don't matter about the deadline. The Yankees put dogs above us gray backs. If that little hound's got any sense at all, it'd find its way back where it came. This ain't no place for a little dog to be roaming around."

Danny glanced along the wall. "Look at the guards. They ain't paying us no never mind. I could walk close by, and maybe he'd come up to me. I could wring his neck and stick him under my shirt real quick."

"Those rags?" Charles said. "It's a small dog, but you ain't got enough shirt left to cover him. Best leave him be."

Danny kept eyeing the animal as they walked along, getting closer but not walking directly toward it as that would bring them too close to the deadline for comfort. The dog looked up at them and wagged its tail. It started trotting toward them.

Caleb stopped hobbling and said, "Don't do it. This ain't no good. I don't want to eat no dog no how."

"The guards aren't looking," Danny said as he whipped his head back and forth, checking the wall.

"Don't matter," Caleb said. "Any one of them could turn around at any second. Don't do it."

Danny continued walking and was several steps ahead of the other two. The dog came up to him, tail wagging double-time, but started to back up when Danny reached out for him. It went back a few steps and barked a couple of times, but not loud.

Danny looked up at the fence once more. The guards were still either not looking his way or not looking at all. It was hard work looking out over a squalid, boring prison camp all day long. The scene never seemed to change.

Danny took another couple of steps toward the dog. Perhaps it was something in Danny's eyes, but the animal backed up and barked again, louder. Danny lunged for it.

"No!" Caleb cried out softly, trying to get Danny's attention without alerting the guards.

Danny, so intent on snatching the dog that he did not notice, crossed the deadline. The gentle breeze from the ocean was shattered by a rifle shot. Danny stopped walking and rocked forward then seemed to hang in the air, his arms slightly out from his sides and his legs bent below him. Two more shots came in rapid succession. "No," Caleb moaned as Danny fell. The dog whimpered loudly, took a few steps away, and then stopped.

Caleb began to hobble toward Danny, in a rush to get to his friend, but Charles caught his arm and said, "Don't."

"I've got to help him," Caleb said as he turned around and stared at Charles' hand on his arm.

"Only God can help him now," Charles said. "There ain't no purpose to you getting killed, too."

Caleb turned back around. The dog was standing over Danny and barking. They couldn't cross the deadline without getting shot. They stood there and looked at their friend's unmoving body as the guards on the fence argued about who had killed him, about who would get the ten dollars from the officer of the day.

August 12, 1864 ~ Train Station, Thomasville, Georgia

Emily dropped her bag and ran across the dirt street. "What are you doing?" she shouted.

The men turned and looked at her. A few were curious. Others held looks of steel, determination to follow through with the murder they were about to perform.

"Bet you didn't expect to see me again," Satterfield said. "You thought you and your darkie boyfriend had escaped from the law, didn't you?"

"Don't listen to him!" Emily shouted at the men pulling the rope taut.

"Put the nigger on a horse," one of them said as he pulled on the rope to test it.

"You can't do that," Emily said. "He's broken no law. He's my domestic slave. He was traveling with me to Richmond to help with my family. He's done nothing wrong."

"That's not what the deputy here says," one of the men said. But he had a curious look on his face.

"I've deputized these men temporarily," Satterfield said. "They're doing their duty, carrying out the law. Get him on a horse now, and let's get this over with."

Two men began to wrestle with Nathaniel but, even with his hands cuffed, he threw them off. They stumbled away and stared at him. Reinforcements stepped in. There were too many of them. Nathaniel was quickly subdued and placed on the horse's back.

Emily noticed that Satterfield was the only other person mounted on a horse. There were no other horses around. That meant the deputized men were locals rounded up to do his dirty work, quite possibly from a Thomasville tavern.

"This is a lynching!" Emily screamed at them. "This is not carrying out the law." She pointed her finger at Satterfield, her arm shaking violently but from rage and not fear. "This imposter is not the law. He tried to rape me."

"Shut up," Satterfield said. "She's lying."

Emily lowered her arm. With her hands balled into white-knuckled fists, she said, "He would have succeeded if my domestic hadn't stopped him. Nathaniel is his name."

"I don't give a damn about his name," Satterfield spat out. "He's a runaway slave. He broke the law, and he needs to be punished for it. Else all of them will run away with no fear for retribution."

"He is *not* a runaway. He is an honorable slave. He is dedicated to his owners, my father and mother, Thomas and Mary Rose." She looked around at the group of men. There were more curious looks and fewer determined looks. A couple of them looked up at Satterfield suspiciously. "He is traveling with me to protect me. He promised my father he would keep me safe." She reached up and pointed at Satterfield again, but steadily this time, her rage changing to reason. "Nathaniel had every right to kill that man for what he did to me, and for what he was trying to do." She pointed at her own chest. "I wanted him to. I wanted to see that animal die for forcing his foul self on me. But Nathaniel let him live. He could have easily choked him to death, but he didn't."

"I got away in time is the only reason he didn't," Satterfield said. "Look here at the bruises on my neck. The only thing that saved me was being stronger than him."

"Stronger than Nathaniel? How many of you men believe something like that? All you have to do is look at the two of them." Emily let her eyes wander over the crowd, making brief eye contact with as many of them as she could. Then she turned her attention back to Satterfield. "And if you got away because you were stronger, how did we get away from your jail? That's impossible." She looked back at the men but kept her finger pointing at Henry Satterfield. "He's lying. Look at him. Pure filth. You can smell him from where you're standing. Moonshine and worse. He's not a Deputy. He's an animal!"

"Why, you!" Satterfield pulled up his scattergun and started to point it at Emily.

One of the men grabbed the barrel and held it down. "You don't go shooting ladies in our town," the man said.

Satterfield tried to wrestle the scattergun away, but two more men grabbed the barrel of the weapon and ripped it out of his hands.

"Thomasville seems to be a wonderful place," Emily said. "Not the kind of place that lynches a slave before they even know what happened. Please, take him down off the horse. And take this man to the real Sheriff around here. He should be arrested for impersonating the law."

Satterfield turned and rushed out of town as fast as he could ride, the scattergun holster empty. Several of the men pulled Nathaniel down from the horse. One of them unlocked and removed the cuffs.

"Thank you for listening to the truth," Emily said to the crowd.

A couple of them tipped their hats and nodded their heads. Most of them did nothing more than turn and walk away. Soon, there was only one man left, an older gentleman in a railroad uniform.

"I believe you dropped this," the man said as he handed the food bag to Emily. "If you're riding the train, it doesn't leave till five o'clock in the morning. You'd get awful hungry before then."

"Thank you. You are so kind. Yes, we are traveling to Richmond, to help my father's Aunt Millie. My name is Emily Rose, and this is my domestic, Nathaniel Whiteeagle."

"I'm Alfred Garrison, the Thomasville railroad clerk. The Atlantic and Gulf Railroad will take you to Savannah. Nine dollars a ticket. There are different ways to get to Richmond from there. You'll need to be careful, though. There's a lot of fighting around Richmond. We've been able to keep the railroad open as far as I know, but that could change at any time. Maybe you'll be able to get through. Do you have a room for the night?"

"No, we've only recently arrived in town and had to sell our horses first."

"There's a hotel not far down the road. You can get a room there. They don't take slaves, however."

"Perhaps I can wait here at the station?" Emily asked.

"Wait here? All night?"

"Yes. The train leaves early. It's so late now it seems a shame to waste money on a room. Besides, I've slept in worse places on this trip. Far worse. If you don't mind, the station is fine."

"Yes, of course. If you wish. You can rest on one of the benches if you'd like. Your slave can sleep over there on the platform." The clerk nodded toward the platform as he winced and shrugged his shoulders. "The platform's not terribly comfortable, but Thomasville would be up in arms if I let a colored man sleep on one of the benches. They're for white folks, of course. Some of the men who left looked a little disappointed they didn't have a hanging. No need to aggravate them."

"The platform is fine," Nathaniel said. "I can sleep anywhere."

"Very well. I tell you what I'll do. I'll stay at the station tonight. If someone comes back, it would be better if I were here. No one to go home to anyway."

"Thank you so much," Emily said. "We appreciate what you're doing, but you're taking a chance by helping us. Why?"

The clerk looked around at the tops of the nearby trees, then back at Emily. "I had a daughter once. She was as pretty as you. I loved her dearly, but she went to the Lord early, too early. Not long after, I lost my wife, as well. Maybe I have a better appreciation for life than other folks. You're welcome here, but if you decide you need a bed during the night, the hotel's only a couple of blocks away."

"I can sleep while sitting on a bench," Emily said, "That's the best way to make sure we get on that train at five o'clock tomorrow morning."

August 18, 1864 ~ Elmira Prison, New York

They listened to the squeal of metal wheels braking on metal rails as the train slowed. When it stopped, they waited for several agonizing minutes. What would Elmira look like? What type of prison was this? How tall were the walls? How fortified was the camp? All eyes were on the inside of the door, wondering what they would see when they were reintroduced to sunlight and the outside world.

Although it seemed like forever, they did not wait long. The wide door to the freight car slid open to a scene they had not expected. There was no prison in sight. Instead, the tall trees around the small Northern town spoke of beauty and peace as a gentle early morning breeze rippled through them, showing the undersides of the leaves.

That was for someone else to enjoy, Caleb thought. The Yankees who lived here could sit back and sip coffee and appreciate the setting. There would be little joy inside a prison wall where guards paced back and forth with rifles in their hands. He could only hope they weren't as eager to shoot as the guards at Point Lookout.

"Looks pretty from here, don't it?" the prisoner next to him said as they looked out. "I 'spect it won't look so pretty from where we'll be."

Caleb didn't respond. There was nothing to add.

A Union soldier on the outside, visible from the waist up, stood in the open door and shouted, "On your feet."

There was no eruption of movement. The Confederate prisoners eased their way up, struggling to regain their feet. A few had to lean on others for support. A few of the ones being leaned on could barely stand themselves. It had been a long ride with little more to eat than they'd been getting at Point Lookout.

Minute after agonizing minute passed. There was no movement. The Union soldiers were waiting for the car in front to be unloaded. One of the prisoners tried to sit back down, but a guard leaned through the door and poked the muzzle of his rifle menacingly toward the man. He shouted at the prisoner to return to his feet. Mercifully, at that moment the other guards motioned for the prisoners to start climbing down.

As Caleb lowered himself from the freight car, with the help of other prisoners, he looked over a town nestled beneath tall elm trees, with green parks and fancy, well-kept houses. There was a prison here, and a Union garrison, but the destruction of war had not touched this place.

Caleb thought about Conecuh's county seat, Sparta, Alabama. It was much smaller than Elmira. Sparta was safely tucked into the Deep South as Elmira was safely tucked into the far North, so neither town had been touched by the torch of battle. But Sparta's log and ax-hewn lumber buildings paled by comparison to the beautiful Victorian homes that lined the streets of this Northern town.

"Everyone who can walk will march two miles to your new home," the guard said. "Barracks Number Three. Those who cannot walk will be carried in carts. We will determine who walks and who gets carried."

They began to file past the guards on their way to fall in behind the prisoners from the first freight car. Caleb tried his best to walk normally, not hobble like a cripple. His wound continued to heal on the surface, but the ball that remained inside his knee kept him from walking properly.

"Do you need to ride?" one of the guards asked him as he hobbled by.

"I'll walk," Caleb answered. He briefly met the guard's eyes then turned and stared straight ahead. Caleb did not want preferential treatment over the other prisoners. If he kept struggling to walk, trying to straighten and bend his legs as he should, perhaps the ball would eventually move out of the way, find another place that would no longer restrict his knee movement. When he got home from the war, if he got home, he wanted Emily to see him walking as she remembered, not hobbling along like some broken old wreck of a man.

They began the walk up the street. The Confederates were dressed every way conceivable, some in nothing more than undershorts. They were filthy and smelled terrible. There was little they could do about it.

Some laughed and smiled as they shuffled along. Others looked around at the town and the nicely dressed townspeople who lined the street and watched them. Spirits seemed to be improved now that they were off the train. A prison in a town this pretty? It couldn't be as bad as Point Lookout. Surely they would serve them more food here than they had been given before.

Their movement up the street could not have been considered marching, but if the Yankees wanted to call it that, he wouldn't argue. Even with the slow shuffle, though, Caleb struggled to keep up. He kept telling himself two miles was not that far. Willing his legs to move ahead, one after the other, step upon step, two miles could eventually be traversed. He might not be able to stand when he got there, but he was determined to make it.

"Walk like a man!" a Union soldier, a Corporal, screamed at Caleb as he came up to him. "You filthy, stinking animal. Trying to slouch off so you can ride in a wagon? Put your feet under you like a man! March like a soldier!"

"I am," Caleb screamed back. He knew better than to shout at a Union soldier. Something had snapped, and the words tumbled out on a raised voice filled with anger. "I don't want no wagon ride. I can march."

"You call that pathetic stumbling around marching? Why, you…"

The Corporal lifted his heavy boot and slung it forward with devastating force, kicking Caleb in his wounded knee. If he had been a whole man, if there was no musket ball in his knee, he could have avoided the main force of the blow. But he could barely stand and hardly walk. There was no time to hobble out of the way of the Union soldier's boot.

Caleb screamed out in pain as he went to the ground. This time, the pain was immediate. There was no shock delay. And the pain was worse than when he'd been shot back at The Wilderness. He had never felt pain so intense, so severe. Caleb writhed on the ground as tears streamed from his eyes.

"You baby. Get up. You better start marching like a man or I'll…"

"CORPORAL!"

John Murray whirled around. It was Major Henry Colt, the camp commander. "Yes, Sir," Murray said as he saluted.

Major Colt had an odd beard that was all gray in front and graying on the sides. In contrast to the gray hair on his chin, his mustache was dark, not a gray hair to be found. His eyes were gentle, usually, but at the moment they were anything but gentle. "What is your name, soldier?"

"Murray, Sir. Corporal John Murray. Barracks Three guard."

"Why did you kick that man, Murray?"

John Murray looked down at Caleb, who was still rocking back and forth and sobbing heavily. "Why, I'm only doing my job, Sir. He was not marching. He was slouching, trying to get a ride he didn't deserve."

"Murray… Murray…" Colt looked away in thought but turned back quickly. "Yes, your name is familiar. I've heard stories about how you treat prisoners. Now I see that the stories are true. Your job is to guard the prisoners, not torture them, *Private* Murray." The Major turned to the young Union officer at his side and said, "Lieutenant, I want you to fill out a demotion order for this man. He is being demoted from corporal to private for mistreating prisoners. Bring it to me, and I'll sign it."

"Yes, Sir," the Lieutenant replied as he saluted.

Major Colt turned back to John Murray and said, "You have lost your stripes. If I see you torture another prisoner, you will be dishonorably discharged. You will lose your pension as well as your stripes. Do you understand, soldier?"

"Ah, yes, Sir, but I was just…"

"Shut up. There is no reasonable explanation for what I saw you do. That is all, Private Murray." Colt wheeled around on the balls of his feet and marched briskly away. The Lieutenant stared at Murray with disdain in his eyes for several seconds before turning to catch up with the Major.

John Murray watched until Colt and his junior officer were out of sight. He stared down at Caleb, anger creasing every surface of his face, and said, "You see what you caused, you animal?" Caleb did not respond. The pain in his knee was too strong for him to talk, but hate oozed around the tears in his eyes as he looked up at Murray. "Maybe the commander is soft," John Murray continued, "But I'm not. I'll find a way to get you back. You're going to pay for costing me my stripes."

September 2, 1864 ~ Richmond, Virginia

"Three weeks to get from Savannah to Richmond!" Emily exclaimed. "It was supposed to be a one day fare. This whole trip has been such a painful..." Her words trailed off as she stepped out of the station. The unmistakable smells of raw sewage and human body odor, tainted with a faint smell of blood, permeated the air. It was nauseating.

She tried to shake off the smells as she began to notice the city around her. The railroad station had been hit by some sort of explosion, a small area burned and not yet repaired. Then her eyes fed across the rolling topography of the city and took in the smoke and dust that swirled about here and there. People and horses were everywhere. Wagons moved back and forth in the streets. People were not only riding and walking and standing around, but they also sat on barrels and benches and anything else that would lift them off the muddy streets. Some were sitting around open campfires, a few of them with something to cook. Some were even curled up on the sidewalks asleep, though how they could sleep among the overcrowded bustle of a huge city was beyond Emily's understanding. A man nearby stretched then stood and started urinating against the side of a building, oblivious to others around him, including the women.

Soldiers were everywhere, in large groups and in small ones. Some were helping fellow soldiers move along, bandages covering various parts of their bodies. There were even wounded Union soldiers, walking along the street under Confederate guard. Men leaned over games at building corners and screamed out their elation or horror at winning or losing as the money changed hands. Emily could see brightly-dressed ladies moving through the crowds, attempting to make arrangements with any man who appeared to have a coin or two. It was apparent these were not proper ladies.

Hawkers moved among the people as well, selling everything that could be imagined. "This isn't what I was expecting," she finally said.

"It appears the war has come to Richmond," Nathaniel said as he watched a work crew filling a craterous hole in the street, packing the dirt in layers as they went. "People for miles around have sought refuge in the city."

"All sorts," Emily said. "Though I'm not sure where they would dig up some of these strange people. It may be from further than miles around."

In spite of there being far too many people, the buildings of Richmond were tall and stately, grand on a scale that was beyond anything Emily could have imagined. She had seen so many things during their travels. Richmond was something new, a wonder on several levels.

"As, ah, interesting as this is," she finally said. "I'm ready to leave. Let's find a carriage quickly. I want to go to Aunt Millie's, get away from the center of Richmond. If I stay around all these smells too long, I might gag to death. This is almost as bad as that stable in Thomasville."

It was not hard to find a carriage for hire. People were hustling a living every way that could be imagined. Anyone who owned a carriage could make a few dollars by shuffling others around the South's largest city. Emily showed the driver the paper with the address her father had written, immediately below the name 'Millie Hanson.'

"Yes, ma'am, I know where that is. It's over that hill yonder. Quite a ways from here. The fare's twelve dollars."

"Twelve dollars!" Emily exclaimed. "The train fare for the last hundred miles was half that."

"I'm sorry, ma'am, but this is Richmond. Yankee soldiers are not far down the road. They've surrounded Petersburg. They're raiding all around here. It's hard to get things through. Why, I have to pay a dollar for a tiny loaf of bread. I've got a wife and three kids at home. They can eat a half dozen small loaves at supper alone. Don't even think about the price of meat. It's the way Richmond is these days."

Emily looked around the street. Other carriages and drivers were sitting and waiting. She said, "Thank you, but I believe I'll check with some of the other drivers."

"Tell you what I'll do," the driver said. "Some of these guys would take you for ten dollars. I'll match that. And this is the nicest carriage around." He motioned toward his carriage which was, indeed, clean and newer looking, the reason Emily had initially picked it.

The driver did look sincere. Since both driver and carriage were the cleanest of the lot, she said, "Okay. Ten dollars, but not a penny more."

The driver helped Emily step into the carriage then turned to Nathaniel and said, "Place the bags inside, then ride up front with me." Nathaniel nodded. He sat up front with the driver as two sad-looking horses pulled them along. The Confederate government had confiscated most of the better horses for the war effort.

After a trip that seemed longer than it actually was, they arrived at the address her father had written. Emily and Nathaniel looked up in amazement. The enormous white house with soaring white columns and sprawling wings on each side sat on a knoll overlooking the surrounding neighborhood. The other homes, stately in their own right, paled by comparison.

Her father had always told her Aunt Millie was well-to-do. Her husband, Carl Hanson, his uncle by marriage, had been successful in the cotton trade. Carl had retired with no financial worries whatsoever, only to die a few short years later.

An older black man walked into the house. At the same time, another black man, also well beyond youth, came walking out, a bundle slung across his shoulder. There were two wagons on the street in front of the house, their horses tied to decorative wrought iron posts.

Each time the front door was opened, the sounds of many conversations floated out. The two older black men could have been slaves, but Millie did not own enough slaves to explain all the voices they heard. Emily had thought that Millie lived alone now that Carl had passed. Perhaps the carriage driver had misread her father's writing.

"Are you sure this is the correct address," she asked.

"Yes, ma'am. This is it."

"But my aunt lives alone."

"Alone? In Richmond? Ah, that's doubtful, ma'am. Nobody lives alone in a house that size," the driver said as he nodded toward Aunt Millie's mansion. "Not these days."

Emily paid the driver after he helped her step down from the carriage. Nathaniel retrieved the bags, and they stood and stared at the house a moment before Emily turned around and said, "Please don't leave yet. Let me make sure we are at the right address."

The driver nodded, so they started up the walk to the front door. The man who had gone into the house came walking out with a bundle over his shoulder. When he saw them walking up, he pointed at them and said something to someone inside the house. He stepped to the side to allow an older white woman, every strand of her hair gray, to step out. "Emily?" the elderly lady asked.

"Yes. Aunt Millie?"

The woman walked as fast as her older legs would allow as she spread her arms for an embrace. Emily rushed to her to save her some steps.

"It is so good to meet you after all these years," Aunt Millie said. "My, my, but you're a beauty. I expected nothing else. Tommy was devilishly handsome when he was young. And your mother was gorgeous. When they got married, Mary was so beautiful every man at the wedding had his tongue dragging behind him. Their wives were a'fuming." She cackled as glossy scenes of the wedding showed across her memory.

"Thank you, Aunt Millie. You look great, too." Emily turned and waved the driver on. He gave a short nod and was quickly on his way.

"I look like a frazzled old lady with one foot in the grave," Aunt Millie said. "But I'm still kicking with the other one."

"You look no such a thing," Emily said. "Daddy has said so many wonderful things about you."

"That boy always did love fairy tales." She cackled again then said, "Oh, I miss my little Tommy so. It's been way too long. We should have gotten together more before the war, but it was so far away. Life separated us by too long a path."

Emily smiled and admired the older woman. She had such a stately presence. And her smile was still radiant, regardless of age.

"I got a letter from Tommy telling me you were coming," Millie said. "But I expected you weeks ago. I have been so worried about you."

"We had trouble on the trip," Emily said. "The Yankees tore up the track going into Georgia, so we had to buy some horses and, well, it's a long story. I'll tell you another time."

"Of course, of course. Come on in."

Millie took Emily's hand, and they turned toward the house. The man with the bundle on his shoulder excused himself and stood to the side to let them pass. Then he walked into the street and placed the bundle in the back of a wagon. He immediately turned around to come back into the house.

When Millie opened the front door, a myriad of meshed-together voices, much louder up close, drifted to the outside. "What's going on?" Emily asked. "I thought you lived alone since Uncle Carl died."

"Hardly. The war has made such a mess of Richmond. Our soldiers need clothes and blankets and other things, so we've turned this big old house into a sewing factory. And I'm right in the middle of it. Why, I can still sew circles around the young ladies who work here." She laughed hard and said, "Just kidding. My old hands are so stiff and sore they're right near useless. But I like to gossip with the ladies while we work. Soldiers' wives, most of them. About all the work being done in Richmond these days is being done by ladies. All the men have gone off to war."

"I saw lots of men downtown," Emily said.

"Those who aren't soldiers or spies are drifters and refugees, hardly what I would call men. A lot of them are useless. They're looking for a handout or something they can steal. We've got to work that much harder to feed them all. Why, we ought to send the lot of them to General Grant. The whores, too."

Emily's head snapped back a little at Millie's bluntness, but she held her smile.

"They'd eat him out of house and home," Millie continued. "He'd have to leave us alone, take his army back up North to get more food."

Emily laughed. Millie once again took her hand and said, “Let’s stop standing around like scarecrows. Come on in.” She led Emily into her imposing home. Nathaniel followed but hesitated at the door.

“Come on in,” Millie said. “Thomas said you would be coming along with Emily. If you stand there, you’ll get run over by all the people going in and out. My goodness, look at the muscles on you. On second thought, nobody’s going to run you down.”

“Ah, thank you,” Nathaniel said hesitantly, not exactly sure how to respond. But Emily saw the twinkle in his eyes. He liked this old white woman. So did Emily. She was frank and fun, and it was impossible not to like her.

“I’ve got two other families living here,” Millie said. “My husband’s two nephews’ wives and their kids. One of the nephews died of yellow fever. The other is in a Yankee prison. Their families lost everything. Both farms were smack dab in the middle of some of the worst battles of the war. Shot to red blazes and mostly burned up. They were lucky to get out with their lives. The fields were practically destroyed. They won’t be no ‘count till well after the war. Poor ladies didn’t have anywhere else to go.” She shrugged and smiled and added, “Might as well make use of this big old house. Besides, it’s fun having kids around. Makes me feel younger myself.”

The wide foyer had a beautiful marble floor. In other times, it would have been stately, indeed. But right now it was haphazard at best. There were lots of freshly made uniforms, stacks of britches and shirts and coats. There were other stacks as well, blankets of different sizes, socks, and small tents. Two women were busily wrapping the goods in bundles and tying them with thin strips of cloth. They handed the completed bundles to the two black men who were loading the wagons out front.

“It’s Friday,” Millie said. “Shipping out a week’s worth of production. It doesn’t look like much for a whole week, but we’re going as fast as we can.”

“All this? Why, that’s wonderful for one week. How could you do that much?”

"Oh, I didn't do that much myself. There are two dozen of us. The best seamstresses in Richmond. And we work long hours. Still, it's pitiful little. Sometimes we run out of material to work with. All we can do is gossip. But I'm babbling now. Come on back to the kitchen. You've got to be starved after your trip."

"Oh, thank you. Yes, we could both use something. I was thinking about getting lunch downtown, but once I saw the place, all I could think about was getting away from it."

Millie smiled a long, sad smile. "Things are scarce, but we can come up with something that might tickle your palate. Thank the Lord I can pay the scandalous prices nowadays. If this war lasts too many more years, I won't be able to. But, then, I won't last too many more years myself."

"Why, Aunt Millie, you're as spry as a fox chasing after a rabbit. You'll be here when the house crumbles down."

Millie laughed and said, "That might be next week the way the Yankees keep firing their cannon at us. But we're trying to hold them off." Then she turned to a young black woman in the kitchen and said, "Carolina, this here is my grandniece, Emily, Tommy's little girl. Lord, what am I saying? You're a baby yourself. You wouldn't remember Tommy."

Carolina smiled at Emily and said, "Pleased to meet you, ma'am."

"And this is her domestic, Nathaniel, wasn't it? They've finished a long trip and have lots of harrowing stories to tell us while they're eating. Scare them up something good. The better the lunch, the better the stories we'll hear." She cackled again.

Carolina smiled briefly, her eyes lingering on Nathaniel, and then she set about her task in a blur of motion.

"Sit here," Millie said to Emily, motioning to a seat at the big table in the middle of the indoor kitchen. She turned to Nathaniel and said, "You can set the bags down in the next room there. We'll get them after lunch. Then sit at the servant's table over here." Millie's instructions were accompanied by finger-pointing that left no doubt what she was talking about.

"I want to hear all about the trip," Millie said when she sat across from Emily. "But first, tell me about little Tommy. How's my handsome little nephew doing?"

Emily smiled. "I never thought of my daddy as little, but he's doing fine…" And so the story went, Emily talking and Millie asking. Emily couldn't help but notice that every once in a while Carolina glanced over and smiled at Nathaniel. She also noticed the twinkle in Nathaniel's eyes as he acknowledged the looks he was getting. Romance among slaves? Why not? They were people, too.

Before she could start on the tales of the trip, Carolina served them. Bacon sandwiches on dark bread with tomatoes.

"It's hard to get fresh vegetables in Richmond," Millie said as she nodded at the plate in front of Emily. "Almost impossible. We grow our own tomatoes out back. We'll have plenty until the first frost then we'll preserve the rest. Eat up, girl. I know you're starving."

"What about you?"

"I've had my lunch. You can talk and eat at the same time, can't you? I'll bet a fat old hen Tommy and Mary taught you not to talk with your mouth full, but I'm eager to hear about your trip so let the bread and bacon dribble down your chin and onto your dress while you tell me all about it."

Emily laughed as she chewed, almost shooting the bread and bacon across the table. When she got control of herself, she told the story about riding horses from Montgomery to Thomasville and running into Sheriff Rufus Tate. Emily also related the story about the three lashes Nathaniel suffered before they could get away. She noticed the concern in Carolina's eyes as she told the story around bites of her sandwich.

"What a devil!" Millie declared. "The Lord will see that he gets his. And that deputy, too. All finished?"

"Yes. It was delicious. Thank you so much." Emily turned to Carolina and said. "Thank you. That was wonderful."

Carolina beamed then looked to Nathaniel for confirmation. He gave it with a nod of his head.

As they were standing up, one of the slaves who had been loading the uniforms came into the kitchen. "Excuse me, Mrs. Millie, but the Lieutenant is here to take the wagons."

They stepped back into the foyer where a Confederate Lieutenant was waiting. The man was short, had an odd round nose which was accentuated by the fluffy, dark mutton chops on the sides of his face, and he looked old even though Emily could tell he was still quite young. Outside they could see a contingent of four Confederate soldiers. Two of them got into the wagons to drive while the other two held their now riderless horses.

"I want to thank you and your ladies for all your hard work," the Lieutenant said to Millie as he bowed. "I'll see you next Friday. If Richmond is still here, that is. Who is this beautiful young lady?"

"This is my grandniece, Emily Rose. She's visiting from Alabama. Emily, this is Lieutenant Rogerson. He and his men come by every Friday to pick up our week's labor."

The Lieutenant bowed low and said, "It is, indeed, a pleasure, Madame." Then he turned to Nathaniel and said, "Is this your slave, Mrs. Hanson? I haven't seen him here before."

"No. This is Emily's domestic. He traveled with her."

The Lieutenant stared at Nathaniel a moment, looking up and down at the black man's lean, muscular body, and then turned back to Millie. "Mrs. Hanson, the Yankees are only a few miles down the road. If Petersburg falls, it might take Richmond with it. We are short-handed. We need every strong back we can get to help build the city's defenses. We've got to protect ourselves. This darkie looks stronger than most. He'll have to come with me."

"With you?" Emily said. "No! Nathaniel is my domestic servant. I need him with me."

"I'm sorry, ma'am," the Lieutenant said. "By order of Confederate command, all able-bodied slaves not otherwise engaged in significant duties are subject to confiscation to work on the city's defenses. The Yankees control City Point, less than twenty miles away. The entire Union army is entrenched there. They might move on us at any time.

We're desperate. We need every able body we can find. We have to confiscate him to help with the work on Fort Harrison."

"Confiscate him? He's a person. You can't walk in here and take him away," Emily protested.

"Yes, ma'am. I can and I must. A slave is property. Property is subject to confiscation by the government for whatever military purposes are deemed necessary. We are in dire straits and need help at Fort Harrison. Your big buck, here, looks like he could do as much work as two men. He'll have to come with me."

"For how long?" Millie asked.

"It depends on how long it takes to run the Yankees away from Richmond," Lieutenant Rogerson said as he shrugged. "Weeks. Perhaps months."

September 9, 1864 ~ Elmira Army Depot, Elmira, New York

"This could get me in a whole lot of trouble," Private Thomas Wilson said. "You sure you can keep your mouth shut?"

"Get you in trouble?" John Murray curled his lip in disgust as he placed the United States Notes into Wilson's hand. He took the two forms from Wilson, one complete and one blank, and tucked them into his jacket. Glancing to the sides to make sure no one was around, he said, "It would get me kicked out of the army. Hell, I'd lose my pension. You don't have to worry about me saying anything."

Wilson stared at Murray a few more seconds. He wasn't sure he could trust this man, but Thomas Wilson needed the money. If he didn't pay off his gambling debts, he would end up in the hospital… if not worse. "Just make damn sure you don't. And meet me back here at ten o'clock sharp. I've got to get that completed form back into the file before anyone misses it."

"Why? That operation was last week. Nobody's going to go looking for it now."

"Maybe not, but I can't take a chance. Ten o'clock. Understand?"

"Sure. I'll be here." And he would. John Murray might need other forms in the future.

Private Thomas Wilson stared for a second, as though not trusting Murray's word, but said nothing as he finally turned and hurried away.

To hell with you, Murray thought. His lips did not move, however, as he watched the other soldier for a couple of seconds before turning around and walking away in the opposite direction. He walked casually, calm and collected.

It was not easy for an enlisted man to find privacy, to find a place to work where no one could see what he was doing. Not his bunk. There was always somebody hanging around in the barracks. Besides, he needed a steady table or desk. The mess hall was out. There were plenty of tables, but it would be full at dinnertime. Even if it wasn't, it was too open and too visible. There was only one thing to do. Use an officer's private desk. And he knew which one, a certain captain who liked to go to the bars as soon as his workday ended. The man would be on his third or fourth beer by now, following each one with a shot of whiskey.

Murray kept watch to the sides and listened for any footsteps as he worked the two thin metal rods in the door lock. It popped open. He darted inside and closed the door then sat at the desk. He couldn't risk lighting a lamp, but there was enough evening sunlight coming in through the small window. Reaching into his jacket, he pulled out the two forms, setting the completed one to the left and the blank one to the right.

It would be simple. All Murray had to do was fill out the blank form to match the completed form, except he would need to change the name and date. And, perhaps, the description of the wound.

He read the completed form and wrote the necessary information on the blank form. The man on the left had his leg amputated because of a shattered thigh bone. That wouldn't do, so on the blank form Murray wrote, "Rifle ball inside right knee." Then, using the signature on the completed form as his guide, he began to forge the chief surgeon's signature at the bottom. It was a piece of cake. John Murray had the gift of good eyes and a steady hand. He could copy anyone's signature, and no one would be the wiser. Slowly and meticulously, he reproduced "Major Eugene F. Sanger" on the signature line then compared the two forms. *Perfect* he said to himself as he admired his handiwork. He stuffed the two forms back into his jacket.

John Murray was a great listener. That was the way you learned things. He had a way of finding secluded spots where he could overhear nearby conversations without being seen. Recently, he had overheard Caleb and others talking and knew that Caleb would not want to go on living if he lost his leg. Perhaps he didn't have to kill Caleb Garner himself. It was easier to get away with murder if he could get someone else to do the killing. Besides, suicide had a sweet symmetry to it. Major Sanger's surgeons would start the dirty work, and, if Murray got lucky, Caleb might complete it.

But even if Caleb lost his nerve and could not take his own life, the Southerner would be a crushed man forever. He would be alive without living. It was the sweetest revenge of all. *That'll show that filthy, stinking Rebel trash,* Murray thought. *He can't cost me my stripes and get away with it.*

Access to the prison medical area was open to Union troops. There was little to hide, so it was a simple matter to slip the new form into the operation tray without anyone seeing. The clerk would pull the form in the morning and schedule the operation for a day or two in the future. Within a few days, Caleb would be a one-legged man. John Murray smiled to himself as he walked out.

He went back to his bunk to wait until ten o'clock. As much as he despised Private Thomas Wilson, he did not want to keep the man waiting. Thomas Wilson could get him almost anything Murray might need. Better not to cross him.

September 11, 1864 ~ Millie Hanson's Mansion, Richmond, Virginia

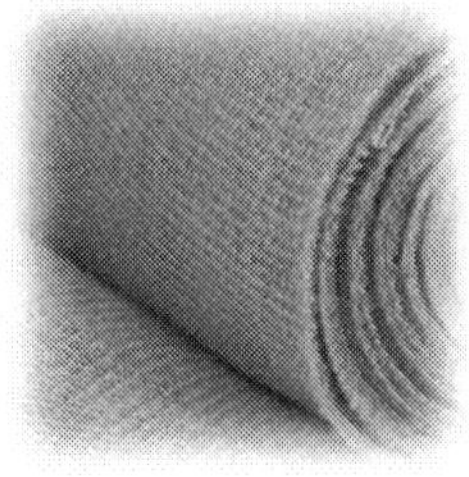

Holding the blanket up, Millie inspected the seams. "I see you inherited your mother's skills. This is about as close to perfect as any beginner is going to get. It's amazing how much you've improved in a few days."

"Thank you," Emily said. "I appreciate you letting me help. I'd go crazy sitting here day after day doing nothing."

"Nonsense. This is the type of work we desperately need. Thank you for helping."

Emily picked up the bolt of cloth and unfurled it on top of the table, allowing enough for the next blanket. "I want to help, but I need to go. Caleb needs me. I've got to get him out of that horrible Yankee prison."

"I know, hon, but there's nothing we can do until your slave is released. You can't go to Belle Plains by yourself. It's far too dangerous. This is not the same Virginia it used to be. There's all sorts of evil going on. We've got to get your slave back first. Thomas trusted him. That's good enough for me."

Emily finished cutting the cloth and looked up at Millie. "But how? We have pleaded with Lieutenant Rogerson twice. He won't even listen to us. He says his hands are tied, that the Confederate army won't release Nathaniel."

"Yes, yes," Millie said as a frown furrowed her face. She became quiet and started pacing around the room. After the third loop, she turned to Emily and said, "I've got an idea. You've got to get a travel pass to cross into Yankee controlled area. They come from General Winder's office. He has nothing to do with the confiscation of slaves, but he might have some pull with those who do. He knows people, important people. Perhaps we could plead our case with him. The General would understand why a young girl should not be roaming around the countryside by herself. Maybe, just maybe, he could pull some strings and get your slave released."

"It's worth a try," Emily said. "Let's go first thing tomorrow morning."

“Yes,” Millie said. “I’m reasonably well respected around here. Perhaps I can throw a little weight around.” Millie smiled as she wiggled her plump body side-to-side, causing Emily to giggle. It was a good release from the dread that had blanketed her for days, building day after day since Nathaniel had been gone.

September 12, 1864 ~ Barracks Number Three, Elmira, New York

When they left Point Lookout, the prisoners were herded into freight cars like cattle. It was both confusing and degrading. Separated because of the disorganized process, Charles and Caleb ended up on different train cars. They managed to get reunited in Barracks Number Three. Charles Pearson had traded places with another prisoner, an arrangement that had included a plump rat that Charles caught, so they were now next to each other.

The reading lessons continued day in and day out. Caleb felt as though he had read the entire Bible several times. As a result, his reading had improved significantly. He would never be able to breeze through words and pages as smoothly as Charles, but he read well enough. He could even sign his own name, though that was the extent of his writing. There were no pens and little paper for him to practice. He learned his signature using a stick and writing in the dirt in the prison yard.

"That's good," Charles said as he watched Caleb scribe his name through the dirt for the tenth time that afternoon. "That's better than all the others. Why, you'll never have to sign with an 'X' again!"

Caleb looked up at his friend and smiled. Suddenly, the full gravity of what he had done gripped him. "I can write my own name! And I can read!"

"You sure can. It was the Lord's will. That's why you learned so easy."

Caleb stared at Charles. "I ain't so sure I'd call it easy. You've been drilling me over and over, like a man in a hurry beating a mule that doesn't want to move."

Charles Pearson got a wry smile on his face and said, "That old mule got up and got going in the end, didn't he?"

Caleb laughed. "I reckon I did."

"Yep. And it was easier than you realize. It takes kids a couple of years to learn to read as good as you do. You did it in two months."

Caleb smiled then said, "Those kids don't go to school fourteen hours a day every blessed day of the week like you've been making me, but I sure do appreciate it. Letters aren't something I'm scared of anymore. They aren't some crazy mystery. I understand them. I don't reckon I could ever pay you back."

"You can read the Lord's word, nowadays. That's payment enough. For both of us. Besides, working on your reading fourteen hours a day made the time pass a lot faster. Considering where we are, anything that makes time go by quicker is a blessing."

"Amen to that. But what are we going to do now? Keep on reading?"

"There are some important things in the Bible, things you need to know by heart. Like the Ten Commandments. Instead of reading them, you should be able to…"

A Union Corporal stepped up to Caleb and Charles and said, "Caleb Garner. The sawbones needs to schedule your operation. Please follow me."

"Operation? What operation? I don't need no operation."

"The sawbones will have to explain. I'm only following orders. Let's go."

Concern on his face, Caleb glanced at Charles. He struggled to his feet with help from his friend. As the Union Corporal walked toward the medical building, Caleb hobbled beside him, struggling to keep up. His limp had not improved even though the wound appeared to be healed. The Corporal slowed down so Caleb could catch up. He looked at Caleb's leg and said, "I would guess the operation is for that leg."

Caleb was led into a surgeon's office. The doctor, a young Lieutenant, looked at the way Caleb was standing, tilting to the side because he couldn't straighten his leg, and nodded his head. "I have your amputation order," he said. "I've scheduled you for first thing in the morning."

"Amputation? What do you mean?"

"Your leg." The doctor waved the papers over his head. "We're going to amputate your damaged leg."

"No! You can't do that."

"You have nothing to worry about, soldier. There is no shortage of medication in the North. You will not suffer."

"But I don't want to lose my leg. There's no infection. It's a lot better, and it'll keep getting better over time. You got no call to take my leg."

The surgeon waved the amputation order in the air again. "I've got the order right here. Signed by Major Sanger himself. He decided the amputation was needed after he examined you."

"He didn't examine me. I ain't never even seen Major Sanger. You can't do this!"

"I can and I must. I have been authorized to do so by this order. I'm sure Major Sanger has his reasons, and I'm sure it's for your own good. He's a fine doctor. He knows what he's doing." The young surgeon set the order on top of his desk and, with a wry smile, said, "Why, he'll even tell you what a wonderful doctor he is himself."

"No! I won't let you do it," Caleb said.

The surgeon waved his hand at Caleb and said, "You are dismissed. Corporal, please accompany Mr. Garner back to his barracks. And please make sure he is here at half past five in the morning for prep. Sharp. I don't like delays. We will begin the operation at six o'clock."

September 12, 1864 ~ Brigadier General Winder's Office, Richmond, Virginia

The unmistakable odor of whiskey seeped through the door as soon as Emily opened it. She glanced at her aunt. Millie's brows wrinkled, and her nose wiggled as she sniffed. They exchanged glances but walked in at the beckoning of a soldier behind a low counter, a mere boy wearing a uniform.

"Can I be of service to you ladies?" the soldier asked.

"I am Mildred Rose Hanson," Millie said. "We wish to see General Winder. He knows me."

"Ah, ma'am, he's busy now. You'll have to make an appointment."

"I'll do nothing of the kind," Millie said. "I need to see General Winder now. Not this afternoon. Not tomorrow. Not next week. Right now." Millie turned to Emily and said, "Come with me, dear."

As Aunt Millie started walking toward the office area, the young soldier put his hand on her right arm and said, "General Winder is in a meeting. You can't go back there."

"Are you going to shoot an old woman?" Millie asked, her eyes opened wide and defiant.

The boy soldier said, "Why, no ma'am. I, ah, I wouldn't shoot…"

"Oh," Millie said with a nod and a smile. "I understand. You want to dance with me. Well, of course." She grabbed his free hand with her left hand and twirled them about, smiling and humming and getting ever closer to the offices.

"But, ma'am…" the young soldier stuttered. Emily was trying her best not to laugh.

"Have you ever danced with General Winder?" Millie asked.

"Danced? With a man? No, ma'am. Why, I wouldn't…"

"I have. He and I are longtime friends. You would do well to remember that." Millie twirled the soldier around once more, with greater force, then released him. He took several steps backward, bounced into the wall and stood there.

"Come along, Emily."

His face horror-stricken, the young soldier hesitated as Millie and Emily streaked past. When he realized they were almost into the office area, he charged after them. Flustered, he said the only thing that came to his mind. "But you don't know where his office is."

"I most certainly do," Millie said as she walked straight toward a door with General Winder's name stenciled on it. She snatched the door open, stepped inside, and then held the door for Emily.

The smell of whiskey was even thicker inside the General's office. He was sitting with two other Confederate officers, all with glasses in their hands. A half-empty bottle of brown liquid sat on top of the desk.

Brigadier General John Henry Winder looked up. His head snapped back slightly from surprise. "What the devil…"

The young soldier came rushing in after Emily. "I tried to stop them, Sir. The lady said, ah, she said she had danced with you."

General Winder stared at Millie then set his glass on his desk and said, "That's true enough. I have. Get back to the counter, soldier. And try your best not to let any other intruders get past."

"Intruders?" Millie said, ripening her voice with as much of an indignant tone as she could muster.

"Yes, Sir!" the young man said as he saluted. He literally ran out of the office.

General Winder turned to the other two officers, who had been watching with amusement, and said, "We will have to continue this, ah, meeting at another time, gentlemen. Please." He waved toward the door.

The two officers tilted their glasses up and drained the remaining whiskey then bowed to Millie and Emily before exiting the office. Both had smiles on their faces.

Winder noticed Emily staring at the whiskey bottle on the table.

"We were celebrating, ah, a Confederate victory," General Winder said.

"Don't try to fool me, John Winder," Millie said. "You were celebrating the arrival of daytime. That's the only excuse you need."

General Winder looked at Millie with a cocked eyebrow. A crooked smile worked its way onto his lips. "Mrs. Hanson, just because we've danced for a few minutes at some social events, that doesn't give you the right to barge in here and…"

"A few minutes, indeed! It would have been longer if you hadn't been so eager to move on to the younger ladies."

"As I recall, you were quite eager to dance with thc young men. What few there were since most of them are off fighting a war. But be that as it may, you have no right to come in here while I'm holding an officer's meeting."

Millie turned to Emily and said, "Be careful where you step, hon. It's thick in here."

General Winder sighed heavily and said, "Millie, I appreciate your war effort. I promise I do. Everybody in Richmond appreciates… Oh, hell. So what if I take a small drink in the morning? What does it matter?"

"Probably a guilty conscience because of those barbaric prisons you are responsible for."

Winder stared at Millie a moment, then turned his head and looked out the window. Seconds passed in silence. "You think I don't care?" he finally said. "We can't even feed our own soldiers. What the hell am I supposed to do? It's the Union's damned fault. They've squeezed us so hard there's damned little left to feed anybody, not just their men."

Millie sighed. Her face turned serious. "I understand, John. I'm struggling to feed the ladies working for me. I can't help you with that."

General Winder turned back around and looked at Millie. "So why *are* you here?"

"I need a favor."

"You need a favor? From me? You've got a hell of a way of asking for it."

Millie smiled then said, "Pour me a small one, John. And freshen up your glass. Emily's too young, but you and I will toast to the great lost cause."

Winder poured a single finger in two small glasses. “Here’s hoping it’s not yet lost,” he said. They clicked them together, lifted to each other then tossed down the burning liquid. “But if it is, people like me will be lost with it. What’s your favor, Millie?”

“It’s for my niece.” Millie patted Emily on the shoulder. “She needs to travel to Belle Plains.”

“Virginia? Why, that’s in the hands of the Yankees. You don’t want to go there.”

“I must,” Emily said. “My fiancé is a prisoner there. I have to see him.”

“A pretty young girl like you? Traveling alone? You can’t be serious.”

“Not alone,” Millie said. “Her domestic will be traveling with her.”

“A slave? Hell, he’ll buck for D.C. as soon as he gets past our lines.”

“Not Nathaniel,” Emily said. “He is dedicated to our family. You, well, you wouldn’t understand. He promised my father he would protect me. He would never break his promise.”

“So you want a travel pass into Yankee held territory for yourself and another one for your domestic slave. Even if you got there without suffering a serious problem, I’m afraid the Yankees would not let you see your fiancé. This isn’t a local jail. Prisoners of war are different. Besides, he may not be there. As I understand it, Belle Plains is a temporary holding point. He could have been moved by now.”

“Oh. I didn’t realize that. How would I know where to look?”

The General thought a moment then said, “I don’t know of a way unless you know somebody in the Union army.”

“I don’t, of course.”

“I suppose you would have to go to Belle Plains to find out. But it would be a dangerous trip. I shouldn’t be selling travel passes to a young lady and a colored slave to cross beyond enemy lines.”

“I shouldn’t have turned my house over to the government for making supplies in support of our great lost cause,” Millie said. “But I did, John. Sometimes you have to go out of your way to help the world along. Don’t you think?”

Winder grunted.

"Selling?" Emily said. "Would I have to pay for the pass?"

"Why, of course," General Winder said. "A hundred dollars for each pass. That's the law."

"Two hundred dollars? I-I don't have that much left. I thought my domestic could accompany me on my travel pass. That's what they did in Alabama."

"Save your money," Millie said as she opened her purse. "I'll be happy to pay for it. And I'm sure General Winder will be happy to accept my money.

"Where is the slave?" the General asked. "He needs to be here to swear an oath."

"We'll have to do the swearing for you," Millie said. "He was confiscated by the Confederate government. Right now he's helping build the defenses at Fort Harrison. We've got to convince the government to give him back."

General Winder jerked his hands up in the air and said, "You don't want much, do you, Millie? A travel pass for a young lady through an area so dangerous she might not survive, and a travel pass for a slave who has been confiscated by the government and isn't even here to do the traveling. I suppose you want me to run down to Fort Harrison and get him released so he can go on this fairytale adventure."

"Would you, dear?" Millie said. "That would be so helpful."

General Winder bent his head down and rubbed his eyes. Finally, he looked back up and said, "You've got a way about you, Millie. No wonder you're rich. And the hell of it is, I would if I could. But I can't help you with that one. I don't have any authority over confiscated labor. I'd get laughed at if I even asked."

"I'll do it then. I'm used to getting laughed at, right before I get my way."

"I have little doubt you will." General Winder pulled some blank forms from a drawer and picked up a quill pen. "I feel like I'm signing your death warrant, young lady." He sighed heavily then asked, "What is your slave's name?"

September 13, 1864 ~ Prison Medical Facilities, Elmira, New York

Caleb had slept little. Although the sky to the east was brightening, the sun had not yet risen when they came for him.

"No," Caleb said. "I'm not going. He's got no right. It's my leg. I don't want it cut off, and I won't let him do it. As God is my witness, he's got no right." His knuckles whitened as he strengthened his grip on the rails of his cot.

One of the two soldiers standing over him started to say something to Caleb but seemed to have second thoughts. Instead, he looked up at the guards by the door and said, "We're going to need some help."

One finger at a time, they pried his right hand loose from the side rail of the cot. While two soldiers held Caleb's arm to keep him from gripping the cot again, the other two pried his left hand loose. They lifted him then tried to walk out of the barracks. Caleb refused to cooperate, so the four Union soldiers held him vertically and drug him out, his bare feet scraping along the rough wood floor.

His feet were bleeding by the time he was drug into the hospital ward. As they were approaching the surgery room, they could hear a round of laughter inside. In a booming voice, the surgeon said, "Why, I've killed more Rebels than any soldier at the front." There was another round of laughter, louder this time.

"No!" Caleb shouted. "Let me go!"

They drug him through the door. It took all four of the soldiers to hold Caleb in front of the doctor. The surgeon pointed at Caleb's bloody toes and asked, "What the dickens is that?"

"Drug his feet," one of the guards said. "He wouldn't cooperate."

"What silliness. No wonder you're late. Listen to me..." The doctor looked at a piece of paper. "Ah… Caleb Garner. Your amputation order was signed by Major Sanger. I will admit he thinks highly of himself, but it is not without justification. He may be cold and obnoxious, but the man is a brilliant surgeon. If he says your leg needs to be amputated, then it needs to be amputated. That is the end of it." He looked at the guards and said, “Place him on that table and get him prepped. I need to get this over with. I’ve got other operations scheduled today.”

“NOOOO!!!!” Caleb screamed as the guards wrestled him onto the table’s surface. “YOU CAN”T DO THIS.”

“As I told you previously, I can. I have my orders, and I will follow…”

An officer with a tall forehead and long goatee leaned around the corner of the door and said, “What’s all the fuss in here?”

“Oh, ah, good Morning, Major Sanger,” the young surgeon said. “I didn’t realize you were here. It’s this prisoner, Sir. We have your order to amputate, but he doesn’t wish to cooperate. He, ah, doesn’t believe his leg should be amputated.”

“They never do. Hmmm. Let me take a look.” As the four guards held Caleb down, Sanger looked over Caleb’s knee. After studying the knee, he looked at Caleb’s face. “Did you say my order? I don’t recognize this wound. Or this man.”

“Yes, Sir,” the Lieutenant said with a nervous strain in his voice. Sanger not remembering? That was unimaginable.

Major Sanger glanced at the order and shrugged. “Yes, this is my signature. Odd that I don’t remember. Hmmm. I’ll examine the prisoner’s leg again.”

Sanger grabbed Caleb’s lower leg and knee and twisted. Pain shot through the damaged leg, bringing Caleb arcing up off the table and screaming at the top of his lungs.

“Hold him down,” Sanger said. Four men grabbed Caleb’s arms and legs and pushed them hard against the table, bruising his flesh. Sanger mumbled to himself as he probed his fingers around Caleb’s knee, pressing hard here and there to feel the different components of the knee. Caleb screamed and fought against the painful probing.

Major Sanger stood back in exasperation and said, “I’m trying to determine if I can save your leg. I cannot do so if you don’t lie still. Do you want me to try, or do you want me to turn around and walk away and let them use the saw on you?”

Caleb became still as he stared at Sanger eye-to-eye. He gritted his teeth, gripped the edge of the cot until his knuckles were white, and said, "Go ahead."

Major Sanger began to work the knee again, straightening and bending. The metal ball still inside his knee scraped into the ligaments and tendons and bone. Caleb gritted his teeth harder, until he thought he was going to chip them, and pressed his fingers against the edge of the table even harder, the nails sinking into the wood. Sweat formed on his forehead and trickled down toward his ears. Strained grunts escaped from his mouth, as did streaks of saliva, but somehow he managed not to scream or move his leg.

Sanger probed for several more minutes then stood back and said, "Interesting. The ball is lodged inside the knee. I can't be sure until I open him up, of course, but it appears the basic structure of the knee is intact. I believe I can get it out without causing further damage."

"But, Sir," the younger surgeon said, holding up the amputation order as he did, "Wouldn't it be simpler to amputate? We've got several operations to perform this morning."

"That would be expedient for today. But what about tomorrow?"

"Ah, tomorrow? I don't understand, Sir."

"Of course not," Sanger said. "Let me enlighten you. This prisoner can be repaired such that he can walk again, though possibly with a limp."

"Ah, Sir, he's a Rebel soldier. We've got sick and wounded all around us. I could have his leg off, cauterized, and bandaged in less than half an hour. It would take three or four hours to do the kind of surgery you're talking about. Perhaps longer."

"Perhaps three or four hours for you. I can finish in less than two."

The young surgeon shrugged. "Four or two. It's still extra time. We could spend that time treating others."

"Use your head, Lieutenant. We spend an extra hour and a half now, and this man becomes mobile again. He can move around on his own. Sure, we could take a shortcut in the operation room. Then both we and the Union army would waste many precious hours in the future."

"How so?"

"Isn't it obvious? Nursing him through a ball removal is considerably less taxing than nursing him through an amputation. If we take his leg, we'll have to carry him around everywhere for quite some time. Then we'll have to provide a crutch and spend the time to teach him how to use it. He would be a burden on the nurses and the guards. It's far better to spend an extra hour and a half now and save dozens, perhaps hundreds of hours of work later. We have a war to win. The Union has better things to do with our resources than nurse prisoners with one leg."

"I'm sorry, Sir. I didn't think of all that."

Sanger sighed and said, "Why doesn't that surprise me? Knock the patient out and prepare yourselves for surgery. You will assist and observe. I am going to teach you fools a lesson."

Sanger snatched the amputation order out of the young Lieutenant's hand and said, "I don't know where this came from. As I said, I have never seen this man or this wound. I can only imagine I thought I was signing something else." He ripped the paper in half then in quarters and tossed the pieces over his shoulder. The ragged little pieces of paper turned and twisted as they fell to the floor.

September 19, 1864 ~ Prison Viewing Stand, Elmira, New York

Why observing the ragged, filthy, animalistic Confederate prisoners was so popular among the town's female population was beyond John Murray's comprehension. The Rebels were not attractive, well-bred, or well-groomed gentlemen. The animals the Southern soldiers had become, in most cases always had been, were disgusting to look at, the lowest of the low. It made no sense. But, sense or not, the ladies crowded onto the two enterprising observation towers that had been set up outside Barracks Number Three, built on platforms high enough to afford a good view over the prison wall.

John Murray had the itch. It had been a while since he had spent the coin to buy a lady of the night in the bar district that had blossomed in Elmira since the army depot was constructed. But he didn't want to spend the money. And he had developed a taste for something a little higher class.

With all the female patrons, the observation tower was bound to be a good place to find a woman. There were several types of ladies who would ogle the half-naked men inside the prison. One of these types would be the kind that Murray needed. It had worked before. Of course, it helped that Murray had the kind of looks that would cause a lady to take a second glance.

He knew Major Colt and the other brass at Elmira were not happy with the viewing towers. The towers were commercial enterprises with no legal connection to the prison. So the brass made rules. Union soldiers were not allowed to visit the towers. And why would they want to? They saw enough of the prisoners from the inside.

But John Murray had a need the brass hadn't thought about. He could not afford to climb the steps to the viewing platform while wearing his blue uniform, so he wore civilian clothes. That was unfortunate since ladies often responded to a man in uniform, but it allowed him a certain amount of anonymity, which was necessary. Unless he saw someone who knew him, and there was little chance of that, he would not have to worry about getting caught and suffering the consequences for not following orders.

He made his way through the crude wooden concession stands that had sprung up between the two observatories, a carnival atmosphere built around the viewing of Confederate prisoners. Murray hastened his steps as he passed by the concession stands. He had no need for ginger cakes or peanuts or even beer or whiskey. His need was more basic.

At the higher of the two observation towers, Murray paid the ten cents admission and moved smoothly up the steps. He hoped he had not wasted his dime. Once at the top, he looked around at the female patrons on the tower, sizing each one up by their body language and their overheard comments. They laughed and pointed and smiled as they looked out over the Rebel prisoners. There was a group of four women, unaccompanied, around the looking glass, taking turns peering through. One of them, a brunette in a peach dress, noticed him. She glanced back, that look in her eyes. This was his lucky day. She was a little on the plain side, but sometimes that was good. Sometimes the plain-looking ones had something to prove.

He stepped over to the looking glass, getting as near to the brunette as possible without being too conspicuous. "Good morning, ladies. I hope the Rebel prisoners are not too repulsive for you."

A couple of them giggled. The brunette said, with a shrug, "They seem to be on the muscular side, although quite lean."

Murray bit his tongue on his response. Another one of the women said, "Why is that man wearing a barrel? Has he no clothes? The Advertiser says they are well provided with attire."

"Of course he has clothes," Murray responded. "We treat the prisoners well." He wanted to say 'even though they don't deserve it,' but cut the statement off. "Wearing a barrel is a form of punishment. This man has broken one of the rules."

"Wearing a barrel as punishment? How silly."

"When a prisoner breaks the rules, they have to be punished. Else they'd run amuck. We'd have no order at all. We cannot make sure the prisoners are treated well and fairly if we do not maintain order."

"I suppose so," the brunette said. "Are you connected with the prison? You talk as though you know a lot about it."

Her eyelids fluttered just enough, the sign Murray was looking for. He took a step closer, but before he could say anything, they heard a commotion from the street below. Something was up, something that was louder than the typical civilian conversation and carnival atmosphere of the refreshment booths below. All heads on the observation tower turned down to look at the crowd, to see what was creating the calamitous disturbance in an already rowdy scene.

Union soldiers! A squad had marched up and stopped in front of the tower, patrons scattering to get out of their way. Four of them, including an officer, separated from the main group and stepped over to the observation tower entrance. They showed the gatekeeper a slip of paper, talked to him briefly, and then proceeded to climb the tower steps without paying admission. The rest of the soldiers stood around the base of the tower, weapons shouldered.

What did the soldiers want? John Murray began to sweat when he saw Major Colt, followed by the Lieutenant who often shadowed him, walk over to the group of Union soldiers at the base of the tower, talk to them briefly, and look upward. Murray snapped his head back to keep from being seen. Would Colt recognize him? It had been a month since Caleb Garner had gotten him demoted. Perhaps Colt had forgotten, but Murray couldn't afford the risk. He hurriedly looked around for an escape route. Nothing. He was trapped. There was nowhere to go other than the stairs. He moved behind the ladies and the looking glass, trying to be inconspicuous.

A Union captain reached the top of the stairs and stepped out onto the tower platform. The patrons looked at him expectantly as he was joined by the enlisted men. "Ladies and gentlemen," the captain announced, "I am Captain John J. Elwell. By order of the United States Commissary General of Prisoners, Colonel William Hoffman, this facility is being appropriated by the United States Army. Henceforth, it will be used for military purposes. All commercial observation of the military facilities at Elmira will cease. I apologize if this has caused you any inconvenience, but I must request that you leave the tower immediately. It will now be manned *exclusively* by officially posted personnel."

What could Murray do? The brunette looked back at him as she made her way to the stairs, but his prior needs would have to wait. Captain Elwell did not know him. He could walk past the Captain and the other three without them realizing he was a Union soldier who was breaking the rules. But Major Colt was another issue. If he remembered Murray…

There was only one choice, delay. It looked as though Colt was nothing more than an observer, that he was not an official part of this appropriation. After all, he ran the prison, not the garrison. Without an official role, he might move on. The longer Murray took to get down, the better the chance that Colt would be gone. Yes, delay was the answer. He leaned against the far corner of the tower and looked out over the barracks as though nothing was amiss.

"Sir," Captain Elwell said. "Please exit the tower now."

Murray did not turn around. He didn't move.

"You, there. Standing in the corner. I'm talking to you."

Murray turned around. Trying to look surprised, he said, "Me, Sir?"

Captain Elwell turned and looked behind him as the other three soldiers were herding the tower patrons to the stairs. He turned back to Murray and held his hands up in a gesture of futility and said, "You are the only other civilian up here. Yes, I am talking to you."

"I'm sorry, ah, Captain. I didn't realize…"

"When I said every one of you, I meant just that. Every one of you. You are to leave the tower now." Elwell pointed toward the stairs.

"Oh, sure. Of course."

Murray made his way toward the top of the stairs but walked as slowly as prudence would allow. As he began walking down the stairs, he surveyed the crowd below for Major Colt. There he was, his back turned as he was stepping away, going back to the post. John Murray breathed a sigh of relief. Perhaps Colt would not have recognized him, but this way he didn't have to worry as he wound his way down the stairs.

He turned the last turn of the stairs and stepped out onto the walk. "I thought I recognized you coming down the stairs, Private Murray." Major Colt was standing directly in front of him. "You may be out of uniform, but you are the soldier who tortures prisoners. I'll never forget your face. What were you doing on a commercial observation tower? It is off limits to military personnel. You have no official business here."

He had to think quick. "Sir, I have a lady friend in town. She's a nice lady. I would not normally dare to go up there, but I got a message that I was to meet her on top of the tower. I had just now run up to find her. I was going to bring her back down immediately. I assure you, Sir…"

"I've heard enough! There's something about you, Private. I don't know what it is, but it bothers me. Be that as it may, you had no military purpose for being on that tower. If you wish to observe the prisoners from above, I'm going to give you a purpose. From now on you are assigned to picket duty. You will walk the walls surrounding Barracks Number Three every hour you are on duty. Exclusively! This is your final chance. Do not let me catch you breaking another rule again. Don't even try to perform any other military duty. You are a picket. That is all!" Major Colt turned sharply on his heel and marched away.

September 29, 1864 ~ Fort Harrison, Outside Richmond, Virginia

Private Jerome Shackleford bent low as he moved along with the other colored troops through the tan, knee-high straw. The white commander, General Hiram Burnham, said if they could catch Fort Harrison by surprise, it would save lives. Union lives. He made as little noise as possible as he hurried up the slope.

Fort Harrison was built on high ground with an excellent view of the James River. Catching them by surprise would be tricky, but Jerome was trying hard to do his part. He was willing to fight, but he did not want to die. If the Lord would keep half an eye on him, perhaps he would make it through the day.

It had been almost three years since he escaped from the plantation in North Carolina. He had to get away. It was a cruel place. He had the stripes on his back to prove it. So he made his escape and ran through the woods for hours, breathing hard and running harder. When he burst from the forest onto a rutted trail with open fields beyond, he saw a white man sitting in a wagon behind a small clump of trees. The man was doing nothing more than sitting there, a scattergun on his lap as though he was waiting for Jerome to come out. Jerome's short escape was over. He was caught. He would be whipped at best, new and deeper stripes across his back, and lots of them. At worst, he would be out of his misery. As he thought about it, maybe that wasn't the worst.

But the white man did not raise the barrel and point it at him. Instead, he placed his scattergun on the floor and motioned for Jerome to come over.

Jerome Shackleford hesitated. He could run back into the woods, but in the distance behind him, the bark of dogs chasing his scent could be heard. They were a long way back, but dogs ran fast and were tireless. There was nothing ahead of him but open fields of cotton. He had no choice. He had to trust this white man.

"Get in there," the man said as he pointed to a secret compartment in the bottom of the wagon. "Quickly."

Jerome scrunched down as thin as he could, which was pretty thin with the scarcity of food for the slaves. He had to turn his head sideways as the white man fitted the boards on top of him.

For the next few weeks, he went from secret place to secret place. There were dozens of others, hundreds, both men and women, who had escaped plantations from Georgia to Virginia. In the dark of night, they were herded onto a boat and hid in the bottom. Another false floor was placed over them.

It was dark at the bottom of that boat, day and night. Jerome was not sure how long he was down there. He lost track of time. As it turned out, it was only two days later when they walked out as free men and women onto the dock at Baltimore. It had felt like longer, a lot longer.

Jerome Shackleford, a free man! It had a wonderful ring to it. At first. Then he slowly began to realize that freedom in the North had its drawbacks. First, there were too many runaway slaves coming in. Most of them, Jerome among them, could not read, which made it harder to find work. They were dependent on the charity of others.

One day Jerome had gone into town with a newly arrived slave, once again seeking a job. The new slave could read and was able to secure steady work, starting the next morning. Jerome was disappointed once again. As they were walking back to the cot at the church where Jerome slept, they passed a poster on a wall. Jerome had seen the poster many times. The letters and words meant nothing to him.

His friend stopped him and said, "Hey, what about this?" as he pointed at the words on the poster.

"What about it?"

"It says it pays sixteen dollars a month."

"What? You'd have to be able to read and write to make that much money."

"Nope. All you have to do is be able to shoot a rifle, and they'll teach you how. It's for joining the colored troops."

"Fight in the war?"

His friend shrugged and said, "If you don't get shot, it's good money."

So here he was, sneaking up a slope toward the Confederate cannon at Fort Harrison. Over two years of fighting and he had not been shot. Yet. He was going to try his best to keep that record intact.

There was a patch of smoke on top of the hill as thunder rolled down the slope. The officers yelled, "Charge!" over and over as they pointed their sabers uphill. Balls were flying in both directions, up and down the slope. More cannon blasts shattered the air. So much for surprise.

Jerome Shackleford and the men with him broke into a full run uphill, bayonets fixed. The sooner they overran the dirt wall of the fort, the sooner the Rebs would quit firing at them. Jerome was in the middle of a group of soldiers that scaled the earthen wall at the same time. The man directly in front of him, a friend, stopped and hunched over. A blade was sticking out of his back. Jerome saw a Confederate soldier pulling his rifle back. As the Rebel did, the bayonet blade sticking out of his friend's back disappeared. Jerome lunged forward with his own bayonet before the Reb could bring his rifle around. The white man's eyes grew large then closed as he dropped to the ground, gravity pulling him free of the Union bayonet.

There was no time for watching a man die, for having any feelings about it one way or the other. It just was. You went right on fighting the next man, else you would die. Jerome had learned that early in the war. He stepped over the man he had stuck and charged further, looking for another gray back to stick.

In the heat of the fighting, he got turned around enough to see the dirt wall they had scaled. General Burnham was coming over the top, rifle in hand and the flag bearer beside him. Burnham was a white man, but he was a good man. He treated the colored troops well. Jerome started to cheer as he watched General Burnham standing on top of the wall. At that moment, General Burnham's hat flew off as his body snapped back. He wavered a moment then fell.

Jerome stood there, staring, but only for the briefest of moments. He didn't want to join the General. He wanted to live. Hefting his rifle and fixed bayonet, he moved ahead, deeper into the fort.

The battle did not last long. At only two hundred strong, the Confederate troops were greatly outnumbered, over ten to one. Almost all of the Confederate soldiers were killed or wounded. Private Shackleford heard a few scattered shots now and then as he continued toward the back of the fortifications. He heard movement to his left and jerked his musket around but held his fire. A dozen or so colored men, chained to a huge log, were standing there staring at him. They were not wearing uniforms. Slaves, he realized. Forced to work for the Confederates. They were chained to the log to keep them from running away when they weren't working.

"You're free now," Jerome said. "I'll get the Lieutenant, and we'll bust those chains off."

He ran back where he had come from. In a few minutes, Jerome returned with another colored soldier who had been a blacksmith at a plantation. He had the skills and the tools. Within minutes, the slaves were rubbing their wrists where the weight of the chains had been removed.

"This way," Jerome said as he motioned toward where the Union troops were gathered. "The Lieutenant can get you to freedom. They'll take you to a boat down on the river."

Nathaniel stepped forward. "Thank you for freeing us, but I need to leave," he said. "I must go back to Richmond."

"Richmond?" Jerome jerked his head back and frowned at this tall colored man. "But that's where the Rebels are. They'll make you a slave again. If they don't hang you for deserting the fort."

"I have a promise to keep," Nathaniel said. "I can cross the countryside at night and return without being seen. The Confederates had a few horses not far from here. I only need one."

Jerome stared at Nathaniel. The man was not only tall, but he was also strong, sure of himself and his purpose. There was no need to stand in his way. Private Jerome Shackleford shrugged and said, "Good luck, brother. May the Lord watch over you."

September 29, 1864 ~ Barracks Number Three, Elmira, New York

The rough-sawn wood floor of the guard platform, hastily constructed in late spring, creaked and groaned as John Murray walked along, bayonet fixed on his rifle. The platform was four feet below the top of the twelve-foot wall that surrounded the thirty-two-acre prison complex, on the outside of the wall so guards could peer over the top and watch the prisoners.

As he stepped inside the sentry box, one of forty along the full length of the wall, he rested his musket against the rough wood and cursed his fate. This was all Caleb Garner's fault. It was even worse since Caleb had somehow managed to keep his leg. The only positive was that being a picket allowed Murray plenty of time to think. But, frankly, with the cloud that had followed him for days, that was not so positive.

Murray did not know what had gone wrong with his plan. All he knew was that Caleb underwent an operation, but the wounded leg was not amputated. It was probably not a good idea to ask around, so Murray decided to remain ignorant. Unless he accidentally overheard the right conversation, he would never know what happened. Perhaps the surgeon had looked more closely at the knee before pulling out a saw, determined that the leg could be saved, and ignored the amputation order. Or maybe they realized the order was a forgery. In that case, all the more reason not to ask around and tip his hand.

Whatever had happened, Caleb was getting better. Murray had seen other prisoners help the filthy Rebel walk around outside the barracks that morning. The walk had been brief, but long enough for him to see that Caleb not only had two legs but could also straighten and bend the damaged leg more than he could have previously.

Murray would have to find another way to get his revenge. He thought about shooting Caleb from the wall. Taking his rifle and aiming and pulling the trigger. Kill him out in the yard. Murray was a good enough shot to do it. But Major Colt would be worse than furious. No matter what explanation Murray imagined, he knew it would not be good enough for the Rebel sympathizer, Colt. The Major would do more than just discharge him and take away his pension. John Murray would be court-martialed and sent to prison. That would not do, of course. He would have to come up with another way.

For the hundredth time, Murray went over everything in his head again. He wanted off this boring wall. Picket duty, walking the platform by himself over and over, was not the way he wanted to spend his days. But his priority was seeing Caleb die, and Caleb needed to be killed without Murray taking the risk of doing it himself.

He would have to find a way to have someone else murder Caleb. How in the world could he do that? If he could convince the military to execute Caleb, that would work. Caleb would be dead without Murray putting himself at risk, but that was easier said than done. The officers at Elmira were too weak. They didn't execute anyone. They let them get sick and die, as though that somehow kept the blood off their hands. It was a bad atmosphere for getting a prisoner executed, but John Murray would have to come up with a way to do it. And this time he would make sure that it worked.

September 30, 1864 ~ Millie Hanson's Mansion, Richmond, Virginia

What was a wagon doing out this time of night? It had to be past midnight. *No telling,* Nathaniel thought. Richmond was a swollen city with lots of people; refugees running from the large numbers of Union troops in the countryside, opportunists trying to take advantage of frightened folks, and Northern spies trying to learn anything of value to pass on to those Union troops.

Nathaniel could not take the chance of riding through the streets on a horse, so he had left the animal outside of the city. He waited until folks should be asleep then began to slink through the streets, hiding behind cover at every opportunity. But now he was caught by surprise, out in an open field of calf-high grass. There was no time to get behind a tree or lean against the covering wall of a building. Neither was nearby. He dropped to the ground and lay still, breathing as slowly and as lightly as possible. The wagon stopped.

"What's dat I see in the grass there? Is that a body?"

Oh, no, Nathaniel thought. The voice was low in the quiet of night, but loud enough to hear. He had been spotted.

"It sure 'nuf looks like something," another voice said. "Or someone. Let's see."

The light around him grew brighter. The people in the wagon had lifted their lantern.

"Who's dat in dem weeds? I see you hidin'. You alive or dead?"

No need to hide any longer. Nathaniel resisted the urge to say he was dead and stood up, lifting his hands high in the air so they could see he was unarmed. The voices were from colored men, slaves. Otherwise, he would have run.

"Whatchu doin' hidin' in dem weeds?" the driver asked. His eyes had gotten wider, the whites easily seen in the soft glow of the lamp.

"I've got to find someone. I need to leave now. It is of critical importance. If you'll go on about your business, and say nothing about this to anyone, I would be greatly indebted to you."

The driver turned to the slave riding beside him and said, "Whatchu think?"

"I think Master Herman was powerful mad at us hours ago."

"You shore 'nuf right 'bout dat. We wuz supposed to be home by suppertime."

"It twern't our fault. It wuz dat mess in town. But if we don't get on home, we'll be even later."

The driver turned back around and said, "Lookie here. We gots to…" He stopped talking when he realized Nathaniel was gone, was nowhere to be seen within reach of the lantern's light. He turned back around, popped the reins, and said, "No, Sir. I ain't been talkin' to no haint." He glanced at the rider and said, "We best not tell Master Herman we've been talking to no haint. He don't believe in ghosts. He'd shore 'nuf get red mad."

"I ain't said nuthin' to nobody," the rider said as they pulled away. "'Cept telling you to hurry up."

Nathaniel was less than a mile from Millie's mansion as he stole his way through the darkness, quick and quiet. He had spent little time in Millie's house, but he had spent enough to know that Millie did not trust the city Richmond had become. She would have a slave awake and on guard at all hours. He would need to get that slave's attention and explain himself before the slave shouted an alarm.

As he approached the home, he was forced to walk into the light of the two large lamps at the front door. There was no choice. He did so with his arms raised in the air and hoped that none of the neighbors could see him. With any luck, they would be asleep at this hour. Besides, Millie's house was so big and so far away from the other houses, if they did see him, they would see little more than a distant figure in a dimly lit area of a dark night.

He tapped on the door, loud enough to be heard but not loud enough to wake anyone.

"Who's there?" A woman's voice. A slave.

"Nathaniel Whiteeagle. Miss Emily Rose's domestic slave. It is urgent that I see her immediately."

The door opened. Nathaniel froze.

"Get inside here," Carolina said. "Hurry. Before anyone sees you." After Nathaniel stepped inside, she looked around as though she could see in the dark then closed and locked the door. "I was so worried about you. Some of those soldiers don't treat colored people none too well."

"It wasn't so bad. Except for the chains. The white officers were decent enough because they wanted us to work."

Nathaniel was surprised when Carolina threw her arms around him. "I'm so glad you're safe. Mrs. Millie's been trying to get you released, but she's not having any luck."

He couldn't help himself. And he didn't want to. He hugged her back. "The Union army released me. Colored troops. Lots of them. The Confederates are all dead or wounded now."

"You could have stayed on their side, gone to freedom."

"And broken my word to Emily's father. I would not do that."

Carolina squeezed Nathaniel, looked at him and shook her head then said, "I'll go wake Mrs. Millie."

"Nathaniel!" Millie said as she bounced her weight down the stairs as though she were a younger and slimmer woman. Emily was directly behind her. "I am so happy to see you. Carolina told me. That must have been a frightening experience."

"There were some difficult moments. It would have been easier had we not been chained in place."

"If our forts are collapsing around us," Millie said, "I am afraid for Richmond. Thank the Lord you're safe."

"Yes," Emily said. "Thank goodness you're free. We can leave right away. Thanks to Aunt Millie, I have our travel passes safely tucked away in my travel bag."

"You'll need to rest before you travel," Millie said. "Sleep late in the morning. You can leave at first light the following morning. That will give me time to find a couple of horses. I'm afraid the Confederacy has long since confiscated ours."

"Is that going to be a problem?" Nathaniel asked.

"For someone else, perhaps," Millie said. "Not for me." She smiled and lifted her eyebrows. "But with travel passes and horses, you're still subject to trouble in Richmond. You might get confiscated again. Here's what we'll do…"

October 2, 1864 ~ Road to Belle Plains, Virginia

The leaves twisted and danced to the autumn breeze, flashing greens that were edged with yellow, orange, and red. The cold was early this year. Emily pulled Aunt Millie's jacket higher and tighter to protect against the bite of the winds. Leaving home in the heat of summer on a trip that was supposed to last no more than a few short weeks, she had not brought a jacket. Aunt Millie's did little to compliment the dress her mother made for her, but it was warm. And she had long since quit worrying about fashion, about appearing to be a proper, well-bred young lady. There was only the burning need to find Caleb, to end his imprisonment, to see him and hold him and get him on the road to home and safety.

"I would have expected to see more people," Nathaniel said. If he was cold, he showed no signs of it other than covering his dark shirt with his black jacket. Perhaps it wasn't that cold after all. Perhaps the cold she felt came from the inside. "It seems as though this land is controlled by neither side. That could present other problems."

Emily did not respond. She wasn't sure what the 'other problems' were, but the problems she knew about were enough. No need conjuring up new worries.

They rode in silence for some time. As they approached a forested area, where trees bordered the trail on both sides, Nathaniel said, "Pay close attention as we go through these trees. The cover will keep us from being seen, but it will also keep us from seeing others."

Emily glanced back at Nathaniel but said nothing. She returned her eyes to the trail and glanced to each side. The dance of the wind-whipped leaves was the only movement. It seemed safe enough.

A few minutes later Emily saw a different movement, the head of a horse emerging from the trees to the right. The horse's neck appeared from behind the leaves as the animal moved toward the road, followed by the front of its body and a man's hand on the reins. As the horse continued to move out into the open, gray sleeves grew to reveal a tattered jacket with a man's face on top.

The horse was sad looking, an underfed farm animal not given to riding. The man was even worse. He had a long, unkempt beard and dull brown eyes, small and sunken. He was a short man. Though he was mounted, he wasn't much higher than the horse's head. As the animal's tail came out from behind the trees, two more ragged Confederate soldiers, on foot, stepped into the open. One was tall, the other medium height with a pot belly. Both were ragged and filthy, looking as though they had been living in the forest for weeks.

"Lookie here," the short man on the horse said. "A pretty lady and a darkie out joy riding through the countryside. Where'd y'all get those fine looking animals? I would've thought the government would have taken them."

Emily stared at the man but did not immediately respond. After a few seconds of silence, she said, "Please, move out of the way and let us through. We are on official business."

"Official business? If the government had official business out here in the middle of no man's land, they'd send troops, not a young lady and a slave. I've got to admire your bravery, ma'am, but whatever business you had just changed. You see, we got into a bit of a row with one of the officers back to camp. Seeing as how he ended up dead, we had to absquatulate real quick. We lit out on foot. We found this one old nag, but since two of us are still on foot, we'll be taking those horses."

"We can't complete our mission without horses," Emily said with as much firmness as she could muster. These men looked desperate, dangerous. She tried not to show fear. "Now, move aside. If we are late getting to our destination, your officers will arrest you for delaying us."

"If our officers could find us, little lady, they wouldn't go to the trouble to arrest us. They'd string us up on the spot for killing an officer and taking French leave." He pulled his right arm around, a musket in his grip, and pointed the barrel at Emily's chest. The rifle seemed every bit as long as the man. The two men on foot raised their muskets as well. "So whatever else we do won't make no never mind. But, thanks to the two more horses you were kind enough to bring us; we'll be able to make our getaway. Now, get down off those horses before this here rifle goes off in my hands. When you dismount, keep your hands high in the air. I don't mind shooting the nigger, but I wouldn't want to shoot a woman as pretty as you. If you don't give me no trouble, I'll let your slave live, too."

Emily hesitated. The man on the horse said, "Lady, you better do as I say, or I'll put a great big hole in you. My friends here will put two holes in your darkie. NOW GET DOWN!"

Emily and Nathaniel dismounted and stood to the side, arms raised. The two men on foot stepped forward, took the reins, and then led the horses back to where the third man waited.

"Don't put no hole in her yet," the taller of the two said. "I want to have a little fun with that pretty girl first." He grinned widely, showing brown, rotted teeth.

"Why, I wouldn't put a hole through a lady who was cooperative," the rider said as he dismounted. "You two get a hold of that darkie."

They laid their muskets against a tree and got on either side of Nathaniel, getting a firm grip on his arms. These men were ragged and filthy and stunk as bad as anything Nathaniel had ever smelled, but they were strong. He could probably whip either one, but both of them at the same time would be difficult. He tried to figure out how to get them one at a time, without getting Emily shot, but his planning came to a halt when the taller man pulled out a long, wide hunting knife and held it against Nathaniel's throat. "You make one move, and I'll slide this pig sticker across your brown neck faster than you can say please."

The short man, a menacing grin on his face, set his musket against the tree with the other two, and then walked over to Emily.

"No," Emily said. "Please…"

"Don't worry girlie," the man said. He snatched Emily's arm, jerking her toward him. The man was strong for his size. His grip bit deep into her arm, pain shooting all the way up to her shoulder. "This won't take long. Me and my friends will be finished with you and on our way in no time at all. If you're a good girl, we'll let you two live. Why, it would give us a bit of a reputation if y'all spread the story."

"I'm next," the tall man said, but his eyes and the sharpened edge of his hunting knife never left Nathaniel's throat.

The short man slung Emily to the ground. "Let's see what you've got under that dress." He jerked her skirt all the way up, exposing her underwear. Emily squirmed to get away.

"Damn! You've got the lumpiest bottom I've ever seen on a lady. What the hell? Let me look at you." He pulled her underwear down several inches. "Why, you ain't lumpy at all. We've hit the jackpot, fellows. This here lady's underwear is full of greenbacks. United States banknotes. Lots of them."

"How much?" the third man asked.

"Plenty enough so's we can get these gray threads off us and go up North where it'll be safe. We'll count it later. Right now we're going to have some fun."

He used both his hands to tug at her underwear, so he left her hands free. She beat on his head and shoulders, but the man ignored the blows as if her fists were made of cotton. Desperate, she grabbed his beard with both hands and jerked as hard as she could.

"Damn!" the man yelled. "Quit that." He grabbed her wrists and squeezed so hard she had to let go. "Son of a bitch, that hurt. You do that one more time, and I'll poke my knife in you."

Sitting on her legs, the man moved down toward her feet to keep his beard away from her. He started tugging on her underwear again. Emily was desperate. She leaned forward and swung her arms around with her fingers extended, as far as she could reach out. Her nails gouged into flesh. She pushed harder. The man screamed, a deep, painful scream. "MY EYE!" he shouted, his hand covering his left eye. Blood oozed from a deep scratch that started on his temple and disappeared beneath his hand.

"You bitch! I'm going to show you." He pulled a knife from his belt and lifted his arm to plunge the blade down into Emily's chest.

"Hey," the tall man shouted. He pointed his knife toward the man on top of Emily. "Don't kill her yet. I ain't had my turn." He took a step forward, releasing Nathaniel as he did so.

"This bitch is dying right now." The short man's arm reached its peak, the blade poised to start back down.

Now free on one side, Nathaniel's hand slid into his boot and emerged in a blur. A silver flash flicked through the air as the long blade of his knife disappeared into the short man's neck. The man's small, sunken eyes grew large and seemed to bulge as his body recoiled around the force of the blow. He stopped moving. He sat atop Emily with his arm raised, a blade in his hand and Nathaniel's blade sunk deep in his neck, as though frozen in that position. Three seconds later the knife in his hand slipped through his fingers and fell harmlessly to the ground. He tumbled over onto Emily, his blood splashing on her dress. She pushed him to the side as she started crying and reaching down to pull her underwear back up.

Without waiting to see if his knife had found its target, Nathaniel swung his free fist and caught the soldier with the pot belly hard on the jaw. The man staggered back, releasing Nathaniel as he fell to the ground. The tall soldier turned back around and lunged toward Nathaniel with his knife. Nathaniel was unarmed, but he was too quick and too strong. His arm flashed out and his large hand covered the other man's hand on the knife handle. He folded the tall man's arm around, forcing the blade deep into the man's belly. The tall man's eyes grew large as Nathaniel, his hand still covering the soldier's hand, jerked the knife out and stabbed again in one smooth motion. He made a third quick thrust of the blade. The tall man's eyes held a bewildered look as his body collapsed to the ground.

When he fell, the knife came out of their hands and bounced on the trail. It never came to rest before it was in Nathaniel's hand. The man with the pot belly had gotten to his feet, but instead of lashing out, he held his arms up in surrender. Emily, her underwear up and her blood-soaked dress down, was trying to stand.

Reaching out with a quick flick of his wrist, Nathaniel swiped the blade across the third man's throat. A stream of blood squirted out. He convulsed once then slumped to the ground in a bloody heap.

Nathaniel turned to Emily and asked, "Are you all right?"

"Why did you kill him? He was giving up."

"I was keeping my promise to your father."

"You did *not* promise my father you would kill somebody who was holding his arms up in surrender."

"No. I promised your father I would protect you. This man was a deserter, desperate. He had nothing to lose. He knew about the money you are carrying. If I had let him live, nothing would have stopped him from coming after you. And me. He would have found us and slit our throats in our sleep. I had no choice."

She stared down at the man's body then glanced at the other two corpses. She looked up at the slice of blue sky between the trees right and left. Looking back at Nathaniel, she said, "Okay. We move ahead. We have to get to Caleb."

"First, we have to bury them," Nathaniel said as he jerked his knife out of the first man's neck. He cleaned the blade on the man's clothes then said, "As long as they're missing, the army won't waste time on a search. Too many deserters and too many missing in action. They write it down in their records and move on to the next battle. But if they find bodies, someone might come looking for the killers. Unlikely, but better to leave no evidence. The horse can run free. The saddle and muskets and everything else will have to be buried with them."

"It will take a lot of time to bury them."

Nathaniel slid his knife back into his boot then looked up at Emily and said, "One shallow grave. We need to keep the bodies hidden for only a week or two. We don't care after that."

October 4, 1864 ~ Belle Plains, Virginia

"Union soldiers ahead," Nathaniel said. "We have to be careful. Our passes are from the Confederacy. They may not take kindly to us crossing into the territory they are controlling."

"Why not?" Emily asked.

"Spies," Nathaniel shrugged, as though it should be obvious. "They might think General Winder sent us here to gather information."

"What nonsense. Everybody knows the Yankees control Belle Plains. There's nothing we can tell General Winder that he doesn't already know. As if he could do anything about it if he did know." Nathaniel stared at Emily in silence, his brows furrowed in a frown. "I learned from Aunt Millie. We ride in like it's our camp. Pretend we're in charge, and they have to answer to us."

"Fine," he said.

Two soldiers on horseback were riding along the rutted trail, coming toward them. The soldiers tipped their blue hats in greeting then disappeared behind them. Nathaniel could feel their eyes on his back, but, for a change, he did not turn to look. Appearing nervous or worried would not be wise.

"See," Emily said in triumph.

Nathaniel grunted.

Passing the sentry, however, was not so easy. He said, "This is a Confederate travel pass, ma'am." He looked at her as though she were crazy.

"Of course it's a Confederate pass. There is no Union office in Richmond."

"Yes, ma'am, but you can't enter a Union military camp with Rebel paperwork. Why, I'd get discharged if I let you through."

"Then give me a Union pass."

"Ah, I can't give out passes. I'm only a guard. And I can't let you in. I've got to follow orders."

Emily slid down from her horse and walked over to the sentry and stood practically toe-to-toe with him. She put every bit of force she could muster into making a stern face and, speaking slowly and clearly, said, "I am here on important business. If you cannot give me a pass, then find someone who can. Now! Otherwise, when I am finished with your commander, and I *will* speak to him, I will have him demote you and place you on permanent latrine duty. Do you understand me?"

The sentry looked about nervously. "Ah, yes, ma'am." He glanced behind him. "I'll get the Lieutenant. He's over there." He pointed at three soldiers walking toward the rows of white tents that were some distance away. Putting his hand to his mouth, he shouted, "Lieutenant Grier, Sir."

As the officer turned around, the sentry motioned for him to come to the gate.

All three of the soldiers walked over.

"What is the matter, Private?"

"This lady wants to talk to the commander, but all she has is a Confederate travel pass. I told her I couldn't let her through, but she insists."

"Hmmm," Lieutenant Grier said as he quickly looked Emily over then glanced at Nathaniel. "Mind your post, Private. I'll take care of it." He turned back to Emily and said, "Please follow us. We'll walk into the camp a short distance."

Nathaniel dismounted, and introductions were made then they led their horses as they walked alongside the Lieutenant. The other two Union soldiers lagged slightly behind. The Lieutenant asked, "What is your business with the commander? He's quite busy at the moment. It would be difficult to see him, particularly with a Confederate pass. Perhaps I can help?"

"I would be most grateful if you would," Emily said. "I must find a Confederate prisoner who was brought to this area; to a place they call the 'Punch Bowl.'"

"A prisoner? Miss Rose, the Punch Bowl is a temporary holding area. Captured Confederates do not stay here. I am afraid I would have no idea about a particular soldier."

"Yes, I understand that this is a temporary facility. But you have records, don't you? You must know something that would help me. His name is Caleb Garner."

The Lieutenant got a concerned look on his face then shook his head slightly as he said, "Ma'am, we've had thousands of prisoners through here. I don't even see all their names, much less remember them. When they're transferred to somewhere else, the records are sent to headquarters. The only records we hold are the prisoners we currently have, but there's very few of them at the moment."

"Oh?"

"Yes, ma'am. You see, we're only a transfer point. We keep prisoners here until they can be loaded on ships and sent elsewhere. Mostly downriver to Point Lookout, on the other side of the bay." Lieutenant Grier pointed vaguely to the southeast, toward where the mouth of the Potomac River emptied into the Atlantic Ocean, some sixty or so miles away. "If he came here recently, we might have a record of it."

"He was captured in May."

The Lieutenant shook his head quickly. "No, ma'am. We wouldn't know. Those records are long gone. I would guess that he's at Point Lookout." Then he turned to one of the soldiers behind him and said, "This is Sergeant Major James Ross. He was here in May, but I doubt he would remember an individual soldier."

The Sergeant nodded and said, "Pleased to make your acquaintance, ma'am. I talked to a lot of the prisoners, but there were thousands of them back in the spring. I would help if I could."

"Anything you could tell me would be appreciated," Emily said.

"What did you say his name was?"

"Caleb Garner."

"Hmmm. That sounds vaguely familiar, but I can't place it. Where's he from?"

"Alabama. Conecuh County."

"Conecuh?" His face wrinkled in thought. "That's sounds familiar. Very familiar." He stared into the distance a moment before smiling and saying, "Oh, yes! I remember. A young man from Conecuh County, Alabama. Seemed like a nice enough fellow. Are you a friend of Conecuh's?"

"Conecuh's?"

"That's what I called him. There are so many Calebs. Conecuh was easier to remember."

Emily took a deep breath. "You saw him? How is he? Is he okay?"

"Ah," Ross started. He hesitated a second before continuing. "He's okay. But, well, he was wounded in the knee. It was pretty bad, I'm afraid. He had trouble walking and had to use a limb to help him get around."

"Oh, no." With the thought of Caleb being wounded, her heart pounded hard in her chest as her hand went to her mouth. In the next second, she realized that 'wounded' meant 'still alive.' She pulled her hand away from her lips and said, "He's alive! What else can you tell me? He's not sick, is he?"

"He was doing well enough when he left," Ross said. There was no need to bring up the infection in Caleb's wound. It would only stress this beautiful young lady. "It's been some time. If he's still ali… ah, I mean he's at Point Lookout. That's where he was sent."

Emily's eyes widened. "I must get there right away!"

"To Point Lookout?" Lieutenant Grier asked. "I seriously doubt they would allow prisoners of war to have family visitors."

"I'm not his family. Not yet, anyway. But I don't want to visit him. I want to buy his freedom. I want to take him home."

Nathaniel's head popped back slightly. He realized Emily's words implied that they were traveling with cash. He frowned at Emily but could only see the back of her head. There was nothing he could do. The words were spoken. They had to trust in the nature of these Union soldiers.

"Buy his freedom?" Sergeant Major Ross said, looking at Emily as though she had gone crazy.

"I'm afraid there isn't a procedure for that," Lieutenant Grier said. "I don't believe you can purchase freedom for a prisoner of war. In fact, General Grant was adamant about no longer even exchanging prisoners."

Emily's heart sank. "There must be some way," she pleaded. "I know it's been done before."

Lieutenant Grier could not bear the crushed look on Emily's face. "I've never personally heard of it, but that doesn't mean it hasn't happened. Sergeant Major Ross has been here much longer than I have. Perhaps he has heard of this before."

"I don't recall ever hearing anything to that effect," Ross said. "But Confederate soldiers are not here long enough for something like that to happen. Maybe it can be done at Point Lookout." He shrugged.

"Don't worry. I'll do it. I must."

"Good luck," Ross said. He hesitated a moment before continuing. "I would like to be of further assistance, but I must be leaving. I have been transferred to Pensacola, Florida, to Colonel Spurling's command. I was taking my leave with Lieutenant Grier. My ship is at the dock now. Please, if you find Conecuh, give him my regards."

"Of course," Emily said. "I will find him. I've heard too many stories about the prisons on both sides of this war. I have to get him out so he will be safe. How do we get to Point Lookout?"

"By boat," Lieutenant Grier said. "Just down at the docks there. You won't be able to take your horses with you, however, but you won't need them. You cannot ride up the peninsula into Maryland, not through the prison compound."

"They will have to come back to the landing here on the return trip," James Ross said. "Perhaps they could entrust their horses to the Union army while they're gone?"

"Of course," Grier said. "Leave them with the landing commander. You can pick them up when you get back. While you are making arrangements for your horses, I'll write a letter of introduction you can use to get passage on a Union supply ship. Ross, since you are on your way to the landing, perhaps they can ride along with you. Tell the landing commander to keep their horses safe per my instructions. I'll have a runner bring the letter down in a few minutes."

"Of course," Ross said. "Follow me."

They remounted and rode out of camp with Emily beside Sergeant Major Ross and Nathaniel lagging a step or two behind. "With the war going on, it is dangerous to travel. Are you armed?"

"No," Emily said. "There were times on this trip when a weapon would have been welcome, but I have no experience with them. Nathaniel is a slave. He is not allowed to carry a firearm. He knows how to use them, though. My father taught him. They used to go on hunting trips together back on our farm."

"Here," Ross said as he pulled a small leather pouch out of his inside jacket pocket. He pulled a derringer out of the pouch and held it up. "This is mine personally. I'm not sure why I brought it. I don't need it. I use this." He patted the pistol strapped to his side. "I've only fired the derringer a few times for fun. You are welcome to it. There are eleven balls left in the pouch, along with everything else you need for reloading." He held the pouch out for Emily.

"I-I wouldn't know what to do with it."

Ross turned to Nathaniel and asked, "Do you know how these small guns work? If not, I can give the two of you a quick lesson. It's very similar to a musket."

"Yes," Nathaniel said. "I have experience with different types of firearms. I can show her what to do."

"Very good. Here, then. Take it."

"But it's yours…" Emily began to protest.

Ross waved her words off. "It gets in my way, and you are in need of it. Now, there are two barrels, one over the other. If you have to shoot someone, use both. The balls are small. If you shoot a big man one time, it might do little more than make him mad. You'll need to shoot twice to bring him down. But you must shoot at close range. The accuracy of a derringer leaves something to be desired."

October 5, 1864 ~ Barracks Number Three, Elmira, New York

"Stinks out here," Caleb said as he coughed against his arm, which was only partially covered by the sleeve of his tattered jacket. Exposed skin peeked through the holes and ragged shreds of cloth. It was cold in New York for this time of year. Caleb hugged himself as he walked along. "The smell is so awful it's got me clogged up and coughing."

"Me, too," Charles said as he coughed into his cupped hands, using the coughed breath to warm them. He rubbed his hands together then pressed them down into his pants.

"You've been coughing for more than a week," Caleb said to Charles. "It may be something besides the smell. You need to go see one of those Yankee sawbones."

"Naw. If I go see one of those blue butchers, I'll come out with a twelve inch incision in my back and a cough that's worse than ever."

Caleb laughed. "Maybe we should get out of the cold. Smell's better inside. A little."

"I don't know. Being out here is better than being cooped up inside those barracks all the time. The stink sinks into the walls on the inside. Out here we can get a breath of fresh air when the wind is a'blowin' the right way."

"It ain't blowing where it ought to be blowing today. This is about as bad as the stink's been since we got here."

"It's that damned pond," Charles said as he pointed toward the back wall of the compound. "Just outside there. What they call Foster's Pond. Any fool can see it don't flow proper. We take leave of ourselves, and it goes right into that pond and nowhere else. Stays right there. It wouldn't be so bad if there wasn't so many of us. There's twicet as many prisoners as there ought to be in this place. Maybe three times. That's a lot of slop jarring for one little pond. Why, I bet there's catfish in there bigger than me."

"Catfish? Up North?"

"Oh, sure. People in the North take leave of themselves like we do. The catfish love it. They eat all sorts of bad stuff. When you think about all the bad things a catfish eats, well, it don't make sense why they taste so good."

Caleb grunted. He took another step and stumbled. While the ground was well trampled, there were lumps here and there where muddy footprints had dried. Charles reached out to catch him, but Caleb had already caught himself.

"You're walking better since that Yankee doctor fixed your leg up."

Caleb coughed and said, "I don't walk near as good as I read nowadays, but, thank the Lord, I can stretch and bend my leg without feeling like there's a torch a'burning inside."

"If you start walking as good as you read, you'll be running races sure enough. Why, you almost read better than me."

Caleb laughed. "Not hardly. But I can read good enough, and it's thanks to you. I owe you more than I could repay, being a dirt poor farmer. I can't wait to read something for Emily. She'll be right proud of me. If she ain't married somebody else, that is."

As they rounded the corner of the barracks building, the one they slept in, they saw a small group of prisoners standing out front.

"I'm sure she's back home waiting on you," Charles said as they walked toward the other prisoners. "Women are like that. When they get that special one in their head, it don't come out easy. Men ain't that way nowhere near like the ladies. Why, she may even have written a letter to President Lincoln demanding that he let you loose."

Caleb laughed again, but the laugh was cut short by a coughing fit. Charles coughed, too, as did one of the prisoners in the small group. Another one of the prisoners said, "Well, I'll be. I knew yawns were contagious, but I didn't know coughs were."

"Must be," another one of the men said. "Damn near everybody in this God forsaken place is coughing."

"It's the stink," Caleb said. "It clogs you up."

"If that's the cause," the first speaker said, "Then it's a wonder we don't pop our heads off from coughing 'cause it stinks worse than a herd of sick mules in this place."

"It ain't the smell," another man said. "It's the exchange of invalid prisoners both sides have agreed on. Every one of us is a'coughing up a storm so's the Yankees will put us on the invalid list. The sick ones will get sent back home."

"Most of the coughing is real," a different man said. 'It's sickness. All sorts of sickness. We woke up to four men dead in our building alone this morning. All of them got the cough real bad a few weeks ago. Got worse and worse till they died."

"That's sure cheerful news," Charles said. "But I 'spect they had a different sickness. Caleb and I don't have nothing more than a little cold. It's right chilly around here for this early in the fall. Easy to catch a cold."

"You look healthy enough," the first man said. "I 'spect you're trying to get on the invalid list to go home."

"If it would help," Charles said, "I'd cough up a dust cloud. Going home would be a dream I can't even hope to have."

"Bribe one of the guards. I hear they're more than willing to say you're an invalid and put you on the exchange list if you've got a little something to barter."

"I ain't got no money," Charles said. "All I got is these rags I'm a'wearing and a small size rat I caught this morning. I don't expect the guards have much use for a rat. They get fed well."

"You better cough up a storm, then. Make them think you really are sick."

October 5, 1864 ~ Point Lookout Prison, Maryland

It had not been easy finding passage. The letter of introduction Lieutenant Grier had given them helped. Emily and Nathaniel came downriver on a small freighter carrying supplies, their horses left in the care of Union soldiers camped at Belle Plains Landing.

"We're going back as soon as we unload, Miss," Captain Anderson said as they landed on the shore. "Best be here on time. We won't be waiting for you. It takes longer going back to Belle Plains seeing as how we'll be going against the current."

"I understand," Emily said. "How long before you leave?"

"We have to unload then I've got some business to attend to. It'll take three hours, maybe four. But if I were you, I'd be back here and waiting in three hours. No more."

"Very well. Where is the prison commander's office?"

"You see these buildings off to the right, the ones arranged like the spokes of a wheel?" Captain Anderson pointed toward the large wooden buildings to the right of the docks. "That's the hospital complex. What you want is one of these buildings to the left of the hospital, the one with the flag out front. That's it right there, ma'am." Emily followed the Captain's finger and picked out the correct building. "The commander is Brigadier General James Barnes. It's doubtful you'll be able to see him. But if you ask for Barnes, you should be able to get far enough up the chain of command to find someone who could tell you what you want to know."

"Thank you, Captain Anderson. You have been most helpful. We will be back here in three hours.

As they walked across the sand, Emily pulled her coat around her. Although it was almost midday, the air was crisp, and the winds bit hard on exposed skin. They walked in silence. Nathaniel had said little since they left Belle Plains. The tall colored man was not usually given to a lot of talk, but since he had killed the three Confederate deserters, he had said practically nothing.

There was a guard on either side of the front door. One of them said, "Can I help you, ma'am?"

"Yes. I'm here to see General Barnes." Emily made a move toward the door as though she had been granted full run of the place.

The two guards glanced at each other. The one who had spoken shrugged and opened the door for Emily. "The sergeant at the desk there can help you, ma'am," the guard said. He nodded toward a soldier with three stripes on each arm, sitting at a desk and writing in a book.

"Thank you," Emily said, still acting as though she was at home and the Union soldiers were her personal servants.

"We are here to see Brigadier General James Barnes," Emily told the sergeant.

"Ah, do you have an appointment, Miss…?"

"Rose. Emily Rose. And this is Nathaniel Whiteeagle." She thought it best not to mention that Nathaniel was her domestic slave since they were in Yankee-controlled territory. "I do not have an appointment. I had no method available to me for making an appointment. We have traveled a long way and have suffered great hardship to get here. I need to see General Barnes on an urgent matter. Now."

"I appreciate the hardships you have endured, Miss Rose, but General Barnes is a busy man. You must have an appointment to see him. If you will state the purpose of your visit, I may be able to arrange a day and time for you to come back…"

"I will NOT come back," Emily said, raising her voice. She had worked hard to maintain her composure during weeks of struggling through things she should not have had to endure, but no more. This close to Caleb and she was being thwarted by rules and regulations. She would have none of it. Her frustrations boiled over. "I have three hours before I have to be back at the docks. I cannot come back another day without further hardship on top of what I have already suffered. Nathaniel and I have been traveling through a South that is virtually in flames. I will spare you the details, but we have been imprisoned, beaten, and almost killed on multiple occasions. I am not going to stand here like a polite little ninny and put up with your rubbish. I want to see General Barnes, and I want to see him now!"

She thrust her finger down on the book that the sergeant had been writing on. He backed up and stared at her, his eyes wide and his face covered with shock. He fumbled for words, "Ah… Yes, ma'am. I'll, ah, see what I can do. But I've got to have the reason for your visit. The general's staff won't even talk to me if I don't have a reason."

Nathaniel said nothing, but his eyes flickered with delight as he watched Emily's rage.

She stared at the sergeant a moment longer before answering, "You have a prisoner here. Private Caleb Garner. I wish to purchase his freedom."

"Purchase his freedom?" the sergeant repeated. He looked confused. "But, ma'am, you can't…" His words trailed off as he thought better of what he was about to say.

"Can't what?" Emily almost shouted. Her finger was still firmly pressed against the ledger on the sergeant's desk.

"Let me talk to General Barnes staff. I'll, ah, see what I can do."

Emily lifted her finger and said, "See that you do." Then she took a step back and waited for the sergeant to return.

It didn't take long. The sergeant came back into the reception area with an officer in tow, a man with a huge, bushy mustache and dark, shiny hair hanging well below his collar.

"This is Captain Daniel Carrington, Miss Rose. He is an assistant to General Barnes. He can be of service to you."

A brief smile flashed across Emily's face as she curtsied, but the smile was gone before she stood straight again. She was not in a smiling mood.

"I am afraid General Barnes is unable to see you today, Miss Rose," the captain said. Captain Carrington stood erect and talked with the soft sounds of a velvet tongue. Emily chose to ignore the implications of the Captain's words. She stared at him directly in the eyes and said nothing as he continued. "He offers his apologies, but he must attend to urgent prison business. Items that were previously arranged, of course. Could I be of assistance? I will do what I can."

"You have a prisoner of war. Private Caleb Garner. I wish to negotiate his release. I am prepared to pay a reasonable sum."

"Excuse me? Pay for a prisoner's release? Why, madam, that is highly irregular…"

"Please! Spare me your bargaining ploy. I know it's been done before many times. With that precedent established, we need only negotiate the amount. Now, if you cannot help me, I demand to speak with Brigadier General Barnes."

The smooth-talking Captain was motionless for a moment, his mouth open but no words coming out. Emily stared at him with as much venom as she could conjure into her eyes. Finally, the Captain found his tongue again. "If you do not mind waiting a few minutes, I will discuss this with General Barnes."

"We will make ourselves comfortable here."

"Of course." Captain Carrington stepped away, his walk almost as smooth as his voice.

As she waited, Emily ignored the desk sergeant and looked around at the wood structure. It was simple but functional and spacious.

Captain Carrington returned in a shorter time than she had expected, waving a piece of paper in front of him. "I'm sorry," he said, "There was no reason for me to bother General Barnes with your request."

"What? Bother him? Do the needs of a lady mean that little to the Union army? I bet President Lincoln would…"

Her words trailed off as the soft-spoken Captain broke in, "It's not that, Miss Rose, I assure you. I would do what I could, but there is nothing I can do. I looked up Caleb Garner's record. I am afraid the prisoner was transferred to the Elmira facility in New York back in August."

October 9, 1864 ~ Prison Medical Facilities, Elmira, New York

Major Sanger stepped over to the cot where Charles Pearson was sweating and coughing convulsively. Charles was a small man, but he looked tiny as he rocked back and forth from the force of his coughing. "This man will be dead soon," Sanger whispered. "I would lay odds on it. And we are forced to wait on him hand and foot until he dies. Or pulls through, but my money's on dying."

"There are plenty like him," Major Colt said, also in a whisper where the prisoners could not hear.

"Yes. And we do not have the staff to take care of them all. They need to be sent home with the prisoner exchange."

"Colonel Hoffman's order specifically states that men too sick to travel are not to be placed on the exchange list. I must say that I am not in total agreement with that sentiment."

Sanger glanced at the next cot, where Caleb lay, coughing and holding his chest. His eyes followed down the row of cots, prisoner after prisoner, all of them sick. Many were rocking back and forth, racked with coughing fits. A few were completely motionless, perhaps dead or very near it. "Hoffman is sitting at his desk in Washington without a clear vision of our situation." He hesitated a moment, looking down at a sick Confederate who seemed to be watching him, and then whispered, "Let us return to my office where we can talk more freely."

Once they were in the privacy of his office, Sanger lowered himself into the chair behind his desk as he motioned for Colt to take the visitor's chair. "Hoffman's conditions make no sense," he announced. "I understand the man was a prisoner himself, early in the war, but he seems to have forgotten the conditions that exist in a prison facility. The men who are near death are our largest burden. We need to use our resources to help the living, not the dying. What does it matter if they die here or die a few days after reaching home? I dare say that, given the choice, they would prefer to die at home than here. They likely would prefer to die in transit trying to get home than to die here."

"I must admit," Colt said. "As heartless as it might sound on the surface, I agree with you, though, perhaps, for different reasons. The sickest of these men have suffered enough. They deserve the chance to see home again. That hope alone might help them live a few days longer than they would have otherwise. And if they die in transit, well, they would also have died here."

"I understand your sentiment. But how do we do this against Hoffman's order? What about the camp commander, Colonel Tracy? And the other three officers on the selection committee?"

"Hoffman is not here. He is sitting in his pleasant office in Washington. We do what should be done then tell Hoffman we followed his orders to the letter. He'll never be the wiser. Tracy is here, of course, but he is indifferent. I regret it, but he is more concerned about the affairs of the garrison than that of the prison. He seems to care less whether prisoners die or not. As far as the committee, you need not worry about the other three officers. I will convince them if need be. I suspect it will take little effort. They will likely agree with us out of hand."

"So we are in agreement. We get the sickest of them out of here quietly and efficiently. Then we will be able to better care for the remaining prisoners, the ones who have a chance of surviving."

"Yes. Under the circumstances, I believe it to be the humane thing to do."

"I'm not sure Colonel Tracy will perceive it that way," Sanger said.

"Perhaps not. If it becomes necessary, I will discuss it with him. Better to let it lie for now. We can always claim confusion about the specifics of the orders."

There was a knock on the door.

"Come in," Sanger said.

The door opened, and a surgeon stepped into the office. "I'm sorry," he said. "I didn't mean to interrupt…"

"Quite all right," Major Colt said as he stood. "I was on the way out. We have completed our business." Colt turned back to Sanger and nodded his head and said "We are in full agreement, Major. I will discuss this with the rest of the committee." He turned and walked out of the office.

"Have a seat, Lieutenant," Sanger said as he motioned to the chair. "Can I help you?"

"It's the invalid prisoner exchange, Sir. There will be three trains, about sixty boxcars in all. They want us to provide a doctor with each train. We are understaffed now. We cannot spare three doctors."

"Then the War Department will have to provide the doctors or provide replacements for our doctors. I have already requested doctors and support staff, but have heard nothing from the application as of yet. We cannot send our doctors away without some sort of assurance that they will be replaced. If they are not, then the prisoners will have to travel without doctors."

October 11, 1864 ~ Elmira, New York

The mood in Elmira's streets was not festive as it had been with the arrival of the first trainload of Confederate prisoners back in July. The ragged, sick, skeletal men who walked down Elmira's streets were to be pitied. There were one thousand two hundred sixty-four prisoners, though no one in the crowd cared to count them. Most walked in one fashion or another, many leaning on each other for strength. About three hundred of them, too sick to walk, had to be carried in carts. Their eyes held no luster. For many of them, their hearts held only a vague hope of reaching home before they died.

A few ladies rushed out from the sidewalks to give paper-wrapped sandwiches to the worst of the prisoners. Or to the ones who still had enough meat on their bones to look halfway handsome. Otherwise, it was a sad, slow procession.

Caleb walked. Even though his limp was still pronounced, he refused to ride. He wanted to walk out of Hellmira. He didn't give a damn if any of the residents made fun of his awkward gait.

Charles Pearson was in a wagon. He could no longer stand. He was almost too sick to talk, so Caleb said little as he walked beside the wagon.

A young lady ran out from the side and handed Caleb a sandwich. "For you and your friend," she said as she nodded at the wagon Charles was riding in. She smiled at Caleb as he took the sandwich. The smile quickly turned to tears as she whirled around and ran back to the sidewalk.

Caleb opened the wrapping. It looked like beef. He wasn't sure, but it didn't matter. It was food. The sandwich was cut into halves, so he leaned over the wagon and held one of the halves to Charles' mouth. Charles was too sick to hold it on his own, but he tried to eat. He took two bites, chewed them as best he could then said, "That's all for now. Save it for later."

While he stuffed Charles unfinished half sandwich into his pocket with one hand, he started eating his half with his other hand. Tears began to stream down his face. He could not remember the last time he had tasted something so wonderful. It had not happened in all the years he had been in the Confederate army. And these people ate like this every day! It was all he could do to keep from bawling like a baby.

~ O ~

John Murray was not on the wall. It was not his shift. Instead, he was in town in civilian clothes, watching the sunken-in animals the South called soldiers as they made their way toward the trains. He had to know who was leaving. He had to know if Caleb was among them. The bastard was not sick enough to be called an invalid. The rules were too soft. Anyone who was too sick to return to the front in sixty days was to be exchanged. So what if Caleb couldn't run, could barely walk? Murray knew by watching from the wall that Caleb's limp was getting better. He might be able to get back to the front within sixty days. He wouldn't be able to run, but these Rebels were idiots as well as animals. They'd go back to the battles and stand there and fire even if they couldn't get away when the Yankee troops overran them.

He surveyed the pathetic stream of prisoners as they walked and rode along. Looking anxiously back and forth, he checked each one of the men stumbling along in the wide street. There, a man with a limp, one hand holding onto a wagon! He recognized the limp. Murray looked closely at the man's face. He was too far away to see detail, but John Murray would recognize that face from twice as far away. Caleb! "Damn!" he said under his breath. He had to do something. He couldn't stop Caleb from leaving with the exchange, but he had to do something.

Perhaps it was time for Murray to leave Elmira. That would be easy enough. A transfer to somewhere… Where? He would have to figure that out. He would have to put himself in a position to intercept Caleb before the filthy animal made it home.

Or did it make sense? He might be jeopardizing everything to try to extract his revenge. As much as he wanted to see Caleb dead, it might not be the wise thing to do. He had to think.

October 14, 1864 ~ Washington D.C.

Because they had passed so many Union soldiers in the row upon row of defenses on the southern approach to Washington D.C., Emily was surprised to see even more soldiers throughout the city. Almost every third person on the streets wore a blue uniform. How could there be so many soldiers? No wonder the South was losing the war.

There were plenty of colored people, too. But this was different from what Emily was used to. The blacks were not accompanied by their owners. They had no owners. These were free men and women, relieved from the shackles of bondage, escaped to the safety of the North. It made her think about Nathaniel. He was still riding beside her, a step or two behind. He could ride off in a different direction, be free of slavery, and there was nothing she could do about it. Not here. But he didn't. She wondered why.

"So this is our great capital," Emily said.

"Not since Alabama seceded," Nathaniel replied.

"Oh, yes. Of course. After all we've been through, how could I forget?"

They rode another half block in silence then Emily said, "It smells better than Richmond."

"Yes, but not that much better," Nathaniel said. "Piles of garbage are everywhere. The only difference is the Washington piles are smaller than the Richmond piles."

"I wonder if the vendor carts have better food than the carts in Richmond?"

"Eat at your own risk in either place."

They knew little about Washington D.C. and had no specific destination, so they were in no hurry as they rode along. Trolley cars, carriages, government wagons, and horseback riders sped past them. It seemed as though most people in D.C. were in a big hurry to get somewhere. Men in suits, government workers of one sort or another, practically ran along the sidewalks. Even though they were on foot, they moved faster than Emily and Nathaniel. Government business was important here. Or so they appeared to think.

Just as in Richmond, there were ladies, obviously prostitutes, canvassing the men, particularly the soldiers. The only difference was the ladies in the Union capital appeared to be cleaner and better dressed. Emily was sure that was not her imagination. She could still conjure up a clear image of downtown Richmond in her mind. It was not a pretty picture.

In defense of the working ladies in Richmond, Emily realized, it was difficult to buy nice things to wear in a city under siege. Even if you had money, which few people did, elegant clothes were not available for purchase.

"It appears," Nathaniel said, "That Washington D.C. has suffered a similar fate as Richmond. The war has generated an influx of people of all types. Some, perhaps, not so desirable."

"They would consider Sparta quite backward. Our little town is a farmer's crossroads compared to Washington D.C. But Sparta is cleaner than this. And nicer. And it doesn't stink. That is, it doesn't most of the time." They rode another block before Emily said, "We need to find a place where you and I can both get a room. Just the one night. I want to be on the train to Elmira as early as possible."

"Perhaps we should ask someone for recommendations."

"Of course." She held her tongue for several seconds, then said, "Nathaniel, why…" her voice trailed off.

"Why what?"

"The colored people here are free. You could be, too. Why do you not leave me?"

"I told you. I promised your father I would protect you. I mean to see that promise through."

A half block later, Emily turned around and looked at Nathaniel and said, "Thank you." The tall black man nodded his black bowler and looked ahead as he continued riding.

The tinkle of music created on makeshift instruments wafted through the air. Up ahead, Emily could see a group of black men on the sidewalk, a short way from the far corner, playing for a growing crowd. One man was playing the harmonica. A young man, not much more than a boy, was beating on two upside-down metal pails. A third man snapped his hands back and forth making the most compelling clacking sounds. The last man plucked a string that was connected to a roughly carved wooden box with a long handle. Somehow it all worked together. "Let's stop and listen," she said. They did.

Emily edged her way through the crowd to get a better look while Nathaniel stayed some distance behind, seemingly content with looking between the heads of the people near the front. A black man stepped up to Emily and said, "How do, pretty lady."

Before she could take a breath to answer, Nathaniel had somehow negotiated the crowd and wedged between Emily and the strange black man. "I am accompanying this lady," he said.

The other man took one look at Nathaniel and began backing away. "I's just being friendly. That's all. No intent, you see."

"Of course," Nathaniel said. "By the way, we need accommodation for the night. Can you recommend a hotel?"

"Why, the Willard Hotel would be the best place for the lady. That's where all the important white folks stay. And for you, there's a colored hotel a few blocks down to the right…"

"I thought blacks were free men here," Emily said. "Does the Willard not accept black guests?"

"Lawd, mercy no. We may not be slaves no more, but we ain't white folks neither. I hear tell there's some towns up further north that treats blacks a mite better than they do here. I don't know. I ain't never been no further north than here."

"Thank you," Nathaniel said as he nodded toward the other black man. The stranger took the hint and wandered away from them.

"The Willard doesn't allow blacks even though they're free," Emily said. "It doesn't make sense. The Exchange Hotel in Montgomery was more accommodating than that."

Nathaniel raised one brow and looked hard at Emily and said, "You didn't sleep where I slept. Or eat what I ate."

Emily put her hand to her mouth but said nothing. Nathaniel had never mentioned it before.

They listened through two more songs then decided it was time to settle in for the evening.

The Willard Hotel was a first class place. Nathaniel insisted Emily should stay there. He asked the clerk for directions to the nearest colored hotel then he turned to Emily and said, "Please do not leave the hotel overnight. Unless it's on fire. The streets may be dangerous. We need to get an early start. I will be back at six in the morning if that is all right with you."

Emily said six was okay so Nathaniel nodded then left. He made arrangements for the horses at a nearby stable. The horses would need to stay in Washington while they took the train to Elmira. Then he started toward the hotel the Willard clerk had recommended.

Less than a block later, he heard someone calling, "Hey, you. Tall guy in the black bowler."

Nathaniel turned around to see a man coming up to him, the man he and Emily had talked to earlier. Nathaniel stood his ground and nodded. "Can I help you?" he asked.

"I see you must have left your lady friend at the Willard. I wants you to tell me how a black man gets with such a pretty white woman. Why, some of these white folks round here would shoot you for being with her."

"I am not her male companion," Nathaniel replied. "I am accompanying her on her travels."

"Huh? I don't understands."

"What is your name?"

"Rooster. Rooster Cain from Beaufort County, North Carolina."

"Nathaniel Whiteeagle. Conecuh County, Alabama. Why I am traveling with her is a long story, Rooster. So you were a slave in North Carolina. How did you get free?"

"I ran away from the plantation almost a year ago, made my way here. It was sure enough scary. I come right near getting caught several times. Spent a whole day in a creek once, underwater and breathing through a straw. The man who was a'chasing me decided to camp out on the bank that night, right where I was at. I couldn't sneak out without making a fuss loud enough to wake him."

"That sounds like a harrowing experience."

"Harrowing? Naw, it was a scary experience. And it was a wrinkling experience, too. When I finally got out of that creek, my skin was so wrinkled it took two days to smooth out." Rooster laughed. "Come on. Let's walk on down to the colored hotel. There's a bar nearby. We can get us a beer while you explain to me how you come to accompany such a pretty white lady."

"It's simple and straightforward," Nathaniel said as they walked along the street. "She is trying to find her fiancé. A white man, of course. He is a captured Confederate soldier. I am a slave of the family. I promised her father I would keep her safe on the trip."

"You're still a slave? Well, bless me blind, but you're in a safe place now. Why don't you leave her? You'd be a free man."

Nathaniel shrugged and said, "I gave my word."

"You gave your word to a white man? That's what you've got to do to survive. That don't count as a real obligation."

"It does to me. This family is different. They treat me like family, not like a slave. I eat my meals at the same table with them."

"With white folks? My goodness. A lot of these Yankees what's trying to set us free wouldn't do that."

"They promised me my freedom at the end of the trip. Already got the papers. They've been good to me. They've always kept their word, so I'll keep mine. Keeping my promise is important to me."

"Man, you're sure enough something. I ain't never heard no colored man talk like that. Here we are, Tater's Bar. Let's go in and have that beer. I'll buy. I gots me a job here in Washington. A regular job for good money."

October 13-14, 1864 ~ Baltimore, Maryland

Caleb and Charles watched as the surgeon made his way through the boxcar, looking at and speaking with the prisoners. He was getting closer.

"Help me sit up steady," Charles said, his voice hoarse from so much coughing. "But hold me from behind, so that Yankee doctor won't see."

"Why?" Caleb asked. "You're too sick to sit up. You need help."

"I don't want to get separated from the exchange for any reason. I want to go home. I may not have no family left, but I want to see South Carolina one more time. That's where I grew up, and I still got friends there. If they ain't all kilt in the war, that is. Besides, my cough has mostly gone away. I'm still a little weak. That's all. If they'll feed us a little better, I'll be okay after a couple of days."

"You're burning up with fever," Caleb argued. "You need to be in a hospital."

The doctor wove his way through the seated and prone prisoners, talking to them one at a time. He reached the man next to Charles, a man who was lying on the worn wood of the boxcar floor taking ragged breaths and moaning periodically.

"The fever will pass," Charles whispered. "Just hold me up but don't let him see you doing it."

Caleb did.

The doctor finished talking with the neighbor and turned to Charles. "Surgeon Campbell," he said. "I'm the medical inspector. How are you doing?"

"Well enough," Charles said. "I'd be doing better if there was more food."

"Don't worry. You will be fed before you transfer to the steamers. You have no problems? No cough? Fever? Anything else?"

"I had a cough, but I'm fine now," Charles lied. "It's gone away. But I'm still hungry."

"Wanting to eat is a good sign." Campbell turned to Caleb. "What about you? You look well enough."

"I'm okay. That main doctor up to Elmira operated on my leg, and it's getting better every day." He didn't mention his periodic coughing fits, and the fire burning in his chest.

Surgeon Campbell nodded then stepped past them, to the next man, a prisoner balled up on the floor. The man did not answer when Campbell tried to talk to him, so the doctor bent down and looked at his face then checked his pulse. The doctor stood and turned to the open door of the boxcar and said, "This man is dead! What in the hell was he doing on this train? He had to have been too sick to travel."

Caleb and Charles watched as the Yankee doctor, the red of anger growing on his face, looked around at the rest of the men in the crowded boxcar. Campbell, smartly dressed in his clean blue uniform, was in sharp contrast to the filthy, tattered clothes of the prisoners. Caleb had become so used to looking at prisoners in rags, he had forgotten how bad they looked. Compared to the doctor, however, the Confederates appeared little better than animals.

Campbell's face was blood red with anger as he jumped down from the boxcar. They could hear him outside shouting orders. He sent a rider to summon the medical director, a man he called Josiah Simpson. Then he issued orders to his staff to separate the dead and those needing emergency care.

"I told you," Charles said. "They're pulling out the sick ones. I 'spect the sickies will get left behind. I don't want to stay in Baltimore. I want to go home to South Carolina. But I'm going to have to walk onto that boat. You got to help me."

"I'll help you."

As Charles and Caleb sat in the boxcar, they couldn't help overhearing Campbell talking outside. The toll was grim. Five dead. Somewhere between fifty and a hundred were too sick to travel and in immediate danger of dying.

When Josiah Simpson arrived, they heard Campbell exclaim, "Forty hours! They were crammed into these cars in unsanitary conditions and traveled for forty hours without medical staff. There isn't a single doctor on all three trains!"

"It appears," Simpson said, "The officers and medical staff in Elmira ignored Hoffman's order not to send those too sick to travel. They emptied their hospital beds, not caring that the trip would cause deaths. Secretary Stanton will hear about this!"

The voices of the Union doctors trailed off as the two men walked away from the boxcar. After the severely ill were removed, soldiers came and herded the rest of them out of the car. Caleb struggled to keep Charles upright, trying not to be conspicuous about it. Charles was little more than dead weight, barely able to lift one leg after another. As he moved along, he mumbled something about South Carolina over and over.

With the help of two other prisoners, Caleb was able to get Charles Pearson onto the back of a wagon as a Union private watched. Caleb was worried that the soldier in blue would separate Charles because he was too sick to walk, but instead, the Union soldier told Caleb to climb into the wagon and help his friend.

After a short ride they got off the wagon and walked along the landing then boarded a steamer in the Patapsco River. "Are we going to South Carolina?" Charles asked.

"We're going to Point Lookout, first," another prisoner said.

"Point Lookout?" Charles said. He turned and stared out across the water, the pupils of his eyes narrow and distant. "We're going back for Danny. You hear that Caleb? We're going to get Danny before we go home."

Caleb said nothing.

October 22, 1864 ~ Elmira, New York

The pickings were slim. If you didn't want to pay for it, there were too many soldiers and not enough women in Elmira. But John Murray wasn't the type to give up. He still prowled the streets searching for the right kind of woman, but he did so in civilian clothes. It no longer mattered that women sometimes responded to a man in uniform. Practicality won out. There was no need for any of the ladies to know he was a soldier. If he had to force the issue a little, the uniform would prove inconvenient. News would likely get back to Major Colt, and that would be a disaster.

Regardless of his looks, he was having no success. He couldn't even keep his mind in the game.

A train crawled to a stop where the sidewalks of downtown ended, doors opening to allow passengers to exit. The train reminded him of why his thoughts were wandering. Caleb Garner had boarded a train on those same tracks and gotten away without John Murray being able to take his revenge. Not only had Murray lost his stripes, but he was also performing the worst job in the Union army now, a damned picket walking the stupid wall. And Caleb was responsible!

Murray had decided, however, that revenge was not worth going AWOL, not worth losing his pension and possibly going to prison. Make that probably going to prison. So the filthy Rebel animal was a week away from Barracks Number Three, and getting further, on his way back home to Alabama. There wasn't a damned thing Murray could do about it. He spat on the sidewalk then kicked the wood wall of the general store. The ligaments in his neck stood out as he strained his teeth together.

To top it off, Major Colt was searching for a reason to cashier him, to dishonorably discharge him and take his pension away. Damn Caleb

Garner! The Union command might as well have stuck a knife in John Murray by denying him the chance to get revenge.

The whole thing was gnawing at him, eating him from the inside out. He spat on the sidewalk again. As much as he wanted to put a bullet in that deadbeat's head, however, it wasn't worth the risks, it wasn't worth traveling around the country for weeks. Besides, he had no desire to go to a stinking Rebel hellhole like Alabama.

But if he stayed in Elmira, he knew that Caleb Garner's escape would continue to chip away at him. Since he could not get revenge, he needed something else to do, something that would occupy his mind. Walking the wall gave your mind way too much time to think about all the wrong things.

No need to ask for a transfer. Colt would say no. The man seemed to enjoy keeping Murray under his thumb. But something like that had never stopped him before. He could always forge his way into a transfer. Maybe an office job in Washington? A small bribe would get him a blank transfer form. He could be at his next assignment before Colt ever realized he was gone. A cushy job in Washington would be nice. Maybe he could win his stripes back. Why not? He could always forge a letter of recommendation to go along with the transfer.

Still, there was the matter of Caleb. Transferring to Washington wouldn't do anything about that. The stinking animal deserved nothing less than death, an end to his miserable little backwoods life. Murray would gladly oblige if he could. He couldn't. Caleb was on a steamer by now, on his way to freedom. If he weren't, he would be soon. Murray gritted his teeth and seethed as the same old thoughts rolled through his mind again and again. He burned deep inside. He spat on the sidewalk then kicked the wood wall until his toes hurt.

When he looked up, he did a double take. Stepping down from the train that had arrived moments earlier was one of the most beautiful young ladies he had ever seen. She was not just pretty or attractive or cute. This woman was a classic, stunning, the kind of woman he had always dreamed of having beneath him. This was what he needed! This would make him forget about Caleb.

After a few minutes watching her, it was apparent she was not traveling alone. She was walking beside a tall colored man, talking with him as they moved along the Elmira sidewalk, coming in Murray's direction. That would make things more difficult. It would have been better if she had been alone.

This far north, it was possible that a white woman and a colored man were a couple, but doubtful. That type of thing was frowned upon, gossiped about, even in the liberal state of New York. Besides, the way he carried her bags and lagged slightly behind spoke of servitude. The colored man must have been in her hire, there to wait on her. And, perhaps, to protect her. He looked more than strong enough to perform that role.

Then another thought passed through Murray's mind. She must have been well to do if she could afford a servant. Perhaps she was better than well to do, perhaps downright wealthy. That could prove to be rewarding if he could only figure out how to take advantage of her. In spite of his bitterness about Caleb, a smile crept onto John Murray's face.

The pair walked straight toward where he was standing. He turned away and stared into the street as they passed by. Good. They were so busy talking and looking around at Elmira they hadn't noticed him. He fell in behind, trying to look like another person in the crowd as he listened to their conversation.

"After all the time this trip has taken and after everything we've been through," the woman was saying, "I can't believe we're this close."

"The trip has been far beyond what we expected," the black man agreed. "But we still have to negotiate his release with the prison's commander. We do not know if that is possible. It may prove to be quite difficult."

The lady glanced at her servant. "We can't fail now," she said. "The road has been too hard and too long. We just can't fail."

The black man nodded but did not reply.

They were Southerners, their accents easily giving them away. Trying to get a prisoner released? That was a joke. The camp commander wouldn't even discuss something of that nature. Unless… Murray had a sudden revelation. Most Union officers were sensible men. Perhaps one of those bags held more than clothes. A large sum of money? It had to be. They must have been carrying a lot of cash with them if they expected to get a prisoner released! For the right price, almost anything could be done. Murray's interest continued to grow.

"Do we have to go to the hotel?" the woman asked. "I want to talk to the commander now."

"We will need a place to stay. Even if we succeed, the earliest train we could catch to go home would be tomorrow morning."

"Yes, but I want to go see the commander, walk right up to him and demand that he release Caleb Garner this instant!"

John Murray stumbled and almost fell, causing the colored man to whip his head around to look. Murray turned as fast as he could rotate, to keep the colored man from seeing his face. With his back toward them, he froze. Because of the shock, it would be several moments before he could trust his legs to walk.

They were here to try to obtain Caleb's release? Apparently, they had no knowledge of the fact that Caleb Garner was in the prisoner exchange, already on his way to freedom.

Who was this woman? A sister? A friend? A wife? Fiancée? Murray had to find out, but the one thing he knew for sure was how good this woman would look with her clothes off while he pinned her to the ground and made her pay for Caleb's mistakes. But how? He needed a plan.

He watched as they stepped into a hotel. Based on the way the woman had been talking, they would go to the prison commander's office this afternoon. They would not wait until tomorrow. He decided to retreat a short distance, in the opposite direction from the garrison, and wait for them. There had to be a way to take advantage of this.

Peeking in through the edge of the front window of the hotel, Murray watched as they registered and disappeared, going to their rooms. He waited.

Less than an hour later, they walked out and turned in the direction he suspected. Since he knew where they were going, he could afford to stay a significant distance behind. They would have no idea he was following.

A plan of action was proving to be more difficult. What could Murray do? The colored man was big and strong and in the way. It was apparent the lady went nowhere without him. If he were going to have his way with this beautiful woman, in all likelihood the colored man would have to die.

Murray waited outside the command building, some distance away, trying not to look conspicuous. If he didn't blend in, the guards might notice him. As it turned out, however, it wasn't a problem. The woman and her black servant left the building soon after arriving. They were not inside long enough for the guards to get suspicious.

Murray had no idea whether they had been able to talk with Colonel Tracy directly, but it was doubtful as they were only inside for a few meager minutes. There was no question they found out that Caleb was no longer in Elmira. Tears streamed down the woman's beautiful face, her cheeks flushed and red. She could have been family, but he saw no family resemblance. Murray suspected she was either Caleb's wife or fiancé. *How in the world could a backwoods farmer get a woman like her?* he wondered.

As they walked back to the hotel, Murray once again fell in behind, closer this time so he could overhear what was being said. But they said little, nothing of significance. When they stepped into a restaurant, he followed, making sure he sat close enough to overhear their conversation. While the pair ordered a late lunch, he ordered only coffee and, with his back to them but his ears listening, pretended to be wrapped up in his own thoughts.

"I have such mixed emotions," the woman said. "I am happy he is going to be exchanged, but this trip, this disastrous trip, has taken so much out of me. I thought I would find him, put my arms around him and hold him close to me. But, once again, he has been ripped away."

"We can take the train back to Baltimore," the black man said. "There should be a ship that could take us…"

"No, Nathaniel. No, I'll not follow any further. I could not bear for him to be snatched away from me again if something else were to happen. Thank God he is on his way home. I'll go home and wait for him there. I'm sure my mother and father need me. I miss them so. I can't wait to see them again."

"I understand," Nathaniel said. "We will go home, then."

"*I* will go home. It's time for you to pull that letter out of your jacket lining. You are a free man, Nathaniel Whiteeagle."

The black man stared at the woman, his mouth open but momentarily saying nothing.

So the servant was a slave. That made sense, the way he always walked slightly behind, always deferred to the woman. Murray committed his name, Nathaniel Whiteeagle, to memory. It was an easy name to remember.

"But I promised your father…"

"No buts. You are free now. Thomas would want it so. After all, he wrote the letter you carry." The woman moved her arm around in a circle. "What about this place? Elmira, New York? It seems as good a place as any."

"Too cold here. Besides, I should see you safely back to Richmond, to your Aunt Millie's."

"To see Carolina again?"

Nathaniel's face was blank for a moment then a smile crept onto his lips, the first smile Emily had ever seen beyond the twinkle in his eyes. "Was I that obvious?"

"Yes. And so was she. Here's what we'll do. Let's go back to Washington. Since we didn't have to buy Caleb's freedom, we've got plenty of money to get you settled in somewhere."

Murray's ears perked up a notch. *Plenty of money!* His suspicions were true. They were traveling with a large sum of cash.

"I can stay at the Willard while we get you settled in somewhere suitable. It shouldn't take more than a week. Maybe not that long. Oh, we need to find you a job, too. That shouldn't be too hard. Washington is a busy place.

"Once we're done, I'll go back to Richmond. I'm sure I can talk Aunt Millie into freeing Carolina. She was talking about it when we were there, about freeing all her slaves. We'll find a way to get Carolina out of

Richmond and on to Washington. Since you'll have a place, I can tell her where to find you."

Nathaniel lifted his coffee cup and sipped, staring into space and thinking. Then he lowered his cup and said, "Washington it is. We'll catch the first train in the morning."

Murray knew all he needed to know. Before they finished their lunch, he drained his coffee and left. Knowing Nathaniel Whiteeagle's name, it was an easy task to get the clerk to tell him the lady's name was Emily Rose. He repeated her name over and over in his head. They would be in Washington for days. It would be a simple task to find her at the Willard, to watch her from a safe distance. He wanted this woman's money. *And* her, if he could, but the money came first. Revenge alone had not been enough to make him chase after Caleb, but things were different now. This was reason enough to fake a transfer and make his way to Washington. The skeleton of a plan germinated in his head.

October 22, 1864 ~ Point Lookout Prison, Maryland

"I never thought I'd be back in this hellhole," Charles Pearson said as they gazed out at Point Lookout from the railing of the steamer that had carried them down from Baltimore.

"It's only for a short while," Caleb said. "The guards told us while you was sleeping. They've got to get all the rest of us together. There's people coming from other prisons, mostly Point Lookout. He said there was over three thousand of us being exchanged. When they get us all together and get the ships provisioned, they'll steam us on down to Savannah."

"That's good to know," Charles said. "As long as it's not a trick to get us to go ashore peaceful so they can stick us back in those tents and watch us chase rats again."

"How else are we gonna go besides peaceful?" Jimmy, a bony-looking prisoner from Tennessee, said. Jimmy was one of the prisoners helping Caleb hold Charles upright when they walked. "They don't need to trick us. We're not much more than ghosts. We ain't got the strength to argue none, let alone fight back. If they say to get off the boat and chase rats, we have no choice but to get off and chase rats."

"True enough," Charles said. He went into one of his coughing fits, which had become more and more common as the trip drug on. The respite in Baltimore had been a short one. "Help me up," he said, his words strained through his coughs. Caleb gripped Charles' shoulder on one side, and Jimmy took the other, keeping him upright. His voice hoarse and weak, Charles said, "Y'all got to help me to stay standing. Else they might leave me here. I don't want to die in this place. Too many ghosts here already. I want to die at home in South Carolina."

"Don't you worry none," Caleb said. "When you get to South Carolina, you'll be a new man. It'll make you well again. Meantime, I'll keep you standing. And I'll make sure the guards don't notice. Jimmy, here, is going to help. We'll have one of us on each side, and we'll keep you standing. They've got us so crowded together, the guards won't see no difference."

When the landing board was extended to the dock, the Confederate prisoners trudged as best they could down to the sands of Point Lookout where they were gathered together and herded toward the prison area. Those who were unable to walk were carried. Except for Charles. With Caleb and Jimmy at his sides, he stepped as best he could. Without them, he would have fallen to his face within a few paces.

"They fed us decent in Baltimore," Charles said as Caleb and Jimmy moved him along. "I don't 'spect they'll feed us none too well in this place. They didn't before."

"Maybe. Maybe not," Jimmy said. "Since we're on our way to exchange, they might try to fatten us up a little, make us look more like normal. If we go back looking like walking skeletons, it'll be the devil for them in all the editorials."

"They may not give a damn how we look," Charles said. "They might think that if we look real bad when we get home, it will frighten others away from joining the Confederate army."

"Hell," Jimmy said, "There ain't nobody left to join. Every man of any reasonable age is in the army. Or was in the army. Now they're either dead, wounded too bad to fight, in a Yankee prison, or run off out west. There ain't no men left."

"I don't think they care about the newspapers," Caleb said, "They'll feed us barely enough to keep us alive for the exchange, so's they can get their own boys back."

"That'll have to do," Charles said. "The folks down South will feed us when we get home. I can't wait to get back around a friend's table and dig into chicken and squash and lima beans and cornbread. Real cornbread. Not that mess the army fed us. I'm going to eat till I throw up. Then I'll eat some more."

"You've been in prison too long," Jimmy said.

Charles had another coughing fit. When he finished and caught his breath, he asked, "What do you mean I been in prison too long?"

"It don't sound like you're getting any news from home. There ain't gonna be no table with food all over it like you're thinking. The Yankees are squeezing us dry. They've got us blockaded. They're tearing up the train tracks. They're raiding here and raiding there. What little food there is ain't getting where it needs to get. What those bastards are doing is working. The whole South is starving."

October 27, 1864 ~ Barracks Number Three, Elmira, New York

Private Wilson slunk around the corner. He looked at Murray briefly then glanced behind himself. Sweat beaded on his forehead. His eyes held only fear and apprehension. The man was nervous and scared, a risk. Murray didn't like having to deal with him, but Thomas Wilson's gambling debts made him an easy target. If he were calmer, less prone to showing his stress, he would do better at gambling. But that was not Murray's problem. He needed what Wilson could get him.

"You took too damned long," Murray said. It had been four days since Emily Rose left with Nathaniel. John Murray was concerned that Emily might leave Washington before he could get there. It would take yet another day to carefully forge the forms and get out of town.

"Don't bellyache to me," Private Wilson said. "You're lucky you got this stuff at all. I work in medical, not HQ."

"What are you talking about? You're a courier. You spend as much time in HQ as you do anywhere."

"Maybe, but it's not easy getting into their supplies."

"Why not? Hell, you're practically a big bug!"

"What do mean, big bug? I'm still a private and get treated worse. I have to toe the mark like everybody else. The transfer form was hard enough to get, but pumpkin rinds and chicken guts? I took a big chance lifting these." Private Wilson rattled the shiny gold lieutenant's bars in one hand while he held the officer's gold braid in the other. "Hell, you're not paying me enough for what I went through. I almost got caught."

"I'm paying you plenty. And I paid you to get these to me two days ago."

"I can always take them back."

"The hell you say. Give them to me."

"You're a hard case, Murray, but you're not getting these till the rest of the greenbacks are in my hand."

Murray pulled the crisp United States Notes out of his pocket and slapped them down onto Private Wilson's outstretched palm. Thomas Wilson made a show of counting the money then handed the form, bars, and braided insignia to Murray. “Peacock about all you want,” Thomas said, “But don’t get caught. The army doesn’t take lightly to impersonating an officer.”

“What’s it to you? You got a problem with me being an officer?”

“Hell, I don’t give a damn if you make yourself general of the whole damned army. But don’t get caught. If you do, you better not mention my name. Otherwise, you’re a dead man.”

“Don’t threaten me, jackass. If it weren’t for my money, you’d be the dead man when you couldn’t pay off your losses. I’m too smart to get caught. You need to worry about yourself. With me gone, I won’t need anything from you. How are you going to pay off your gambling debts then, eh?”

Wilson did not reply. He stared at Murray for several seconds then stuffed the money into his pocket, turned around, and hurried away, looking carefully side-to-side as he went.

“Idiot,” Murray mumbled to himself. He tumbled the pumpkin rinds, the lieutenant’s bars, in his hands then looked at the neat, even stitching of the chicken guts, the officer’s gold braid. Impressive work. The bars looked good, too. They would look even more impressive on his shoulders, but as much as he would have liked a promotion, it would not happen now. Nor would it happen in Washington. As a fresh transferee to the War Department, he would need to show up as a private. That would make him less noticeable, allow him to blend in better. The pumpkin rinds and chicken guts? A precaution only. For emergencies. Maybe somewhere down the road. Maybe never. Who knows where this would end up? Or what he would need to be before it was over?

November 1, 1864 ~ Apartment Building in Washington D.C.

The lady gave a funny look and shook her head slightly. "I'm sorry, miss. We don't have no rooms for rent here. We're full up right now."

"Do you know where we might find a reasonable apartment for Mr. Whiteeagle?" Emily asked.

The lady looked at the black man then back at the young white woman and shook her head as she backed up and closed the door without another word.

"You'd think we were still in slave country," Emily remarked under her breath as they walked away. Then, louder, she said, "Where do all the freed slaves stay? We've walked to ten buildings today alone. It's the same story as yesterday. There's not a room available anywhere."

"They have to stay somewhere. Sooner or later we're bound to find a place with an available apartment."

"Not today," Emily said. "My feet are killing me. I'll do good to walk back to the hotel. We need help, someone who lives here and knows what's available, where everything is."

Nathaniel stopped and snapped his fingers. "I know who. And I know where we can find him."

"Who? And where?"

"Tater's Bar. A man named Rooster."

"Rooster? Oh, yes. I remember you telling me about running into him. That's a marvelous idea. It's early afternoon yet. Let's go to our hotels and rest. I need to get off my feet for a while, but I can meet you later."

November 1, 1864 ~ War Department and Willard Hotel, Washington D.C.

"I do not understand," the clerk said. "I have no record of a transferee coming in from Elmira. We should have received a letter of notification first."

"I don't understand why you haven't been notified," John Murray said. "My transfer paperwork is clear enough, signed by Colonel Tracy himself. Why, you should have a letter on file. It would be a simple matter to verify his signature."

"Of course," the clerk said. "Let me discuss this with Secretary Stanton's office. Please wait here. I'll be back in a few minutes."

The clerk stood and walked down the hall. While he waited, Murray looked on the clerk's desk. There was a letter from Secretary Stanton himself, signed in his hand. Having Stanton's signature might prove worthwhile, but he couldn't afford to take the letter. It would be missed quickly. He might not even get out of the building with it.

There was no time to waste. The clerk could come back any moment. Murray glanced around the desk. Besides the letter and a leather-bound register, a quill pen and bottle of ink rested on top. To the right, there was a waist-high open-shelf case. One of the openings had a small stack of blank paper. It was unlikely that one sheet would be missed.

He did not want to move Stanton's letter. No need to raise any unnecessary suspicions by knocking anything out of place. So he took the blank sheet of paper and placed it on the desk beside the letter. He memorized the position of the pen, then picked it up and dipped it in the ink well. As quickly but as carefully as he could, he starting recreating Secretary Stanton's signature. If he could finish, it would be identical. John Murray had the eye. But quality forgery took time. It could not be rushed.

He listened for boot steps and glanced at the hallway several times as he worked. This copy would be his template for whatever he might need in the future if he could just get it done in time.

He heard a door open and the pounding of hurried steps. The clerk! He had yet to finish the 'on' at the end of Stanton's name. Placing the pen back exactly where it had been, he stared at the two letters and committed them to memory as he folded his copy and stuffed it into his jacket. There was no time to step back around to the visitor's side of the desk.

The clerk entered the room and stopped in his tracks. "What are you doing behind my desk?" he demanded.

"Looking out the window. I'm just amazed at how big Washington D.C. is. I'm from the country. I've never seen a city this large."

The clerk shrugged and said, "After a while in this place, you'll wish you were back in the country."

"Hmm," Murray grunted. He looked away from the window and casually walked back to the other side of the desk.

The clerk held out the forged transfer form and said, "Your transfer paperwork is proper. But there's a problem. Secretary Stanton's office has no knowledge of your transfer. It was not requested and not needed. Based on your military history, they said they cannot use your services here. I'm afraid this is some sort of mistake."

"You mean… How could there be a mistake? I came all the way from Elmira, New York."

"And it appears you will need to go all the way back. This whole thing is some sort of misunderstanding. You are not needed here. Stanton's office is preparing the order for you to be reinstated with your unit in Elmira. Please wait in the lobby. A runner will bring the order to you shortly. Once you have it, you may go."

This was perfect. Murray had not anticipated the transfer being refused, but it left him free to do as he pleased in Washington, no military job to waste his time. If he was a little late getting back to Elmira, that was okay. It was the first of November. It would be easy enough to change the one on the reinstatement order to a later day in the month.

The wait for his return paperwork was short. Since he was in no great hurry to get back to Elmira, he had time to take care of things. First, the money. Money always came first. Second, the girl. He wanted, needed, to find out if she was as good as she looked. Third would have been putting a bullet in Caleb Garner's head, but it was not worth a trip all the way to Alabama. So third would have to be going back to Elmira to finish his enlistment. Not that he wanted to spend more time on the wall, but the war was drawing to a close, and his pension, eight dollars a month, was at stake.

He left the War Department and, after changing back to civilian clothes, walked toward the Willard Hotel. He had talked to a Willard registration clerk that morning and verified that Emily Rose was still registered. She was bound to go through the front door at some point, coming or going.

As it turned out, she was going. Less than two hours later Emily Rose emerged from the Willard Hotel and started walking down the street. He followed some distance behind, on the other side of the street. There were plenty of people walking around Washington, almost too many. Emily Rose would not suspect him.

She stopped in front of a colored hotel where her slave was waiting then they continued in the same direction until they went inside a placed called Tater's Bar. He wanted to go inside and listen to them, but that was out of the question. It was a colored bar. John Murray would be too conspicuous as the only white person besides Emily. There was nothing to do but stand outside and watch and wait.

November 1, 1864 ~ Tater's Bar, Washington D.C.

"I'll be damned. If'n it isn't that tall, quiet colored man. What was your name?"

"Hello, Rooster Cain. I thought I might find you at Tater's."

"Every evening," Rooster said as he dipped his head then brought it back up to emphasize his words.

"My name is Nathaniel Whiteeagle."

"Oh, yeah. I remember now. How in the world could I forget a name like Whiteeagle? I see you brought that pretty white woman with you. How, do, ma'am."

"Good evening, Mr. Cain."

"No, ma'am. It's just Rooster. You go saying 'Mister' to me, and that mean old white owner from Beaufort County back in North Carolina might come up here and whip me again, for being uppity."

"We sure wouldn't want that, Rooster," Emily laughed.

"Y'all do know this is a colored bar, don't you?"

"I don't drink," Emily said, "But surely there's no law against me sitting at the table while you two enjoy a beer. Perhaps they've got something without alcohol."

"Well, maybe the white folks out there won't see you in here. Did you find your man up in wherever it was?"

"Elmira, New York. No. He had already been released as part of a prisoner exchange. He may get home before I do."

"Sure 'nuf? Why, that's a twist of a tale. Darn near beats all I ever heard. So's you're passing through Washington on your way home, then."

"Yes," Emily said. "I am. Nathaniel is going to stay in Washington. He's a free man. My family no longer wishes to hold him in bondage."

Rooster leaned back in his chair and stared at Nathaniel then at Emily before finally saying, "That's powerful. If I'd of had an owner like you, I'd still be back in North Carolina. Even after he set me free." He turned back to Nathaniel and said, "So what you going to do? Gotta make a living somehow."

"I'm trying to find a job. And a place to stay. We're not having any luck on either account."

"Mr. Whiteeagle, you came to the right person. I believe I can help you on both accounts. You know how to read and write, don't you?"

"Yes."

"And you got book learning, too. I can tell. A colored man like you, strong and smart, won't have no problem finding a good job. You got to know where to look. I can help with that."

"That's wonderful," Emily said. "What about a decent place to stay? Something that's not infested with rats."

"Yes, ma'am. Well, finding a nice place to stay won't be as easy. The war is going bad for the South. Yankees are all over Virginia. Plantation owners are having to run away and hide, so their slaves is skedaddling. They're all pouring into Washington. Rents are high, but if'n you gots money, you can find something to suit."

"I'm a slave," Nathaniel said. "Income has never been something I have been concerned about."

"Don't worry," Emily said. "I can pay in advance. You can start paying yourself when you get paid from your job."

"That'll sure 'nuf work. First things first, though. Got to get a regular payday. When I get off work tomorrow afternoon, I'll come straight to your hotel. Uh, that's you, Mr. Whiteeagle. No offense, ma'am, but it would be better if a white woman didn't accompany us while looking for a colored man's job. Anyways, I can take you to several places that might hire you on the spot."

"That's great news," Emily admitted, but she couldn't help showing her disappointment at being left out of the search.

"A place to stay is going to be a little more difficult, but they're out there, even for colored folks. Washington's got all kinds of places, from rat traps worse than the shacks back on the plantation all the way up to places that would make a plantation owner's house look like a shack. You tell me how much you're willing to pay, and I'll pick out some good places that will match your money. We can start looking for a place after you get a job. It might take a little longer, though. I hope you won't have a problem staying at the colored hotel for a few more days."

Rooster turned to Emily and continued, "Now, I don't means nothing ugly Miss Emily, but when we find a place for Mr. Whiteeagle, it would be better if you didn't visit him and go inside. Even though this is the Yankee capital, it don't look proper for a young white woman to be going into a colored man's apartment unaccompanied. Best you take our word that the place is good enough."

"Perhaps," Nathaniel said to Emily, "It is time for you to go home. Rooster will help me find a job and a place to stay. It may be time to go see your mother and father."

"I'm not leaving until I'm sure you are taken care of," Emily said.

"Man," Rooster said. "I wish I could have a pretty white woman fussing over me like that."

Nathaniel frowned at Rooster then said to Emily, "If that is your wish. But you must agree with my wish. When you leave, I will travel with you. When we get close enough to Confederate lines to make sure you can get to Richmond safely, I will return to Washington."

"Agreed."

November 12, 1864 ~ Prisoner Steamer Near the Coast of South Carolina

"He hasn't coughed since early this morning," Caleb said. "He's usually coughing every few minutes."

"Maybe he's getting better," Jimmy said.

"Maybe. But he don't look none too good."

Charles Pearson's face was tainted a dull tannish yellow. His skin was dry and warm, no longer sweating. Overnight he had talked a lot, mostly things that made no sense at all, like he was talking to people who weren't there. But since the sun came up, he said little. He woke periodically, only to look at his friends as though they were strangers, or talk to them as though they were someone else. He had called Caleb 'Jesus' at one point. Caleb was worried.

"How's your friend?" a Union guard asked. Since they left Point Lookout, Caleb and Jimmy had given up the pretense that Charles was okay. It was all too obvious he wasn't. The guard seemed to be genuinely concerned and came around periodically to check on him.

"Sleeping mostly. He ain't doing none too well."

"I hate to hear that. I was going to tell him that's South Carolina out there." The guard nodded his head toward the shrub-covered dunes along the shore.

Charles stirred. "South Carolina? Are we home? Let me see."

The guard helped Caleb and Jimmy lift Charles so that he could see over the rail. "You said you were from South Carolina," the guard said. "That's it. We're passing your home right now. Did you live close to the ocean?"

"No, not too close," Charles said. "But South Carolina is South Carolina. It's beautiful to me all over."

Caleb was surprised. For as bad as his friend looked, and as crazy as he had talked through the night, Charles Pearson was as lucid as he had been in days. Perhaps he was getting better. Was that possible?

"I guess you can let me back down. I done seen it. It was sure a sight to see, too."

Caleb and Jimmy and the guard lowered Charles down to his bedroll. "You'll be back on South Carolina soil a'fore long," Caleb said. "When you get strong enough to walk."

Charles rolled his eyes toward his friend. He feebly reached out his hand and touched Caleb's ragged sleeve a moment before his arm dropped back to the bedroll. Then he said, "Seeing is going to have to be good enough." His eyes closed.

"Don't you worry none," Caleb said. "When we get to Savannah, Georgia, we'll find a way to get you home, even if I have to carry you all the way to South Carolina myself."

"I'll help carry you," Jimmy said.

The guard patted Caleb on the shoulder and said, "I'm afraid your friend is no longer breathing. I'm sorry. So sorry." He turned and walked away.

A tear rolled down Caleb's cheek as he put his arms around Charles Pearson's slight, thin shoulders. He thought about Arlis and Danny and so many other young men he had known and liked. All gone now. He held Charles against his chest as the tears flowed.

November 16, 1864 ~ A Road Outside Richmond, Virginia

"You understand," the Union lieutenant said, "We cannot accompany you to enemy lines. Nor can we guarantee your safety. You are taking quite a chance."

"I don't care who wins the war anymore," Emily said. "I want it to be over. And I want to go home. I would ride through the flames of hell itself if that's what it took to get there."

"It may well take just that, ma'am," the officer said. "I can't stop you. You have a valid travel pass. But I strongly suggest you carry this white flag of truce as you go. Maybe the Rebs won't shoot if they see the white flag."

"I will go with her as far as I can," Nathaniel said.

"That would not be a good idea," the lieutenant said. "I strongly suggest you go back to Washington, Mr. Whiteeagle. This area is not safe for you. The Confederate lines are only a few miles down this road. They send out cavalry patrols to keep an eye on us. I know you have the papers declaring you a free man, but I understand that many Southern soldiers are not honoring those papers. If caught, you would go straight back into bondage. If they didn't kill you first."

"Yes," Emily said. "You need to go back, Nathaniel."

"But…"

"There is no 'but.' You have your freedom, you have a job, and you have a place to live. It is time for the rest of your life. Besides, it's only a few miles. I'll be fine." She held up the white flag the lieutenant had given her and twirled it about in the air. "And I'll make sure Aunt Millie frees Carolina. Thank you for everything, Nathaniel. One of the great pleasures of my life is having known you."

Nathaniel looked uncomfortable, but she could tell in his eyes that he appreciated her words. "Thank you. And I have enjoyed watching you grow into a fine young lady."

"Now, be off with you," she said with a smile. "Go home."

"Yes, ma'am," Nathaniel said. He stared at her a moment longer then turned his horse around and slowly rode back toward Washington D.C.

"Good luck," Emily whispered to his back.

"Good luck to you, ma'am," the Union officer said. "I wish I could send an escort with you."

"I'll be fine," Lieutenant. "Good day."

She nodded to his salute then turned and rode toward Richmond and Confederate lines.

Tired of carrying the small white flag, she had slid the stick through the horse's bridle so that it flapped over one of the horse's eyes when the breeze whipped in the right direction. She had traveled perhaps fifteen or twenty miles, well over halfway. She couldn't be far from Richmond.

Arriving at Aunt Millie's house would be nice. She would appreciate the comforts of the colossal home, but she couldn't stay long. She needed to get home…

A movement to her left caught her eye. A man on a horse pulled out from the trees. Her breath caught in her throat. This had happened before, but this time she was alone, almost defenseless.

The man was young, quite handsome. He didn't look like a thief, but he held a pistol in his hand and pointed it at her. "Get down from that horse, Miss Rose."

"How do you know my name?"

"I said get down. Now!" He punctuated his command by holding the pistol out further. It was aimed straight at her chest. She slowly dismounted.

"I know all about you, Emily Rose. You're the fiancée of Caleb Garner, a filthy, scumsucking Rebel from Alabama."

"Caleb is a wonderful person. He would never hold a gun on a lady."

"Maybe he would if he knew that lady was carrying a lot of money."

Emily was shocked. She couldn't keep her mouth closed. How did this man know so much? Nobody knew about the money except her and Nathaniel… and some dead Confederate deserters.

The man smiled as he dismounted. He did so without taking his eyes off Emily or moving his pistol aim from her chest.

"Give me the money. Now!"

"I don't have any money. If that's what you want, you've got the wrong person. Please leave me alone."

"Do you think I'm an idiot, lady?"

Emily shook her head, more a shudder than an acknowledgment of his question. "I don't know who you are. Please, go away. There won't be any trouble if you ride away from here."

The man, a smirk on his face, walked over to where she was standing. "There won't be any trouble here, either. Not for me. You're a real looker, lady, too good to pass up. We're all alone out here in no man's land, so I'm going to take what I want from you first then I'll find the money and take that, too."

"No," Emily pleaded, shaking her head and backing up.

"Take off your clothes," he said as he moved closer. He was only a few feet away and pointed the gun straight at her face. "Yep. I'm going to see you naked, all of you. One way or the other. If you don't take your clothes off, I'll rip them off for you. If you don't cooperate, I'll carve my initials in your forehead so that jackass Garner will know who took his lady before he had the chance." He stepped closer still. She could see the anger seething behind his eyes.

"Please. I've done nothing to you," Emily continued to plead as the tears began to flow. She stepped back, but he came after her. Moving faster than her eyes could trace, his arm shot out as he grabbed her hand and jerked her back toward him.

"Your stinking boyfriend has. He got me demoted. I don't have time to run down to your backwoods home and shoot that jackass, so you'll have to pay for his sins."

"No," Emily begged. "Please. Take my horse. You can have it. And my bags. Take it all, but please don't hurt me."

His hand shot out so quickly she had no time to react. It slammed into her cheek, above the jawline. He had used his open hand, not his fist, but the blow still made her dizzy, blurred everything around her. The pain was immediate and intense. She tumbled to the ground.

Even though she was disoriented and in pain, the senses she had left screamed at her to get off the ground and get away from this man. She started to roll to the side so she could get to her feet and run, but she couldn't move fast enough. He was on top of her in seconds, jerking at her blouse.

"Get your damned clothes off!" he seethed between his teeth. She saw him glance around, as though he realized he was too loud, that someone might hear. Maybe someone was nearby. She started screaming. His free hand slammed down on her mouth, hard. The scream was stifled into nothing. "Shut up, bitch!"

He holstered his pistol to free his right hand as he continued to stifle her scream with his left. He was so strong. "Let's see what you've got, lady." He jerked her dress up then started to tug at her underwear but stopped. "What the hell? What is this?" The man felt of the pockets on the front of her underwear. "I'll be damned," he said as he looked into one of the pockets. "Banknotes. Lots of old banknotes. I knew you were rich."

Emily tried to scream around the man's hand, but he was so strong and squeezed so hard that he hurt her. She could get little sound out.

"This changes things," he said as he leaned back. "You're struggling too hard, and I don't have time to waste trying to screw you. Hell, with all this money I can get laid as much as I can stand. Sorry, little lady, but I don't need witnesses. Poor old Caleb will have to spend the rest of his life wondering what happened to his pretty little lady. Or maybe I'll write him a letter and tell him."

He put his hands around her throat and began to squeeze. She tried to breathe, but no air would come. Her world started turning black. She could no longer move her arms to try to knock the man away. Tiny little sprinkles of light shot around in the dark, moving in arcs and lines around the periphery of her vision. The sparkles of light grew.

Vaguely, as though it was close but far away at the same time, she heard a funny sound, a 'thunk,' like the sound of Thomas slapping a side of beef as he hung it in the shed after butchering one of their calves.

Somehow air streamed into her lungs. Then she realized the hands were gone from her neck. She sucked deeply, getting more and more air until her chest was full. She opened her eyes and was able to see again. The man was still on top of her, but his eyes had grown huge, and there was a strange look on his face. He turned to look behind him as he was getting off of her and standing up. A knife stuck out of the back of his right arm. It was deep enough that it must have struck the bone.

She saw Nathaniel rushing forward, attacking with his bare hands. The man's right arm was limp, but he reached over with his left hand and pulled his pistol out of its holster. He raised it and fired. Nathaniel slowed but kept running. He was only a few feet away.

Emily struggled to regain her feet. She turned to her horse and reached into her saddlebag as the man fired again. Nathaniel's dark shirt was shiny where he reached up to grab his chest. Blood. Nathaniel went down.

"NO!" Emily screamed. She pulled the derringer the Union soldier had given her out of her bag, pointed it at the man's back, and fired, hitting him in the left shoulder. He dropped his gun and stumbled backward, toward his horse.

Emily aimed the derringer but did not fire the second barrel. She realized that, once she did, there would be no time to reload. The man could retrieve his gun from the ground and kill her long before she could rummage through her saddlebag for balls and powder, much less get them into the derringer. So she held the tiny pistol aimed at his chest. She would fire only if he came at her, and only when he was close enough so that she could not miss her target.

He didn't come at her. Instead, he backed away, leaving his pistol on the ground. While she held her aim, he climbed clumsily onto his horse and rode off as fast as he could, headed back in the general direction of Washington.

Emily rushed over and dropped down to Nathaniel's side, but she forced herself to stay conscious of the receding hoof beats, to make sure the man did not stop and sneak back.

"Nathaniel! Can you talk? Please, talk to me."

Nathaniel made a slight waving motion with his hand but said nothing as his eyes closed.

"NO! You can't die." She shook him briefly, but he was dead weight, not responding at all. She stopped to feel for a pulse. She found it, weak but steady. He was still alive! "We've got to find a doctor," she said, more to herself than to Nathaniel since he was no longer conscious.

Blood was oozing out of his chest and arm. The chest first. Emily ripped strips of cloth from a spare blouse and made a pad. She pressed this against Nathaniel's chest wound and wrapped strips all the way around his body then tied them tight over the wound. It was not easy. Nathaniel was a large man. But she found the strength. She had to stop the bleeding. The arm wound was not bad, but she bandaged it as well. He had lost enough blood, too much. She pressed down on the chest wound to slow the bleeding as Thomas had taught her to do many years ago, in case of an accidental cut.

Nathaniel was in bad shape. Should she leave him and go get help? The Union soldiers couldn't help her. They had already told her they could not come this far. The Confederates wouldn't help. She could not trust them to assist a dying black man. They would likely help him die sooner. She could go all the way to Aunt Millie's for help, but it was a long trip to Richmond and back. Would Nathaniel live that long? While she was gone, the man who shot him might come back for his pistol. If he found Nathaniel alone and unconscious on the ground, the man would kill him.

There was only one choice. She had to get Nathaniel Whiteeagle onto a horse and take him to find help. Washington was much too far. She would take him to Richmond, to Millie Hanson's house. Aunt Millie would know what to do.

Then she realized she was not strong enough to lift Nathaniel and place him onto a horse? He was far too large, too heavy. He couldn't help. He was unconscious, dead weight. She looked at her surroundings.

The land was rolling but gently sloped. She saw no dirt mounds or rock outcroppings where she could tie a horse and drag Nathaniel to the top then roll his body over onto the horse. The ground was too flat.

Not far away, there was an old log, a tree fallen in recent times. The trunk went into the earth, but the top of the tree rose several feet above the ground, supported by what was left of the upper limbs. This tree would have to do. She found Nathaniel's horse and tied it in place about the mid-point of the tree. Then she drug Nathaniel over to where the trunk connected to the roots, almost at ground level.

Emily did not know where she got the strength, but somehow she drug his body up onto the trunk. Using the rope Nathaniel had been carrying on his horse, she tied him in place so she could rest. After several minutes, she summoned her strength and pulled him further up the trunk.

Fortunately, the slope of the dead trunk was gentle. She was able to drag him upward. Unfortunately, she had to take constant breaks. It took every muscle in her body to pull the big slave along, checking his bandages regularly to make sure he was not bleeding excessively. She worried that she would make the wounds worse, but there was no other choice.

Eventually, she got him at the level of the horse then drug him over onto the saddle. After carefully tying him down, she was ready to go. It was late afternoon. Nathaniel was in bad shape. There was no time to waste.

There were plenty of doctors in Washington. And Nathaniel's home was there. But she was far closer to Richmond, to Millie's house. Even though she risked delivering him back into slavery, Richmond had to be her destination. She would worry about Nathaniel Whiteeagle's freedom later. If he survived. Right now, all she could think about was trying to make sure that he did survive.

November 16, 1864 ~ Venus Point, South Carolina

It was cool for November along the Savannah River, the border between South Carolina and Georgia. The whipping breeze off the ocean made it feel even colder for men dressed in ripped and rotting clothes. Huddled together, they started making their way onto the dock then across to the smaller Confederate ship tied on the other side. At the same time, Union prisoners were coming from the Confederate ship, filling in the voids made by the departing Rebel soldiers.

A Yankee soldier stumbled on the deck, not far from where Caleb waited his turn to cross. Two other Yankee prisoners, men in blue rags, their bodies little more than bones with skin stretched across them, took each side of the first man and helped him to a seat on the deck against the rail.

Thinking his eyes were playing tricks on him, Caleb rubbed them and looked again. Yes. The first man was moving different parts of his body, the movements slow but unmistakable. He was actually alive, a living skeleton. How could a human being look like that and still be breathing?

Taking in the rest of the Yankee prisoners with a broad look around, Caleb realized they were in even worse condition than the Confederate soldiers he had been herded with on the Union steamer. How could this happen? In his mind, Caleb had assumed that Southern courtesy would ensure Union prisoners received proper treatment, that it was the Yankee monsters who withheld food while prisoners died of hunger and disease, bodies piled on top of each other in mass graves.

"They're as pitiful as we are," Jimmy said.

"Worse," Caleb responded. "I never understood why they fed us so little in those Yankee prisons, but this is crazy. Those men don't look like they've eaten in weeks. How could we have done this to them? You can't be human and treat other people that way."

"Maybe it weren't so much on purpose. I heard tell that the army is running out of food. And the people back home as well. What with the blockade and the war being fought on our own ground, there isn't enough food for everybody. Any army is going to feed their own soldiers first. They feed the prisoners whatever's left over." Jimmy watched the Union prisoners stumble onto the ship a moment then added, "Don't look like there's been much left over in the South."

It was their turn to cross. With a conscious effort, Caleb lifted his foot onto the wooden footbridge that extended down to the dock. There was little energy left in his body. He trudged along one foot in front of the other, trying not to look at the Yankee prisoners on the other walk. He was tired of looking at living skeletons. He had been living with them long enough. Finally, he stepped down onto the deck of the smaller ship, a Southern soldier helping him as he stumbled forward.

Caleb looked at the man. It had been a long time since he had seen a Confederate soldier who was not a prisoner. The last time, the soldier he had looked at was a dead man: Arlis. God, he was going to miss his best friend. He may have been on his way home, but home would never be the same. He would miss roaming around Conecuh County with Arlis on their hunting and fishing trips. He would miss Arlis' teasing him about Emily. He would miss Arlis never missing a target. Arlis was special, and that special was gone.

Closing his eyes, Caleb thought about the others. He would miss his brother, John, whom he had not been able to watch after even though he had promised to do so. Caleb would miss all his new friends, Danny Talley and Charles Pearson and so many others he would never have met if there hadn't been a war. These people he had watched die were but a few of the thousands and thousands of dead on both sides of this inglorious conflict. There were so many people to be missed. After thinking about it, Caleb decided there may not be a single person left in the country who wouldn't miss somebody.

The next few hours were a blur. Caleb was aware of sailing a few miles into a harbor and being herded onto the streets of Savannah, Georgia. They lined up for a handful of doctors to inspect them, local doctors. It was not news when the doctor told him he was sick. He found out it was pneumonia, not that having a name for it mattered. While his leg had gotten better, his limp less pronounced, the rest of him had sunk into a gripping sickness, coughs that came from deep in his chest and hurt with a savagery he had never known, a feeling of heat throughout his body, shivers in spite of the heat, and almost endless sweat. It sometimes seemed like he gave out more fluids than he took in.

"You are in no shape to travel," the doctor said. "You'll need to spend a few weeks in the hospital before you can go home."

He had been gone so long. Now he was back on southern soil. He wanted no further delays. "I-I want to go home," Caleb stuttered. "I'm well enough to ride the train. Please let me go."

The gray-headed doctor looked over his reading glasses and peered down at Caleb and said, "Son, you're not far from being dead now. You wouldn't survive the trip home. And if somehow you did, they'd be burying you not long after."

Caleb could only stare back at the doctor. Was he that sick? He wasn't sure. He knew he didn't feel good. In fact, he felt bad, even beyond bad. But he had felt bad for so long it seemed as though that was normal. Still, everything was, well, fuzzy. That was the best way to describe it. Maybe the doctor was right.

"I was taking care of sick folks before you were born, son," the doctor continued. "You'll have to trust me on this one. A few weeks in a hospital bed with some decent food then you'll be in good enough shape to go home. *And* survive after you get there. Now, follow this man and we'll get you assigned to a hospital. Believe me, the time will pass quickly enough. Seems like it goes by faster every year."

November 17, 1864 ~ Millie Hanson's Mansion, Richmond, Virginia

Emily looked at herself. Not physically. She was sure she looked far the worse for wear, but that was not important. She looked at her life, at what she was doing. This was a far cry from the dreams of a few short years ago, a young girl's dreams of finding a man and marrying and having children on the best farm in Conecuh County. Instead, here she was, sneaking into Richmond, Virginia, in the dark of night, a slave near death on the horse she tugged along, worrying about getting caught by soldiers who would ask too many inconvenient questions. And who would likely not care whether a black man died or not. The only thing they would regret about his death is the labor that black man represented. But she cared. Greatly. If there were any way to keep Nathaniel from dying, she would find it.

He *was* still alive, though barely. Emily stopped and checked his weak pulse regularly, hiding behind bushes and trees and buildings and whatever else was convenient. There were few people about at one or two in the morning. Or whatever time it was. But there were enough to make her keep to the shadows, stay on a trail unseen.

She checked her makeshift bandages, looked for fresh blood flow that would mean she had to tighten the bandages or add new ones. Between checks, she made her way toward Aunt Millie's mansion, reversing the turns they had taken when leaving Richmond. Traveling by memory was difficult, especially in the dark, but there were few turns. Perhaps it was the gravity of her situation, her desperation to get Nathaniel to safety that aided her, but she found her way.

She remembered Nathaniel knocking on the door in the early hours of the morning when he had escaped from Fort Harrison. Now it was her turn to bang on the door and hope someone would wake up to let them in before she was seen. She jumped from her horse and beat against the solid wood of the beautifully carved door. Aunt Millie had told her it was custom made for their home by the best craftsman in Richmond. Now, all it represented was a barrier between her and safety.

"Who's there?" came Carolina's voice on the other side.

"Emily Rose. I've got Nathaniel. He's hurt badly."

The door slung open. Carolina, fear spread on her face and her eyes wide, said, "Where?"

"Help me get him down from his horse. He's been shot."

"We'll need help," Carolina said.

She disappeared inside but was back within seconds with two colored men, Millie's slaves. Millie was immediately behind and embraced Emily as though she were going to squeeze the life out of her. They got Nathaniel down from his mount and carried him to an upstairs bedroom then Millie sent the men to walk the horses around to the stable in the back. Even though her neighbors would likely be asleep at this hour, she didn't want to take a chance. No need to draw unwanted attention to her house.

Carolina and Emily stripped off Nathaniel's shirt. Emily carefully untied and lifted the bandages she had applied to his shoulder and his chest.

When Carolina saw the chest wound, she gasped loudly, placing her hand on her mouth.

"We need a doctor," Millie said. She rushed out of the room.

"Get some hot water," Emily said. Carolina nodded and, with tears in her eyes, rushed down the stairs.

Carolina was barely gone when Millie returned. She had hastily put on a dress and was pulling a coat over it.

"Clean the wounds and make sure you keep a compress on them," Millie said. "Especially the chest wound. I'll go get a doctor. Be back in a few minutes."

"Can't you send someone else?" Emily asked.

"This isn't the Richmond it used to be, hon. It's too dangerous for a slave to be out this time of night. And getting a doctor to leave the hospitals is practically impossible. Too many sick and wounded soldiers. I doubt even my personal doctor would come if I sent a slave, but he won't deny me if I show up in person."

With that, she was gone. Emily looked down at Nathaniel. He was a big, strong man, but the wound in his chest looked terrible. Blood still seeped from both wounds in spite of her efforts, but not as much. The flow was slowed to a trickle. And it seemed as though his pulse was stronger, although that could have been her imagination.

Minutes later Carolina returned with a steaming pot of water, and they went to work. They were long finished cleaning the wounds and putting on new bandages when Emily leaned back in a nearby chair and closed her eyes. She was so tired. She drifted off but was startled awake by the pounding of feet coming upstairs.

Millie rushed into the room, the doctor immediately behind her. He looked tired. His eyes were red, and the bags under them were dark, but he carried himself with precision. Even in the early morning, he was dressed in a suit.

After a quick look at Nathaniel, the doctor said, "Good work on the bandages. Get them off."

As Emily and Carolina removed the new bandages, the doctor took off his coat, rolled up his sleeves, and then opened his bag. He pulled out several instruments and dipped them in the pot of steaming water. Then he began probing in the chest wound.

Sometime later, both bullets lay in a porcelain bowl on the table beside the bed. "The one in the chest missed his heart," the doctor said. "Some damage to his lung. Would have killed most men. I've got to get back to the hospital. Bandage him like you did before and change the bandage three times a day. If he bleeds, hold a compress in place to stop it." The doctor, unhappy as well as tired, rolled down his sleeves and put on his coat then left the room.

As Emily and Carolina were taking care of Nathaniel, they heard the doctor talking loudly from the bottom of the stairs, his voice rising as he spoke, "For Christ's sake, Millie, he's a slave. And not even your slave at that. I've got soldiers to help. I'm working damn near around the clock now. The next time something like this happens, the darkie will die. Hell, he'll likely die in spite of my coming out here. This whole trip was probably wasted!"

December 12, 1864 ~ Savannah, Georgia

"It's been mite near a month," Caleb said. "I think I'm well enough to go home."

"No," the doctor said firmly. "You're malnourished, you've been sick enough to kill weaker men, and your leg is not fully healed. If it were only a matter of putting you on a train, I might give in. As long as you had someone to travel with you, someone who could follow my instructions. Unfortunately, that's impossible."

"Why? Some of the others are trying to get back to South Alabama, too. I'm sure one of them would do what you said."

"That's not the issue. That devil Sherman got here two days ago and has laid siege to Savannah. The blockade controls the harbor. You can't leave while the Yankees have us surrounded."

"I heard, but I got my exchange papers. They're supposed to let me go free."

"Humph. They were supposed to be civil as they marched through Georgia, too. They were supposed to leave our God-fearing families alone. Instead, those devils burned our people's homes to the ground and stole their livestock and livelihoods. The only people left to stand up to them were old men, women, and children, cause the husbands and daddies were gone off to war. Or dead. Sherman didn't care. They burned them all out. If his men didn't kill them right then and there, they left them to die. Children out trying to forage a living in the countryside, no place to stay, no place to sleep, nothing to eat but handouts from others who have little to hand out. And those devils destroyed the railroad track, too. Why, you'd have to walk every step of the two hundred miles to Macon to catch a train. Forget your paperwork. Sherman would have no more respect for your exchange papers than he did for the women and children of Georgia as he burned them out of house and home."

Caleb stared at the doctor in disbelief. He said nothing.

"Even if Sherman's men honored your papers and let you through," the doctor continued, "You're not well enough to walk two hundred miles. It would kill you. I'm sorry."

No longer able to endure the rigors of battle, Caleb was not required to return to the front. He was a free man. But what good was being free when he could not get back to Alabama? All Caleb wanted was to see his home again, to see his mother and father and to stand out on the orange soil that made them work so hard. And, most of all, to hug Emily Rose and find out if she still wanted this half-broken man. But at every turn, something seemed to stand in the way of reaching Conecuh County. He was beginning to wonder, as he had done many times in battle and even more so in prison, if he would ever see his home again.

"Sick or not, we still have to get you out of the hospital," the doctor said. "When Sherman takes over this city, and there is no doubt that he will, you could be imprisoned again. They would not give a Confederate soldier proper treatment. It would be dangerous."

Caleb thought back to Point Lookout and Elmira, about the way he and his fellow soldiers had been treated little better than animals. Better? After he thought about it, he realized he was only fooling himself. They had been treated worse than animals, far worse. He decided he would rather die than go to prison again. "If I can't go home, what can I do? Where can I go to be safe? I can't go back to a Yankee prison. I would take a quick death over a slow one."

"There are quite a few exchange soldiers still in Savannah. We must protect you. We have reached out to the community, and the people of Savannah have responded. Families all over the city have volunteered to take in convalescing soldiers until Sherman has gone. Once the Union army leaves our fair city, and you are well enough to travel, you may safely go home. Mind you, you will still have to walk the first two hundred miles. It will be months before they get the rails fixed. If ever."

"I don't care if I have to walk the whole way. I want to go home."

"I understand. Meanwhile, you'll be staying with the Talbot family. Gather your things. They will be here any moment."

There was little to gather. Caleb was ready before the doctor walked out of the room. His limp kept him from walking at a normal pace, but he followed the doctor through the halls as best he could. At the front desk, he was introduced to a smiling, middle-aged couple, Barnett and Ester Talbot. He followed them outside and climbed into the buggy they drove. It was not a gray, weathered farm wagon, but a true-to-life black carriage. Not the fancy enclosed ones, but it was nice enough. He had never ridden in a real carriage before.

They cheerfully passed small talk back and forth until Caleb asked if they had any children. Their smiles disappeared. "We had a son and a daughter," Barnett Talbot said. "Our son, Edward, was an officer, a Lieutenant. He died of yellow fever early in the war."

"I'm sorry for your loss," Caleb said.

"Our daughter, Sarah, left for France before the war," Ester Talbot said. "She was studying art in Paris. She was quite gifted. Her letters came regularly, once a month or more. She loved Paris and sent us the most beautiful sketches she had done of things around the city. Sarah went on and on about how wonderful Paris was. Then the war started. She couldn't get home because of the God-forsaken blockade. We couldn't even get news from Europe, much less personal letters from Sarah. So we have heard nothing from her since the war started. We don't know what's become of her."

They fell into an uncomfortable silence. Trying to think of something to say, Caleb looked around at the buildings lining the streets of Savannah. It was a pretty town compared to the other cities he had seen since he had been in the army. "I'm sure she's fine," he finally said. "And this here war is almost over. As soon as it's done, they'll get rid of the blockade, and your daughter will be able to come home again. Yes, you'll see her before too much longer. I'm sure of it."

A smile came back to Ester's face. "Yes, of course. That will be so wonderful."

Barnett said, "I believe you are correct, young man. It won't be long. Well, here we are. This will be your home until we get rid of Sherman."

Barnett Talbot stopped the carriage in front of a home that, while not the largest or most elaborate in Savannah, was a world apart from the log cabin where Caleb had been raised. Caleb looked at the house in dismay. It was hard to understand how people could have enough money to live like this. It made him think of his grandfather, Absalom Garner, Sr. His father, Sam, had always told him that his grandfather was a rich man back in South Carolina, a prominent land owner. Junior and Senior had had a serious falling out. Sam Junior left South Carolina, met Sarah in Georgia, married her then moved on to Alabama. Sam Senior was so aggrieved by whatever it was that came between them, something that Sam Junior had never fully explained, that he no longer recognized the existence of his older son. Sam Junior was written out of the family will, so Caleb had grown up a poor farmer.

"We've a formidable force defending the city, under General Hardee," Barnett said as he stepped down from the carriage. "Perhaps they can come to some mutual agreement and Sherman will march on to other places."

"I doubt it," Ester said. "Sherman has several times as many men, and they are much better equipped."

"Ah, my dear, but battles are not always won by the larger forces. Hardee is entrenched in good defensive positions. And they've flooded the rice fields, so the approaches to the city are narrow and easier to defend."

"For our sake, I hope so. But it doesn't look promising to me. I am afraid we will have the Yankees at our doorsteps in short order."

Barnett smiled and wobbled his head and said, "Perhaps. We do lack for supplies." He opened the front door of his home and motioned for Caleb to enter. "Here we are. I hope this will be suitable for as long as you are here."

Caleb stepped inside and glanced at the tall ceilings and expansive rooms with ornate trim. It was like something out of a dream. "Suitable? This is like nothing I've ever seen. It's beautiful. I wish Emily could see it."

Barnett and Ester smiled. "Your wife?" Ester asked.

"We were supposed to get married after the war. If I made it home."

"That shouldn't be too much longer," Barnett said.

A black man in a long tail coat and ruffled shirt came walking into the room. "You're back," he said.

"Yes, Janus. This is Caleb Garner, the soldier who will be staying with us for a while. Caleb, this is Janus Slade, our house servant."

Caleb nodded at Janus but got only a cold stare in return. The slave's skin was dark, but his facial features were sharp, not typical for a colored man. He held his chin high in the air. "I will attend to the carriage, Sir," he said.

"Thank you. When you return, please show Mr. Garner his room and find some clothes that will fit him. Do you think you can repair his uniform?"

Janus looked Caleb up and down. He finally said, "It will be difficult to repair. I will do my best." He turned sharply on his heels and walked outside.

"Please," Ester said. "Come into the kitchen. There's coffee. Sugar, too. The blockade hasn't stopped everything."

"That would be a dream sure enough," Caleb said. "Thank you."

The kitchen alone was as large as the Garner family home back in Conecuh County, quite possibly larger. The coffee was something out of heaven, far better than what passed for coffee in the hospital. And Caleb couldn't remember the last time the sweet taste of sugar had passed over his tongue.

Janus stepped through the back door and into the kitchen. "The carriage is parked and cleaned, Sir." Then he turned to Caleb and said, "Follow me."

Janus Slade had to wait for Caleb to limp up the stairs. He said nothing as he stood at the top staring down at Caleb, his eyes showing no kindness. The room was richly furnished with dark wood trim and flowered walls. The furniture was hand-carved, intricate, beyond anything Caleb could ever have imagined.

A couple of minutes later Janus returned with clothes in his hand. He laid them on the bed and said, "These should fit. Leave your uniform on that table. I will do what I can with it."

"Don't know that I need it anymore," Caleb said. "War's over for me."

"My Master has instructed me to do my best to repair it. I will. If you wish not to have it back, you should take that up with him. Do you require anything else?"

"Do you have a Bible? I like to read a little every day."

Janus' eyes widened in dismay as he spoke, "You read?"

"Yes. Don't you?"

"Mr. Garner," Janus said, his chin held even higher and his eyes dark and determined, "It is illegal for slaves to learn to read in the state of Georgia. Do you think me a criminal?"

Caleb stared at Janus a moment. The colored man's face showed nothing other than contempt. "Have I done something to you, Janus? Made you mad somehow?"

"I have no idea what you are referring to, Mr. Garner. I will bring you a Bible shortly."

"You look at me like you hate me, like you'd stick your nose up in the air at my dead body."

"I do not know what you mean. I am here to perform servitude for you. How else am I supposed to treat a Confederate soldier?"

Caleb thought he picked up a strange inflection in the words, 'Confederate soldier.' He said, "I fought for my state, for Alabama. It didn't have nothing to do with colored folks. My family don't own no slaves. We're practically slaves ourselves, slaves to a land that don't yield much of a living. I ain't done nothing to you."

Janus Slade looked down at Caleb, staring at him eye-to-eye, and said, "I have no idea what you are talking about. As I said, leave your uniform on the table. Let me know if I can get you anything else." With that, he turned sharply on his heels and left the room.

December 21, 1864 ~ Savannah, Georgia

"The situation has changed," Barnett Talbot said. "General Hardee and his entire army abandoned us yesterday. It was the prudent thing to do on his part. Rather than be brutally beaten and occupied, Mayor Arnold and his delegates rode out to make an offer: We will put up no resistance as long as they protect our citizens and our property. To Sherman's credit, the Union army has agreed. They began entering the city yesterday."

"That makes good sense," Caleb said. "With no army, you couldn't fight back."

"Quite right. We will, in fact, get along with them well. Ester and some of her friends are working on a plan to get supplies from them then bake cakes and other goods to sell back to the Union soldiers. With a smile, of course."

"But what happens when they leave? If you cooperate, won't the Confederate army be mad when they come back in?"

"I don't believe so. Simple survival. Better to keep the city of Savannah intact for future use than to upset the Union and have them burn it down. So we will be friendly to them while they're here, endear ourselves to them as we need to, then we'll curse them like rabid dogs once they've gone. When the Confederate army comes back in, if they do, I believe they will see the wisdom in that. We are, ultimately, saving the city for them."

"That's pretty smart thinking. So what does that mean for me?"

"We are going to move you to a bedroom in the attic. You'll sleep up there but stay down here with us unless we find out that Union soldiers are going house-to-house. If we hear anything, even a knock on the door, it would be best for you to hurry up to the attic where you are unlikely to be found."

Caleb shrugged. "How long do you think Sherman is going to stay?"

"Who knows?" Barnett said. "But he will not spend the duration of the war here. I suspect a matter of weeks. The winter is upon us so he may decide to rest easy for the winter then leave in early spring. So far they are living up to their agreement and being quite civil. Still, Confederate soldiers are at risk, even if you are exchanged prisoners, so we have to take precautions." Barnett turned to his house servant and said, "Janus, please gather Mr. Garner's things and take them to the attic room. When you've finished, make the spare bedroom appear as though it has been vacant for quite some time."

"Yes, Sir."

Barnett turned to Caleb and said, "The doctor will come around periodically to check on you. He will tell us when you're well enough to travel, but there will be little opportunity to leave until Sherman is gone. Now, when you settle in, please come back down for coffee." He motioned for Janus to proceed.

"Follow me, Mister Garner."

Caleb marveled that an attic room, which was not finished or decorated as was the house proper, was still much grander than his home in Conecuh County. Boards on the sloping walls and the ceiling were neatly cut, fitting together tightly. It was nothing like the hand-hewn logs he had grown up with. While the door, hidden at the back of a small alcove, was not readily evident, the room was, nevertheless, furnished as though it was a room in the house proper. He would lack no comforts.

"Where do you sleep?" Caleb asked Janus as the colored man was sorting his things upon a dresser that was far nicer than any piece of furniture Caleb's family owned. And this was one that was stored out of sight in the attic.

"Where do I sleep? Why? What business is it of yours?"

It had been like that for nine days. Janus Slade had been cold and condescending the entire time. He never volunteered any information to Caleb. Nine days were enough. It was time to get some things out in the open, even if it meant he got kicked out of the house with Yankees roaming all over town.

"I was only being civil," Caleb said. "Conversation. I've never done anything to you. Like I told you before, I was born a poor Southern farmer. I don't own no slaves, and I don't reckon slavery is a good thing, not that I ever thought about it much one way or the other. I didn't fight so's the rich folks could own you colored folks. Why risk dying for something I don't even believe in? I fought for Alabama. I fought for my home. And, more than anything else, we needed the enlistment money. That's all. It cost my younger brother his life. And it's cost me my health. Hell, I don't even know if I'll ever be able to walk like a real man again."

Caleb ran out of words. He stared at Janus as the colored man stared back at him. It seemed as though Janus Slade's chin lowered slightly.

Suddenly more words came rushing out of Caleb's mouth. "I'm hiding out till I can go home, get back to my maw and paw and my woman. She's waiting for me. Prettiest girl in Conecuh County. Probably all of Alabama. I got nothing against you, and I don't want to hurt you. What do I have to do to prove to you I bear you no ill will?"

Janus Slade continued to stare into Caleb's eyes. He tilted his chin up then back down and said, slowly and deliberately, "Teach me to read."

January 3, 1865 ~ Millie Hanson's Mansion, Richmond, Virginia

The central courtyard was surrounded by Millie's huge home. Marble-paved and containing several life-size statues, it was spacious but private, opening to the outside only through a small wrought iron gate nestled into the shrubbery. You could not look from the outside and see the gate. You had to know it was there.

Several of the mansion's windows overlooked the courtyard. Millie and Emily looked out one of those windows, watching Nathaniel and Carolina below. It was a warm day for winter. Carolina had taken him outside to enjoy the early afternoon sunlight. They stood, hand-in-hand, leaning against each other.

"I suppose that's obvious enough," Millie said.

"I knew it the first time they looked into each other's eyes," Emily said. "There was something there from the start. It was plain to see it was more than mere infatuation. I love Caleb, but it didn't start like that. We knew each other growing up. We went to church together. There were times when I thought he was the most awful boy I'd ever met. Eventually, it changed. Our love grew, but slowly, over the years. I think you have to be a little more mature to experience the kind of instant love that Nathaniel and Carolina seem to have." She nodded toward the couple standing on the cobblestones below.

"I believe you are right."

"What about you? Did you fall in love with your husband, Carl, at first sight?"

"He was tall, handsome, dashing, and quite rich. I was so infatuated I couldn't hold a cup of tea without spilling it. When he started talking about marriage, I jumped. I was so happy. But I was a young girl at the time. As I became older, I realized I had only thought I was in love. Over the years I began to see the real man inside of him, all his faults and quirks, all his idiosyncrasies. He had his share of them."

"You must have tolerated him. You stayed with him all those years."

Aunt Millie stared at Emily for several moments before turning her gaze back down to Nathaniel and Carolina. Finally, she said, "More than tolerated. Far more. It made me fall truly in love with him, a love deeper than I was capable of or could even understand when I originally met him. I suppose that sounds ridiculous."

"I… No. I think I understand."

As they were watching, Nathaniel bent down and kissed Carolina, a deep, lingering kiss.

"I believe we have crossed over the threshold into eavesdropping," Millie said. "Perhaps we should close the curtain." She reached up and pulled the drapes together, killing the streaks of sunlight across the walls and floor, greatly reducing the light in the room. "I guess you're right. I've got to let Carolina go. It's not fair for me to keep her here when her heart is with someone else."

"Yes, Aunt Millie. It's the right thing to do."

"My, how the world has changed. A few short years ago we would have thought little of splitting slave couples apart. Now, I'm going out of my way to put them together. It's a shame it has taken this horrible war and all of its bloodshed to open our eyes."

"Aunt Millie, in the last few weeks I've been around you long enough to know your heart is far softer than you let on. I don't think you would ever have split up a slave couple, even before the war. As far as other Southerners are concerned, I have seen few changes of heart because of the atrocities of this war. It's almost as if the flow of blood has become a routine way of life, something that has made the South even more determined in its efforts to prolong slavery."

"The flow of blood routine? I hope you're wrong. That would be sad, indeed. Perhaps, in my own small way, I can help start the healing. Yes, you convinced me some time ago. In fact, I wrote the paper last week. I suppose it's time to give it to her."

"I'm proud of you, Aunt Millie," Emily said. "I'll call them in."

Once the four of them were gathered at the servant's table, Millie said. "It's past time for this." She lifted something and held it out. "Here. This is for you, Carolina."

Nathaniel held his usual stoic look, but Emily could see the curiosity in his eyes. He wanted so badly to be back to normal, no longer spending long hours in bed. He was up much of the day, walking around and trying to do light work. But everyone knew better. He still had a long way to go. He struggled to perform that light work and had to rest afterward. It would be weeks before he was ready to travel. When he was, Emily knew she would have a problem convincing him to go back to Washington and freedom. Nathaniel was back to insisting he see Emily safely home to Conecuh County before accepting his freedom. Now more than ever, he had said.

Carolina cocked her head sideways and looked at Millie, who held a leather pouch in front of her. "Go ahead," Millie said. "Take it. Before I change my mind."

Carolina reached out, tentatively, and lightly gripped the leather pouch. Her eyes were a storm of anticipation, curiosity. She feebly mumbled, "Thank you."

"Oh, for crying out loud," Millie said. "The present isn't the leather folder. It's what's on the inside. And the leather folder, too, if you want it. Go ahead. Open it up."

Carolina untwirled the string and lifted the flap. She pulled out a sheet of parchment. Aunt Millie's flowing but awkward letters were all over it. She looked up at Millie and said, "I can't read."

"It's your papers. I am setting you free. I know Lincoln did that a long time ago, but the Confederacy doesn't recognize what Lincoln did. This declaration will be recognized by our government. You're free to go, wherever you want to go."

Tears began to stream down Carolina's face. She looked at Nathaniel then back at Millie. "This is the only home I've ever had."

"True enough," Millie said. "You were born in the slave's quarters out back. But things have changed, Carolina. For better or for worse, the world is going to be different. I hope it's for the better. A privileged old woman like me has trouble adapting to change, but even I can see what's coming. There's no sense trying to stand in the way of fate and getting trampled by it. So you're free to go anytime you want to."

Carolina burst into a full cry. Nathaniel put his arm around her, trying to console her.

"I didn't mean to make you cry. It was supposed to make you happy."

"I am," Carolina sobbed. She let go of Nathaniel and hugged Millie. Her chest continued to heave a few more times, but she managed to reign in the crying. Finally, she let go of Millie and stepped back and said, "Thank you so much, Mrs. Millie, but I don't know where I'd go. I mean… Do I have to leave?"

"Why, of course not. You're always welcome here, Carolina. I still have enough money to pay you a small salary. But Emily and I thought, well, you and Nathaniel… I mean…"

Emily had never seen Millie at a loss for words. She seemed to have words at her command when everyone around her was dumbstruck. Not this time. Emily had no choice but to come to her rescue.

"Nathaniel has made some friends in Washington. And he has a good job. Well, had a good job. I believe he can get it back once they understand what happened. Aunt Millie and I thought the two of you would want to move there. You'll need that paper. Oh, and a travel pass for both of you. Aunt Millie can arrange that."

Nathaniel looked down at Carolina then back up at Emily and said, "I guess we are that obvious. This…" He looked down at Carolina and reached for her hand, holding it in his as he continued, "Is a new experience for me. I do not wish to lose it, but I must see you safely home before I can enter a different life. Caleb should be home by now. I will make sure you get home to see him. Once the two of you are together, and I have paid my respects to your parents, I will take my leave."

Emily looked down a moment, lost in thought. Then she looked back up and said, "I want so much to hold Caleb, put my arms around him and not let go." Tears began to well up in her eyes. "After all he's been through, he needs me."

“And you need him,” Nathaniel said. “But travel in the South is more dangerous than ever. I cannot let you go alone. I gave my word. I almost broke it when we were in Washington, and that invited a near disaster. That will not happen again.”

“But how will you get back to Washington?” Emily asked. “You have your paperwork, but there are a lot of people in the South, people like that awful Sheriff, Rufus Tate, who would not honor your freedom if you were traveling alone.”

“Rufus Tate would not honor my freedom if I were traveling with Jefferson Davis himself,” Nathaniel said. “But fortunately there are few like him in the South. As long as I am with you, I am your slave, and that should be honored. The Union is in control of Pensacola and much of Mobile. Once you are safely home, I can make my way to either place, whichever is the clearest path. It may be difficult, but it will not be impossible to arrange passage back to Washington on a ship. When I get back, I will return to Richmond for Carolina.”

“That would not be wise,” Millie said. “Once you get free, you need to stay free. I still have enough pull in this town to get Carolina to Washington. I know people, even in Richmond, who are antislavery. They will help. All you need to do is find a way to let me know you are home.”

Nathaniel squeezed Carolina’s hand lightly. “I can do that.”

“It will take time,” Emily said.

“Nathaniel is a man of his word,” Carolina said. “I knew that right away. He will do what he says he will do. And I will wait as long as I have to.”

February 1, 1865 ~ Talbot Residence, Savannah, Georgia

The tapping of boots against wooden steps sprung them into action. Janus stood and rushed to the open door, laying a towel over his arm and assuming a position of servitude. Caleb closed the book they had been reading, A Tale of Two Cities, placed it on his nightstand, next to the Bible he read every night, and then stretched out in bed.

Moments later, Barnett Talbot stepped inside. “Good afternoon,” he said. “I was wondering where you were, Janus.”

“Checking to see if Mr. Garner required my services this afternoon. Perhaps some tea?”

“You seem to be taking good care of our guest. I, ah, appreciate that. But it may not last much longer.”

Caleb’s head snapped up. “I’m leaving?”

“General Sherman is leaving, marching off to the Carolinas. The Union army will be gone by sunset. The city’s strategy, our strategy, has worked. The Union believes we are in sympathy with them, so Savannah remains intact. Now we no longer have to placate those barbarians. Unfortunately, the same can’t be said for the Carolinas. I dare say they will get no better treatment from Sherman’s band of thugs than the rest of Georgia received.”

“I can go home!” Caleb shouted.

“Very soon,” Barnett said. “On his last visit, the doctor seemed to think you were close to being well enough to travel. He should check you once more before you leave. A prudent precaution, of course.”

Home! Caleb looked at Barnett Talbot then at Janus Slade. A rash of images flashed through his mind: The forests of Conecuh County, the cabin where he was born and raised, the Sepulga River, and, most prominent of all, the beautiful face of Emily Rose. After all this time, was it finally true? His pulse raced, but words escaped him.

"If you wish," Barnett said, "You can come down from the attic. Perhaps back to the bedroom? Until you leave, that is."

"That's fine. Mr. Talbot, I can't thank you enough for all you and Mrs. Talbot have done. But it's been almost three years since I seen home, since I seen Emily. I'm ready to leave. When can I see the doctor?"

"I'll arrange for him to come here tomorrow. If he says okay, then we'll get you packed and ready. You can leave the first thing the following morning."

"He'll say okay. I'm ready. I know I am."

"Very well." Barnett smiled broadly then turned to his slave and said, "Janus, please bring Mr. Garner's things back to the guest bedroom."

"Yes, Sir."

Janus began to gather Caleb's belongings, which seem to have grown in the time he had stayed in the Talbot's home. As he worked, they listened to Barnett Talbot's receding steps down the stairs.

Once it was quiet, Janus turned to Caleb and said, "I must thank you. It is comforting being able to read the Good Book on my own. And Gulliver's Travels was exciting. I can't wait to finish A Tale of Two Cities after you leave. You have opened up new worlds for me."

"You learn fast," Caleb answered. "A lot faster than I did. Thank you for bringing the other books up here. I ain't never read anything other than the Bible before. It was fun reading something new."

"I learned fast because you are an excellent teacher. Of course, when Mrs. Talbot sits down for our nightly Bible reading, I will still have to pretend that all I can do is listen."

"What would they do to you if they knew?"

"You and I could both go to prison. Or worse. Would the Talbot's turn us in? I doubt it, but I would not run the risk. When you are a black man in Georgia, Mr. Garner, you learn not to take chances."

February 3, 1865 ~ Railroad Station, Savannah, Georgia

"We don't know how much of the track the government has repaired," Barnett said. "It's been several months since Sherman came through. Surely some repair work has been done. Janus, stop the carriage at the railroad station. We'll inquire about the status of the tracks."

There were a few people in front of the station, but most of them were walking by, some on the road and some along the tracks. Barnett and Caleb stepped inside. Other than a wrinkled old clerk with a thin face and body and a long gray mustache, they were the only ones on the inside. Caleb walked up and said, "Could I get a ticket to Gravella, Alabama?"

"Gravella, Alabama?" the railroad clerk said absently as he opened his fare book. "Don't hear that one much. Let's see…" He fumbled through the pages of the fare book for some time before announcing, "Here it is. The Alabama and Florida Railroad. Seventy-five miles south of Montgomery. You would have to change trains four times. Let me add up the fares."

"Fares?"

"Of course. Hold your horses a second." The clerk added several numbers on a scrap of paper already covered with writing, poking the numbers into tiny blank spaces between other numbers and letters. Paper had become even harder to find late in the war. "That would be twenty-nine dollars and twenty-five cents."

"What? That's almost thirty dollars? I ain't got no money to pay for a ticket like that." Caleb patted the chest of his Confederate uniform, which had stitching holding tears and rips together and holes where there was nothing left to hold together. Janus had done the best he could, but there were limits to what could be done. "I'm a Confederate soldier. They always put me on the train for free before."

"That's because you were going off to fight. The way you're limping looks like your fighting is over."

"Don't worry about money," Barnett said. "I can pay for the ticket."

"Ain't no need to worry about money or tickets," the clerk said. "It don't matter no ways, now."

"Why not?"

"Sherman tore up the track all the way to Macon. Those nice rails you see outside don't go too far. In any direction. Once you get out of Savannah, the rails is all Sherman's neckties now. Twisted into useless loops."

"Hasn't the government effectuated repairs?" Barnett asked. "That was months ago. Surely some of the track has been repaired by now."

"Can't. Sherman burned down all the factories. We got nothing to repair with. I don't guess the rails will be fixed till after the war, if ever."

"Factories destroyed? I don't understand," Barnett said. "I heard he left our towns intact, that they were not burned down like Atlanta was."

"Technically that may be true. His orders was to destroy only those buildings what was capable of supporting the Confederate war effort. It appears his soldiers took a pretty liberal view of what could help the war effort. Not much was spared. They weren't supposed to trespass in people's homes, either, but those blue devils raided houses and stole people's valuables at gunpoint. Mark my words, they'll all have to answer to the Lord one of these days. And I dare say that nary a one of them will escape the flames of hell."

"How am I going to get home?" Caleb asked.

"You got a horse?"

"No, Sir."

"Probably just as well. Somebody would steal it. But without a horse, you'll have to walk."

"Walk? All the way to Gravella, Alabama? How far is it?"

"Montgomery is three hundred and thirty miles from here. Add seventy-five miles to Gravella, so that's four hundred and five miles along the railroad bed."

Caleb's jaw went slack. He stared at the clerk with his mouth open.

"You'll have plenty of company," the clerk added. "There's thousands of folks walking around the countryside right now. Refugees from all the places Sherman burned down, slaves trying to follow

Sherman, and white folks running away from him. Whole families living in the woods. Most of them don't know where their next meal is coming from."

"But..." Caleb was stunned. Words wouldn't come. His country had gone to the trouble to get him released, but nobody was doing anything to help him get home. Then he thought about it and realized there was nothing they could do. The war was over, it just hadn't ended. The South had lost. The Confederate government could not repair railroads. There was little manufacturing capability left. All the government could do was work to delay the final collapse and pray for a miracle on the field of battle. No, pray for several miracles. One wouldn't be enough.

"It's not all that bad," the clerk said. "What you've got to do is walk to Macon. General Sherman was kind enough to leave Macon be. It's a hundred and ninety miles along the railroad track. Or where the railroad track used to be. You can catch the train in Macon and ride to Columbus then Montgomery. The train from Montgomery don't stop at Gravella on the way south, only on the way back. But you can go to Evergreen. It's close. Five miles away. The fare from Macon would be..." Once again he added some numbers in the quickly dwindling spaces on the scrap of paper. "Thirteen dollars and fifty cents. A mite better."

"I spent six months in Yankee prisons. I ain't got no money."

"You being a wounded soldier and all, maybe they'll waive the fare in Macon."

"I can give you money for the fare," Barnett said. "I'm sorry, but I cannot spare a horse. Do you think you can walk two hundred miles? You can stay with us longer if need be."

Caleb looked at Barnett then said, "I got to get home. I'll walk."

"I feel sorry for you," the clerk said. "I really do. For you and all the rest. Lots of soldiers like you. I can't help you, and I can't help any of them, neither. The trains ain't running into or out of Savannah. I come down here because I don't know what else to do. I'm sure you can find some companions to walk along with. I hear there's a lot of Confederates leaving Savannah today. Men who used to be prisoners like you."

Barnett thanked the clerk, and they left, walking outside to where Janus waited in the carriage. Barnett told Janus about the conversation with the clerk.

"You should have plenty of company, Mr. Garner," Janus said. He pointed at the tracks that headed west out of the station. "Three groups of soldiers have walked by since I've been waiting, all headed toward Macon I assume. Most of them were wearing their uniforms. I guess because they're heavy enough for this time of year, but some of them seem to be a sight worse than yours. Maybe it's all most of the soldiers have got to wear."

Caleb looked at the track. There was a group of five soldiers, four in gray uniforms and one in civilian clothes, walking along. The man in civilian clothes must have been a soldier as well. He was missing his left leg from just below the knee, a sure sign of a battle wound. He walked on Yankee-issue crutches and struggled to keep up with the other men. Another had a slack right sleeve on his Confederate jacket. It dangled at his side, useless. One of the other three was a couple of inches shorter than the rest but appeared to have the most energy as he walked. This said little as none of them moved lithely along. All of the men were thin, walked with shoulders slumped, and had stringy, unkempt beards.

"I'll catch up with those men," Caleb said. "Better hurry." He crawled down from the wagon. "I thank you for everything, Mr. Talbot."

"Ester and I have enjoyed having you stay with us," Barnett said. "We appreciate your service to the Southern cause." Caleb glanced down at his injured leg but held his tongue. No need giving voice to his thoughts. "Oh, I asked Janus to fill your blanket roll with supplies, food and drink for the trip."

Janus pulled the roll from the front floor of the carriage and handed it down to Caleb. He whispered, "Thank you. I wish you well."

Caleb nodded then slung the roll over his shoulder. It was heavy. Janus had packed it generously, so much so that carrying it would be a burden for a man who still walked with a limp.

February 9, 1865 ~ Washington D.C.

He looked at his full beard in the mirror of the cheap room that had been his home for weeks, ever since he was strong enough to leave the small town in Virginia. The beard was neatly trimmed and made quite a difference in his appearance. It would be hard for anyone to recognize him. And it complimented the officer's uniform, the lieutenant's bars on his shoulders. After all, few officers were clean-shaven. He studied his reflection and smiled. He honestly looked like an officer. Unless someone knew him personally, this would fool them. Where he was going, no one knew John Murray personally.

The Virginia doctor back in that small town had been sympathetic. Murray was given permission to live in the doctor's office, downstairs from the doctor's residence, until Murray was healthy enough to travel. Getting that permission was simple. He told the doctor he was a spy for the Confederacy, wounded by Union troops while on a mission. He also said he had to get to Washington to complete his assignment as soon as he could travel. Then he swore the doctor to secrecy. The Southerners would believe anything as long as those beliefs fit their desires.

He may have left Virginia too soon, however. By the time he rode the short distance back to Washington, his right arm was useless. Pounding pain had returned. But that was weeks ago. Now his wounds had healed enough to leave Washington. And it was none too soon. While the old lady who ran the boarding house had been sympathetic at first, thanks to his made-up story about getting wounded by Confederates while trying to find his brother's body in Virginia, her patience seemed to be waning. She was getting more demanding about paying the rent on time. She also wanted to raise the rent to the regular price. With his wounds healed, she no longer felt he needed a discount. To top that off, she was getting more reluctant to allow him to perform chores as a method of payment.

He had needed more medical treatment after arriving in Washington, so he found a nearby doctor. Unfortunately, that doctor would not treat him for free as the small town Virginia doctor had, and the man was getting persistent about his bill. Murray, persuasive with his promises of payment in the near future, had kept the doctor at bay by paying barely enough to string the man along.

Thank goodness Murray had had the foresight to use a false name. Since neither the doctor nor the landlady knew his real name, it would be a simple matter to dodge the doctor bills and the past due rent. All he had to do was get out of town unseen. That was easy enough to do. The old lady went to bed early.

Placing his uniform at the bottom of his bag, he packed the few things he carried on top of it. He was not sure he would ever need a Union officer's uniform, but it was comforting to know it was there if he did.

Even though it was late in the evening, he decided it was best to check the situation before walking out with a packed bag. He set his bag by the door to his room and walked out without it. A short walk through the rambling old house revealed that the coast was clear. The landlady was asleep, as were the other boarders. He slipped back into the room and retrieved his bag.

His right arm still bothered him. It would be a few more weeks before it was fully healed, so he carried the bag over his left shoulder. It was a shame that damned slave had come up from behind him. The colored man ruined everything. Murray would be rich, now, enjoying the pleasures that Washington had to offer if not for that. Under an assumed name, of course.

Murray was not sure how he had missed the colored man, how he had let the slave come up from behind undetected. He had watched the white woman for quite some time. She showed every sign of traveling alone. What he was sure of, absolutely definitely sure of, was that the damned slave was an expert with a blade.

Not only did Murray have to fire in a hurry, but he also had to use his left hand to hold the pistol. He was an expert marksman with his right. With his left, well, he did the best he could. The second bullet hit the big colored man somewhere in the chest. Maybe it killed him, but Murray didn't think so. It was possible the slave could have bled to death before the lady could reach help, but he could not depend on that. Best to be on the safe side and assume that the slave was still alive, still a threat to Murray's plans.

Those plans had been changed because of the weeks of delay. He had to give up the idea of completing his enlistment and receiving his pension. There would be no going back to the Union army now. Oh sure, he could fabricate a story that would explain his wounds and all the missing time, but he was already under suspicion in Elmira. Colt wouldn't believe him. Murray would be cashiered at best. And by now, there was no doubt whatsoever that he was wanted as a deserter. He might even get arrested before he could return and explain away his absence. With handcuffs on, they wouldn't even listen to his tale.

Besides, he was sick of being a picket, walking the stupid wall over and over. Even if he could talk his way out of a dishonorable discharge, which was a fantasy, going back to walking the wall was not something he wanted to do. He had had more than enough. No, there would be no going back, for many reasons. He had no choice but to kiss his pension goodbye. Time for a new life.

There were still fortunes to be made out west, one way or another. He had heard a lot of stories about people getting rich not just in California, but in other western states as well. The gold rush may have been over, but silver was still plentiful. And there were lots of other opportunities. Sure, he could work hard and establish a commercial enterprise in a fast growing area. That would make him a decent living. But Murray wanted more than a decent living. And he wanted it now, without all the hard work. He would have to find another way to get his hands on wealth, a quicker way.

But first things first. He needed seed money if he was going to get wealthy, and he knew where to get it. He was packed and ready to travel south. John Murray had banknotes to steal and scores to settle.

February 16, 1865 ~ Millie Hanson's Mansion, Richmond, Virginia

"No, Miss Emily, please," Carolina said. "If you go, you know he'll go with you. I can't stop him."

"But he doesn't have to," Emily said. "And he shouldn't. I can go home on my own. He needs to go back to Washington."

"He's a bull-headed man. He ain't going to change his mind. I know your family treated him well. Maybe that's the problem. He was bad mistreated before that. Your momma and daddy come along and fixed all that for him. He loves the Rose family. And he's bound and determined to see you home safely. I can't stop that, and I wouldn't try. But he was hurt serious, almost died. He's not well enough to travel yet. If y'all got in a tight spot, he wouldn't be as good as he was before. He needs a few more weeks, two or three, perhaps. Please, Miss Emily. Stay a little longer."

Emily Rose looked out the window at the barren tree limbs. If you looked close, you could see the oval-shaped dots of brand new buds on several of the trees, scattered along the length of the limbs, particularly the small limbs. In a few weeks, the light reddish-green of new leaves would be dancing to the March winds, and air would be warmer. As much as she wanted to go home, perhaps waiting was best. "I understand, Carolina. I wouldn't want to hurt Nathaniel in any way. I'll wait a little longer." She nodded with more certainty than she felt. She couldn't escape the feeling of dread inside that she'd made a wrong decision, that she needed to be home.

February 24, 1865 ~ Savannah, Georgia

Savannah was a pretty town. And it was still intact. Sherman had failed to do his job here. John Murray wondered why it had been spared the torch, why it was better than Atlanta. Sherman must have had good reason. Otherwise, he would have treated Savannah as he had every other part of the South.

But that was not Murray's concern at the moment. He was looking for Caleb Garner. Caleb had been ill, and his leg was not healed when they shipped him out of Elmira. With any luck at all, the Rebel animal was still in town, too sick to travel. It would have taken months for Caleb to heal. That is, if he was still alive.

Murray stopped his horse at the Home Guard office, a place hastily restored after the Yankees marched away to wreak their havoc on the Carolinas. Once inside, doing his best to imitate a Southern accent he said, "I'm, ah, Joseph Garner. I'm trying to find my brother, Caleb." He had used the first given name that popped into his head, that of Private Joseph Thomas, the soldier who pilfered things to help pay his gambling debts. He had no idea whether Caleb had a brother, but the chances were good. These Southerners were prolific breeders. "He was in the prisoner exchange back in November."

The man behind the desk, an older man with a hollow look to his eyes, stared at Murray for several seconds without saying anything. Was his attempt at a Southern accent that bad? Murray could forge the written word better than any man he had ever known, far better, but imitating accents was something altogether different.

He was about to say something else when the old man finally spoke. "I don't reckon I know where he is. We ain't got no records here. They might have some records out to Venus Point. Can't say. Not sure that sort of thing was recorded. If it was, they might not tell you no ways. Military records and all. Say, you're not from around here, are you?"

"Ah, no. We're from South Alabama."

"Don't sound like no Alabamian I ever talked to."

"Oh, well, we moved down from Pennsylvania some years before the war. Our sympathies were with the South. I guess I still have some Pennsylvania in me when I talk."

"I reckon you do. Well, wish I could have helped you. Good day to you."

Murray stared a second longer then turned on his heels and walked out. *Idiot Southerners!* He briefly thought about trying to find a ferry that went to Venus Point but gave up on that idea. It was doubtful that records existed. Most of these idiots didn't even know how to read and write. If they did have records, the stupid old man might have been right. They wouldn't tell him what he needed to know. But no matter. Caleb was sick. He would have been taken to one of the hospitals in town. It would be a simple matter to go to the hospitals until he found which one.

First, though, he needed to work on his accent. If he was going to be Caleb's brother, he needed to sound more like a Southerner. Time to go to a bar and have a few beers and listen.

February 26, 1865 ~ Georgia Countryside

Caleb sat on the ground, looking out from beneath the makeshift lean-to. The framework was constructed from fallen limbs that lay scattered about on the ground. They had no ax or saw to cut fresh supports. Several of them had knives, but no one had the energy to whittle a limb from a tree.

The top of the lean-to was covered with smaller limbs, scrap boards from a nearby home that had burned, and anything else they could find. It was not large, so the six of them huddled together trying to stay dry and warm.

The weather had been rainy for days. No matter how hard they tried or what they put on the framework above them, the lean-to still leaked here and there. Considering the materials they had to work with, they knew it would, so they built it on the highest part of the old railroad track bed, with the ground sloping toward the open side. The water that dripped through ran in small rivulets under the lean-to and out into the open then down to the standing pools on the sides of the track bed. The trick was to sit in an area where there was no leak and no rivulet. If you moved around, you would get wet.

"I wisht this rain would quit so's we could get going," the man with the amputated leg, Jesse, said for the hundredth time.

"I wish Caleb had another bottle of wine," Walter said. Walter was slightly taller than average and still had all his limbs. But something was missing inside the man. You could see it in his eyes. He typically said little but drank a lot if there was something to drink, which there hadn't been since early in the trip. "Those two bottles he had were gone the first night."

"Yeah," Jesse said. "You drank one of them all by yourself. And part of the other."

"I can't help it if y'all drink too slow. And since you've got me thinking about drinking, we need to get going so we can find someone else with some bark juice or some John Barleycorn. There's bound to be somebody along the way who's making a batch right now. Maybe they'll share a little like the last man did."

Between the six of them, they had no money for purchasing liquor or beer. Their only cash was the fifteen dollars Barnett had given Caleb to buy a train ticket in Macon, and Caleb was the only one in the group who knew he had it. The bills were safely tucked into his sock. Since his socks had holes in them, he slept with his shoes on.

"I'm happy I don't have to lug those bottles no more," Caleb said. "They was right heavy that first day."

"Why, hell's bells," Albert said. "I'd lug the damned things for you if we had some. And I only got one arm."

A hollow laugh echoed out from under the lean-to, but quiet quickly overtook them as they sat and watched the afternoon fade into evening. There was little movement other than Albert shifting his legs around, something he did regularly. Caleb thought since an arm was missing, perhaps he needed the reassurance of knowing he still had both legs.

An old friend, reddish-gold rays of sunlight, greeted them the next morning. Bright colors danced on the surface of the pools on both sides of the track bed as the water receded. The pools would soon be gone, giving way to the dirt and decayed leaves that made up earth's winter surface. They decided to leave the lean-to standing in case anyone behind them might need it. There was no worry about a train hitting it since the metal rails lay around on either side of the track bed, twisted in knots. It would be a long time before a train conductor saw this part of rural Georgia again.

Caleb's limp had improved since leaving Savannah, which was encouraging, but he still had trouble keeping up. The six of them tended to string out along the bed, not staying in a group, with Walter's long legs in the lead, and Jesse pulling up the rear as he hobbled along on his crutches. Jesse would periodically call out to the others to wait on him. They didn't answer, but they quietly stopped and waited until Caleb then Jesse caught up. Once they were a group again, they turned back toward Macon and resumed walking, often without saying a word.

That afternoon they came to a place where the train used to cross the river, but the track no longer extended over the water. The timbers of the trestle lay haphazardly on the shore and in the water below, splintered, burned, and broken. Twisted metal rails were scattered in and among the shattered timbers. Sherman's men had done their job well.

"This ain't no little creek where y'all can carry me and wade over," Jesse said. "This is the Ogeechee River. The train track's been a'following it pretty much ever sincet we left Savannah, but the river's turning north. We got to go west. We're going to have to build a raft to get acrosst. Only we got no tools to build with. I'm beginning to wonder if I'm ever going to get home."

"Look down there," Caleb said. "There's smoke coming up through the trees. It's got to be a house, over that crest, there."

"And a rope stretching all the way across the river," Albert said as the pointing finger on his only arm traced a line in the distance. "Lookee there."

"If somebody lives here, I bet he's got some red eye. Hell, cheap old popskull would be fine," Walter said.

"Let's get down there and find out," one of the other men, a former sergeant named Edgar, said. "I bet he's got a raft and can pull us across the river. We can pick the railroad bed up again on the other side."

"As long as he don't charge to take us across," Jesse said.

They turned quiet as they started down the slope, weaving through the trees toward the smoke that rose into the air. Once they were far enough so that the bank of the river came into view, they could see a log home and two smaller log buildings. Several people were milling about. Sure enough, there was a raft tied to the shore, at the same spot where the rope that crossed the river was anchored.

"Howdy," a plump man with a red beard that reached almost all the way down to his waist said as they walked into the opening where the buildings stood. The red hair on his head was almost as long as his beard. Two men with muskets hanging between their arms and sides walked up to the group and stood on either side. "Soldiers on your way home, eh?"

"Easy to tell," Jesse said.

"Sure enough. We've seen a lot of Confederate soldiers straggling home lately."

"Former *guests* of that sorry-ass Yankee hospitality," Albert said. "We got exchanged. On our way home. Say, how much further is it to Macon?"

"You're pretty much halfway from Savannah to Macon. Thereabouts."

"Well, hell," Albert said. "I was hoping we were a mite closer than that."

"We need to get across the river," Jesse said. "That your raft?"

"Yessir. I run the ferry. You got any coin? Can't run a business giving rides for free."

"Hell, no," Albert said. "All we got is a need to get our tails home. Ain't nobody following this track got any money. Most all of us were prisoners. The damned Yankees didn't pay us nothing for being prisoners. They hardly even fed us."

"Yessir. That's a sad tale for sure. I noticed there wasn't much money coming through with the soldiers going home. Lots of would-be customers, but it's hard to make a living if those customers can't pay. I can't help folks for free. It cost me plenty to run this place. Do you have anything of value?"

"You got any popskull? John Barleycorn? Anything?" Walter asked.

"Yessir, we've got some of the best red eye you'll find in these parts. Beer, too. But it ain't free either. My name's Red, and that building there is my tavern." He pointed toward one of the two smaller buildings. "Let's step inside and sit down. We can discuss business better in there."

They followed Red into the small log building. The two men carrying muskets followed behind them. The tavern was simple. A half-log, cut lengthwise, was propped on two shorter logs and served as the bar. Behind it, there was a simple wood table: a rough-sawn board with four limbs for legs. On top of the table, there were several glasses of various styles, a huge jug of gold liquid, and a smaller jar of reddish-brown liquid. The stools scattered along in front of the bar were nothing more than short logs turned upright.

Red sat on the cut surface of the first log and nodded at one of the two men with muskets. The man set his rifle against the wall and poured

Red a drink from the jar with the reddish-brown liquid. The plump man, Red, held the drink out and said, "Yessir, this is some pretty fine stuff. Hits a man the right way when he needs it." He took a sip then said, "Two big shots for two bits. I don't cheat my customers."

"We ain't got no money," Walter said.

"That's a shame," Red said as he took another sip. "Yessir, I understand about you not having no money as long as you understand that I can't give stuff away. This here is my business, my livelihood. That's how I pay these fellers here." He pointed at his two men. "So, since you've got no money, what do you have? I'm willing to work with you men, being Confederate soldiers and all, but you need something of value. We've had a few come through who didn't have nothing to barter. They tried to swim across. Some made it. Some didn't. Even had a one-legged man try to swim across. Heck, he didn't even get halfway. So what is it? Do you have anything on you that's worth something?"

Five of the six former soldiers looked at each other. The sixth, Walter, sat and stared at the jug of liquor on the table behind the bar.

"I ain't got nothing," Jesse said. "'Cept my crutches. But I need them if I'm going to get home."

"Hellfire," Albert said. "I'd give you my boots, but I need them for the trip, too. I can't walk on those track bed rocks in my bare feet.

Red looked down at Albert's boots and said, "I said something of value. Your toes are about to pop through those ragged things." He looked back up and continued, "Ain't none of you got a ring or watch or pistol or anything with any value?"

"I got to have a drink," Walter said. He stood and walked around the bar, stepping toward the table where the booze rested.

"Don't put your hand on that jug unless you can pay for it," Red said. "It might come back with fewer than five fingers."

Walter acted as though he didn't hear the plump man. He reached for the whiskey, but the man who had served Red's drink grabbed Walter before he could reach the jug. With a strong hand, he jerked Walter back, hard and fast.

"Leave me alone!" Walter shouted. He lunged toward Red, trying to reach the half-full glass the plump man held in front of him. Red jerked his hand back.

The silver of a blade flashed in the sunlight that came through two small windows set high in the front wall. A knife had found its way into Walter's hand. His arm swung back, building momentum for the plunge forward, toward Red. A shot rang out. Walter's hand stopped in mid-swing. It hesitated a moment then came straight down as his body fell to the floor. The knife tumbled across the rough-sawn boards.

Caleb froze. His eyes grew large as he watched Walter twitch then become still, a pool of blood growing around the edges of his torso and a red hole in his back. Caleb had seen many men die in battle, and many more die in prison. Those deaths had been senseless, but they did have the excuse of war. This was different. Walter died for no sensible reason whatsoever.

The man who had grabbed Walter's hand picked up his musket and held it on them as the other man reloaded.

"You kilt him," Jesse said, his mouth hanging open and his eyes wide.

Caleb took a step backward. He wanted so much to get home, to let his eyes rest on Emily Rose's beautiful face once again. It would be senseless to die now, after everything he had been through and all the miles he had traveled? Absolutely senseless.

The other four former soldiers stepped back as well.

"Don't look so afeared," Red said. He took another sip of whiskey before continuing. "Pure case of self-defense. If my man, here, hadn't shot him, he was, sure enough, going to poke me with that pig sticker. I'm sure you all seen it clear enough. If you don't mean me no harm, I don't mean you no harm."

"Oh, no," Edgar said. "No harm. We don't mean no one no harm."

"Fair enough then," Red said as he bent over and picked up the knife. "This will have to do as compensation for burying the man. Oh, don't worry about the sheriff. He's a friend of mine. I'll make the report next time he's down this way. Y'all won't have to be here. You're free to go on home. And speaking of that, let's get back to business. Any of you have anything valuable, something worth the fare to get the five of you that's left across the river? Otherwise, you'll have to swim across. Or go back the way you came."

February 27, 1865 ~ Savannah, Georgia

Three days had been wasted knocking on doors. Not the whole time, of course. Murray had spent a great deal of time listening to others in bars and working on his Southern accent back in his hotel room, standing in front of the mirror and watching his mouth move as he spoke. But he had rapped his knuckles against doors and banged door knockers until he was sick of them.

The first hospital he visited had explained that the exchange prisoners were hidden in resident's homes. They also explained that there was no record of who was hidden or whose home they were hidden in. On purpose. They didn't want any paper around for Sherman to find. Caleb could have been anywhere. All Murray could do was ask the townspeople. One at a time. A needle in a haystack.

Murray learned that most of the former prisoners had left Savannah within a few days of Sherman's departure. Caleb was probably gone, too. If not, he would make his way out of town soon. It was doubtful Murray would find him going door-to-door. It was too slow a process. And he had knocked on so many doors and asked so many people about Caleb Garner, the repetition was making it difficult to say the name.

But he had to keep trying. Searching in the wealthier part of Savannah, he walked along the brick walk and knocked on the front door of another mansion. Within moments, a colored man answered the door.

"Good afternoon," Murray said. "I'm Joseph Garner, from Alabama. I'm looking for my brother, Caleb Garner. He was part of the prisoner release a while back. Our family believes he was staying at a home here while he recuperated." No need to mention hiding from Sherman's men. That went without question.

"Not at this residence, Sir. I can ask my master if he knows the name. Please wait here."

Several seconds later an older white man came back. His hair was gray, not a single strand of dark to be found, but his suit was impeccable. It seemed out of place for a South that had been ravaged by war. "May I help you," the man said.

Murray repeated his story.

"I see. We had two soldiers staying with us, but they're both gone now. Neither by that name, though. Still, it does sound familiar. Let me think." He put his fist to his lips and blew into it, looking down as he concentrated. "Oh, yes. I remember hearing Barnett Talbot mention that name. More than once. I believe the gentleman was staying at the Talbot home. It's two streets over. Close by. Perhaps your brother is still there. I'll give you directions."

Murray found the Talbot residence and tied his horse out front. If Caleb was still there, this was going to be tricky. Chances were if Caleb had brothers, none of them were named Joseph. So if the servant or Mr. Talbot, whoever answered the door, went inside and told Caleb that Joseph Garner had come to find him, they would soon know Caleb had no brother named Joseph. Mr. Talbot would be forewarned that something was up. In that case, Murray would need to keep his hand near his pistol. He might have no choice but to kill everyone in the house. He didn't want to do that. Too messy. Besides, he wasn't a wanton killer. He only killed for good reason. But if he had no choice, he would do whatever it took. He gathered his nerves and rapped his knuckles on the door. After a short wait, a black man opened the door.

"May I help you?" Janus Slade said.

"Yes, please. I'm looking for Caleb Garner."

"And you are?"

"Joseph Garner. I'm his brother. I have come to get him, and I was told he was staying here."

"Ah, I see," Janus said.

"Who is it, Janus?" came a voice from inside the home.

"A Mister Joseph Garner, Sir. Caleb's brother."

A well-groomed, middle-aged gentleman appeared at the door. "Barnett Talbot," the man said as he extended his hand for a shake. "Yes, Caleb mentioned that he had several brothers. But he is no longer with us. He left, what? Not quite a month ago. He should be well on his way home by now, though getting home might take quite some time. The tracks were destroyed by Sherman as I'm sure you know. He was going to have to walk all the way to Macon. He was traveling in a group, along with some other released prisoners.

"And his health?" Murray asked.

"Quite good," Barnett said. "I'm not sure how much you know, but you'll be happy to hear his pneumonia has fully healed. He still walks with a limp from a wound he received, but it continues to get better. I don't believe it will be permanent. I dare say that he will be walking normally in a matter of months."

"I'm sorry I missed him, but that's wonderful news. Thank you so much, Mr. Talbot. Well, I'm happy to know he's on his way home. I will go back and wait on him." Murray smiled and nodded and left.

There was no sense chasing after Caleb through the Georgia forests and hills. No telling where he was. And if he were with a group of soldiers, that would make Murray's task even harder. One or two of them might be armed. Perhaps all of them. These backwoods types were religious about their weapons. No, taking on a group of former soldiers might not be wise.

He had been kicking a plan around in his head all morning. He could put on the lieutenant's uniform then forge a letter from Secretary Stanton, complete with a signature that no one would be able to refute. The letter would state that John Murray was a special agent on secret assignment to locate a traitor to the Union, Caleb Garner. Murray could also forge the order for Union soldiers to execute Caleb on the spot, at the moment of capture. With those two papers, he could travel by boat to Pensacola and convince the commanding officer to provide him with an escort to help find Caleb. All Murray had to do was set the execution in motion. He wouldn't even have to be there when the firing squad pulled their triggers. He could be safely riding away, with a smile on his face and not even a trace of blood on his hands. At least, as far as the law was concerned.

It was a good plan, but there were problems with it. Murray was not sure if the Union forces in Pensacola had access to telegraph. It was doubtful since they would have to use Confederate telegraph lines, but on the off chance they did, it would be an easy matter to telegraph the War Department in Washington to verify Murray's cover story. Of course, it would not be verified, and he would be jailed.

Besides, it was highly doubtful the Union commander would provide him with a military escort for going deep into southern territory. It was too dangerous.

As much as he liked the boldness of the plan, it had too many potential pitfalls. Better to take a simple approach. He would ride due west across Georgia and Alabama, straight to Conecuh County. It would be an easy matter to find Caleb's house and wait for a moment when he could catch Caleb alone. Once he did, he would put a bullet in the man's head. Then he would find Emily Rose's home and do whatever he wanted to her before killing her and taking her money. With the money safely in his bags, he would go out west where no one would ever know.

Doing the killings himself brought in an element of risk he would prefer to have avoided, but it couldn't be helped. He would have to be careful. He would have to get away undetected and go out west as quickly as he could ride.

There was one other thing he had to be mindful of, Nathaniel Whiteeagle. The big slave might still be alive and protecting Emily Rose. But that would not matter. Aside from an occasional ache in bad weather, Murray's right arm was now fully healed. If the slave survived, Murray wouldn't miss the colored man's heart this time. John Murray was too good a shot.

February 28, 1865 ~ Millie Hanson's Mansion, Richmond, Virginia

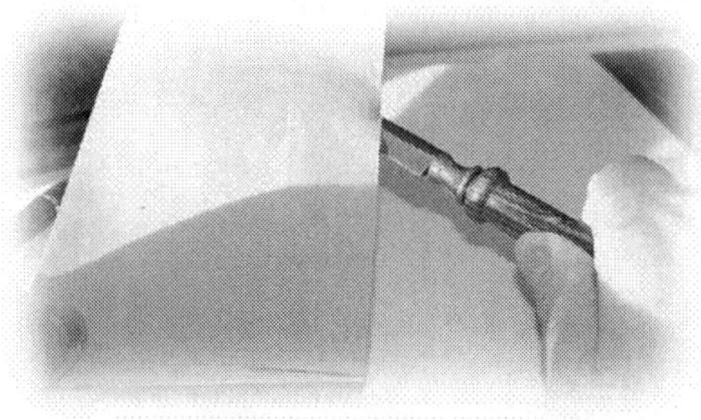

"A letter from Thomas!" Millie shouted as she ran through the house. "It got through."

"What?" Emily asked.

Aunt Mille stopped in front of Emily, who was seated beside Carolina at the servant's table. Millie held her chest and took a couple of deep breaths before continuing, "I got a letter from your father. Mail from that far away is so rare nowadays. If this letter got through, maybe things are getting better. I'll read it to you."

She opened the envelope, her fingers taking meticulous care not to damage the paper. If the inside had not been used, she could always fold it inside out and reuse it. The letter was only one short page. "It's…" Millie started. She stared at the paper a second then said, "It's his handwriting, but there's not much here. The letters are larger than he normally writes."

"His eyes might be going bad," Carolina offered. "It happens as people get older."

"Yes, of course. It's quite short. Oh dear. Oh, no."

"What is it?" Emily asked.

"Your mother. I'm so sorry. She passed away. Consumption."

"No," Emily gasped. Her hand went to her mouth as tears began to roll down her cheeks. "I won't get to see Momma again. Never."

"Oh, you sweet dear," Millie said. "God will watch out for her. She was too good a woman. He will take her under his arms." Millie's tears also began to flow as she reached out to hug Emily.

Carolina cried, too, though she had never met Emily's mother, couldn't even remember what Emily said her mother's name was.

"It's… Do you want to read it?"

Emily nodded as the tears continued to roll, the skin on her face turning red.

Millie handed the sheet of paper to Emily.

Dear Millie,

I laid Mary to rest yesterday. It was consumption. After Emily left, her cough got worse and worse until she couldn't get out of bed. There was nothing the doctor could do. It finally took her. I will miss her dearly.

I have not heard from Emily. I fear the worst. I could not bear it if something has happened to my baby. I would never forgive myself for having let her leave on such a dangerous trip.

If she contacts you, please let me know.

Sincerely,

Thomas Rose

"I'm so sorry, dear," Millie said. She hugged Emily again.

"Thank you," Emily said. She collapsed back into her chair. Carolina patted her on the shoulder. The tears had slowed, but they still came.

"If he doesn't know you've been here," Millie said. "That means none of my letters have gotten through, none since your arrival. With the Yankees burning Atlanta and raiding here and there all through the South, the mail has become so unreliable. I'm surprised his letter got through."

Emily looked up at Millie with red eyes and said, "I must go home. My father needs me. I cannot wait any longer. I must leave right away."

Carolina nodded. She stood and said, "I'll let Nathaniel know so he can start packing."

March 21, 1865 ~ Union Command, Milton, Florida

"Conecuh County?" Sergeant Major James Ross said. "I met a Rebel soldier from there. Nice fellow. Can't remember his name at the moment. I called him Conecuh. Met his fiancée, too. Beautiful lady."

"You've been to Conecuh County?" Colonel Andrew Spurling asked. He eyed the sergeant major suspiciously.

"Oh, no. I've never been anywhere in Alabama. She came to my last post, Belle Plains. She was trying to find Conecuh. He was a prisoner of war. She wanted to buy his freedom."

"I doubt that went well."

"I don't know, Sir. I was in the process of being transferred here. She was still trying to find him when I left."

"Regardless of your *friends*, Sergeant Major, our mission is to cut off the resupply and escape route for the Confederates at Mobile. We will be destroying the Alabama and Florida track through Conecuh County. We are to destroy their ability to make war at every opportunity. We will wreak havoc and destruction in a manner that will destroy their will to fight. Do you understand?"

"Yes, Sir."

"And if your friend has returned and does anything to impede our mission, then he is to be dealt with accordingly. We will take him prisoner if possible. If not, well, you understand what you have to do."

"Yes, Sir. He was a prisoner who I befriended in a different setting. I am fully aware of the need for our mission, and the importance of bringing about a victory over the rebelling states. You can count on me."

"Excellent, Sergeant Major Ross. Please instruct the other officers to gather their men. I will address all three cavalry brigades as a unit before we depart."

It did not take long to bring the three brigades together. This would be a major raid deep into the heart of the South, cut off from any hope of Union reinforcements. Tensions were high, but expectations were higher. The men had been up and ready for some time.

"Gentlemen," Spurling began, "Our objective is to destroy the supply and escape route through an area that has enjoyed full Confederate control for far too long: Evergreen, Gravella, and Sparta in Conecuh County. We will bring the reality of war to areas that have not suffered the destruction and the struggles of battle. It is our job not only to destroy railways, trains, military facilities, supply facilities, and anything else that can be used to the benefit of the Confederate soldier, but also to destroy the very will to fight in one of the few areas of the South that has seen no true combat.

"Anyone who fires upon us is to be fired upon. We will capture if we can, or kill if we must. Anyone who stands in the way of our destruction of the Confederate ability to make war is subject to be fired upon. Anyone. You may see young boys and withered old men in gray uniform. They will have muskets that will be aimed at you. Just because they are far too young or too old to be soldiers does not mean they won't pull that trigger. You will treat them like any other Confederate soldier. Unless they raise their hands in surrender, you are to shoot to kill. No exceptions.

"We will move swiftly and decisively. Do not get comfortable at any stop as we will stay nowhere for any length of time. We will ride long hours. You may miss some sleep. You can sleep when we return to Pensacola. The success of our mission will depend not only on destroying the Rebel ability to make war, but also on how fast we can accomplish our goals. If we move slowly and lag behind, we run the risk of allowing the Confederates time to gather their forces in sufficient strength to fight back. If they do, many of you could lose your life. I will NOT let that happen. I will push you hard.

"With God's blessing, we will accomplish our goals, shorten this war, and be back here in a few days. I wish you well. Move out!"

March 22, 1865 ~ Rose Residence, Forks of Sepulga Community, Alabama

"Oh, Daddy," Emily said as she encased her father with her arms, squeezing as hard as she could and feeling very much like a little girl again. "I have missed you so much."

"I didn't hear from you," Thomas said as he hugged back, careful not to squeeze as hard as the loneliness inside him wanted to. He didn't want to hurt his little girl. "I was afraid you were dead."

Emily leaned back but did not break her embrace as she said, "We couldn't get a letter through. The South is such a mess. Much of the railroad track is destroyed. Many buildings, even homes, are in charred ruins. Former slaves and former soldiers are on the roads and in the forests, small groups and large groups. Some of them are traveling alone. They seem to be wandering around aimlessly. There are areas where the rule of law no longer covers the land. If it hadn't been for Nathaniel…" She let the words lie as she renewed her hug.

After they finally released, Thomas looked over at Nathaniel, who had stood stoically to the side during the lengthy greeting, and said, "I am so indebted to you. I couldn't have lived with myself if something had happened to my Emily." Thomas extended his hand.

Nathaniel only nodded as he shook Thomas' hand, but Emily could see the release in his eyes. He had fulfilled a promise that meant so much to him. He was now free to find a new life.

"Where is Momma buried?" Emily asked. "I want to go see her."

"Out back, near the trees. I thought she would want to be close to home, especially if you made it back alive. She would want you to say goodbye to her. Come. I'll show you."

They stepped outside and walked toward the forest in the back, not too many steps behind the house. As soon as they rounded the building corner, Emily saw the stone marker. Thomas had spent money on a nice one. It made Emily feel good inside. She wanted her mother to be recognized for the wonderful woman she was.

Emily walked up beside the grave and held Thomas' hand as the warmth inside her dissolved into tears. They streamed down her cheeks as she said, "Hello, Momma. I missed you more than I can ever explain. I wish I could have gotten home sooner so I could have hugged you one last time. I tried so hard."

Thomas squeezed her hand lightly and said, "She knows you did. She's up there smiling down at you right now."

Emily glanced at the sky and smiled, but the tears continued to flow.

When they finally went back inside, Emily turned to her father and said, "I like that she's so close to the house, Daddy. But I thought you were going to start the family plot back in that small clearing in the forest. You and Momma talked about how you wanted to be surrounded by nature on your land."

Thomas looked away a moment then turned back and tensed his lips in a grimace before finally saying, "It ain't our land."

"What? What do you mean? That's always been ours. The forest and the open fields on the other side, where we used to grow cotton and vegetables. I don't understand."

"I sold it right after your mother died. The livestock, too. Except the horses. I kept them for pulling the wagon. And because I knew how much you love to ride."

"You sold our family farm?"

"Not the house and the yard. Mary is buried on property that's still ours. But I sold the forest and the fields. All of it."

"Why?"

"Emily, your mother's death took something out of me. It took everything out of me. I didn't want to farm anymore. I didn't want to raise cotton or keep after the animals. It wasn't in me once she was no longer here. When I thought about it, I realized it hadn't been in me for years. I was only going through the motions. So I sold the land for all of us. Mary was gone, and it looked for all the world like you weren't coming home, either. I was afraid you were… Well, I put out the word and got an offer. It wasn't as much as I'd have liked, but with the war going on and the South losing, it was better than I expected. I took it. That's what Mary told me to do before she passed. She knew me well enough to know that my heart was not in the place any longer. And she wanted me to sell it for you."

"Me?"

"Yes. She didn't want you to live a farmer's life, not here in the defeated South. She said it makes you old before your time, that you were so beautiful you deserved better. So she told me to sell it for you. I'm going to stay here for what few years I've got left. I don't need much. Most of the money is yours. You can buy yourself a nice place somewhere out west, maybe in a city where there's more opportunity."

Emily stared at her father in disbelief. She had always assumed, as the only child of Thomas and Mary Rose, that she would inherit the farm. She never thought about the work of running a farm, at least not when she was younger. As she got older and fell in love, she assumed that Caleb would be beside her, that they would live together in this very home, the best farmers in Conecuh County. Somehow, she had never thought about whether she wanted to be a farmer's wife or not. It was the way things were, the sort of thing you grew into without question. Now it was not just questioned, it was tumbled down, laying in pieces at her feet. She was stunned. She said nothing. She could think of nothing to say.

"You need to leave," Thomas continued. He glanced at Nathaniel and nodded at the tall colored man. "Both of you. The South is going to surrender any day. It's inevitable. No one knows what that's going to mean for us, but you can rest assured that Yankee soldiers will be around here for a long time. It ain't going to be the same. And there ain't going to be the kind of opportunity for a good life like you deserve. Both of you."

"Nathaniel is going to Washington," Emily said. "He's got a good job there. But what about me? Where would I go?"

"Out west," Thomas answered. "The open range in Texas where the land is too big for the Yankees to control. Or further west. California if need be. Somewhere you can be free, where you can find a good life, where you won't be shackled by being a beat down Southerner. If you still want to farm, there's plenty of land out there. But if you want to do something that could make a better living, an easier living, there's cities, too."

"I love you, Daddy. And I loved Momma so much. If that's what she wanted me to do, that's what I'll do. But not without Caleb. I won't leave till he comes home and says he wants to go with me."

March 23, 1865 ~ A & F Railroad Station, Montgomery, Alabama

"This here is my home," Jesse said. "South of here a piece. I'm not done with the walking yet, but I'm close enough so's I can just about smell it."

"You take care," Caleb said. "I hope everything is okay when you get home."

"Me, too. My wife don't know about my leg yet. Kids either. I didn't know how to tell them. Didn't write no letters no ways. I guess they'll know when they set eyes on me. It'd be sorta hard to miss."

Caleb smiled then said, "They won't care a flit about your leg, Jesse. They'll be so happy to see you home it won't matter none. I 'spect they've been mighty worried about you ever getting home again."

"I reckon you may be right. And I'll be happy to see them. Maybe I can do enough to make some sort of living for us. Anyways, I won't be going into that next station with you, but I sure do appreciate what you did for us back in Georgia. If you hadn't had that five dollars on you, I'd have tried to swim acrosst. Don't reckon I'd have made it with one leg. I might be at the bottom of that river now, the catfish picking my bones clean."

"I'm glad five dollars was enough."

"Enough? Heck, did you see the way Red looked at those bills? And it was United States Notes, too. Money your friends in Savannah got off Sherman's men. I think he'd have taken us acrosst the river three times for that five dollars if we'd have asked him to."

Caleb laughed, but the laugh died quickly. "It left enough money from what Mr. Talbot gave me so we could get some good food. Thank goodness the trains are letting us ride for free."

"You're powerful right about that. I was sick and tired of walking by the time we got to Macon. If they'd wanted me to pay to get home to Montgomery, I might have had to make my home right there in Macon instead."

Caleb looked around at the station. He was eager to get going, to complete his long three-year ordeal and get home to see Emily. It was early yet. If there was a train soon, he could be home before the day was over.

"You take care," Jesse said, "I wisht you a good trip. You ever get up this way, come find me. I'll introduce you to my family."

They shook hands, and Caleb stood there for some time watching Jesse hobble away on his crutch. When Jesse was little more than a dark speck well down the road, Caleb turned and walked into the station.

"I need to get home to Gravella," he told the ticket salesman. "They let me ride for free all the way from Macon to here."

The salesman eyed Caleb's worn and patched up uniform. "Welcome to the Alabama and Florida Railroad, soldier. You can ride free with us, too. Glad you made it home." He wrote on a small piece of paper and pounded it with his stamp then handed it to Caleb. "Here's your ticket. It goes to Evergreen. Closest I could get on the train going south. Only the northbound train stops at Gravella. I didn't think you'd want to go all the way to Mobile and back to avoid a short walk up the road."

"You're right, for sure. The sooner I get home the better. Thank you so much."

"You're welcome, son. You've got quite a wait, though. The train is not on its regular schedule. Hell, nothing much is anymore. It doesn't leave till close to midnight. It'll get to Evergreen in the morning. You'll be in fine company, though."

"How's that?"

"There'll be over a hundred regular troops on the train with you. Going down to Mobile. They'll be fighting the Yankees down there. If they don't run into them sooner."

March 23, 1865 ~ Conecuh County and Gravella, Alabama

Gravella, Alabama, was a smudge on the map, hardly worthy of the name 'town.' But the railroad came through, as did the highway from Montgomery to Mobile. Where these two crossed, a few rough buildings, the town of Gravella, had grown. John Murray arrived on horseback early that morning. Making casual conversation with the locals, he found out where the Garner home was located. He rode by. As Murray expected, it was nothing, a small log cabin. The fields were strewn with weeds. There was little livestock. The few animals he saw looked undernourished. As far as he was concerned, the place was little better than a pigsty.

The clerk at the Sepulga General Store was talkative enough. Caleb had not returned from the war. Nobody knew if he would be returning. Most people assumed that Caleb, like his brother early in the war, was now dead. So many Southern boys were. If he was still alive and did come home, he would find only problems and sorrow. Sam, his father, had passed some time back. His mother was losing her memory. She might not even recognize him.

Murray returned to the railroad crossing at Gravella that evening, intending to wait it out. He was sure Caleb had caught the train in Macon and would be home any day. All he had to do was watch and wait.

There was a tavern, such as it was, close to the crossing. Murray sat through several drinks, sipping slowly and listening to surrounding conversations. There were only a few, and those died early. By eleven o'clock, he was the only person left other than the owner.

"What time does the train from Montgomery stop?" he asked.

"You mean from Mobile?"

"No. Montgomery."

"The train from Montgomery don't stop here. Southbound, it only stops in Evergreen. Northbound, out of Mobile and Pollard, stops here."

"What about the southbound?" Murray asked. "If somebody was traveling from Montgomery to Gravella, would they have to stop in Evergreen and come back to Gravella on horseback?"

"More likely walk. Lots of walkers around here. But it's not far. Only five miles, straight back up the road. Two-hour walk if you ain't already tuckered out."

"What time does the southbound get to Evergreen?"

"It's supposed to get there a little after four o'clock in the afternoon, but with all the troop movements and the war going so crazy, the times are all mixed up. I ain't heard it pass through Gravella yet today, so it's running late. Or it ain't gonna run at all. Might run in the morning. No telling. You through with that glass? I need to close down."

"Sure." Murray slid the glass over to the owner. "So I haven't missed today's train?"

"Not yet."

Murray nodded and left. It was after eleven. Should he go to the trouble of riding the five miles to Evergreen? Being on the road this late might cause some suspicions if somebody was up. That would not be a problem in normal times, but these were anything but normal times.

He could stay in Gravella and set his bedroll out a short distance from the rails. If the train came through, it would wake him up. Then he could ride to Evergreen. But what if Caleb was on the train? During the time it took Murray to get to Evergreen, Caleb might get past him. Sure, he could always go by Caleb's farm. But it would be so much easier to jump Caleb on the road with no one around. After that, it would be a simple matter to find Emily Rose and get the seed money he would need out west. If she was back home. If not, she was bound to be home soon. He would wait on her, too, if necessary.

But everything had to go his way. When they found Caleb's body, the first thing they would do is question strangers. Murray was not only a stranger, but he had also been asking about Caleb. So he was going to have to find a way to hide Caleb's body so that no one would discover it before he could finish with Emily Rose, get her money, and leave. It was messy any way Murray looked at it. He stopped his horse as he tried to decide what to do. The more he thought about it, the worse it sounded.

In the quiet of late evening, he could hear sounds, scraping sounds and horse's hooves and men's voices. What was going on? He looked toward the noises, moving his head back and forth to pick out something in the dark. There, a man climbing a telegraph pole. He was wearing a hat. A soldier. Below the pole, there were dozens of soldiers on horseback.

Murray had expected to see Confederate soldiers in this area, but not so many of them. He needed to hide. He glanced at his surroundings then back at the soldier near the top of the pole. There was something about the hat. He looked more closely. The man reached up and cut the telegraph lines. A Union soldier!

Union soldiers this deep into the South? Cutting the communication lines? This was a raid, a Union raid in Conecuh County!

The ground reverberated, and the air shook. Horses, lots of them. More cavalry arrived. Two groups of men dismounted and began to tear up the tracks through Gravella. There was no need to worry about a train getting to Evergreen. Any train coming from Montgomery would stop here, derailed. He no longer needed to ride south.

Union soldiers, however, were inconvenient. He was here to get rich and leave some bodies in his wake. That might not sit well with the Union commander, especially since one of the bodies would be a pretty young lady. Better to wait until the raiding party was gone. They wouldn't be here long for fear of Confederate troops arriving to chase them off.

He led his horse back into the woods to the southeast, far enough away where he would not have to worry about being seen or heard, but close enough so that he could see what was going on. Then he muzzled his horse, tied it to a tree, and laid out his bedroll. Might as well get some sleep.

March 24, 1865 ~ Gravella, Alabama

John Murray was jarred awake by the screeching of metal and the booms of collisions. He looked out from the trees to see a train bouncing across the earth, derailed by the torn up track. It was a northbound train. The engine came to rest with flames licking up around the boiler and cabin. He glanced at his watch. Four-thirty in the morning.

Murray could see that there was a lot of activity around the train, but he wasn't sure what was going on. The sky was still dark. There was a set of field glasses in his saddlebag, standard issue for Union officers. He had taken them during his time at Elmira, and no one had ever been the wiser. He pulled them out and lifted them to his eyes. Adjusting the focus, he could see that the Union soldiers were carrying torches, setting the rest of the train on fire. Freight cars were mostly wood. They caught quickly, shooting flames high into the night sky.

Caleb would not have been on a northbound train. When the fire began to burn out, he lowered his field glasses and settled back on his bedroll.

A few hours later, he was awakened again by the loud screech of metal on metal. This time, there were no sounds of collision. A quick look told him it was a southbound train. He glanced at his watch. Seven-thirty in the morning. The daylight allowed the train conductor to see that the tracks were destroyed. He had stopped the train before it derailed.

Gunfire broke out. There must have been Confederate soldiers on the train. Murray scrunched down behind the tree. No one should be shooting in his direction, but there was no sense taking a chance.

~ O ~

Emily stepped outside to look around at the land that was no longer a part of the Rose family. She would miss it, but she understood why her father had sold it. Perhaps he was right. Perhaps it was time to get away, to move out west and start a new life. If only Caleb would come home. If he was still alive and able to come home. It had been so long since the prisoner exchange. They were invalid prisoners, all sick, and Caleb was one of them. As painful as the thought was, she had to face the reality that he may not be coming home, that he may already be buried somewhere she might never find.

She looked up at a flock of blackbirds taking to the air, going out for the day. The birds didn't care about war, about the ugly scars men cut into the earth, cut into themselves and their hearts. Their existence was so simple. They flew out every morning in search of food. They congregated at night to rest.

Her reverie was broken by the sound of hooves pounding the trail. Someone was moving fast. She ran back to the front of their home to see who it was, why they were in such a hurry. Nick Stallworth was driving his wagon down the trail, whipping his horse into a fury and going too fast for the narrow, winding path. Emily waved him down.

"What's wrong, Nick?"

Nathaniel came rushing outside.

"Yankees," Nick said through heavy breaths as though he was the one who had been pulling the wagon and not his horse. "It's a raid down to Gravella. Lots of Yankee cavalry. The train from Montgomery got stopped. Those devils captured a bunch of our boys. I'm riding down the road to warn everybody, to tell them to stay away from town."

Emily whirled around and shouted, "The train!" to Nathaniel. "Caleb could be on it. Get the horses. We've got to get to Gravella fast."

"But Miss Emily," Nick protested. "You're supposed to stay away. For your own safety."

Emily waved him off and ran toward the house. Nathaniel was running toward the barn. Nick shook his head and turned his attention back to the road, taking off in a hurry.

"Daddy! There's a raid in Gravella, and they've taken some Confederate soldiers from the Montgomery train. Caleb could be one of them. Nathaniel and I are riding into town."

"What are you going to do?" Thomas said. "If you interfere, they might take you prisoner."

Emily looked into her father's eyes. "I've got to do something," she said. "I can't sit here knowing that Caleb could be on that train. I just can't."

Nathaniel came rushing inside. "We're ready," he said.

"I understand," Thomas said. "Please don't take any needless risks." He looked up at Nathaniel and said, "It looks like I'm still depending on you."

Nathaniel tipped his black bowler to signify that he understood then he and Emily rushed out the door. Thomas stood there and listened as the pounding of horses hooves faded into the distance. He was so worried. Emily was young and in love, and that could be a deadly combination in a dangerous situation. He couldn't stand there. He had to do something.

~ O ~

The battle had not lasted long. The Confederate soldiers were too few and too poorly equipped. They had put up a stiff resistance, considering, but a short resistance, surrendering in the face of unbeatable odds. The Yankee cavalry lined them up outside the train, along the Mobile to Montgomery road. There were over a hundred of them. Regulars. On their way to reinforce the Confederate installations in Mobile.

Sergeant Major James Ross walked along the line of prisoners. These were tough men, some battle hardened. Others were too young or too old but many of them, even the young kids, looked almost as tough as the regulars. Then he recognized a face. This man was not a regular, not any longer. His uniform was torn and rotted. It had been heavily patched but was still in tatters. He seemed completely out of place from the others.

"Conecuh!" he said. "What are you doing here?"

Caleb turned and looked at the Yankee sergeant. "I know you," he said. "You're… Ross. That's it. I met you in Belle Plains."

"Yes. Sergeant Major James Ross from Battle Creek, Michigan. Your leg must be better. You no longer need a crutch."

"Still walk with a limp," Caleb said. "But it's slowly getting better. What are y'all going to do with us?"

"You are a prisoner again. We are taking you to the prison at Ship Island."

"But I'm home. After all this time and all the battles and hospitals and prisons, the war is supposed to be over for me. I was exchanged. You can't take me away now. I haven't even made it home to the farm."

"You were exchanged? Do you have your paperwork?"

Caleb pulled the exchange papers from a jacket pocket and handed them to Ross.

"Let me talk to the Colonel."

Ross stepped away and walked over to where a small group of Union officers was standing. He showed the paperwork to Colonel Spurling. "This man was exchanged out of Elmira as part of an invalid prisoner exchange," Ross said. "The papers say he is to be given free passage to his home. He lives only a few miles from here."

Spurling looked over the paperwork then glanced up at Caleb. "The paperwork is in order," he said. "And a Union soldier somewhere is free because this man was exchanged for him. We cannot do him the disservice of putting him back into prison. Arrest him as a formality only. Then we will release him as an exchange prisoner. That is the proper way to handle it. And it makes the numbers look better. As soon as you release him, he can be on his way home."

Sergeant Major Ross saluted sharply and said, "Yes, Sir."

He stepped back over to where Caleb was standing. "I must arrest you," he began. He could see Caleb's shoulders physically droop. "But it is a formality only since you were on the train with the regulars. As soon as we record it, you will be released as an exchange prisoner. You will be able to go home."

A tear rolled down Caleb's cheek as he said, "Thank you."

"My pleasure." Ross smiled. "Follow me. We'll take care of this now."

~ O ~

Murray watched the sad parade from the trees. The Confederate soldiers being lined up in the street were not returning prisoners. Their uniforms, irregular as they were, were in far better condition than those who had been exchanged. It could be hours before the Union soldiers were gone. *Might as well get comfortable,* he thought.

Before he looked away, however, a face caught his eye. His jaw dropped. One of the Confederate soldiers paraded from the train looked familiar, way too familiar. Even from this distance, he could see that the uniform was in poor shape, not like the others. He picked up his field glasses. Caleb Garner! He was home. But he wouldn't be for long. The Union cavalry would consider these men prisoners of war. They would take them to Pensacola or Mobile, wherever, to get them out of the war, off the field of battle. Damn! Caleb was slipping through his fingers once again, even if it was to go back to prison.

Hold it, he told himself. Caleb was handing some papers to the Yankee soldier. It had to be his exchange paperwork. The soldier went over and talked to the officer then pulled Caleb out of the line. They were letting him go. That meant that Caleb would not escape Murray's vengeance. All Murray had to do was wait until… *Hold it,* he said to himself one more time. Murray thought about his original plan. Here was a chance to put it into action, to have Caleb executed by the Union army. Of course! Caleb would be dead and Murray would not be arrested for murder.

He had forged the paperwork, the secret assignment and the execution order, while he was still in Savannah, in case an opportunity arose. The forged papers were in his saddlebag, below the Union officer's uniform. With the telegraph lines cut, they would have no way to contact the War Department for verification. Nor could they contact anyone else. They would not be able to question him. This was perfect! It was time to become a lieutenant in the Union army.

~ O ~

As Caleb walked behind James Ross, a Union officer on horseback, a Lieutenant, trotted through the groups of soldiers and stopped beside them. He dismounted and stood in front of Ross. The eyes that looked out from above the man's full beard seemed familiar to Caleb, but this was a Union officer. He could not have known this man. The familiarity must have been a coincidence.

"Where are you going with that prisoner, sergeant?" the Union Lieutenant asked.

"To arrest and release him. A formality. He's an exchange prisoner."

"He is NOT to be released under any circumstances, by order of the Secretary of War, Edwin McMasters Stanton."

Ross stared at the officer a moment then asked, "Who are you, Sir? I do not recognize you."

"Lieutenant John Murray." Murray had considered using an alias, but with the telegraph cut, and the fact that those lines were Confederate telegraph lines, there was no way they could try to verify the forged paperwork or find out that John Murray was wanted for desertion. Besides, with any luck at all, word of what he was about to do would get back to Elmira. That parlor soldier Major Colt would find out how badly he'd been outsmarted by the man he had wronged. "I am on special assignment for the War Department, hunting down this traitor to our great nation. This man is to be executed for treason. Immediately!"

"I ain't done nothing," Caleb said. "I'm just a soldier. I ain't even that anymore."

Ross stiffened and said, "Sergeant Major James Ross. I will have to relate this to my commanding officer as he has given me other instructions. Please follow me."

"Of course." Murray foraged through his saddlebag and pulled out the papers then he tied his horse to a hitching post and followed Ross as they walked back to where the small circle of Union officers was standing.

"Colonel Spurling, this is Lieutenant John Murray. He says he is on special assignment for Secretary Stanton."

Murray saluted and said, "Here is my letter of assignment, Sir." He handed the forged document to Colonel Spurling. "It is signed by Secretary of War Edwin McMasters Stanton himself."

"I can see that," Spurling said. He looked at the letter for several moments before saying. "Yes, that's Secretary Stanton's signature. I've seen enough documents from him to know. So you are to track down Caleb Garner?"

"Yes, Sir. The spy is this man right here." Murray pointed toward Caleb.

"I ain't no spy," Caleb said.

"He was in the Confederate army," Murray said, "But he was pretending to be a spy for us. He passed along information about a Confederate attack, but it was a trap. An entire company innocently walked into it. They were shot down to the last man, even when they held up their arms in surrender. The wounded got the bayonet. Caleb Garner is responsible for the wanton murder of one hundred sixty-four good men, brave men. I have orders that he is be executed by firing squad at the first opportunity. Here is the execution order." Murray handed over the second forged document.

"I ain't done nothing like that," Caleb said. "You got the wrong man."

"We were not notified that there would be any agents working in this area," Colonel Spurling said.

"They would not have known to notify you, Sir. The War Department is not aware of my location. They knew that my search started in Savannah, Georgia, but, of course, I was working undercover. I followed the trail all the way through Georgia and into Alabama. I was unable to let Secretary Stanton or anyone at the War Department know where I was or where I was going. It's the inherent danger of being a special agent for the Union while traveling through the South."

"In a Union officer's uniform?"

"No, Sir. I wear civilian clothes when I am under cover. I saw your men and knew it would be safe to pull my uniform out. It's been too long since I've been able to wear the blue."

Spurling stared at Murray a moment before looking at the papers again and saying, "I would prefer to verify this with the War Department. There is no way we can contact them from here. Can this not wait until we return to Pensacola?"

"I have my orders, Sir. From Secretary Stanton himself. You can read on the execution order. It states that Garner is to be executed immediately upon capture."

"Yes, I read that. Still…"

"I am to complete my mission and return to Washington with all due haste. I have another mission waiting on me, one that could prove critical to shortening the war."

Colonel Spurling turned to James Ross and said, "It appears we have no choice but to carry out Stanton's orders. We cannot afford to delay our mission by spending undue time on this. Please assist Lieutenant Murray and do it quickly. I do not want to tarry in this area long enough to get trapped by Confederate forces."

"No!" Caleb shouted. "I didn't do nothing."

At Spurling's wave, two Union soldiers grabbed Caleb and began to walk him back toward the train.

Murray turned to Ross and said, "We can place him in that first passenger car while we get this arranged."

Caleb protested loudly, but the two soldiers shoved him into the passenger car. They tied him to the seat at Murray's instruction.

Murray said, "I'm tired of hearing him complain. Those hundred and sixty-four Union soldiers never got a chance to complain." He pulled out a handkerchief and gagged Caleb. Then he pulled a small black cloth bag from his coat pocket, glanced at Ross, and said, "Hooding." He pulled it over Caleb's head then pulled the strings snug and tied them around Caleb's neck. "I don't know why they require us to use these things," he said. "I guess so he won't see who shoots him. Not that it matters." It didn't matter to Murray at all, but it looked official. Looking official was important.

"Let's get this set up," Murray continued. "Better leave a watch on him. This man is much more dangerous than he appears."

Ross nodded to the two men who had drug Caleb into the car then turned to Murray and asked, "What now?"

"First, we'll pick the location. Somewhere close will be fine. I have no problem with the townsfolks watching. It would teach them a lesson. But that's not important now. What's important is following Stanton's order and me getting back to Washington as soon as possible. We'll need six men for the firing squad. That will be enough since your commander is in a hurry. And six bullets should be more than enough to make sure he's dead."

"Yes, Sir," Ross said. He looked down at Caleb and the black hood covering Caleb's head. How could this be true? Conecuh a spy? It made no sense. But orders were orders. The consequences of not following orders were beyond significant.

~ O ~

Emily and Nathaniel stopped at the edge of Gravella and looked at the throngs of Union soldiers, the line of Confederate prisoners, the train wreckage, and the smoke rising from several fires around town.

"If he was on this train," Emily said. "He has been taken prisoner. I brought the money. Maybe we can buy his freedom here."

"I wouldn't offer the money," Nathaniel said. "This is a raiding party. Raiders often use war as an excuse to be criminals. They intend to destroy everything related to military activity, no matter how remotely. But I suspect their larger goal is to break our spirit, which this raid into the heart of the South will surely do. That is often the more important objective. There are few laws or restrictions on raiders. Union soldiers will steal jewelry and other valuables from people's homes while their commanders turn their heads and look the other way. If you offered a bribe, the army would take your money then take Caleb, too. They might even put you in prison for trying to bribe an officer."

"But… What can we do?"

"Try to reason with their conscience, and hope they have one. Caleb was an exchange prisoner. Caleb was set free, which means a Yankee soldier was set free as well. It would be against the rules of the exchange to take him prisoner again now that the Yankee soldier has gone home."

Emily nodded. It made sense. They rode forward. At the same time, Union soldiers were walking their way.

~ O ~

Murray recognized the white woman and the large black man riding into Gravella. What in the hell were they doing here in the middle of a raid? The bigger question was, would the woman recognize him? Perhaps not with the full beard he now wore. Caleb hadn't. But better to linger behind, keep his distance and let the soldiers on the perimeter handle it. They had orders not to let anyone pass. Alive. That was standard procedure for a raid into enemy territory. He said nothing to Ross about them.

"This way," Murray said as he pointed toward a dirt alley. "Let's see what's behind these buildings."

There was a narrow cleared area behind the two log stores that were part of Gravella's tiny commercial district. The clearing ended quickly, in front of the woods that ran up the slope of the small hill to the north.

In the cleared area, some scraggly weeds grew in the orange, rocky soil, but little else. There were a few broken pieces of wood, china, and other trash scattered here and there.

"This is perfect," Murray said. "We'll do it right here, get rid of that animal and be done with it. What about the firing squad?"

"Everyone has an assignment. We weren't expecting something like this to come up. I-I…" Ross fell silent.

"You what?"

"It's, well, he seemed like such an honest person. I never thought he could be a spy, let alone a double agent."

"People can surprise you. In my business, you learn to be suspicious of everyone." Murray glared at Ross as he emphasized the 'everyone.' "Once again, what about the six men for the firing squad?"

“We can use the two men who are guarding him now.” Ross looked back toward the street, as though he could see through the log buildings. He finally said, “I’ll pick four others from the men outside, but it will take time to find four I can pull away from other tasks.”

“Okay,” Murray said. “Don’t take too long. I’ll go to the train to relieve the two guards and send them to you. You gather the other four as fast as you can and have them set up in a line along here. We’ll tie him to that sapling there. When you get the men in place, come help me with Garner. You could do this by yourself, but if I need to, I’ll help you drag that traitor along to speed things up. We need to get it over quickly. It’s critical I get to my next assignment as fast as possible.”

As they were walking back through the small dirt alley, they could hear shouting, the sound of people and horses moving around. A woman screamed. Ross rushed back out to the street. Murray rushed as well but lingered behind.

“What is the commotion?” Ross asked a corporal as they walked over to where a large group of soldiers had gathered.

“This woman and Negro are demanding to be let through. Something about a prisoner.”

“Demanding?” Ross said. “That’s ridiculous. They must leave immediately or be arrested.”

“I told them that. When I did, she tried to ride past us.”

Sergeant Major Ross looked at the two. He stared a moment before saying, “I know that woman. In fact, I’ve seen both of them before. But where?”

“That doesn’t matter,” Murray said from behind. “They cannot be allowed to interfere. Have them leave or risk being arrested and detained.”

“Ah! Belle Plains. That’s where it was. I can’t remember her name, but she is Conecuh’s fiancée. The Negro is in her employ.”

“Conecuh?” Murray said as he continued to linger back, trying to make sure the woman didn’t see him.

“Conecuh is the man you are about to execute. That’s what I call him. It was easier to remember than his real name.”

"I don't give a damn what you call him or whose fiancée she is. Have your men get them out of here right now! We have a job to do, and we don't need any interference from Rebel civilians." *I can easily find her later,* Murray thought. *After the raiding party is gone. Then I'll slit her throat and get my money. I also owe that colored man a knife blade, but I'll repay it with a bullet.* "You seem to be awfully familiar with the enemy, Sergeant Major Ross. You have your orders, and you don't need me to follow them. Are you going to follow through or not? If not, I can file an insubordination charge against you."

Ross could hear hooves pounding in the background, getting closer, but assumed it was men from the raiding party. He gathered himself. There was no other choice. "Yes, Sir, Lieutenant Murray. I will follow the orders Colonel Spurling has given me." He turned to the Union soldiers who were holding Emily and Nathaniel back. "Corporal, please make sure these two leave in an orderly fashion. If they do not, arrest them and detain them with the other prisoners."

The sound of hooves pounding against the road grew louder. Dust billowed into the air as a wagon rushed toward them, coming from the same direction that the woman and colored man had come from. The Union soldiers at the perimeter raised their rifles, but the wagon came to a quick halt. There was an older man, gray-headed and barrel-chested, sitting on the bench seat of the wagon.

"Emily!" they heard the old man shout.

"What the hell is it now," Murray said. As the soldiers were trying to turn Emily and Nathaniel around, Murray and Ross walked over to where the wagon had stopped.

"What are you doing with my daughter?" Thomas Rose asked.

"She is going to be arrested for interfering with official government activity if she doesn't leave now," Murray said. "The Negro, too."

"You can't arrest her. You have no right. This is the Confederate States of America!"

"I have every right," Murray said. "Our business here has been ordered by the President of these United States. *All* of the states! If she does not leave, she will be arrested. Don't try my patience, or she will be executed by firing squad, along with my prisoner."

"You can't do that!" Thomas shouted. His musket was propped up in a wooden sleeve between the end of the seat and the outside boards of the wagon. He reached over and unconsciously put his hand on the tip of the barrel.

This was getting out of hand. Murray had to take control of the situation, or his ruse might be discovered. He reached for the pistol at his side, pulled and fired. Thomas Rose clutched his chest and fell forward. There was a growing splotch of red on the front of his shirt as he tumbled out of the wagon and onto the street.

The woman screamed again. She sent Union soldiers sprawling as she rushed toward where Thomas lay.

"Why did you do that?" Ross asked.

"He threatened us and reached for his rifle," Murray answered. "Simple self-defense."

"If he had tried to lift it, my men would have disarmed him without bloodshed."

"I couldn't take that chance. Hell, you were standing in front. I probably saved your life."

"You animal!" Emily screamed at Murray. "You shot my father for nothing. He was not going to hurt..." Her words stopped, and she became quiet, staring at Murray hard. Suddenly, she shouted, "I know you!"

"What are you talking about? I've never seen you before."

"You didn't have that beard, but I'd recognize those eyes anywhere." Emily pointed her finger at Murray's face. "This man tried to rape me. He was going to kill me and take my money. He would have succeeded if Nathaniel hadn't stopped him."

James Ross looked at Murray.

"That's ridiculous. She's making it up because I shot her father. Come on. We've got an execution to perform. I'll send the two guards to you. When you have the squad ready, you can come get the prisoner. And get those Rebel sympathizers out of here now!" He turned and left.

Reluctantly, Ross turned toward Emily and Nathaniel. She sat in the street and bent over her father, whispering in his ear. "You need to get him to a doctor," James Ross said. "Please. You must go." Ross gave some orders to his men then turned and left, following behind Murray.

~ O ~

Emily leaned down to Thomas' face and whispered in his ear, "I love you, Daddy. We'll get you to a doctor."

"I love you, too." His words were weak, raspy. "Don't waste time on a doctor. Tell Nathaniel to get down here and listen."

"I'm right here," Nathaniel said from the other side.

"I tied my best two horses in the woods on that rise to the north. You see those two tallest pines, the ones that stick out from all the others?"

Nathaniel looked up and said, "Yes, I see them."

"The horses are halfway between them. The money from selling the land is in one of the saddlebags. Emily, you find Caleb and leave. Y'all can make a new life for yourselves out west. Just go. Don't look back. Caleb don't even need to go home. There's nothing there for him." His lips stopped moving. He said no more.

Nathaniel checked for a pulse. There was none. He shook his head. The tears flowed heavily as Emily held her father's head in her lap and rocked back and forth.

Nathaniel patted Thomas on the shoulder then stood. "Who is being executed?" he asked.

"A Confederate spy," one of the Union soldiers said. "A man from around here. I believe his name is Caleb Garner."

Emily's head jerked up, her eyes wide. "No!" she screamed. "Caleb's no spy. He's a farmer. That's all. You can't let them do that."

The Union soldier shrugged and said, "We're only following orders, ma'am. That man you said tried to kill you is a special agent for the War Department. He has an execution order for Caleb Garner. The prisoner is being held in that first passenger car on the train there. They're trying to get the firing squad together now."

"You can't!" She gently laid Thomas' head down then jumped up and started to run toward the train, but the soldiers restrained her. "Let me go! I've got to stop this. You can't shoot Caleb. I love him. Please," she begged.

"Ma'am, if you don't leave, we'll have to arrest you. They might even execute you as well. It would be better if you took your father and left town."

"You've already killed my father!" Emily shouted. "You can't kill Caleb, too. I've got to stop it."

She tried to break her way through the Union soldiers. It took several of them to restrain her.

"Ma'am," the corporal said, "If you bust into that train, they might shoot you. You can't… There's nothing you can do. I'm sorry."

Emily went limp in the arms of the Union soldiers. "She passed out," one of them said.

Nathaniel stepped over to the soldiers who were holding Emily's motionless body. "She was in love with the man you are executing," he said. "I understand there is nothing we can do. Please allow me to take her home. And her father as well. We wish to bury him in peace."

Nathaniel Whiteeagle took Emily from the Union soldiers and placed her on the seat of the wagon. Several Union soldiers reached down and lifted Thomas and put his body in the back of the wagon. Without looking back at the raiders or Gravella, Nathaniel turned the wagon around and began driving toward the Rose home.

~ O ~

"You will stand in a line right here." James Ross indicated the position with a wave of his hand. It had taken too long to find four additional men he could pull away from the activities of the raid, but he finally had his six. "We will tie the prisoner to that small tree at the edge of the woods. You will fire on my command. Wait here while I go get the prisoner."

Ross walked down the street, reluctant to do what he was about to do and powerless to stop it. He stepped into the train car and looked around. Lieutenant John Murray was not there. Something must have come up to pull him away. Or perhaps Ross had taken so long to find the firing squad, Lieutenant Murray had come looking for him. It did not matter either way. Ross had his orders. The Lieutenant must have been serious about Ross taking care of this by himself. *What a dirty, rotten job!*

He stuck his head out of the car and commandeered the first soldier he saw. They untied Caleb from the train seat and hauled him to his feet. "I am sorry to have to do this," Ross said. "But I have my orders."

Caleb tried to say something through the gag, but his reply was nothing more than a muffled grunt. He struggled to get free, but couldn't. His hands were firmly tied behind him. The two Union soldiers virtually drug Caleb to the waiting firing squad. He would not cooperate by walking. He struggled every step of the way, trying his best to go backward. James Ross was as gentle as he could afford to be with his Confederate friend, but he had his orders. He and his men forcefully brought Caleb to the execution area.

They tied Caleb to the small tree. Sergeant Major Ross stood behind the firing squad and said, "Private Caleb Garner, the United States of America has sentenced you to death for treason to our great country." Caleb continued to grunt loudly, moving back and forth and pulling against the ropes that bound him. "It is my duty…" Ross' words trailed off a moment. He took a deep breath and continued, "It is my duty to carry out the execution. On my order, men... Ready... Aim…" He hesitated. He looked around for something, anything, a messenger telling him to stop, an angel from heaven coming down to intervene. There was nothing.

He hated this. It wasn't what the war was truly about as far as he was concerned. Somehow, executing a poor Alabama farmer seemed so stupid, so wasteful. But he had no choice. No choice. "Fire!"

Six shots rang out. The front of Caleb's uniform was instantly splotched with dark, wet spots as his body slumped forward, the rope keeping him from falling to the ground.

Ross was trying his best not to shed tears in front of the other men. He couldn't help it. The tears flowed anyway, large and heavy. He walked over and cut Caleb down, gently lowering Caleb's body to the ground. “I am so sorry,” he whispered. “I hope you find peace with God. Maybe he will forgive you for what you did.”

Ross knew the gag wouldn’t matter, that Caleb’s spirit would be free to talk to God when he flew into heaven, but it wasn’t right to leave his dead body gagged. He had to take it out. He reached down and untied the hood then lifted it over Caleb’s head.

Sergeant Major James Ross gasped loudly. The six members of the firing squad gathered around and looked down at the dead man dressed in Caleb’s Confederate uniform. It was Lieutenant John Murray.

~ O ~

Emily stood at the crest of the rise and looked out through the pine needles and young leaves of early spring toward the town of Gravella below. The southbound train was now on fire, the flames high and bright, even in the mid-morning sun. They slapped at the sky as though they would burn the heavens.

Shots rang out, the firing squad. Emily's heart trembled, beat heavily. Had Nathaniel failed? He said he would do his best to save Caleb as he hurried off, but the terrible sound of the firing squad’s rifles was unmistakable. Had Nathaniel not gotten there in time? Tears formed in her eyes as her heart sank.

She patted each of the three horses, the two Thomas had tied here and the one from the wagon, to steady herself more than to steady the horses. Looking to the east, Emily could not see the wagon, but she could see the smoke rising from where she and Nathaniel had set it afire.

They had carefully laid Thomas’ body to the side of the road where he would be found. She knew the people of Gravella would honor his wishes by laying him to rest beside Mary on the small plot of land that still belonged to them.

Sounds! Dried leaves crunching and small limbs cracking. She turned back toward town and looked downslope. There was Nathaniel, climbing through the trees, the large, lean black man having no trouble at all negotiating the slope.

Some distance behind him, she saw Caleb! Her hands went to her mouth. Her heart pounded so hard she could feel it in her ears and in her eyes, in the tears that streamed down her cheeks. He struggled, but he was alive and breathing, and he was making it up the slope well enough.

She rushed down to him, hugged him and kissed him and placed her fingers on his face to feel him, to sense that he was as alive as he looked. It had been three long years, years that had not dimmed her love in the least. All the time and all the trials and tribulations had only served to make her love stronger.

Tears burst from Caleb's eyes as he looked at her. She began wiping them away with her fingers, but he reached up and gently took her hands in his. "You don't have to wipe them away," Caleb said. "It's all right for a man to cry when his dreams come true."

She laughed and cried at the same instant, almost choking. They hugged each other and kissed and squeezed and closed their eyes to every world except the one they held in each other's arms.

"We need to leave quickly," Nathaniel said when the kiss looked like it would go on forever. "I'll travel to Pensacola. It isn't that far. From there I can get passage on a Union freighter going back to Washington. Once I get home, I'll send word to your Aunt Millie."

"I hope you and Carolina have a wonderful life together," Emily said.

"Who's Carolina?" Caleb asked.

"I'll explain on our way to Texas," Emily said. "Here." She handed Nathaniel three hundred dollars in United States Notes. "My father would have wanted me to give this to you. That should be enough to give you and Carolina a good start. I'll miss you, Nathaniel."

The two of them hugged, a white woman and a colored man who shared a bond that had nothing to do with a romantic relationship and everything to do with shared life experiences, a profound human friendship, and saving each other's life along the way.

"Thank you for everything you've done," Caleb told Nathaniel. "When you took that hood off me in the railroad car, and I saw who you were, well, I can't describe the feeling of relief that came over me. Especially when I saw that Yankee on the floor with a gag in his mouth."

"It was my pleasure," Nathaniel said. "We need to leave before the raid is over. Let's mount."

They waved one last goodbye as they parted, Caleb and Emily going west and Nathaniel curving around to eventually go south.

THE END

AUTHOR'S NOTES

Caleb Garner

Private Caleb Garner was in the Confederate army for almost three years. He marched thousands of miles across America, fought in most of the major battles, was wounded twice, and was held in three different Union prisons, including the infamous 'Hellmira' prison in Elmira, New York.

Caleb was selected for an 'invalid' prisoner exchange in the fall of 1864. (For the purposes of the exchange, 'invalid' was defined as prisoners too sick to return to the front within sixty days, but not too sick to travel.) After a five and a half month journey, Caleb's train rolled into Gravella, Alabama, (now Owassa, Alabama) on March 24, 1865, three weeks before the war ended.

On that same day, Union Major Andrew Spurling led a raid into Conecuh County to destroy the railroad track and limit the Confederate capability to reinforce Mobile. The train from Montgomery reached the damaged track and came to a grinding halt at seven-thirty in the morning. After a short skirmish, over a hundred Confederate soldiers who were riding on the train were taken prisoner.

After three long years of war and captivity, Caleb was a mere handful of miles from home, a relatively easy walk, when he was recaptured. Since he was an exchange prisoner, it was an 'administrative capture.' It was recorded then he was released. That was the last record of Caleb Garner. He simply disappeared.

Caleb was not killed in the raid. Nor was he among the prisoners Spurling's men took to Ship Island in Mississippi. And he never showed up on a Conecuh County census again.

Most people believe Caleb died not long after returning and was buried nearby, possibly in an unmarked grave since no gravestone bearing his name has ever been found. Even in civil war times, however, it was hard to die without a trace. We have no trace.

There are other possibilities. Many former Confederate soldiers migrated out west, to Texas and beyond, to avoid the crushing burden of Union occupation. It is possible that Caleb did as well, and that his heirs are living out west today.

Historical Accuracy

Conecuh is a story woven around and through the actual events in Private Caleb Garner's life. While I endeavored to make this book as historically accurate as possible, I had to whip out my literary license on many occasions. Sometimes it was because I needed to alter the facts slightly to keep the story flowing. More often, however, it was simply because we do not know the exact details. I had to make things up.

If you run across something and think, "I'm not sure it happened that way," please remember that my primary goal in writing ***Conecuh*** was to entertain you, not subject you to a history lesson.

Language

Racial slurs were in common use at the time. I have limited the use of such terms to the few scenes where I believed it was necessary to convey historical accuracy and the emotions of the moment. I sincerely hope that no one takes offense. We are all Americans. We are strongest when we stand together.

ACKNOWLEDGEMENTS

There is an old saying that it 'takes a village to raise a child.' That can also be said about the creation of a historical novel. There are many people in the village that created ***Conecuh***:

My cousin and her husband, Sherry and John Garner, related the story of John's great uncle, Caleb Garner, while we were working on a previous novel. (Sherry is one of my early manuscript readers.) I was intrigued. As I read the information she sent me, a timeline of Caleb's life and related information, a story began to form in my mind. A novel was born.

Halfway through the first draft, John and Sherry discovered that a genealogist had made a mistake, that they might not be related to Caleb after all. Or, if related, it was likely more distant. By then, however, I was hooked on Caleb's story. Great uncle or not, the novel had to be written.

I am deeply indebted to Sherry for all her research, inspiration (humorous and otherwise), and for the title of this novel. I knew I couldn't use the working title, but was at a loss until she suggested ***Conecuh***. Simple but profound. I loved it.

A great big Thank You to Sherry's daughter, Robin Robinson, for helping with the research and for sending me lots of material relating to Caleb's story.

Another whopping Thank You to the Evergreen Public Library Historian/Archivist, Sherry Johnston. Sherry assisted in our research efforts and provided some critically important material about the history of the area. It is interesting to note that I had already named Caleb's fictitious friend, Arlis Johnston, before I met Sherry. The fact that they have the same last name is purely coincidental. A little freaky, but a coincidence none the less.

Author and historian Myra Singleton Johnson provided comments on early manuscripts and loads of inspiration. Writing novels is not easy. At times, it can be extremely frustrating and quite lonely. Having people who believe in you is immensely important.

Marilyn Parker is a dear friend with a keen eye. She is my final reader. I am always amazed at what she caught when I thought I handed her a clean manuscript. I greatly appreciate her holding the key to the last gate.

Another Thank You goes to Command Sergeant Major James Ross, US Army Retired, for loaning me his name. It was a perfect match for the James Ross character in the book. Hats off to James as well as to all military personnel, both active and retired. Thank You for your service.

As always, I cannot thank Mutt Suttles enough for his beautiful art. Mutt is a friend and an exceptional artist. I am honored beyond words to have his work grace this cover.

This book would not have been written without the very heartbeat of my life, my beautiful and brilliant wife, Dr. Charlotte Hughes. She reads my gruesome rough drafts with a smile, maintains that smile through many versions of the manuscript, and is a fountain of inspiration, selflessly encouraging me to pursue my passion. I tip my heart to her.

Finally, I would also like to tip my heart to all my readers. Thank You for making thousands of hours of work worthwhile.

PHOTOGRAPH AND ILLUSTRATION CREDITS

Public Domain: Flickr
Front Cover – Elmira Prison
Back Cover
July 1, 1862 ~ Alabama Hospital #2, Richmond, Virginia
April 23, 1863 ~ Trail From the Sepulga Trading Post, Sepulga, Alabama (Don DeBold)
July 13, 1863 ~ Falling Waters, West Virginia
July 23, 1863 ~ Manassas Gap, Virginia
May 6, 1864 ~ Directly North of Orange Plank Road, Wilderness, Virginia
August 12, 1864 ~ Point Lookout Prison, Maryland
August 12, 1864 ~ Train Station, Thomasville, Georgia
August 18, 1864 ~ Elmira Prison, New York
September 2, 1864 ~ Richmond, Virginia
September 12, 1864 ~ Barracks Number Three, Elmira, New York
September 13, 1864 ~ Prison Medical Facilities, Elmira, New York
September 29, 1864 ~ Barracks Number Three, Elmira, New York
October 9, 1864 ~ Prison Medical Facilities, Elmira, New York
October 13-14, 1864 ~ Baltimore, Maryland
October 22, 1864 ~ Elmira, New York
November 12, 1864 ~ Prisoner Steamer Near the Coast of South Carolina
March 21, 1865 ~ Union Command, Milton, Florida
March 23, 1865 ~ Conecuh County and Gravella, Alabama
March 24, 1865 ~ Gravella, Alabama

Public Domain: Pixabay
September 2, 1862 ~ Conecuh County Courthouse, Sparta, Alabama
April 19, 1864 ~ Rose Residence, Forks of Sepulga Community, Alabama
August 12, 1864 ~ Point Lookout Prison, Maryland
September 9, 1864 ~ Elmira Army Depot, Elmira, New York
September 12, 1864 ~ Brigadier General Winder's Office, Richmond, Virginia
November 1, 1864 ~ Tater's Bar, Washington D.C.

CC0 Public Domain: Pxhere
August 29, 1862 ~ Thoroughfare Gap, Virginia
August 26, 1863 ~ Rose Residence, Forks of Sepulga Community, Alabama
July 28, 1864 ~ Point Lookout Prison, Maryland
February 1, 1865 ~ Talbot Residence, Savannah, Georgia
March 22, 1865 ~ Rose Residence, Forks of Sepulga Community, Alabama

Public Domain: Matthew Brady (All photos between 1861 and 1865)
May 14, 1864 ~ "Punch Bowl" Holding Area, Belle Plains, Virginia
September 30, 1864 ~ Millie Hanson's Mansion, Richmond, Virginia
October 14, 1864 ~ Washington D.C.
December 21, 1864 ~ Savannah, Georgia

Public Domain: Thure de Thulstrup (1864)
Front Cover Battle Scene

HERB HUGHES

Public Domain: PublicDomainPictures.net
August, 1861 ~ A Forest Near Sepulga, Alabama
June 2, 1864 ~ Rose Residence, Forks of Sepulga Community, Alabama
August 12, 1864 ~ Thomasville, Georgia

Public Domain: National Park Service Photos
May 5, 1862 ~ Countryside Near Williamsburg, Virginia (M. Boyce)
July 17, 1864 ~ Point Lookout Prison, Maryland (Jamie Kennedy)
November 17, 1864 ~ Millie Hanson's Mansion, Richmond, Virginia

CC0 Public Domain: Max Pixel
February 3, 1865 ~ Railroad Station, Savannah, Georgia
February 16, 1865 ~ Millie Hanson's Mansion, Richmond, Virginia
February 28, 1865 ~ Millie Hanson's Mansion, Richmond, Virginia

Public Domain: Picryl
February 24, 1865 ~ Savannah, Georgia
February 27, 1865 ~ Savannah, Georgia

Public Domain: Alamy, Royalty Free
Front Cover Train

CC0 Public Domain: Harris Brisbane Dick Fund, 1933
August 30, 1862 ~ Henry House Hill, Virginia
October 4, 1864 ~ Belle Plains, Virginia

Public Domain: Sachse E., & Co. (1864)
October 5, 1864 ~ Point Lookout Prison, Maryland
October 22, 1864 ~ Point Lookout Prison, Maryland

CC0 Public Domain: Stilfehler
March 9, 1862 ~ Rose Residence, Forks of Sepulga Community Alabama,

Public Domain: Missouri Historical Society
August 29, 1862 ~ Forest Around Stuart's Hill, Virginia

Public Domain: Timothy H. O'Sullivan (1863)
July 2, 1863 ~ Big and Little Round Tops, Gettysburg, Pennsylvania

Public Domain: Alexander Gardner
July 9, 1863 ~ Conecuh County Courthouse, Sparta, Alabama

Public Domain: Altairisfar (Jeffrey Reed)
May 12, 1864 ~ Conecuh County Courthouse, Sparta, Alabama

Public Domain: US Army Photo
May 30, 1864 ~ Union Camp near Mechanicsville, Virginia

Public Domain: Quadell
June 13, 1864 ~ Hammond Hospital, Point Lookout Prison, Maryland

Public Domain: Painting by Gari Melcher (1860-1932)
June 27, 1864 ~ Rose Residence, Forks of Sepulga Community, Alabama

Public Domain: Pexels (David Debert)
July 6, 1864 ~ "Hellmira" Prison, Elmira, New York

Public Domain: Carl Nebel (1851)
July 17, 1864 ~ Train Station, Sparta, Alabama

CC0 Public Domain: Ian Slater
July 27, 1864 ~ Rural Southwestern Georgia

CC0 Public Domain: David Haskiya
July 29, 1864 ~ Rural Jail, Southwestern Georgia

Public Domain: Civil War Photograph Collection (1864)
October 2, 1864 ~ Road to Belle Plains, Virginia

Public Domain: John Whelan
October 5, 1864 ~ Barracks Number Three, Elmira, New York

Public Domain: Zoro
October 27, 1864 ~ Barracks Number Three, Elmira, New York

Public Domain: (Charleston, South Carolina)
November 1, 1864 ~ Apartment Building in Washington D.C.

CC0 Public Domain: Hmaag (2015)
November 16, 1864 ~ A Road Outside Richmond, Virginia

Public Domain: Robert N. Dennis Collection (1861 to 1865)
November 16, 1864 ~ Venus Point, South Carolina

Public Domain: Wikimedia Commons
December 12, 1864 ~ Savannah, Georgia

CC0 Public Domain: Marathon (Golden Yard, Hampstead)
January 3, 1865 ~ Millie Hanson's Mansion, Richmond, Virginia

Kalorama Triangle Historic District, Washington D.C.
February 9, 1865 ~ Washington D.C.

All others are Public Domain or Public Domain, Author Unknown

Author **HERB HUGHES** worked in the computer industry for over two decades then built a successful private business before retiring to write novels.

Conecuh is his fifth novel and second historical work set during the civil war. Earlier novels include:

TENNESSEE YANKEE – Historical fiction, civil war.
Killing Rhinos – Science fiction, prison colony planet.
The Joystick Murders – Detective novel, set in the year 2042.
A BLOODY WONDERFUL WAR – Humor/adventure.

All novels by Herb Hughes are available from Amazon.

www.herbhughesnovels.com

Available from:
BOOKS FROM THE POND
Athens, Alabama

www.booksfromthepond.com

Made in the USA
Middletown, DE
05 June 2020

96650815R00201